D0097283

Dedicated to my parents

Acknowledgments

To the late Bob Bailey, my eighth-grade English teacher. Your words are forever etched in my yearbook and in my memory:

"Kathy, please, please keep writing. You have a talent that must not be wasted..."

You left us way too soon, Mr. Bailey. I'm sorry you're not here to read my first book, the one I promised to dedicate to you. I'm sorry I never got a chance to thank you for your pep talks and for the impact you had on me.

Thank you for your humbling words to a 13-year-old who simply enjoyed writing, for being the first person to point out "a rare gift for writing" in her adolescent musings, for igniting a lifelong passion for writing, and as such, for *your* gift of encouragement.

The pain of your untimely passing was immense for so many of your students. I think I speak for them all:

Your inspiration is as everlasting as your legacy.

Michael Kaye: Thank you for being the first person to believe in this book, for believing in my abilities from the get-go, for your advice, honesty and patience with my doubtless annoying perfectionism. You were my safety net, always there to guide and encourage me when I wanted to abandon it all. I could not have done this without you.

Lenore Skomal: As an agent and a person, you're one of those rare people who goes that extra mile for others. Thank you for all your hard work, dedication and perseverance. Thank you for teaching me patience, trust, and above all, appreciation.

Thank you Sahar Jahangiri, Khushnood (Klassic Designs), Deborah Dove, Layan Afifi, Elle Kaveh, Steve Passiouras, Eva Natiello, Jason Kurtz, Foojan Zeine, and Khatereh Yavari for your help and support.

Thank you to everyone who read and gave me feedback on my manuscript.

Thank you Zari Faripour, my ex-mother-in-law but forever friend, for all your time, help, encouragement and support. I am truly humbled by your generosity.

storyteller who reminds us that writing is an art. Kaveh playfully weaves an unmistakably personal story that engages the reader with the skills of a storyteller. Through moments of deep sensitivity or anxious mystery, she keeps the reader moving with curiosity and empathy that builds page by page. This book is a must read in a globalized world where stereotypes have no place and empathy is the key to our collective future."

— Maryam Zar,
writer, activist, policy adviser, former correspondent in Iran; Los Angeles commissioner on the Commission on the Status of Women; founder of Womenfound

"Ms. Kaveh is a very talented writer with a distinct voice. She skillfully weaves a family's personal struggles into a work of universal importance. She tackles multiple and difficult themes with such grace and raw honesty that the writing seems effortless. An impressive piece of work."

— Shahrzad Ardalan,
radio show host/producer

"The stories of Iranians immigrating to the U.S. are many and the experiences hardly monolithic. In *And Sometimes Why*, Kathy Kaveh reveals with heart-breaking honesty and humor the way one family's decisions post-immigration result in addiction and dysfunction despite the best of intentions. A frank exploration of how no amount of privilege or planning can protect children from the unintended consequences of their parents' actions, even when those choices are made out of an abundance of love."

— Marjan Kamali,
author of *The Stationery Shop* and *Together Tea*

"A fascinating story of a young girl's life prior and after the Iranian Revolution. Ms. Kaveh's poignant novel portrays the hardships, struggles and hypocrisy endured by the Iranian people, especially the youth."

— Ketab Sara Co.
(Global publishing house; Tehran,Iran headquarters)

"Ms. Kaveh's *And Sometimes Why* is beautiful, powerful and politically relevant. (Kaveh) does an extraordinary job of capturing a young girl's physical and emotional journey growing up caught between two worlds. Her sense of humor makes the heart-wrenching parts (of the story) all the more powerful. While this is Ms. Kaveh's first novel, she is no novice. She is an obviously talented writer with a solid debut."

— Reza Goharzad,
journalist and political analyst

And Sometimes *Why*

A Novel

Kathy Kaveh

Copyright © 2021 Kathy Kaveh

The moral right of the author has been asserted.

All rights reserved.

No part of this publication may be reproduced, stored in a retrieval system, or transmitted, in any form or by any means, without the prior permission in writing of the publisher, nor be otherwise circulated in any form of binding or cover other than that in which it is published and without a similar condition including this condition being imposed on the subsequent purchaser.

Published by Greenlight Publishing

ISBN 978-0-578-78285-0

Typesetting services by BOOKOW.COM

Thank you to my brother, Kurosh, for being the most genuinely decent person I know, and for all your help and patience in countless ways and through all the versions of this book, from the first "final draft" to the last "Final Final Final Final FINAL DRAFT!" This book would literally be lost without you.

My parents, thank you, quite simply, for everything.

Last, but most importantly, thank you to my son, Kameron, for being you, with your pure, generous heart and your unconditional love. You are my everything. Thank you for all your patience and hard work in helping your old-school mom with the barrage of technical/computer/digital issues and for creating my website (etc.?!) Above all, thank you for teaching me the true meaning of courage.

Foreword

On a late summer night in 2002, I recalled the childhood memory of packing up my dolls before moving to America. I wrote about it as a journal entry, much like thousands of others like it in notebooks and computer files I had amassed since I was 13 years old.

I had no idea that I had just written a chapter of what would become a novel. Nor was that my intention. But as more memories flooded back to me, I realized that while the literary world is ripe with novels and personal accounts about the French Revolution, the Russian Revolution, the Holocaust, and other such major historical events, to my knowledge, no one had ever written a novel, a memoir, or a personal, non-historical account about the Iranian Revolution.

So I set out to do just that: write the first novel about an Iranian family and their life in the aftermath of the revolution. I created fictitious characters and plot lines, mixed with true personal and historical events, to introduce the literary world to the realities of life in Iran. My goal was to debunk the many stereotypes associated with Iran and Iranians. It does indeed snow in Iran, we don't ride camels as a form of transportation, we're not religious fanatics, we're not terrorists. But when a lot of us left Iran after the revolution, we faced (and continue to face) these stigmas, stereotypes and prejudices.

Writing the book was effortless, editing it endless. I wrote almost 800 pages in fewer than six months. According to a fellow writer who read the first draft of my manuscript, I had essentially written the equivalent of 10 books in one. The storyline and structure of my book were so complex that cutting and editing it became a herculean task. In the time I took on this task, many books about Iran and the revolution were published. Each time a book like *Funny in Farsi* or the *Persepolis* series came out, a part of me felt proud that Iranians were finally being recognized in the American literary marketplace, but a part of me admittedly felt a pang of defeat — that someone else had beat me to it and that my "original idea" was anything but. The more books about Iran came out, the more the anecdotes and jokes I had written about became commonplace, the more pointless, trite and cliché the once-original ideas in my book seemed. Halfway through editing my book, I abandoned the whole project.

Ten years later, with the knowledge of how hard I had worked on it, I decided to re-commit myself to pursuing my book.

I faced a slew of personal and not-so-personal setbacks in the quest to publish my book.

I was one of those rare and lucky writers to immediately get an offer and sign a contract with a seasoned agent representing a reputable NY-based literary agency. My agent taught me to be tough skinned and accept rejection as part of being a writer. But it wasn't the rejections that bothered me; it was the reason behind the rejections that hurt. The positive rejections from many of the big and small publishing houses, the feedbacks about my "undoubtedly fierce talent," "beautiful writing," "powerful storytelling," etc., made it even more difficult to accept them rejecting my book because I didn't have a strong-enough "platform." A what? I asked my agent what that even meant. It meant that I didn't have enough of a social-media presence, that I wasn't well-known enough as a writer — or a person — to sell enough books. It was akin to the oxymoron of when companies won't hire you because you have no experience, but you can't get experience if no one will hire you. The old days of when a writer's only job was to write a quality book were long gone. With the advent of social media, writing a good book is no longer enough. A book is more than a creative endeavor; it's also a product. And today's writers have to also be PR agents, social-media strategists, marketing managers and self promoters of their "product." You have to be a writer and a businessperson; the latter, I am not!

When my agent said that there was no question about the quality of my book and that 10 years ago (before social media), it would've been published on its own merit, I felt like I had been punched in the gut. Because 10 years ago, the book was ready. It was only the fear of it not being original that made me believe I had missed the proverbial boat, and that trying to publish it was just a pipe dream and a waste of time.

Years later, I went the route of self-publishing, only to fall prey to one of the many scam self-publishing houses pretending to be legitimate.

Brick-and-mortar bookstores all but disappeared. Playing Candy Crush, tweeting, gaining followers on Instagram, and getting "likes" for endless selfies replaced reading as a pleasurable pastime.

Defeated, disillusioned and distraught, I once again abandoned my publishing goals.

Shortly thereafter, my eighth-grade English teacher and mentor passed away unexpectedly. His untimely death had a profound effect on me and all the students who were blessed to have had him as a teacher. When I had promised Mr. Bailey to acknowledge him in my first novel, I didn't take it seriously that I would indeed write a novel someday. I remembered that promise, as well as my promise not to waste what he had called my "gift for writing." As I mourned his loss, I re-evaluated myself as a writer.

Although many writers, agents and editors I've spoken to are equally disappointed and saddened by the shifts and new realities of the publishing industry, I realized that my ego was the main culprit, complicit in holding me back. It was my ego that had me believing that I had to be the first to write about a subject, that I had to be published by the big leagues. It was my ego that had blinded me to my true beliefs about what it means to be a writer. I set aside my ego and acknowledged that I write because it's my passion. I had written this book because it was a story that covered a lot of important issues, some of which transcend culture and nationality. My book isn't just about the Iranian Revolution. It's also about how certain events affect us, change us and shape who we are, for better or worse. The themes of prejudice, bullying, forgiveness, acceptance, rejection and addiction are universal. This book isn't just about the Iranian experience. It's about the human experience.

Everything's been done; everything's been said. But no one has done it, no one has said it the way someone else has. Each person's style, voice, perspective, interpretation and vision is different from another's. Each person's reality of the same event is unique. I remembered Mr. Bailey saying that writing isn't about the subject, but about the passion in the writing and the voice of the writer. Imagine if all the powerful stories about the Holocaust were never told because every writer thought that Anne Frank already said it all in her diary. Imagine if all the powerful books and movies about the Civil War never came to fruition because the writers or producers thought there was nothing left to say after *Gone with the Wind.* And on that note, imagine if perseverance wasn't one of Margaret Mitchell's strong suits and she hadn't pursued her publishing quest just *one* more time after her 37th rejection, depriving American readers of the second most popular book of all time, rivaled only by the bible.

So even if my story about the Iranian Revolution is not the first of its kind, Iranian-American writers are still a minority in the literary world and I'm proud to be one among them.

An estimated 3 million Iranian-Americans live in the United States. The majority of us are educated professionals who have contributed significantly to American society, economically, culturally and personally. But we are still under-recognized as a people and even less so as creative individuals.

My quest in publishing this book is to give a voice to Iranian-Americans who are still considered a minority in the United States in general, and the literary world in particular.

According to Wikipedia, "Iranian Americans are among the most highly educated people in the United States.[1] They have historically excelled in business, academia, science, the arts, and entertainment."[2]

While people of different colors, religious backgrounds and ethnicities are fighting for acceptance and taking pride in who they are, Iranian immigrants continue to face prejudice and silently accept that being Iranian is still synonymous with being a "terrorist." Prejudice and xenophobia stem from fear and ignorance. As writers, part of our job is to educate, to replace fear with familiarity. I recently read an anonymous post on the Internet by someone who said that Iranian-Americans who hyphenate their ethnicity should "just pick a country and better yet, go back where they came from." Perhaps someday a statement like that will be as unacceptable and ignorant as saying the equivalent about African-Americans. As my character Ari says, *"Maybe if we educate Americans about (how much good there is in our country), there won't be so much prejudice against Iran."*

I'm honored that I'm just one of many writers who is slowly, but surely removing the stigmas attached to Iran and its people, what we continue to deal with inside our country and abroad. This book is for my fellow Iranian-Americans and the all they've endured. "No matter how the revolution has impacted

[1] "MigrationInformationSource–SpotlightontheIranianForeignBorn". Migrationinformation.org. June 2006. Retrieved 15 February 2010.

[2a b] "Iranian-AmericansReportedAmongMostHighlyEducatedinU.S". Payvand.com. 24 November 2006. Retrieved 15 February 2010.

Iran, one thing I have seen in Iranians is resiliency. Our culture has stayed rich in tradition and artistry, our people ripe with success. At some point, we have all tapped into our strengths and shown our malleability."

Unlike Miryam, the protagonist of this book, maybe we as Iranian-Americans will no longer whisper when someone asks us where we're from, no longer feel shame from all the bullying and the ignorance surrounding who we are. Perhaps someday we will no longer change our Iranian names to their Americanized versions, no longer say we're "Persian" instead of "Iranian" because of the political connotations of being Iranian. Perhaps someday we will no longer be the world's nomads and feel proud and blessed that we have not one, but two countries to call home.

So even though I'm not the first person to write a novel about the plight of Iranian-Americans, I certainly hope I'm not the last.

Author's Note:

This book is a work of fiction. I have done my best to research the political, economic and historical events related to Iran and the 1979 revolution, as well as to informally and formally interview people in and out of Iran about their experiences and opinions on various subject matters and incidents depicted in this book. I have also loosely woven in snippets of certain personal memories, anecdotes and experiences about growing up in Iran and the United States. But while the basic, historical premise of this book is factual, this book is not a memoir and is not intended to be regarded as such. The events, characters, dialogue and opinions in this book are fictitious.

The characters are not based on any persons, living or dead, and the events or opinions expressed throughout the book are not meant to represent my or my family's experiences, nor do they reflect our personal, political or religious beliefs.

I know that I cannot possibly capture the plethora of subjects, individual stories, experiences or opinions of every Iranian, in or out of Iran, relating to the revolution. Nor was that ever my intention. Mine is simply one account of a fictitious Iranian family's journey in the aftermath of the revolution.

Though I have combined research, interviews and personal accounts with imagination, this book is not meant to be a journalistic endeavor or to represent the experiences of any particular individual, family or culture as a whole.

Parts of the narrative are from a fictional character's childhood perspective. Therefore, the sometimes-light-hearted depiction of revolution and war from a child's viewpoint is just that; it is in no way meant to diminish or disrespect the plight of Iranians during the revolution and especially not meant to mitigate the experiences of the many soldiers who fought and/or lost their lives in the Iran-Iraq war. My father, a physician, served as a surgeon on the frontlines of this war and saw the atrocities first-hand. The protagonist's childlike viewpoint of the war does not in any way portray my understanding of the magnitude of the war's impact on Iran, its people, or my respect for the soldiers and their families.

I have no personal, political, or religious agendas or motivations in writing this book. My intention is neither to glorify, nor to condemn any country, government, political ideology, political figures, culture, social class, ethnicity or religion.

I have the utmost love and respect for my motherland of Iran, pride in my fellow Iranians in and out of Iran, as well as for my homeland of America and the American people.

Kathy Kaveh

PART I

Prologue

I had just woken up when Grandfather poked his head through my half-open door and asked if I wanted to go to the bakery with him. I nodded excitedly. I was 5 and had never been out of the house that early.

I got dressed quietly. Grandmother was still asleep, but she would be getting up for her morning prayers soon. If she heard me, she might not let me go. She might scold me back to sleep or God forbid, make me pray with her.

I put on my favorite blue summer dress with the white flowers and walked slowly to the back door. Grandfather was already there, brushing the lint off his beige pants. He looked up when he heard my blue clogs clicking on the linoleum. He opened his large hand with a smile. I looked down shyly and placed my hand in his.

We left the house just as dawn broke. The air was cool and smelled clean. We walked the curvy Tehran alley that led to the local bakery, grocer and flower shop. The sidewalk was rocky and dented like the face of an aging beggar, but the smooth street was newly re-paved, glistening with shiny black asphalt.

Grandfather nodded to the flower shop's elderly owner, who was sweeping the dead autumn leaves off the sidewalk. He was brushing away the leaves hurriedly, as if scared that the vibrant leaves on the flowers inside his store would see them and wilt at the sorrow of what their own future held.

When the man saw Grandfather, he stopped the swish of his broom, bowed and whispered, "Good morning, *Agha.*" Grandfather nodded back in acknowledgment. I felt proud to be walking with this powerful *Agha*, this man who wore a suit even to pick up bread.

Grandfather held my hand tightly, but didn't speak during our walk. And I wasn't my usual talkative self that morning. I didn't want to do anything wrong. I wanted him to enjoy my company so he would take me to the bakery again the next time I stayed at their place. I wanted to earn my position as his companion.

His smile would widen when along the narrow way, I kicked the acorns that had fallen from the trees hovering above. Any other adult would have scolded me. Something about my shoes, about how a young lady should walk. But he never did.

I can still hear the birds chirping loudly to compete with our footsteps in giving the silence a melody. I can still smell Grandfather's after-shave, the morning air and the hot *Sangak* bread folded under his arm in the crinkly white paper. I can still taste the steam from the warm bread. I can still feel Grandfather's strong hand cupped gently around mine.

We did not exchange a single word that morning, but it was the safest, most loved I had ever felt.

A week later, he died.

No one ever made me feel like that again, until Ari.

Chapter 1

I used to think Ari was my cousin. Because that's what Iranians do; they call anyone even five times removed their cousin. I have 657 cousins. Some are actual cousins, others are cousins of cousins and still others are just, cousins.

So I thought Ari was my "cousin" because our parents used to be good friends in the good-old Iran days, before either of us was born.

His full name is Aryan. I think it's a rare and beautiful name. Very fitting of the rest of him. It's as scarce and cool as say, Luke, is in America. My name is one of the most common Persian names. It's like Jane. Only Leila — as common as Jennifer — is a more popular name than Miryam (the usual spelling and pronunciation of which is Maryam.)

But Ari hates his name.

"They might as well have named me Hitler," he always says.

But just because Hitler believed that the Aryan race was supreme, and that Jews are not of the Aryan race, doesn't mean the term Aryan itself is anti-Semitic. The name Aryan simply pertains to the Aryan race, which Iranians are descendants of, but it has nothing to do with Hitler or anti-Semitism.

Ari's dad, Mr. Tabaii, was my mom's *khastegar,* a candidate for an arranged marriage. The way that works is that Ari's grandfather liked the way my grandfather did business, so it was a given that their kids would someday marry. Of course there's a lot more to it than that. Ancestry, social class, economic status, yada, yada, blah and blah were equally important factors. But essentially, two people who may not even be able to stand the sight of each other should marry because it just makes good — economic and social — sense.

They met when my mom was 19 (ripe for marriage…tick, tock, tick, tock until she rots) and Ari's dad was 30 (had enough escapades under his belt to settle down and satisfy the virgin lust of his grateful bride.)

They were attracted enough to each other, got along on the few occasions they dined alone and actually had a lot in common. But to my grandparents' horror, Mom didn't want to get married just yet.

So after endless discussions, the families ended the courtship amicably. Before he married Ari's mom, Mr. Tabaii even sought Mom's approval and permission. For years, his wife, Soraya, didn't know that he had almost married Mom. And when she did find out, she and Mom had become such good friends that she no longer cared.

Mr. Tabaii worked for the Shah (the former king of Iran.) I didn't really know what that meant. I still don't. I never asked. To me, anyone who worked for the Shah just "worked for the Shah." I was too young and politically ignorant to understand any details. We knew a lot of people who "worked for the Shah." So in my uncurious mind, they all had the same job, void of description. They just "worked for the Shah."

At the prime of their lives, our parents, 20- and 30-somethings with nothing in the world to lose but time, led the grandest of lives. They wore haute couture, dined with royalty — that is, "ate with the Shah" — and vacationed in places some people could only dream of visiting. Our photo albums depict pictures of my parents pointing at the Eiffel Tower, riding camels in Egypt, smiling on balconies in Greece and riding gondolas in Venice.

Even when we kids came into the picture, everything continued in the life-styles-of-the-rich-and-famous fashion. Raising us involved a few minutes a day of peek-a-boo, dressing us to replicate the pages of *Kids Vogue* and showing us off. Our nannies did all the grunge work: the diaper changings, late-night feedings and vomit wipings.

Ari and I were part of this life, but, damn, we were too young to appreciate it. He was born in November of 1968, eight months before my parents' wedding. And I came into the perfect picture not a day short of nine months after my parents got married.

Ari and I were apparently the best of friends. We played together in *Shomal* (the Caspian Sea), slept with our heads together when dinners at restaurants dragged late into the night and even took baths together (but, damn, I was too young to appreciate it.)

As all good things must come to an end, Ari's parents' good-only-on-the-outside marriage ended when Ari was 6. Mr. Tabaii had been having affairs left and right. Or as the British say, left, right and center. As usual, everyone, "all of Tehran," as Mom says, knew about the affairs except Soraya. When she found out, it was blow after blow after blow.

They divorced immediately, and Soraya got full custody of Ari without a battle from his father.

After the Tabaiis divorced, our families slowly, but completely, lost touch. I never saw Ari after that and forgot he even existed until after the Iranian Revolution.

Chapter 2

It's a beautiful, warm Los Angeles day in June 1993.

Even the freshmen are partying, but I don't have time to celebrate the end of my school career. I've been busy preparing for my parents' visit from Iran. Making three trips to the supermarket (it always takes me a while to remember what they like to eat), cleaning the house, making sure Nader gets a haircut, and most importantly, getting rid of all evidence that I smoke.

Mom's eyes twinkle proudly when she first sees me. But by the time we get onto the freeway, her critical eye takes over. I look unkempt, I'm wearing jeans again and my face looks too pale. And I'm driving too fast.

Dad, on the other hand, has barely spoken, as usual. He's still staring at me from the passenger seat with a look of sorrow and joy combined, as if he gave me up for adoption 22 years ago and we just reunited at the airport.

I pull into our driveway and pop open the trunk. My younger brother, Nader, runs out to greet Mom and Dad, while Cyrus, my middle brother, trails slowly behind.

"You're here!" Nader yells and throws himself in Mom's arms.

She grabs him so hard she almost knocks him down.

Dad laughs and looks over at Cyrus.

"How are you, son?" he asks and pats him on the shoulder. "Still growing?"

Cyrus chuckles nervously and fake-punches Dad's arm. They hug and kiss each other, then proceed to pull the suitcases out of the trunk.

"Help them out, Nader," I say when I see Dad struggling with a large suitcase.

But Mom won't let Nader go. She has officially started the long ritual of worshipping him. He's 12, going on 3.

"*Elahee man ghorbooneh oon reekhtet beram,*" she says in Farsi as she kisses his forehead.

Literally means, "I hope to be sacrificed for your face." He's the best looking out of the three of us, but nothing to die for, really.

Iranian expressions are loaded with themes of death and demise, even when they're about life and love. What people don't realize about stereotypes is that they're stereotypes for a reason: they're usually true. And just by virtue of their language, Iranians are correctly stereotyped as exaggerators. For example, while "shut up" in English simply means "shut your mouth," the Farsi version of shut up, "*Khafeh Sho,*" means "choke to death." But, of course, this is all just my ignorant opinion. Dad would argue for five hours about the billion-year tradition of the Farsi language, a language so rich that it actually differentiates between a silent fart and an audible one.

Dad and Cyrus drop the luggage in the middle of the living room, where Mom continues to beat her chest in a show of love for Nader.

"Fadayeh oon ghad o heykalet beram." (I hope to die for your height and your body.)

"Mom, stop it!" Nader yells and wipes his face with his sleeve. "Stop the fight! Stop the fight! Miryam?"

Instead of knock-knock jokes, Nader the film buff annoys everyone by quoting lines from movies, then asking us to name the movie. Cyrus always begs me not to encourage Nader, but it's a game I've actually grown to love.

I shake my head and frown. "No clue."

"No, not *Clue*," Nader says. "*Rocky IV*."

"Oh give me a break," I say. "Like I'm supposed to know some random line from Rocky freakin' four."

"Vatch your langvage, young lady," Mom says, glaring at me.

"What did I say?"

"Freaking," she says.

Cyrus, Nader and I crack up.

"Dat's not a bad vord," I say, imitating her accent. "You're tinking of fucking. Not da same ting as freaking."

"Hey, hey," she says and slaps the back of my hand. "Don't talk like dat in front of your little brodder."

Nader is hardly like a 12-year-old in many ways. Maybe because he was basically raised by a bunch of teenagers. The word "fuck" is G-rated to his ears.

I smile at Nader. Even though Mom knows better than to go near Nader's hair, he's combing his fingers through it as if Mom messed it up when she kissed him. He catches my smile, let's go of his thick, spiked-up hair and looks away shyly. He's often self-absorbed and self-conscious at the same time.

Mom approaches Cyrus. His turn to be slobbered over.

"Jiggereh man."

Then mine.

"Maman fadat besheh."

(Cyrus is her liver and she wants to sacrifice herself for me. No doubt after resurrecting from her earlier death for Nader.)

In the past five minutes, Nader has been drenched with kisses, Cyrus has been hugged bearishly, I've been looked up and down admiringly, and Mom has sacrificed her body and soul 58 times. Meanwhile, Dad remains standing in the corner watching us all with a fatherly look that only another father can appreciate.

After all the butchering and worshiping officially die down, we all just look around awkwardly like strangers in an elevator. Then Ari walks through the front door and makes me feel awkward in a whole other way.

"Oh hi," he says to my parents. "You're here. Welcome back."

He smiles at them shyly, as if he's not part of our nuclear unit and no one standing here would ever sacrifice themselves for him.

Little does he know.

Chapter 3

"Every syllable of every word in the English language has a vowel in it," my second-grade teacher, Mrs. Ambler, explained. "And what are the vowels again?"

"A, e, i, o, u," the class answered in unison.

"And sometimes y," Mrs. Ambler said. "Don't forget sometimes y."

"Why y?" I asked. "What word starts with y as a vowel?"

"Good question, Miryam," she said. "It doesn't mean that it *starts* with a vowel. Y becomes a vowel in a syllable that doesn't have any other vowel in it. It could be anywhere in the word. Like in 'happy' or 'cry.' Or in Tony's name.

Or in Patty's name. Or in the word you just used to ask your question, Miryam. The word 'why.'"

Tony, Patty and I smiled, proud to have been part of Mrs. Ambler's explanation.

"So 'why' is a word where y is a vowel?" someone asked with a giggle.

"That's right." She smiled. "So let's try that one more time, everyone. What are the vowels?"

Twenty high-pitched voices repeated, "a, e, i, o, u. And sometimes y."

Mrs. Ambler took half a point off my test the following week because I had jokingly written that the vowels were "a, e, i, o, u. And sometimes why."

Chapter 4

I wish Ari wouldn't disappear whenever my parents visit. And he's always evasive about where he's going. Which is why I'm always paranoid that he's dating someone without my knowledge. As close as we are, he never talks to me about his love life.

Until a few years ago, he always included me in his social life. But ever since he graduated college and started working as a computer software developer, he hasn't had much of a social life. On the rare occasions he does go out, he no longer asks me to join him.

My parents are having their annual party at our house to re-unite with their friends in Los Angeles. I find Mom talking to her friend Mrs. Hekmat and prepare for small talk.

"So, Miryam," Mrs. Hekmat says as she sips her white wine. "Do you have a boyfriend now?"

"No, she does not," Mom says, giving me a dirty look.

Mrs. Hekmat smiles sympathetically at me, as if apologizing for asking me the taboo question in front of Mom.

"Well, in time a nice young gentleman will come and sweep her off her feet," she says to appease Mom.

Mom gives me a suspicious look, a "Jim-never-vomits-at-*home*" look.

"Jim never vomits at *home*" is a line from the farce movie *Airplane,* where a paranoid wife questions every random thing her husband does, including throwing up. Thanks to Nader, it's become an inside joke among us kids whenever someone is acting suspicious.

I look away and smile at one of the guests swaying to the Persian music. I complain about these parties only because I'm not good at socializing. But I do love having the house so alive. Music and laughter fill the air as much as the smell of Mom's *ghormeh sabzi* cooking in the kitchen. The slipcovers are off the couches, the Persian carpets are rolled out, and the little crystal dishes on the coffee table are actually filled with candy and pistachios. Mom can turn even a dungeon into a home.

Mom sees Nader sitting on a nearby sofa and yanks him up.

"Nader has a nice little girlfriend," Mom says to Mrs. Hekmat. "Jennifer, is it?"

Nader nods, but with obvious annoyance.

"I'm not surprised," Mrs. Hekmat says. "Such a handsome man he's becoming."

I look around to make sure Cyrus didn't hear her. He's self-conscious enough about his looks without constantly needing to hear how handsome his little brother is. Not that Cyrus is ugly. He's just an average, typical-Iranian-looking guy. He's hairy, has olive skin, and a large, boney nose. He's not really bad looking. But he's never exactly been popular with girls either. I'm sure it has more to do with his shyness than his looks, but it's hard to say. Maybe he's shy around girls because he thinks he's ugly.

I stand up on my tiptoes and see that Cyrus is away in the patio. So I smile at Mrs. Hekmat's compliment to Nader — as if I had any role in how he looks.

"You see how tall he's gotten since you last saw him?" I ask. "He's taller than Cyrus now."

"Miryam," Nader groans. "Cut it out."

He walks away and I chuckle. Nader thrives on attention, no matter that he acts aloof. So I give him lots of it. A 12-year-old who lives without his parents 11 months out of the year needs to be doted on.

"You should see his girlfriend," Mom says to Mrs. Hekmat. "She's beautiful."

I nod, then frown. Mom has never even seen Jennifer.

"He's a real playboy already," Mom continues with a smile. "I just wish he'd rub off on Cyrus."

I give her a dirty look that I know she'll never interpret as my loath for her chauvinism and walk away. She yells after me, "Bring out some tea, would you?" I pretend not to hear her. I do have my limits when it comes to being treated like a girl.

In my next life, I don't care if I come back as a dog. As long as it's a male dog. Instead of a bitch.

My parents don't know how lucky they are that my feelings for Ari make me feel guilty even when I check out guys with my friends Bee and Paige, let alone date.

I don't think I'd be much of a girlfriend to any guy. Except for Ari himself, of course. But as unrequited loves go, I stay up crying for him at nights while he snores away.

The part of me that sees Ari as a brother has never met the part of me that prays for him to be my lover. When I stick my tongue out at him in sisterly jest, I forget that he's the same guy I wish would suck my tongue in loverly passion. And when I imagine him gazing deeply into my eyes, I forget that our eyes see each other strutting around the house in a towel all the time without a second's thought.

Bee says that I purposely fell in love with Ari knowing I couldn't have him so that I would never join the real dating world and disobey my parents. Spoken just like a girl who's been allowed to date since she was 14. I love vicariously living the life of an Iranian girl with freedom. It shocks and thrills me when she says things like she, her parents and her latest boyfriend all went out for Chinese food. A scene like that with my parents would involve an ambulance taking Dad to the ICU.

"Didn't I ask you to bring some tea for the guests?" Mom asks as she passes by me.

She's gone into the kitchen before I have a chance to ignore her. I peel an orange and continue watching the men do shots in the patio. Two of the men clink glasses.

"After you," one of them says, lowering his glass.

"No, please, after you," the other one says, lowering his glass even more.

They do this until they're both practically crouched on the ground, still begging the other to go first. When they can't get any lower, they clink glasses one last time and finally down their shots.

Cyrus, meanwhile, has had three shots. Maybe if he, too, picked up on these polite Persian rituals called *taroff*, he wouldn't drink so much.

He flinches and puts down his shot glass. Dad laughs and pats him on the back.

Cyrus certainly has come a long way from when he was single digit in age and Dad would give him tastes of wine and champagne. Mom and Dad would get a kick out of him licking his lips after drinking an entire glass of wine in one gulp at the age of 7. But you'd think they'd be slightly worried when a few years later, he would beg them for a drink on a random weeknight when even my parents were drinking Pepsi.

They obviously don't realize Cyrus' penchant for self-destructiveness or they wouldn't be so blasé about him drinking. Every time they visit, they destroy all of my and Ari's hard work with Cyrus.

I grab my crystal wine glass from the table and take a sip. Dad's friend, Mr. Arastoo, walks out of the bathroom and towards me.

"Why are you sitting here all by yourself?" he asks.

"Oh, I'm fine," I say with a smile. "I'm just observing."

"You'd rather be out with your boyfriend instead of here with us old folks, huh?" he says with a chuckle. "Well, it's only once a year when your parents visit."

"Don't be silly, this is lovely."

Besides, haven't you heard? I'm not allowed to date until a nice young gentleman comes and sweeps Mom and Dad off their feet.

I stand up to continue the conversation with Mr. Arastoo. But after we establish that the weather is indeed uncharacteristically warm considering it's only early June, we have nothing more to say and our silence makes the room uncharacteristically quiet considering 30 other people are chattering and laughing nearby.

Mom saves me with a come-here glare.

"Excuse me," I say to a-relieved-looking Mr. Arastoo. "I think my mom needs me."

He nods gently and I walk towards Mom.

"That's your second glass of wine," she whispers.

"So?" I say with a frown.

"So, I don't want you drinking in front of my friends."

"What? Cyrus is on his second *bottle* of tequila."

"That's different. You're a lady. And another thing. Don't peel an orange if you're not gonna eat it. Don't you know there are starving children in Africa who would kill for the orange you just left to go dry on that plate?"

I mumble an apology and walk away to my bathroom. I smoke two cigarettes in a row and open the window to let the built-up smoke escape before walking back to the living room.

"Where have you been?" Mom snaps.

"Sorry," I say as I cover my mouth with a tissue, pretending to dab my lipstick. "I was in the bathroom."

"Go mingle," she says. "You're not a child anymore. You have to be sociable at these parties."

She walks away leaving her half-empty wine glass on the coffee table.

Doesn't she know that there are alcoholics out there who would kill for the rest of the wine she left to go bad?

I pick it up and down it.

Chapter 5

I cried every day in kindergarten. My parents had enrolled me in *Farhang America*, a private American school in Tehran. They wanted me to learn English and become friends with the better class of kids that attended private school. But before I learned English and found those classy friends, I struggled to communicate with them and understand the strange language in which they teased me for being a crybaby.

But by the second grade, I spoke better English than Farsi and had more American friends than Iranian ones. I had finally started to fit in.

Then the revolution ensued.

It was March 14, 1979. I specifically remember the date because Persian New Year was exactly a week away. The revolution had been in full swing for a while. But leave it to me to have been the only living creature in all of Iran — and possibly the world — not to know what was going on.

All I knew was that I missed watching the Pink Panther cartoons on TV while doing my homework. Both channels showed news, news and still more news. Everything north, east, west and south, was news. Demonstrations, arrests, American hostages.

And closer to my world, my parents were whispering all the time, Dad fired two of our maids and my American teachers at school were absent for 12 days and counting. My parents explained nothing to me, except that I should go to school, keep my mouth shut, come home and stay home. It was all very vague, but I obeyed, never questioning much.

No one told us why we were being dismissed from school early almost every day or why our teachers suddenly didn't care about homework. But I was 8 and the only thing occupying my mind was the upcoming two-week New Year's vacation.

But even I could no longer ignore what was happening that Wednesday afternoon in March when I was reading a *Little Lulu* comic book at the kitchen table. I heard Mom shrieking and I ran upstairs in a panic that mimicked the sound of her voice. She was on the floor crying and Dad was holding her crouched body, his arms vibrating to the rhythm of her convulsions. Newspaper pages were scattered around them. I started crying and screaming hysterically, only because Mom was. Dad ran to me, covered my screaming mouth and dragged me out.

Everything else is sketchy. Some water. Our maid, Zohreh, putting me to bed. Waking up in the middle of the night to Mom's swollen eyes. Holding her tight as she stroked my hair and whispered "sorry" in my ear.

I finally got the full story in sketches similar to the day's memory. My parents had read in the newspaper that Ari's dad had been executed for political reasons. I didn't know who he was, but I was terrified about his death. Until we left Iran, I was scared that because my parents knew someone who had been killed by the new government, they, too, could be killed.

The next day, my parents called Ari's mom. Afraid that her phone was tapped, she came over our house with Ari to talk to my parents in person. The adults told us to go play in my room. I made Ari play Barbie fashion show with me while our parents talked in the living room until way past our bedtimes.

Ari's mom was terrified. She was banned from leaving the country, but she sought to get Ari out any way she could. She asked for my parents to be on the lookout for any family leaving Iran who could take Ari with them.

My parents committed to making sure Ari would escape the country that had killed his father.

I've never talked to Ari about his dad. I can only wonder what had gone through his mind the day he found out. The day when I got my first glimpse of how the revolution was going to change every Iranian's life forever.

Chapter 6

My friend Paige does a ballet move, picks me up and spins me around clumsily. "Happy graduation!"

Looking at my family, you'd never guess that they're dressed to attend the same event today. My parents look like they're going to a black-tie wedding, while Cyrus and Nader are dressed perfectly for a baseball game. Mom's blue eye shadow is only slightly less inappropriate and sparkling than her diamond necklace. Nader's shorts are six sizes too big for him, as fashion dictates, and Cyrus is sporting his usual jeans and T-shirt, stating that he won't let fashion dictate him.

But they're all wearing the same smile, their eyes twinkling with the same pride. I'm thrilled that I'm the cause of it all, the reason we're all together for a change, being festive and loving.

Just last night, I had gotten into fight number (I've lost track) with Mom about how she treats me like a 12-year-old. So I yelled at her and then she yelled at me for yelling at her in front of my father. As usual, I had trouble verbally apologizing and did so instead with inane gestures like helping her unpack her suitcase. By the time I had hung up her tenth black skirt, I felt more angry than sorry and stormed out. If I really were 12, that would've been the point I would've locked myself in my room, listened to Depeche Mode's "Little 15" over and over and written in my "journal" (distinctly different from diary) about how my parents, you know, like, suck.

But I'm not 12. I'm 22, so as usual, I brushed it all under the intricately patterned Persian carpet. And Mom and I both woke up today pretending everything was fine.

Dad puts his arm around my waist and squeezes me. Mom snaps another of her famous unposed pictures.

"Good goin' Sissy," Nader says and kisses my cheek.

He gets a kick out of calling me Sissy. He insists that it's just an innocent nickname for his sister, but we both know that there's also a double entendre not so hidden in there. He's a little too smart for my good.

I smile and move my hand towards his hair, pretending I'm gonna mess it up. He jerks his palm up and pulls himself back in a panic. I crack up. I love this narcissistic kid.

"I can't wait to get my diploma," Cyrus says.

"Don't be in too much of a hurry," I say.

He shoots me a give-me-a-break look. But I feel like an adult today and that's the kind of thing adults are supposed to say.

"You be kviet, young man," Mom says. "You get your grades up before you even tink about graduating."

"Oh God," Cyrus mutters. "Here we go again."

"Mom, leave him alone," I whisper.

"Vhy you alvays protect him?" Mom asks. "Is dis da vay you are vit him ven ve not here? You say leave him alone? So he goofing off?"

I walk away so she'll stop talking about Cyrus, especially in front of Paige.

I actually really do look after Cyrus when my parents aren't here. More so than I do Nader, who's half his age. But when they're here, I put on my protect-Cyrus gear. I step in as the punching bag when they aim for him. No one, not even my parents, understands Cyrus. Everyone thinks he's grumpy and spoiled. But he's just shy and sensitive. When he does talk, it's usually sprinkled with sarcasm. And the more people pick on him, the more he shuts out the world. It's a fine line trying to let Cyrus just be without making him think he can do whatever he wants. I'm always wary of slipping off that line. It's almost a curse that I know him so well. It's a huge responsibility having the confidence of someone so fragile in your hands. But at least he knows I'm on his side, no matter what. We could go months without really talking – as we often do – and still remain on the same wavelength.

"Don't worry about her," I say to him.

"Do I ever?"

"Shhh," I whisper.

Dad senses the tension and changes the subject. He kisses me and tells me how proud he is.

"You know, your mother and I sacrificed everything for your education. We left our home, we started a whole new life just so you kids could get a proper education."

He's not trying to be preachy. This actually is the appropriate day for him to give me the speech he's given me every day since we moved here from Iran.

"Now let me see what we sacrificed everything for," he says in a sing-song voice, pointing to the leather folder in my hand.

I show him the piece of paper that reads, "Thank you for participating in today's ceremony. Your diploma will be mailed to you shortly."

Paige moves closer to us and opens her folder.

"Hey," she says. "Generic diplomas."

It's the kind of day when you laugh at anything, even that.

Mom starts where Dad took off. "You know, Paige, Mr. Mirashti and I leave our children all alone in America and live der in Iran so we can pay so dey go to eskool like dis."

Paige nods seriously and acts as if she, too, hasn't heard this speech before.

"Mom," I say, "There are at least a hundred other Iranian kids who graduated right here today and I bet all their parents are here from Iran saying the same exact thing."

"First of all, not all da parents have to live der in Iran. Ve lost all our money, young lady."

"Second of all?" I say.

She looks at me with a confused frown.

"Never mind," I say.

I kiss her cheek and hug her tightly. "Well, thank you. I know how hard it was for you."

"Vhy you talk in pass tense? Is still hard. I have two more boys. And dey *really* have to estudy because dey marry vomen."

"What my mom means," I say wanting to die in front of a confused-looking-but-still-smiling Paige, "is that traditionally, and I emphasize traditionally, men are the breadwinners of the family. Because now that I, a mere female, have a college education, I can go to Mr. Cray and get my job at Pavilions back."

My parents are both very embarrassed about my working as a checkout girl at Pavilions supermarket. It was on their list of "300 jobs unsuitable for a proper Iranian girl." Stripper, hooker, checkout girl. They translated checkout girl into check-*me*-out girl.

"Don't be silly," Mom snaps. "Of course vomen have to vork at good job too. Not cashier." She glares at me. "But is more important for da man. No, Paige?"

I *know* she just asked the wrong person the wrong question. I mean, what would Gloria Steinem say right about now? But leave it to Paige to nod and say, of all things, "Absolutely."

Mom must be forgetting that being a cashier was actually my dream job when I was little. "Wow look at all that money she has," I would say when the checkout girl at our local grocery store would open the cash register. How come they don't think it's cute anymore? I start to tell Mom and Paige the story just to lighten the mood, when I notice Ari walking towards us with a bouquet of red roses.

"Congratulations, angel," he says and kisses me on both cheeks.

"Thanks, Ari," I say giddy as a schoolgirl with a shaky voice. "When did you get here?"

"I've been trying to find parking for the past half hour. Then I couldn't find you guys. Sorry I missed the ceremony."

I just continue to smile, not trusting myself to open my mouth beyond a stretch of my lips. I grab the flowers excitedly, as if he's a professor handing me back a test I got an A on.

"He's looking bubblicious," Paige whispers in my ear.

I smile proudly, as if he's mine to blow.

He does look extra polished today. Ari has *GQ*-style taste in clothes. He doesn't buy clothes often, but when he does, he only buys the best. But he's not a label lover. He says that usually designer clothes cost what they do because they're high quality. But he'll buy a Zegna tie just as easily as a Walmart shirt if he thinks it's nice and of good quality. And he'll get a compliment regardless. He's always appropriately dressed too. He'll wear jeans and a T-shirt to the movies and look just as good as when he wears a suit to a fancy restaurant. I'm not the only one who thinks so either. Everybody always comments on Ari's sense of style. He was even voted "Best Dressed" in his high-school yearbook.

He took time off from work to come to my graduation today, and since it's "Casual Friday," he's wearing jeans, a white button-down shirt and he just now realized it's too hot and took off his black blazer. The jeans round out his butt perfectly. And the white shirt accentuates his olive skin and makes his eyes look a lighter shade of brown than they really are.

He catches me staring at him and winks. I don't even attempt to wink back. I smile and turn quickly away.

I see my friend Bee and wave her over. She's surrounded by her large Persian family and I don't feel like doing the polite thing of saying hello and kissing everyone from her mother to her step-uncle on both cheeks.

Bee was the first person I met when we moved to Los Angeles. Our homeroom teacher had asked her to be my "buddy" on my first day of school because we were both Persian. But Bee was tight with the hip (aka American) crowd and wanted nothing to do with the new Iranian girl, lest I tarnish her image. The only thing she said to me that day was, "Do NOT speak Farsi with me." I was intimidated by her and hated her from day one and all the way through high school. We didn't become close until college, when she finally deemed me cool enough to befriend.

Her real name is Behnaz. But on her first day of school in America, her third-grade teacher had stuttered trying to pronounce her name during roll call. She kept mumbling, "B...B..." and Behnaz opted to say, "B is fine. Just call me B." And Behnaz didn't know that Bea was a correct Americanized option for her name and had written "Bee" on all her homework assignments. So Behnaz became Bee from then on. It's one of the more ridiculous ones, but most Iranians have an American version of their names. Reza becomes Ray, Shahrokh becomes Sean, Farhad becomes Fred, and so on. Almost all Persians do it, but they make fun of every other Persian who does it. The award for the most ingenious, but absurd, Persian-to-American concoction I've heard goes to a guy I knew named "Asghar" who went by "Oscar."

Bee walks towards us and immediately starts flirting with Ari. She takes her graduation cap off and flings her long, blonde-dyed hair at him. I don't mind when she flirts with him because Ari never pays any attention to her and I know that she doesn't even realize when she's flirting. She does it with every guy. She's not exactly a dumb (fake) blonde, but she's more pretty than she is smart, and she's always relied on her looks for attention.

She runs her finger through her hair and complains about the humidity.

"Congratulations on your graduation, too," I say sarcastically.

"Oh yeah," she says with a laugh. "Congrats, you guys. Come here!"

She hugs Paige and me at the same time. She hands her camera to Ari and asks him to take a picture of us. She stands in the middle and wraps an arm around each of us.

"Your hair was covering Miryam's left eye and Paige's right eye," Ari says to Bee after taking a few snapshots. "But that's how all you guys' pictures are."

Bee throws her head back and laughs. Ari smiles at me and hands Bee her camera.

"Damn," she whispers to me. "Did you see the way he smiled at you?"

I know his smile was meant to mock Bee more than to flirt with me, so I play dumb and pretend I didn't notice.

"Behnaz!" Bee's mom hollers towards us. "Come here. We're taking pictures."

She doesn't ask Paige or me to join them and for that, I'm grateful. To say I've never felt comfortable with Bee's family is putting it mildly. They've always been very judgmental of my parents for going back to Iran and leaving us here. I know it's not anyone's idea of a sound decision, but it's not anyone's business either. My parents, on their part, judge hers for being too lenient and letting Bee date any guy she wants to.

Bee blows air kisses at Paige and me, then struts back to her family.

I walk with Paige to where Dad, Cyrus and Nader are huddled around a young girl. This has Nader written all over it. He's a kid with a taste for the finer things in life.

"Merci," the girl says, blushing purple.

No doubt one of them just told her how pretty she is. Well, we know it wasn't Cyrus.

She really is pretty. She and her parents are here for her older sister's graduation. My parents end up knowing her parents from Iran, so hugging, kissing and sacrificing themselves for each other ensue.

"Wow, what a small world," Paige says to me.

"Not really," I say. "Just small Iran flocked to Los Angeles. Or better known as 'Irangeles.'"

"Right," she says, as if apologizing for forgetting this factoid.

"How's Jennifer?" I whisper to Nader without looking for his reaction.

Never too early to teach the kid to respect women.

When the family leaves, Dad pats Nader on the shoulder, like he just graduated something too, and they share a laugh.

"Typical," I say, walking away with Paige.

"Oh, lighten up, Mir. It was cute."

"Cute? Maybe to you. You're not the one treated like you're 12 while your 12-year-old brother is treated like he's 22."

"You're so bitter towards your family," she says with obvious annoyance. "You actually are like a 12-year-old who's like embarrassed to be seen at the movies with her parents. And speaking of embarrassing, I cannot believe you dragged me into that fiasco with your mom. About women working. I was mortified."

"Fiasco? That was just about the tamest conversation I've had with my mom since she got here. She's more, I don't know, soft around other people."

"Which is more than I can say for you. Why are you so mean to her? So she's a little old-fashioned. Seriously, Mir, all that stuff you constantly make fun of, how they sacrificed everything for you, I don't think you really get it."

I want to defend myself and say I do get it, I do appreciate it and she could never understand that I made just as many sacrifices as they did. Probably more actually. But as usual, I see Paige's point and end up apologizing to her for I don't know what.

"Don't apologize to *me*," she says. "Apologize to *them*. Anyway, forget it. There's my dad and Babs."

Paige calls her mom by her first name, or rather, by that ridiculous shortened version of Barbara. Paige shortens everything. She would even shorten Bee's name if she could. She would just smack her lips together and make a B sound.

Paige's last name is Turner. Her father, a book publisher, was ecstatic when the ultrasound showed that she was a girl so he could create a pun with her name. "Paige Turner. My bestseller." It makes her sound like a prostitute if you ask me, but it is pretty witty.

Paige is one of the nicest, most uncomplicated people I've ever known. Case in point: she would go to Baskin Robbins and order a scoop of vanilla. Her mom told me that when Paige was 7, she once put a dollar bill under their car's windshield wipers after a drive through heavy rain and when her mom asked her why she had done that, she had said, "Just giving them a tip for all their hard work. They must be exhausted."

She walks over to her dad as her mom walks towards mine.

I go stand by Mom to make sure East doesn't say anything embarrassing to West.

Mrs. Turner isn't very worldly. And like Paige, she's lived in the same vicinity her entire life. Aside from Bee and me, I don't think she knows any foreigners. And certainly none from as alien a country as Iran. I sometimes wonder if she even knows where that is. Or if she thinks it's the same place as Iraq. People like Paige's mom baffle me. It's not like I expect people to learn about my country, but I would assume that with so many Iranians living in Los Angeles, something like her husband having an Iranian co-worker (which she tells me every time she sees me) wouldn't exactly be newsworthy either. Everyone in Los Angeles knows at least one Iranian. It could be their dry cleaner or the president of their company. To my chagrin, we're all over the place.

And she pronounces Iranian "Eye-ranian," which I believe is the biggest pet peeve of every Iranian on the planet. But she is very sweet and at least she's intrigued, rather than repulsed, by my nationality.

I don't even know how I actually relate to Paige, a girl whose family personifies the perfect American life. Storybook Christmases, three generations of women sitting around the Thanksgiving turkey and actual conversations at an actual dinner table are the norm in their lives. Paige got accepted to Columbia, NYU and Princeton, but chose to go to UCLA so she could stay with her family. She rejected Ivy League schools for the familiar ivy growing outside her childhood home.

"Hello, Mrs. Mirashti," Paige's mom says to mine. "Congratulations."

"Yes, tank you," Mom says. "You too. You must be so proud of Paige. Miryam tell me she going to become doctor."

"Dentist," Mrs. Turner says. "Yes. But she still has to apply to dental school. Let's hope she gets accepted into some good ones."

"I'm sure she vill," Mom says, nodding. "I kill a lamb for her."

I turn red as a slaughtered lamb's blood and scramble to change the subject immediately. But it's too late. Mrs. Turner's eyes are already popping out of their sockets.

"Excuse me?" she says, looking at me to translate.

"Kill lamb," Mom says. "In our culture, ven ve have a vish from God, ve kill a lamb and give da meat to charity or da hungry people and ask God to make our vish come true. Is called a 'nazr.'"

"That's fascinating," Mrs. Turner says. "Well thank you very much. I appreciate that."

"Yes, yes. Is good deed for good result. I kill da lamb for her as soon as I go back to Iran."

"You kill the lamb yourself?" Mrs. Turner asks in shock.

I don't know whether to laugh or cry. So I just whimper and beg for God to make this conversation end. Wish I had a lamb to kill.

"No, no," Mom says, laughing. "Of course not. Ve buy a good lamb and give it to professional lamb killer."

Note to self: kill Mom and give da meat to da hungry people.

"Fascinating," Mrs. Turner says again.

"Yes, yes," Mom says. "And sometimes..."

"Mom, that's enough. She gets the point."

Mom gets quiet and just smiles. Finally, the silence of the lambs.

Chapter 7

Principal Clarkson walked into our third-grade history class as we scrambled to our assigned seats. Suddenly, all the chatter about how we had spent our holidays lulled into a silence uncharacteristic of kids still hyper from vacation. Everyone sat up straight. We were terrified of him, simply because he was our principal. I, for one, was petrified of authority figures in general, so I went one step further and stopped breathing.

It was our first day back to school after the Persian New Year holiday in April 1979.

After an insincere-sounding, "Welcome back," he said, "I wanted to let you know that some of your teachers will be absent again today and in the days to come. And we were all hoping that good things would be in store for the New Year. But unfortunately, most of your teachers will be gone permanently."

He sounded rehearsed, like even though it was only 8 a.m., he had already given his speech a dozen times. He read aloud the names of the teachers not returning. Our school had some Iranian, but mostly American, teachers. It didn't register just then that all the American teachers were leaving, only that most of the ones I loved were.

Mr. Clarkson handed us each a sealed envelope to give our parents. I hated those envelopes. They always meant trouble.

Substitute teachers once again presided over almost every class. But whereas all the students usually took advantage of substitutes to ensue chaos, that day, everybody was on their best behavior. I felt the familiar faint feeling in my stomach all morning and finally threw up in English class.

I threw up a lot as a kid. Come to think of it, I still do. I purge anything unsettling, be it food, drink, thoughts or emotions. Maybe that's why I've always been thin. The accidental bulimic.

I came home that day feeling like I hadn't really gone to school. The bus dropped me off and I practically tiptoed up to my room in keeping with the day's silence. I waited for Mom to come and ask me how school was. But she just sat on my bed and smiled weakly. She looked really out of it, like she had just woken up. Had she been crying again?

"I have something for you," I said after she watched me change from my grey uniform into my home clothes.

I handed her the ominous envelope. She ripped it open and read the one-page note to herself. I waited for her to holler at me for something I didn't recall doing. I consoled myself by thinking that all the kids had gotten envelopes so I had accomplices for whatever I had done wrong. Mom looked angry, but didn't say anything. And I didn't dare interrupt her silence. She sprang up suddenly.

"Your father and I want to speak to you after supper," she said in Farsi.

Very proper Farsi. Father, not Dad. Speak, not talk. Supper, not dinner.

Dad had always been very dramatic, very much into the introduction, main paragraph, supporting paragraphs, conclusion thing. He never realized how torturous the introduction part could be for a kid who just wanted to hear her punishment and get it over with. But that night, there was no introduction, no nothing. It's as if he was tired of the whole Mr. Brady routine of, "Marcia, your mother and I love you and we're always here for you, but…" None of that anymore. He talked to me like an adult and I didn't like it one bit.

"Miryam, they're closing down your school," he said as he studied my face.

"Who is?" I asked.

"The new government. Your teachers are all going back to America."

Long pause. *All of them? All at the same time?*

"Can't they find new ones?" I asked.

"Honey, it's all Americans, not just your teachers. They've either been deported or they've chosen to leave Iran for good. All the international schools are going to be closed down. Everything American, English, French. They're all going to be replaced by Iranian public schools."

I barely knew what the old government was, let alone understood that everything was changing because of the new one.

I stared blankly at Dad, hoping he could read my jumbled thoughts.

Mom nudged him.

"Your mother is going to call all your friends' moms and find out what new school they'll be going to and we'll send you to the same one. It won't be that big a change. You'll still be with your friends, just in a different school and with different teachers. Don't your teachers change every year, anyway?"

I nodded. "I want to go wherever Lisa, Larry and Amy are going."

Mom looked at Dad. It's like she was mute.

"No, honey," Dad said. "Not them. Lisa and Amy are American, so they'll probably be leaving Iran. If they haven't already. And Larry. Well, you'll only be going to school with girls from now on."

He looked down, then continued almost to himself. "Boys in one school, girls in another."

"So Larry and I can't…"

"Larry isn't Iranian either, so he'll probably be going back home too. Where is he from?"

"Hong Kong," I said, realizing just then that Larry, Lisa and Amy hadn't been in school that day.

I continued listening to Dad without understanding him. The Shah is gone, he kept saying.

How can the Shah be gone? The Shah is the Shah, the king. Who is higher than the king?

Khomeini. *What's a Khomeini?* No, it's not a title. It's a person. No he's not the new king. He's the religious leader of the new government.

There was that government word again.

Don't mention the Shah's name in public anymore. And don't say anything bad about Khomeini.

I don't know Khomeini. Why would I say anything bad about him?

Khomeini is the leader of Iran now. *Like the Shah.* I SAID DON'T SAY THE WORD SHAH ANYMORE. *But we're not in public.* Get in the habit of not saying his name regardless. *Sorry.* It's just that you can get into trouble if you say anything wrong, honey. Nobody is safe right now. American embassy was burned. Americans were taken hostage. *What's a hostage?* A prisoner. *Why? What did they do?* They didn't do anything. *Then why are they in prison?* They're not in prison. They're hostages to punish America. *What did America do?* Nothing. It's complicated. It's not just Americans, it's everybody. Just do as we say. And stop crying.

I didn't have a school to go to for two weeks. But instead of joy, I felt a misery worse than being at school struggling with a math problem on the blackboard every day. I waited anxiously for Mom to find me a new school so I could escape a home in which she cried behind closed doors and Dad cursed the bold headlines of every local and national newspaper.

Even little Cyrus was acting up. Screaming, crying, banging on walls, throwing toys out his second-floor bedroom window onto the street, neighbors coming in to snoop more than to complain. The minute he'd start his antics, our maid Zohreh would drag him to the basement so Mom wouldn't hear him and get more upset.

"That Cyrus is a disturbed child," one of our neighbors said to Zohreh once.

All I did those couple of weeks was read comic books and walk around on tiptoe, scared to draw attention to myself.

One day, while reading *Little Lulu*, I panicked and ran to Mom for comfort.

"Oh my baby," she said. "Of course the new government isn't going to confiscate your American comic books. And they're not going to hurt us even if they do find out you like to read American books. Don't worry so much."

I felt a little better, but just to be safe, I hid *Little Lulu* and *Richie Rich* under the Persian books in my desk drawer.

Chapter 8

Dad and Cyrus haul the suitcases out my bedroom and drop them by the front door. Dad holds his lower back and bends backwards exaggeratedly, complaining to Mom about how heavy the suitcases are. *How much did you shop, woman? There'd better not be any magazines or CDs in there or you're on your own at Mehrabad* (Tehran's international airport at the time.)

Mom shoos her hand at him as if annoyed at a fly's buzzing sound. She continues hugging Nader and me at the same time.

"Will you please take care of your brothers?" she asks me.

"Of course I will. Don't worry. We'll be fine."

Mom and I are both crying like we are *not* the same two people who bickered every minute of the past month, and if we had just one more day, we could prove our love to the world.

I look over at Dad to see if he's crying yet. But he's still just frowning at the suitcases. He always panics about the customs at the airport in Tehran. If the customs people find any fashion magazines, CDs, American movies, alcohol, pork products, hell a million things that are illegal in Iran, they confiscate them and punish you accordingly. If they find a videotape of *Basic Instinct*, for instance, they'll scold you, confiscate it and probably rewind Sharon Stone's peep show scene amongst themselves a thousand times. But if they find a bottle of wine, which they'll also take to enjoy themselves, they'll threaten you with jail.

But my parents have never had any problems at customs. Young people are more likely to have all the good stuff like the latest music, so they don't bother checking older people's suitcases. That's why we always ignore Dad's departure-day paranoia. All of us, including Dad, know that there is at least one illegal item in Mom's suitcases. You'd think that by now he would check her suitcases before zipping them up. But for some reason, he never does. So it's not until they get home when he sees all the illegal things Mom snuck in. She even smuggled in cognac once.

"You don't even drink cognac," I said, watching her wrap a sweatshirt around the bottle.

"It's for cooking," she said. "Duck with cognac sauce is one of your dad's favorites."

"I'm sure he'll appreciate the sentiment when they're hauling you both off to jail."

I chuckle to myself, opting not to remind Dad of the cognac. As it is, he's scolding her about the tube of pork salami hidden in her sweat socks last time.

"You are so cute," I whisper to Mom so Dad doesn't hear how amusing I find her antics.

She smiles without asking me what I mean. I smile back, feeling a sudden lump in my throat. I curse myself for not giving her reason to smile more often.

Dad looks at his watch. He never starts with the goodbyes until it's absolutely necessary. And that was five minutes ago.

His face changes from one of a man in control into that of a lost child as he approaches me. I don't move. I just let him hold me. He kisses me and tells me with a choked up voice to take care of my brothers. I don't answer. I close my eyes and sniff his neck before kissing it.

The cab outside honks. I grip Dad tighter. "No!"

"It's OK, honey" he whispers in English. "We'll be back next year."

He starts to move away, but I pull him back. I sob on his shoulder and feel his silent whimpers. When I finally let him go, Mom comes and takes over. I land in her embrace and bury my face in her shoulder-length hair. I sniff her neck, her hair and her cheeks, memorizing the scents of Chanel No. 19, Pantene and Revlon pressed powder.

The cabdriver rings the doorbell. Dad opens the door and asks him to help with the suitcases. They always take a cab to the airport because we hate airport goodbyes. I particularly hate the picture of that plane taking off on the billboard above LAX's departure ramp. Surely it's a welcome sight for burnt-out executives going to Hawaii. But to me, it's as if the drawing of that plane with its nose tilted upwards is snickering about once again snatching my parents away.

I walk over to Nader and clasp his arm. He lets his tears fall without wiping them. I peer over at Cyrus. As usual, his face is expressionless, his demeanor unaffected. But I know how hard these goodbyes are for him despite his lack of emotion. I once heard him crying in his room for hours after saying goodbye to my parents.

Cyrus helps the cabdriver with the suitcases. I look at the cabdriver's tired, haggard face and think that as miserable as his existence might be, I would do anything to trade places with him right now. He's not crying. He'll drop these two people off and not care that he'll never see them again. He is completely detached from this scene and the emotions attached to it. I'd be willing to go home to his whining wife, his teenage daughter's new nose ring and his 6-year-old son asking where babies come from. As long as I don't have to say goodbye to my parents. Again.

Mom cries harder as each suitcase disappears into the cab's trunk. Dad hugs Cyrus for a long time before grabbing Mom's arm and ducking with her into the back seat. The three of us stand on the sidewalk, waving. I start making gag sounds.

"Gross," Nader says. "What's wrong with you?"

"I have to puke," I say.

"So what else is new?" he says, making a face. "Jim vomits everywhere."

"Be quiet," I say, trying to savor the last moments of my parents being close by.

The cab pulls away from the curb and drives off as I do my freeze-frame. I always take a mental picture of the last image of my parents. I never know when, or if, I'll see them again, so in tribute to the pessimist that I am, I like to capture a final memory. Just in case.

I close my eyes and lock in the picture of Mom brushing the mascara-tainted tears off her cheeks and Dad fake-smiling, while blowing a final kiss our way.

I stand there long after Nader and Cyrus go inside. I think that if I get in my car and drive fast enough, I can still catch up to the cab and see my parents just one more time. They're still within reach. In a nutshell, nut being the key word, I obsess. About something I should be used to by now.

Chapter 9

We stood trembling with fear in a line so straight even a ruler would've been proud. The principal yanked our hands to her eyes and inspected our nails. She wasn't looking for dirt, but for nail polish, which was anti-Islamic. Nothing else concerned her. We could've had long, filthy or chewed-up nails and she would've given us a pat on the back, as long as she couldn't find even traces of wiped-off nail polish from the weekend. Our toenails also went under scrutiny, but not until it was time for midday prayers when we took off our shoes and socks, then wiped our hands, feet, and faces with water in accordance with the pre-prayer cleansing ritual.

It was month two at my new public Iranian school, but I still wasn't used to it. I missed *Farhang America*'s bigger playground, my pretty classmates with their blonde hair in pigtails and the always-smiling teachers. Here, the girls all looked the same in their black scarves and long black coats, and the teachers wore their frowns proudly.

Instead of picking teams for volleyball, we gathered in our schoolyard to beat our chests in the name of Allah and chant "Death to America." Competition and fun went from beating the other team to beating our chests harder than one another. And instead of playing outside, we spent part of our lunch-hour praying in dungy basements, murmuring Arabic words whose meanings were alien to most of us.

I had found a few friends, but they didn't replace Larry, Amy and Lisa. I no longer felt the calm from Lisa's hands traveling down my head as she braided my hair every day during math class. Here, some girl I didn't care to know sat behind me, and I wouldn't have let her touch my hair even if it wasn't tight in a ponytail and under the black scarf that hid the fears braided in my mind.

I never did understand why we had to wear the Islamic uniform at school in the first place, considering it was an all-girls school. Even the male custodian wasn't allowed to do his job until every girl had gone home for the day.

Looking back at my class pictures, I recall the color of my classmates' scarves more readily than I do their faces. The hippest girls, those who by then would've been wearing makeup and strutting around the fourth grade in a mini skirt, showed their sense of style by wearing beige, white or other controversial-colored scarves instead of the authority-preferred black. The most fashionable was Sayeh, who walked into class one morning wearing a polka-dotted lime-green scarf. She was a rebel who caused a roar of silent applause.

The only tolerable part of my days was English class. I spoke better English than Mrs. Razemi and sometimes, if I corrected her too much, she would let me take over the class. It was much more fun teaching actual students than my dolls. I also got to grade my own homework and test papers. And Mrs. Razemi knew that if she questioned my grading, I'd degrade her in front of the class for her horrible accent.

But even all that started getting old. So I got really excited when Mrs. Razemi announced that we would be starting sex education soon. I figured we were in for a few months of giggles. Little did I know that sex education at a public school in Iran would last a single afternoon. Mrs. Razemi started and wrapped up our sex education by teaching us only what she deemed important: pre-marital sex was a sin, neither God nor the government would condone intercourse before marriage, and our husbands were the only men allowed to see our naked vaginas.

One of the girls, Salma, asked what sex even was. The class snickered.

"Ask your parents," Mrs. Razemi said sternly. "It's not my job to tell you what it is. It's my job to tell you that it's wrong."

"Well, if we don't know what it is, maybe we'll do it and not know we're doing it and go to hell."

Those of us who knew very well what sex was roared with laughter.

"One more word out of you about sex and *I'll* send you to hell," Mrs. Razemi said, giving the rest of us an I'm-warning-you look.

"But I want to know why it's so bad," Salma persisted.

"Because it's dirty and it makes you smell of sin."

"Smell where?"

"Enough!" Mrs. Razemi screamed, slapping her ruler on the aluminum desk.

"Do you have sex?" Salma asked.

Mrs. Razemi dragged her to the principal's office as Salma screamed, "What did I say? What did I say? I just wanted to know if that's why your underarms smell all the time."

Chapter 10

THERE comes a time when you let go of all your high hopes, your notion that if you work hard and get an education, you will be rewarded for the rest of your life. There comes a time when your parents' screams from across the Atlantic are so loud, the phone becomes an unnecessary vehicle of communication. That's the time you take a job as a receptionist.

After being unemployed for so long, even people like Ari and my parents, who had told me never to accept second-best, were so proud of me when I got this job, you'd think I had become the first woman president.

Life's been going along in its humdrum ways. And after the past few months of unrest at home, humdrum is music to our ears. I've been rising before the sun does, going to work, sitting in two hours of rush-hour traffic, bringing home minimum wage, and passing out in front of the television at nights. Living the American dream.

Sometimes people get bored and fed up with the mundane. Middle-aged men have affairs and middle-aged women start dressing like 13-year-olds. People ruin years of marriage, hurt the mother/father of their children, drink, do drugs, do all kinds of crazy crap to escape the ordinary. And not that my life went one step beyond an intense ecstasy trip, but even a slightly unpleasant chaos that meanders between ordinary and intense can make you appreciate the boring routine that most people can't admit to appreciate. All of a sudden, making dinner and having the boys gather around and talk like civilized people has become intensely satisfying. Somehow, giving my boss, Elizabeth, a phone message makes me feel important. Like I'm contributing something to the world. Because she returned that phone call, a business transaction took place and the American economy moved forward a milli-inch. The economy started doing better with thousands of other random acts like it and the president could devote more time to social issues, foreign affairs and the environment.

I feel like a pretty big grain of sand, believing I'm a crucial part of that insignificant stretch of beach. That's what normalcy does to you. You're not going to change the world, but you're not going to destroy it either. You'll contribute, just a little, and everyone will at least nod in appreciation. And when you die, world leaders will not gather at your funeral, but passersby won't spit on your grave either.

Imagine what I'd sound like if I had gotten a job at, say, Greenpeace.

More than my own sense of self-worth is Ari's sudden motherly worship of me. When I laid out the simple, but eye-catching Haft-Seen table for Persian New Year last month, he kissed me on the forehead (for four seconds) and told me that I'm the reason our family has stayed together.

So I followed suit and made the boys get up in brand-new pajamas before the commencement of spring. To any American looking through our window, seeing people in their sleepwear, looking at their watches and kissing each other on the cheeks at the stroke of 4:21 a.m. on an average March Wednesday, we would have seemed beyond abnormal. But as none of us was even slightly annoyed at waking up for the occasion, we were finally the epitome of normalcy.

Chapter 11

The Iran-Iraq war had been in full swing for more than two months on the day Dad picked me up from school because he had gotten off work early. He frowned when I asked him why almost all the houses we passed by on our drive home had duct tape in the form of an "X" on their windows. He didn't seem to like my question and took a few moments before answering.

"It's because of the war. If there's bombing."

His vague answer made me think that "X" stood for "No," as in, "Do Not Bomb This House."

What can I say; it was my first war.

"Why don't we have one?" I asked. "I don't want our house to get bombed."

He frowned again and gave me a puzzled look. "We're not going to get bombed. It's just a precaution."

It wasn't until a few weeks later, after the bombings actually started, when I finally understood that if a bomb were to go off far enough to cause only shaking, the windows armored with duct tapes in the shape of an "X" would break and fall off in a big chunk instead of shattering all over the place.

A few times a week, the radio and television sounded red sirens to have people practice the emergency procedures in case of a dropped bomb. The sirens weren't very spontaneous. They always went off at around 6 p.m., when most everyone was home from school or work. I guess it was meant to be a family experience.

I sat in front of the TV every day after school, waiting for the red siren, or "*ajireh ghermez*." Even with the TV volume on low, the monotone, ear-screeching sound was deafening. Once it sounded, we were supposed to dash to our safety zone. For my family, it was our basement.

We never knew if these drills were just for practice or if there were actual enemy planes about to drop bombs. Living in Los Angeles now, I've seen some emergency broadcast tests for earthquakes. But I don't exactly dash under the nearest table every time. It's a test. It says so. And if there were an actual earthquake, I'd feel it. But it was different with bombs. Every time we heard the red siren, we had to make like bombs were dropping on our heads like hail and run for cover under the umbrella of the basement.

The first time I heard the red siren, I turned ghastly white and froze in my chair by the breakfast table, where I was doing my homework. Zohreh was in the kitchen cooking *lubia polo* for dinner and Mom was in the hallway walking with a stack of books on her head. She has mild scoliosis and always tries to improve her posture by walking with books on her head like a teenage girl practicing to be a runway model.

Tom suddenly stopped running after Jerry. The TV screen went blank and what sounded like a cat-in-heat's meow heralded the red siren. The books fell from Mom's head with a bang. Zohreh screamed herself into hysterics, telling Mom that it was all over and "they" had come. She yelled at us to pray with her.

"Khanoum, oomadand! Tamoom shod! Ya khoda besmellah! Ya Khoda! Salavat befrestid, salavat!"

Mom screamed back at her to calm down. She ran upstairs to get Cyrus and Nader, while Zohreh dragged me down the long, winding stairs to the basement.

Dad, holding Cyrus' trembling hand, and Mom carrying baby Nader, wobbled down the stairs soon after. My parents were so pale, they were blue. Twenty minutes later, Dad's transistor radio sounded "*ajireh sabz*," the green siren, and we were deemed safe to return to life.

Upstairs, Mom gave a still-screaming Zohreh a tranquilizer. Cyrus and I fell asleep two hours before our bedtime. I woke up in the middle of the night and panicked that I hadn't finished my homework.

But the next day at school, none of the other girls had finished their homework either. And Mrs. Koopaii didn't even check. The whole day, we just talked about the siren and how we had handled it. She reminded us that it was all for God and dismissed us an hour early. It was the most fun I had had in school since *Farhang America.*

The second time the red siren sounded, Mom gave Zohreh a tranquilizer immediately. That was the only difference.

But by the third red siren, no one panicked. Everyone was more annoyed than scared. Nothing had happened during the first two and we took for granted that these were just practice drills. Zohreh refused the tranquilizer, called it "devil candy," and opted instead to pray, very calmly, until the green siren sounded.

Cyrus just held Mom's hand instead of biting it and my parents were just going through the motions. As for me, I was ecstatic. No bombs, no real worries, but the perfect excuse to ignore my homework.

As the drills continued but people started taking them in stride, the government decided to re-instate panic by not sounding the green siren for hours, each time making us think there was a real threat. But at any point, it could have been real. And no one could take the red siren in jest. So even if it meant putting life on hold and sitting in the basement for three hours, we did it. We weren't as scared, but we were wary. The government had become the boy who cried wolf, but we were the villagers who could never afford to ignore him.

When we waited long hours in the basement for the green siren, we got antsy. We got hungry, tired and bored.

And that's when the war became fun.

Every day after school, I'd run home excitedly, praying there would be a siren. I'd fill a picnic basket with sandwiches, sodas, pistachios, fruits, and milk for Cyrus and Nader. I decorated the basement with knick-knacks and photos of happier times. I took down books, blankets, pillows and toys. I turned the basement into a cozy family room. I even asked Mom to buy me some yellow paint so I could add a touch of sunshine to our hideaway, but she scolded me and said I was taking my enthusiasm a little too far.

It got to a point where I'd get downright angry if there wasn't a drill or if the green siren sounded before we could play gin rummy. Sometimes I'd ask everyone to stay in the basement even after the green siren sounded. But they always ignored me. Once upstairs, everyone would do their own thing. No more chaos, no more rallying together, no more family. Just boring old life as usual. I hated it. So much that I wished we'd really get bombed so everyone would take the basement seriously again. I mean, it had gotten so bad that even Mrs. Koopaii saw no reason why we couldn't just do our homework in the basement while waiting for the green siren.

This war sucked, as far as I was concerned.

And then it happened. The Iraqis dropped a bomb on an uninhabited area close to Tehran. Thankfully, there were no casualties, but the entire city rattled. Zohreh fainted on the quilt I had laid out in the basement. Dad screamed at Mom to stop Cyrus from screaming so he could hear the radio. Mom screamed at Dad to do something about the maid.

I smiled and opened the picnic basket.

"Who wants chicken and who wants bologna?"

Chapter 12

I've always had this morbid thought about how fascinating it would be to die on your birthday. If I were turning 67, maybe I wouldn't care about my birthday. But I'm 23 today and there's still this narcissistic part of me that thinks it's weird that people go about their daily lives and newscasters report on mundane events when it's my birthday.

I'm thumbing through *Health* magazine with a cigarette dangling from my mouth when Nader walks into the living room and glares at me.

"Happy birthday, oxymoron," he says. "Emphasis moron."

I chuckle. "Witty."

He smiles. "I need help with my math homework."

"From a moron?" I ask.

"Witty."

"Yes, I am," I say. "But if I help with your math, your teacher will flunk you."

"Flunk me? Flunk *him*."

"*Back to School*," I say, trying to sound bored with his movie game.

"Damn you're good," he says.

"No. You're just losing your touch. That was too easy. And ask Ari for help with your math."

"Ah flunk it," he says.

He grabs his backpack and tells me he's going to the library without asking for a ride — or permission. I know that he's way too lazy to walk more than a block. Or to study on a Saturday.

I sigh. "Have fun at Jennifer's house."

The highlight of my day is going with Ari and Cyrus to a family session with Cyrus' shrink. I shake Dr. Rubenstein's hand firmly, knowing he'll read into it. But other than that, I opt to stay quiet throughout the session. I am, after all, the mother figure and we all know what shrinks think of mothers. It's all our fault.

We follow Dr. R. into a small office and I look for the cliché couch. But there isn't one. The three of us sit on normal chairs and face the stalky man in his mid-50s. His legs are disproportionately short for his relatively large upper body. He looks like a cartoon character who was hit on the head with a frying pan till he couldn't shrink anymore. I stare hard at the notepad in his hand as he talks to Cyrus.

"Do you feel like you haven't done a good job raising Cyrus?" Dr. R. asks.

Silence. They all stare at me.

"Me?" I ask with a frown. "I'm not his mother."

"That's not what I asked," Dr. R. says.

"Well," I say, fidgeting in my seat. "I don't really know how to answer that. I mean, Ari helped raise him."

I know that the only reason I'm watching my every word is because he's a psychiatrist. If anyone else had asked me the same question, I would've bawled and said, "This is all my fault."

"What I'm asking, Miryam," he says, "is whether you feel responsible for Cyrus' drinking and general behavior. Do you feel like you failed him? Or are you angry that he failed you?"

"Um, neither really."

He waits for more, but that's all I got. He looks at Ari when he continues. Like, forget her.

"The first step in healing is to remove all blame," he says. "On all your parts. Because it won't solve anything. Our job is to figure out where to go from here. Clear enough?"

Now he looks at me. I nod. Yes, as the Rain Man of the family, I'm following you.

"Cyrus has a number of issues," Dr. R. says. "But they're interconnected. We can't solve the whole without understanding and dealing with the parts. So the first step is to deal with his depression."

"Depression?" I blurt.

Shit. Now it looks like something obvious has passed by me.

"Yes," Dr. R. says. "Cyrus is suffering from moderate, but chronic depression."

Suffering? We're the ones he's making suffer.

So much for not blaming.

The doctor talks about the role of anti-depressants, about the brain-poison that is alcohol, and about honesty.

"I also want to make sure you understand that depression is a chemical imbalance," he continues. "Cyrus may have been born with it or certain events may have triggered it, but that's irrelevant. The point is that this is not his fault. And it is not *your* fault. If he had diabetes, would you blame him or yourselves?"

Ari shakes his head no. Dr. R. looks at me. I'm thinking about the *Three's Company* episode where they go to a shrink because they're all angry at each other for how they spent the money Chrissy won at the racetrack. Chrissy had bought some weird stuffed animal…I think it was a giraffe. Yes, it was definitely a giraffe and then Jack was…

"Miryam?" Dr. R. says. "Are you following?"

"Yes, yes. He has diabetes."

"Well, he doesn't actually…"

"And it's not his fault," I quickly add.

"OK," he says. "Close enough. Any questions?"

We all shake our heads.

"Great," he says. He brings his wide hands together in a loud clap. I jump in my seat. He smiles at me and I stare at his notepad, relieved that he doesn't jot down anything, like, "Mother figure startles easily."

He ushers us to the door and makes a marked point to tell Ari, and only Ari, that we should have more of these sessions. As in, there's a yacht I'm looking to buy. And leave the mute ditz at home next time.

Just as I'm walking out the door, Dr. R asks to speak to me privately. I give him a look of surprise quickly turning into panic.

"I wanted to mention that it might not be a bad idea for you to seek some counseling for yourself as well," he says when we're alone.

"Why?" I ask, trying not to sound defensive.

"A girl who's always had to take care of others without anyone there to take care of her yearns for attention on the inside. I just don't want you to think you're fine and then one day become self-destructive as a way to look for someone to save you." He studies my face. "Do you know what I mean?"

I move my head in a way that could be interpreted both as a yes or a no, kind of like when I would be stuck between choice "a" and "c" on a multiple-choice test in high school and doodle something that could pass between either one.

He talks about dysfunction and turning dysfunctional in order to deal with dysfunction.

"What's going on with Cyrus is that by acting dysfunctional, he is forcing those around him to be functional and stable. If he starts taking care of himself, you and Ari might abandon him the way your parents did. You may someday do the same. Subconsciously, you might think, 'if I'm a mess, my parents will have to remain in their parental roles so they can bring me out of the mess.' Or 'if I'm a mess, I won't have to deal with the painful reality that those around me are a mess.'"

"Are you saying I'm dysfunctional?" I ask.

"There's dysfunction in most families," he says. "And you have to face up to that in your own family, if that is indeed the case, instead of turning dysfunctional yourself. I don't mean you, per se, but you in general."

But I, per se, am the one you're talking to and you're calling me dysfunctional in general

"It's a very unhealthy way of staying a child," he says.

"Staying a child?" I say, mock-laughing. "I've been an adult since I *was* a child."

"No argument there," he says, shaking his head. "But that's just the point. And it's something you might want to think about and process. You don't have to see me. But I think it's a good idea for you to seek some counseling for yourself, not just for your brother."

I sigh and try to think of some way to tell him that I kind of understand what he's saying without actually agreeing to see a therapist. But thankfully, he himself looks at his watch and ushers me to the door.

Ari asks me why the doctor had wanted to talk to me.

"Nothing important," I mumble.

He gets quiet. The kind of quiet where he's emphasizing that he's trying to be quiet.

"You were like a zombie in there," he says in the car. "Not paying any attention. Do you even give a shit anymore or am I officially on my own trying to glue this family together?"

"Glue?" I say with a chuckle. "Try scotch tape."

"No, glue!" he yells. "*Crazy* glue!"

I seesaw between anger and fear towards Ari. I try to sound calm. Rational. Adult. Like someone who doesn't need to see a therapist.

"I just don't think the doctor's approach is working," I say. "Like it's gonna do any of us a shred of good to hear that it's nobody's fault. 'Get in touch with your inner child.' 'Listen to your soul.' All this crap people throw around without knowing what it even means. What the hell is he actually doing for Cyrus? He said this is the third medication he's prescribed him, he's hanging by a thread in AA and I don't think Cyrus had depression before, but $3000 later, he sure does."

"You didn't even know that he was diagnosed with depression a month ago," Ari says with a sarcastic chuckle. "You didn't even know he was on medication till today."

"Maybe I was like a zombie in there because the guy talks to me like I'm a moron," I continue, as if Ari just interrupted my speech. "Like he has to spoon-feed me his useless psychobabble."

"Oh, so *that's* your problem?" Ari yells. "Your little princess ego is bruised? *Fuck my brother and his problems as long as I'm respected and acknowledged?* And you think you actually know more than the doctor does?"

"Don't talk to me like that!" I scream back. "That's not what I said. I may not be a shrink, but I know my brother and..."

Cyrus groans, opens the car window and bangs his head on the dashboard. Even when Cyrus is sitting right in front of you, it's easy to forget he's there.

Ari and I stop arguing and mumble an apology to each other, only because of Cyrus' obvious frustration. Or guilt. Or whatever he's feeling. When we get home, Ari and Cyrus go to their rooms, while I pace in the living room trying to keep calm. Calm, shocked, petrified, livid, what's the difference at this point? I feel like crawling into a hole and hibernating there until...

Until what? Ari pulls me out of the hole and carries me into the sunset? Cyrus kneels above the hole and tells me it's not my fault? Dr. Rubenstein throws me some of Cyrus' antidepressants until I can climb out of the hole? Until Nader turns 18 and throws Mother's Day flowers over the hole? Until my parents come for their next visit and I yell from inside the hole, "Everything's fine. Don't worry. We're fine?"

At night, I decide to listen to Bee's advice to "get a life" and go out with her and Paige to a club to celebrate. They rhetorically remind me that it's my birthday, not realizing that I had actually completely forgotten. Thank God for Bee and Paige. They're the only friends I need. Together, they meet both ends of the human spectrum as I dilly-dally in the middle. An English teacher could line us up as props on a lesson in superlatives. Paige is tall, I'm taller, Bee is a ladder. Paige is pretty, I'm prettier, Bee is a goddess. It also works internally. Bee is smart, I'm smarter, Paige is a genius. Bee is nice, I'm nicer, Paige is a doormat. I'm like the middle child of this friendship triangle, my role in it symbolizing my place in the world at large.

I don't talk to them about the therapy session or the argument with Ari. Just last week, Bee said she was sick of hearing about Cyrus, his drinking or anything else going on with him.

"He's a normal teenager going through normal teenage stuff," she had said. "Let his shrink deal with it and start saving money for all the therapy you're gonna need in the future."

I don't want another lecture from Bee or sympathy from Paige, so I lie and tell them Ari and the boys took me out for a nice birthday lunch. Paige smiles and tells me she's happy things are better at home. But Bee's in a mood because she just dumped her boyfriend for asking her to marry him. He was perfect. And madly in love with her. But she doesn't believe in marriage.

"He's left me like 10 messages today apologizing," she says while we're waiting for the bartender to give us our drinks.

"Apologizing for what?" I ask.

"I don't know," she says. "Loving me too much."

Her sarcasm is obvious. But so is the look on her face that says she's not going to give us a real answer. So we just let her be Bee.

"The problem is the feminist movement," she says. "It's not about women having a choice. It's about oh, women can do everything men can do? Then let 'em do it. But you're still a woman, so don't forget, after you bring home the bacon, you gotta fry it too. Feminism just gave men an excuse to demand more from women. We're expected to do the work and still do all the other shit that caused the feminist movement in the first place."

"No," I say. "A man who truly gets it will chip in with the housework and everything else in a marriage."

"Give me one fucking example," she says.

I'm about to blurt Ari's name, but I stop in mid-blurt. He does help with the kids, but the only way he would even recognize an oven cleaner is if Cyrus were inhaling it.

"Every single Iranian guy in America thinks he's modernized," she continues. "'Oh, my wife can work if she wants to. Or stay home if she wants to.' But once you get married, it's like 'oh you gotta work because that's what every American wife does and you have to cook *khoreshteh fesenjoon* from scratch because that's what every Iranian wife does.'"

She goes on and on and I let Paige, whom we've pegged Switzerland, deal with her. The Swiss Alps have a volcanic eruption. Instead of nodding and agreeing the way she does about everything, Paige lectures Bee on the advancement of women since the feminist movement. I forgot that this is the one issue that gets Paige all riled up.

I just drink and smoke and ignore them both. I'm already living what they're arguing about, so I don't need this on my one night off.

Whoever designed a martini glass never intended for it to be carried around in a crowded bar. More than half of it spills as I follow Bee and Paige all over the club. (Actually, maybe it's a business ploy.) We finally plop somewhere and as they continue their conversation, I conjure up ridiculous scenarios and amuse myself in my head. At one point, I'm oblivious to the fact that a bunch of guys are surrounding us. One of them asks me what I'm thinking about.

"I was just thinking how interesting it would be if someone were to turn 9 years old on 9/9/1999," I say. "Or die at the age of 99 on 9/9/99."

I want to continue because there's a lot more where that came from, but I notice how everyone is glaring at me.

"Oh crapezoid," Bee says to one of the guys. "I'm sorry. My friend here sometimes sounds like a philosopher on crack. She's a little nuts."

"And you are beautiful," he says to her. "Your face is perfect."

"Why thank you," Bee says, smiling a perfect smile.

Everything physical about Bee really is perfect. Her only "flaw" is her chest that's as flat as an old, opened can of Coke. Which frankly, I'd kill for. My nipples are larger than her boobs. But she hides her natural beauty with too much makeup. Sometimes she looks like a whore and I want to tell her so, but there's really no nice way to tell your best friend she looks like a whore. Actually, sometimes she calls herself a whore, maybe to beat other people before they say it. She's had a few sexual partners, but that hardly makes her a whore. By American standards, that is. By Iranian standards, the fact that she's even kissed a guy makes her a whore. Hell, by Iranian standards, *I'm* a whore. (OK, so I'm exaggerating, but I'm Iranian so it goes with the territory.)

"You know," I say to the guy who told Bee she's beautiful, "even though people, myself included, take physical compliments or insults so personally, they are the most impersonal remarks when you think about it. Bee is beautiful. Perfect, as you said. But it has nothing to do with her. Or with her parents if that's what you're thinking I'm thinking. It's like if you told her, 'Wow, the sky is absolutely breathtaking tonight' and she said, 'Why thank you.' You know?

It's just as ridiculous when you really think about it. It's a God thing. And yet people equate looks with identity."

The guy stares at me.

"Miryam, be normal," Bee whispers.

"There's no such thing as normal," I say. "And if someone is normal, they're abnormal because they're normal. Because if you…"

The guy fishes a lighter from his pocket and flicks it towards the unlit cigarette I've been holding for five minutes. Probably just to shut me up.

Chapter 13

"Oh my God!" Mom screamed. She let go of the steering wheel and started hitting herself on the head.

"What happened?" I asked, looking around "What's wrong?"

"My scarf! I forgot my scarf!"

I had always known it would be a matter of time before Mom left the house without wearing her scarf. Even though it had been about a year since the revolution, she still wasn't used to the fact that wearing a headscarf in public was national law.

No wonder everyone at the grocery store had stared at her. They probably thought she had done it on purpose.

"Kids, help!" she screamed. "Get out the toilet paper!"

Cyrus and I giggled while wrapping half a roll of toilet paper around her head.

"Mummy!" I said excitedly. "Mommy's a mummy!"

She laughed, probably more from relief than from amusement.

Thank God toilet paper had been on Mom's shopping list and we managed to get home without any incidents.

But when my turn came, I wasn't as lucky.

I hadn't forgotten to wear my scarf; I simply didn't wear one outside of school because I wasn't yet required to do so by law. According to Islam, girls don't have to start covering themselves until age 9, when they are considered a woman.

I was only 8 the summer Auntie Negin was visiting from Shiraz and she and I walked to the corner grocer to buy her cigarettes.

We were talking casually, about nothing significant enough for me to recall, when a gang of teenage boys turned the corner and walked towards us. They stared at me and whispered amongst themselves. I ignored them and continued talking, but it seemed like Auntie Negin was no longer listening. I was looking up at her, oblivious to what was going on when she suddenly grabbed my waist and swung me aside. I looked over at the boys and watched in fear as they threw fistfuls of rocks at me, yelling, "*Marg bar bi hijab!*" (Death to those who don't wear the Islamic attire.)

I still had two months before I was forced to shed my shorts for long pants and to cover my long hair with a scarf. But the boys obviously didn't care how old my bare, tanned legs and sunlit hair were.

Auntie Negin held me tightly to her side and quickened her pace. The boys threw the last of the rocks in their hands towards me, then laughed as they walked past us.

Auntie Negin got quiet, but vigilant, for a long time. It wasn't until after she bought her Winstons and lit one that she talked. She didn't say anything about what had happened and tried to get my mind off it by pointing out pretty flowers and asking me about the upcoming school year. But I could tell she was scared. She was walking fast and kept looking behind her.

"Auntie Negin, please don't tell Mom what happened," I said when we got close to our house.

It took a while before she asked, "Why not?"

"Because she'll worry," I said. "She's always worrying lately. She's so sad all the time. When she found out that religion and Koran classes will be mandatory this year, she started talking to Dad about leaving Iran and moving to America. If you tell them about this, they'll start talking about America again. And I don't want to go to America. Please don't tell her."

She didn't answer and continued walking quickly. When she hadn't said anything by the time we reached our house, I grabbed and pulled at her arm impatiently.

"Please don't tell," I pleaded again.

"I won't tell, honey," she said.

The look on her face reassured me that she wouldn't. I sighed with relief. I was spared worrying once again about leaving the only home I knew.

Chapter 14

I stumble into the house and feel for the light switch. The shot of bright floods the blackness and strains my eyes. I plop down on the sofa and kick off my black heels.

I'm about to open the birthday present Bee and Paige gave me at the club when the phone rings. I run to pick it up before it wakes anybody up.

"Hello, beautiful," Ari's mom says on the other end.

"Hi Soraya joon," I say cheerfully. "How are you?"

I'm surprised to hear her voice. It's not like her to call so late at night. She calls Ari on Saturday mornings and I'm usually asleep. So I never get to talk to her.

"Fine, honey, how are *you*?"

"Fine, thanks, but I think Ari is asleep," I say, hoping she'll know that I'm cutting the conversation short only because I'm thinking of her phone bill.

"I know, honey. I called to talk to you."

I smile and wait for her to wish me happy birthday.

"I know you're usually up late," she says. "I wanted to call and give you my condolences."

I freeze and repeat her words in my head. I'm quiet for a long time, making Soraya think the connection went dead.

"Hello?" she yells. "Hello? Hello?"

"I'm right here, Soraya joon," I say with a shaky voice. "Condolences about what?"

She doesn't say anything.

"About who?" I ask.

Silence.

"Soraya joon, say something! What are you talking about?"

"Oh honey, I'm so sorry. I thought you knew."

"Who? Just please tell me who!"

"Your parents are fine. It's not them. But I don't want to be the one to tell you. I think you should call your parents."

"Fine," I say quickly, not having the patience to drag it out of her. I mumble "goodbye" and hang up.

I call my parents, but there's no answer.

I run to Cyrus' room. But just as I'm about to open his door without knocking, I notice that Ari's lights are on. I knock quickly and run in without waiting for a response.

"Ari, what's going on? Who died?"

Chapter 15

SOMETHING isn't quite right when a 9-year-old says, "Ah, the good old days," and she means it. And instead of laughing or pinching her cheeks, the adults nod their somber heads and drift into nostalgias of their own.

It was our first trip to Shomal since the revolution and I felt very adult sitting with Mom and her friends, talking about how things just weren't the same anymore.

Shomal, which literally means "north" in Farsi, is the Caspian Sea area north of Tehran, where we vacationed during summer and the New Year's holiday in March.

When I think of Shomal, the image that immediately comes to mind is that of Mom's face in the car's side mirror on our way there. Her face said it all. Her hair would be pulled back with a bright bandana, her eyes would be closed, her cheeks pink, and her smile frozen, never melting under the sun's blaze. Her peacefulness matched the joy inside me.

Shomal was where even adults became kids. We always went there with a big group, sometimes as many as 30 people. Our villa had 12 bedrooms, a vast living room and a wide terrace, all nestled among acres of wilderness. But with everyone crammed inside, it felt as cozy as a bed and breakfast. Most of the rooms had bunk beds, but even that wasn't fun enough for some guests, who would drag their mattresses close to the brick fireplace and sleep next to it; others would put cots covered with nets to ward off mosquitoes and sleep on the veranda overlooking the sea.

All the villas in Shomal had names. Ours was "Mazraeyeh Maryam." Or in English, "Miryam's Meadows."

Age and gender disappeared in Shomal. Forty-year-old women would play ping-pong with 6-year-old boys; sore-loser old men would call grinning little girls "cheaters" during bingo; girls with no use for bikini tops would sun next to women in double-D ones; expert swimmers would dive into the sea with first-time swimmers wading behind; heck, even cats and dogs got along as they strolled in the woods with their owners.

At the end of each activity-filled day, we kids would put on improvised shows for the adults, singing, dancing and asking them to judge our juvenile talents.

All the women chipped in with our many maids to cook all kinds of food, enjoyed with heaps of pickled garlic, a trademark treat we only had in Shomal. Whether true or not, everyone said that garlic in our bodies would repel mosquitos. Pickled garlic was as much a signature of Shomal as were cold pitchers of fresh watermelon and cantaloupe juice.

Everything in Shomal was child-like. Even the plates we used there weren't quite so adult. They were still china, but not as nice as our set in the city. And they were bright yellow. No one would care if I accidentally broke one of those. There were no carpets. I could spill and drip water on the checkered black-and-white marble floor and not be scolded. And instead of central air-conditioning, every room had a ceiling fan that whizzed round and round and round.

The sofas were orange, and the walls were decorated with cartoon sketches of donkeys and caricatures of old men with funny faces. My favorite was of an old man mooning a stuffy-looking old lady. The modest decorations consisted of knick-knacks that different guests had brought over the years as a memento of their stay.

The women walked around with shorts and colorful bikini tops, while even the stuffiest of men would shed their suits to show off their hairy chests and chicken legs.

More than half the fun was in getting there for me and Cyrus, who never asked, "Are we there yet?" As anxious as we were to arrive, the five-hour car ride competed for our excitement with our usually weeklong stay at the villa. We never had enough linens in Shomal. So Mom would load the car with pillows and fluffy blankets for us to take. Dad would blast the air conditioning and Cyrus and I would snuggle under the blankets. I would doze off to the voice of my favorite Persian singer, *Googoosh,* dancing through the car speakers.

Nestled between Mom's bare legs would be a basket filled with chicken and Mortadella sandwiches, fruits, sunflower seeds, pistachios and a thermos of tea. The best-tasting sandwiches I've ever had were the warm, soggy ones on our way to Shomal.

Our arrival there was heralded by dozens of street vendors selling hand-woven baskets. Once I saw them, I would roll down the window to suck in the delicious sticky air, the same one my parents complained about. But I loved whiffing the humidity that smelled, felt and tasted like Shomal. When Dad would draw open our villa's rusty red gate, my heart would bounce along the long dusty road to the main house. I itched to get out and run in my meadows with open arms like Julie Andrews in *The Sound of Music.*

Before the revolution, we went to Shomal mainly to enjoy the sea. City slickers swimming and sunning by the seashore with the super-sized seashells. But after the revolution, when the government stamped swimming, sunning and any other "s" a sin, the adults sat around talking about Shomal memories instead of making new ones.

Just one day in Shomal after the revolution, I knew that the joyful air in one of my favorite places had been tainted forever.

Even though we kids could still swim in the sea, adult men and women couldn't be on the beach together. And the women could only go swimming if they donned *chadors*, thin, usually black, cloths that covered them from head to toe. They had to pile clothes on, instead of taking them off, in the 110-degree humidity and practically drown in order to swim.

Every day, I watched the somber-looking grownups sit in the villa instead of play with us on the beach. They watched the sunsets from the terrace, played cards, talked (about the revolution, what else?) and drank. At night, they talked and drank some more. It just wasn't the Shomal it used to be.

As I sat listening to the women talk about all the fun they used to have in Shomal, I knew I had been gypped. Just when I had started to enjoy life, just when I was old enough to appreciate how good we had it, it was all taken away.

I left the group of women and was walking over to watch Dad and my uncle play backgammon when my second cousin Yasmine whispered in my ear to follow her.

All the adults loved Yasmine. So I copied everything she did, hoping I'd get the same attention. My version of the theory of relativity. I didn't realize that she got so much attention because she was so pretty. She was tall, had straight golden-brown hair and large hazel eyes. Everything else about her was petite though. Her nose and mouth were like miniature hand-crafted art objects. She looked like a little china doll with oversized eyes. And her white skin earned her the nickname Snow White.

I told Yasmine I was too scared to go outside at night, but she said it would be worth my while. All sorts of animals roamed outside. And only Yasmine had more influence on me than my own misgivings.

I followed her through a maze of bushes and plopped down where she told me to on a patch of wet grass. It was pitch black. Wolves were howling somewhere.

Maybe 10 miles away, maybe right next to us, but they were there. And so was my fear. Yasmine went behind a cherry tree while I sat hugging my knees and taking in the sweet smell of gardenias.

"Oh my God, what are you doing with that?" I shrieked.

She grinned as she shook the uncorked bottle of red wine.

"I snuck it back here an hour ago," she said. "I knew you'd act suspicious and ruin the whole thing, so I brought it here without telling you. Don't worry, they'll never miss it. There were six more bottles just like this."

"They're gonna come looking for us," I said.

"You wouldn't be thinking that if we were in our bedrooms. You're just scared because we're out here. When do they ever come looking for us in this huge place? We could be anywhere."

I silently scolded myself for being so immature.

Yasmine took a swig and handed me the bottle. My eyes had adjusted to the dark and I could see her squint a little too clearly to want to follow suit. But I was also excited. I had never done anything like that before. Shomal was fun again as I took a big gulp. My throat burned. I screeched and made a face.

"It's OK," Yasmine said with a laugh. "You won't even taste it after a while. Just pretend it's medicine."

But I don't sneak 10 miles into the woods to take medicine. That's where I'll likely be hiding to avoid *taking it.*

She took another swig, didn't even flinch.

"Do you do this a lot?" I asked.

She laughed. "Of course not. But we're in Shomal. Why should our parents have all the fun? What are we supposed to do for fun? Besides, I thought this would be a neat thing to do since it's probably the last time we'll be together like this."

"What do you mean?" I asked before taking two quick gulps in a row.

"You guys are moving to America and we're moving to France in two weeks."

There wasn't a family around us that wasn't considering leaving Iran at the time. For my family, the consideration stage had officially yielded concrete plans. Once the school year was over, we were going to move to Los Angeles.

My parents had told Ari's mom of our plans. She was ecstatic that Ari could finally leave Iran. Originally, she had sought a trustable family that would simply take Ari out of the country and enroll him in a boarding school abroad. But my parents convinced Soraya that leaving home would be hard enough for him without also having to attend a boarding school. They said he could live with us in America, that it was important for him to be part of a family and grow up with values, discipline and love. She was so grateful that she cried the entire time they discussed the details, including the financial arrangements.

I thought my parents wanted to move to America because I had gone to an American school and I already knew how to speak English.

Which is what made me ask Yasmine, "Why are you moving to France? You don't speak French."

"I'll learn," she said with a confidence people like me will never even understand.

Half-intoxicated, we sat rocking ourselves in silence, the chirp of crickets and howl of wolves our pubescent rock 'n' roll.

I panicked once again about the prospect of leaving home. My parents were thinking of me, Cyrus and Nader, of our future. But I felt like I was doing *them* a favor because they were the ones who were so miserable all the time. I wanted to stay in Iran. I wanted to come to Shomal and drink wine with Yasmine. I wanted to create more happy memories here.

The bottle was almost empty. I was feeling dizzy, which was a good thing. Yasmine plucked fistfuls of grass and threw them at me, laughing.

"You seem really happy about leaving," I said sadly.

"No, no, no, no, no, no, no," she said.

Each "no" was like the turn of a crank that made my head spin faster.

"I'm very sad about leaving," she said with a pout. She raised the bottle above her head, then took the last gulp. "A votre santé. That means 'cheers' in French."

"You don't speak French," I reminded her. And myself.

Bitter, perhaps jealous, drunk.

"No, but my parents got me a tutor. I know how to say the really important stuff."

My head spun faster, which was not a good thing. I started hiccupping. Yasmine imitated me. Then she pulled down her pants and peed, saying alcohol makes you pee a lot. I realized I had to pee too, and squatted next to her. We giggled at the silence magnifying the swishing sound.

Happy drunk.

"Let's go back," she said and almost tipped over as she pulled up her pants. "I want to be drunk around the adults. It'll be fun."

The idea thrilled me. But I knew I would somehow mess up and give our secret away. I was cool in Yasmine's eyes at that moment, and I wanted to keep it that way.

"I'm going to bed," I said.

Sleepy drunk.

Snow White and the Seven Drunks wobbled towards the light from the villa. I concentrated on the sound of my hiccups, the crunch of dead leaves under our feet and the intermittent howl of animals.

I fell climbing up the four wide steps in front of the side door. Yasmine yanked me up, giggling. I feigned a smile and pretended I wasn't in pain.

"Listen to me, Miryam," she said, pulling up my limp shoulders. "Brush your teeth extra hard before you go to bed. Grownups can smell alcohol from a mile away."

She hugged me extra hard, petted my head and said that we'd be best friends forever and ever and ever. And I tried extra hard not to vomit on my friend.

It was only 9 o'clock and still an hour before my bedtime. But I went to my room through the back hallway, then locked my door. It was the first time I ever locked my bedroom door. It was the first time I had something to hide from my parents.

The ceiling fan wasn't on, but I stared at it as it went round and round and round, like a dragonfly on speed, until I passed out.

Chapter 16

"Ah crap," Ari says as he sits up in bed. He quickly throws his white flat sheet over his bare legs and blue boxers. He looks down and rubs his head.

"Ari?" I give him a look of desperate pleading. "Who died?"

"Your grandmother, honey. She had a stroke last night. Your parents said not to tell you because of your birthday. We were gonna tell you tomorrow."

I sit on his bed and stare down. His words echo through my head. I try to picture Grandmother's face, but nothing registers. All I see is the dark-blue carpet.

"I'm sorry, Miryam," he says, sliding across the bed towards me. "We didn't want you to find out today. Who told you?"

"Your mom," I say, trying to sound annoyed. "She just called and gave me her condolences but wouldn't tell me who died. So fucking frustrating."

"We were trying to keep you from finding out all day," he says with a sigh. "Your parents called when we got back from the therapist's office."

"But I talked to my parents," I say, shaking my head. "They called this morning to wish me a happy birthday...before we went to the shrink...they didn't even talk to Cyrus or Nader."

I frown, trying to remember the sequence of events.

He nods, acknowledging my confusion. "They called again in the afternoon to talk to Cyrus and Nader. You were in the shower, so they told them, but asked them not to tell you yet. They told me to make sure you enjoy your birthday. I called Bee and told her and Paige to take you out tonight because Cyrus and Nader didn't feel like celebrating. And my mom of all people lets it out."

"Bee and Paige knew?" I ask, not sure why that makes me angry.

Is it that they knew before I did or that they didn't tell me? Or that maybe they took me out for my birthday only because Ari asked them to? That it was a pity party? Or that they made me drink in celebration and acted like nothing was wrong?

"We were all just trying to help, Miryam. We didn't want to ruin your birthday."

"Who cares about my birthday? I must've looked like such an idiot going around as if nothing was wrong, drinking and laughing while I'm supposed to be in mourning." I shake my head and randomly repeat snippets of his word jumble. "'Told them not to say anything,' 'told me to make sure you have fun,' 'told them to take you out for your birthday.' What's with this family and always having to fucking hide things from each other?"

"It wasn't our idea. Your parents just wanted you to enjoy your birthday."

I feel a lump in my throat and suddenly well up with tears. But I'm not sure if I'm crying about my grandmother or out of anger. I'm not sure about anything I'm feeling and when Ari tries to hug me, I wail and shove him away. He strokes my hair and pulls me back to him. He flinches at the touch of my cold hands on his bare back.

"How did Cyrus and Nader take it?" I ask as I unwrap myself from him and wipe away my tears.

"They'll be fine. We knew you'd take it the hardest. Cyrus was really worried about you."

I think of how just today at breakfast, I had remembered Grandmother stuffing eggs down my throat. I feel guilty and wonder for a split second if it had anything to do with her dying. Like I caused it on some supernatural level by thinking of her as a torturer. Then I remember that she died last night. I sigh with relief.

I blow my nose in the tissue Ari hands me and I flop backwards on his bed. He lies back with me and stares at the ceiling. The sound of cars passing by outside seems to suddenly grow louder, drowning out my sobs and shallow breaths. My eyelids are shut tight as oyster shells, silently creating droplets of pearls that fall on my face when I intermittently open my eyes. I let Ari hold me. Being in his arms feels nice. Even the crying feels good, more cathartic. I cry until I feel worn out.

I roll my head to the side and see that he's looking at me. He smiles. My heart sinks. It's the kind of smile he hasn't given me in a long time. The smile he used to give me when there was an inside joke between us, when we weren't supposed to laugh in front of adults but were cracking up on the inside, when we were just kids and nothing was too serious and we were one happy-go-lucky soul. I smile back, but with a slight downward turn of my lips to indicate that I'm still sad. He smiles again. This time, I laugh just a little, not sure why. It's like he's playing with me.

Suddenly, he grabs my arm and smiles.

"Where is it?" he asks with a grin.

"Oh no you don't," I yell and pull my arm away laughing.

I have this long white hair growing on the back of my right arm. Ari found it years ago and tried to yank it off. I ran around the living room, screaming for him to leave it alone. Since then, it's become a game where he chases me, threatening to pull it out if I don't obey him about something trivial. I used to be scared that it would hurt if he plucked it. But now, I've simply grown attached to this bizarre stray hair, as if it's the last remaining thread from my security blanket.

"I just want to see if it's still there," he says, grinning and tugging at my arm.

"It's there," I say, pulling my arm even farther away.

He wrestles with me as I giggle. "Let go!"

He pins back my arms and tickles me.

I shriek and squirm, begging him to stop tickling me.

"Let me see it and I'll stop," he says, laughing.

"Shhh," I say, kicking my legs in the air. "They'll hear us and wonder what the hell you want to see so badly."

"I want to see your genetic mutation," he whispers with a laugh.

We wrestle and laugh until we're both gasping for air.

"Truce," he finally says and falls back on the bed.

He picks up my head and puts it on his still-pounding chest. I feel it move up and down and hear his heart beating like a metronome in sync with the rhythm of my breaths.

Our panting slowly dissipates. I feel calm, as if just for a little while, I don't have to think about anything. He strokes my hair. I take a few deep breaths that seem to deflate my insides, then I go limp.

I cushion my cheek on his chest, slowly letting my lips linger in the tangle of dark hair. His fingers express his surprise, breaking the rhythm to which they were stroking my hair. Then they catch themselves and continue.

I move my lips from his chest to his neck. Still lingering, breathing him in. I look up and see that he's staring at the ceiling. He can tell I'm looking at him, but he doesn't look down. I kiss his chin. He swallows hard and my insides churn, knowing he's going to stop me at any moment. I stare at his thick lips, as if aiming. But I don't kiss them just yet. I just look.

I put my mouth on his without actually kissing him. I part my lips and lick his gently, watching him through my half-closed eyes. He's still staring up, still stroking my hair. I close my eyes, feeling them soak with tears again and finally, I kiss his lips. They move slightly, ever so slightly, and I open my eyes just enough to let the tears escape and fall onto his face. His hands move to the back of my neck, where tiny little hairs are standing up on end like perfect summer daffodils. He strokes the hairs gently, as if blowing on the daffodils and releasing their seeds into the air.

He tightens his grip on my hair and pushes my face into his. He opens my mouth with his tongue and kisses me. Kisses me, kisses me, kisses me. The most sought-after, hard-earned, long-awaited kiss in the history of unrequited love.

He tastes like graham crackers. Dipped in honey. Dunked in sweetened tea. He moves from my mouth to my nose, my cheeks and my eyelids, brushing the tears away with his lips. I take his lips back immediately, as if I don't know how I had lived without them until now. I suck them hard and moan.

"Miryam..."

"No, Ari, don't say anything. Please."

I straddle on top of him as my skirt hikes up my bare thighs. I feel him pushing up at me and I moan softly. He grabs my thighs and moves me up and down his body. He's breathing fast and hard, and I'm begging, pleading with God not to let him stop. I take his hand and slide it under my skirt, to the edge of my underwear. He snaps the garter, then pushes one side down. I don't want to get up, scared that he'll escape from under me.

I'm careful to take off my pink Snoopy underwear discreetly. I don't want him to see it and make me explain that I have a stack of Snoopy underwear and I always wear one on my birthday. I tilt to one side, then the other and yank it off before shoving it quickly under the bed. He unzips my skirt and I slide it off, then sit back on top of him. I pull my shirt over my head and fling it to the ground. He looks at my breasts heaving in a black lace bra. He takes a deep breath and looks away, then back again.

He slowly traces the skin outside the top edges of my bra from one side to the other as I unhook the back. He grazes up and down my bare arms with his fingers until I'm dotted with goose bumps. His touch is so soft, so sensual, like a tangible whisper for which every inch of my skin is suddenly screaming. I close my eyes and shake my shoulders so my filled-to-the-rim C-cup bra can drop off completely. I take his hands and cup them around my bare breasts. He circles his finger around my nipples. He moves his hands slowly and gently along the curves of my breasts. Just when I'm relaxing and warming to his touch, he stops. He grabs my shoulders and pushes my back onto the bed. I shiver, watching him look down at my completely naked body. Raw and at his mercy. I stare at his face, into his eyes, for even a hint of what he's thinking. But there isn't any.

"Miryam..."

I quickly kiss him, afraid that my name is the first part of a sentence saying we should stop.

I run my fingers through his hair and push his face to mine, as if it's the only way I can keep him close. I hear the rustle of his hands pulling off his boxers, then feel him on the inside of my thigh. I instinctively open my legs a little. But it's as if my mind and body are out of sync. My body knows exactly what it wants, exactly what to do, but my mind won't let it. All my muscles stiffen and my legs close back up. I moan with frustration. I tell myself to relax. I try to take a deep breath. Just as I'm about to inhale, I feel him pushing inside me. He whispers for me to relax. It's not going smoothly and I'm scared that he'll give up. Or change his mind. I force my legs as wide as I can without having them dangle off the bed.

"Do you need me to do anything?" he asks.

I'm not sure what he means so like a good little girl, I just say "no." Is he asking how to arouse me more? Or is he asking about birth control? I should tell him to get a condom, but I can't risk him leaving the bed for even a second.

You're such a stupid girl. You'd rather risk getting a disease than risk him leaving the bed? Stupid, stupid girl. Tell him to wear a...

I feel a deep thrust that makes me suck in my breath. It hurts more than I had ever thought it would, but I just bite my lip hard without making a sound. He buries himself deeper and deeper inside me like a rock nestled under a bush with tiny leaves.

The painful part must be over. I can relax now.

But with every thrust, it hurts all over again and I feel like my insides are ripping apart. I want to tell him to stop, but I don't. I can't. I open my eyes and watch as he slides in and out of me with his eyes closed. We're both breathing hard, one of us out of pain, but neither of us is moaning. I always thought people moaned a lot during sex. *Why isn't he moaning?*

Right then, he brings his mouth close to my ear and lets out a long, monotonous moan as he clutches my right breast tightly with his hand. I mouth "I love you" behind his back. Suddenly I become aware of what we're doing, that this is actually Ari, inside me, and we are as close as two people can be.

And that it's over.

I pretend not to know that he already came. I wrap my legs tightly around his back and tug at his hair. I grab his behind and push him more into me, forcing him to stay inside, ignoring the pain. But he pulls out abruptly and I have to stop myself from screaming, "No!" The trickle of warm liquid inside me isn't enough to stop the sudden chill swimming across my skin.

"Shit!" he says and slams his back onto the bed.

"What?" I say, closing and tightening my legs.

"Shit, Miryam. I came inside you."

He gets up and walks to his dresser. He takes out a small blue towel and rubs it between my legs.

"Shit! Shit! Shit!" he says.

I clam up and become very aware that Ari is rubbing my naked vagina with a towel. He looks at me and frowns. *What is he looking at me like that for?* I start getting nervous, terrified really. He clutches the towel, covers himself with the sheet and looks down. *He regrets it already. He's not even giving me a forced cuddle.*

"Ari," I say, not knowing what to follow it with.

He sits down and looks at me, waiting for me to say whatever I was going to. But I just stare at him. His face is blank.

I have never wanted to read someone's mind more than I do right now.

He stands up walks away, dragging the sheet with him, and locks the door.

"That was pretty risky of us not locking the door," he says, sitting back down on the bed. "They never knock when they come in here. Shit, can you imagine?"

I don't say anything. He's thinking too logically for me right now. Cyrus and Nader are the last things on my mind.

"Why don't you lie down next to me?" I say like a little girl.

He gets up again and puts on a pair of clean black boxers before lying down on his back.

"I think you should sleep in your own bed," he says. "Just in case."

"OK."

"Just in case, you know. I don't mind if you sleep here, but you know."

You don't mind? *How...sweet of you.*

"Yeah," I say weakly. "I said I would. It's not a big deal."

Except for his breathing, which is still heavy, everything is quiet.

"Do you want me to leave right now?" I ask when he hasn't said anything for a while.

"No, no. I was just saying. Whenever. You can even sleep here. I can always tell the boys you passed out or something. Just wear something. I'm just being careful. I didn't mean it like that."

We're both quiet for a while. I've stopped breathing completely and he's breathing extra hard, as if he stole all my breaths and is living for us both.

"Miryam, I'm really worried about coming, you know, inside you."

"Don't worry. Obviously, I don't have any sexually transmitted diseases and my period just ended two days ago."

I realize how bitchy my tone is only after I stop talking.

But Ari either doesn't notice or doesn't care.

"Oh thank God," he says without looking at me. "About your period, I mean. I'm sorry. I didn't have any condoms. And I thought I'd just, you know, pull out."

He sounds very uncomfortable talking about what he had no problem doing just a little while ago.

"I'm clean, too," he says. "So don't worry."

"I wasn't worried," I mumble.

"Do you think they heard us?" he asks after a few minutes of silence.

"I don't know. I don't think so. Stop worrying."

"I think we were both quiet enough, but what if they could hear the bed move?"

"Ari, I don't know. Tell them you were jerking off or something. What the fuck do you want me to say?"

He looks at me for the first time in a while, and I know he was going to tell me to fucking watch my fucking language or some fucking bullshit like that.

"Are you...what's the matter?" he practically whispers.

I don't say anything.

"I'm sorry," he says. "I'm sorry I hurt you. You were just so tight."

I shake my head even though he's not looking at me. I want to tell him that that's not what hurts, that he's an unfeeling bastard and that he should have more to say to me after we just had sex. After I just lost my virginity to him. But I just grunt.

"I think I should go to sleep now," I say, sitting up and wrapping the sheet clumsily around me.

He slides close to me, turns me around and kisses me on the lips. I don't kiss back. I have this horrible empty feeling inside me and I need to be alone.

"I'll see you in the morning," I say.

"Are you sure you don't want to just sleep here?"

"Yeah, it's OK. I have to call my parents anyway."

I can tell by his expression that he had completely forgotten about my grandmother. Or maybe he's just relieved that I'm leaving. I throw the sheet back on the bed and put on my clothes, aware that he's watching me. I don't know if he sees the Snoopy underwear, but he doesn't say anything. I feign a smile without looking for his and leave.

I go to the bathroom, sit on the toilet and bury my head in my cupped hands. It just feels like the thing to do. I wish I knew why I feel so horrible, why I'm not ecstatic. Everything is jumbled in my head and I have trouble focusing on any one of the million thoughts that creep in and crawl out like sketches of an incoherent dream.

I hold in my pee and have a mini orgasm when I let the drops drizzle out. Now that I've officially had sex, I can vouch that it's overrated. Peeing is *so* much better.

I wipe myself and notice the blood-soaked toilet paper. The amount of blood surprises me. I always thought it would just be a couple of drops, but when I look down in the toilet, I see that even my urine is bloody. Damn that Judy Blume! She said it would only be a few drops when I was 15 and read *Forever.*

I wipe until there's no more blood. I throw the paper in the toilet and stand with my skirt down to my knees, watching it all flush away.

That's it. Twenty-three years of virginity literally gone down the drain. With one flush. That's what it all boils down to, really. Nothing but some blood finding its way to the sewer. I glare into the mirror and just like the first time I got my period, I'm surprised that my reflection doesn't look any different. No stamp on my forehead, no hue of maturity, no womanly glow.

I go to my room, put on a homely pair of pajamas and get under the covers. I start shivering. The racing thoughts stop and turn my mind into a complete blank.

I think of calling Paige or Bee. But I don't want to. They'd shriek like little girls, ask too many questions and analyze it more than I have the energy for. They would make too big a deal out of it while not taking it seriously enough. I feel very protective of my news, like a pregnant woman who wants the knowledge only to herself for a while. Or am I just embarrassed to tell them about his reaction afterwards? That the very first word he said to me after I lost my virginity to him was "shit."

I think about calling my parents, but that thought goes through me like a shot of wormed tequila on an empty stomach. All of a sudden, it hits me. My grandmother is dead. And I practically celebrated her death, again, this time by having sex. What if she were watching me?

I think of her, of my parents, of Cyrus and Nader. The guilt is unbearable. But I don't understand why. It's my body, my life. And I love Ari. It's not like I'm a 14-year-old who just had a one-night stand with some random guy. Why have I been brainwashed to think of my family and to feel guilty about this?

But no matter how much I rationalize everything, the feelings won't budge. I feel dirty and cheap. I feel empty.

This isn't how I'm supposed to feel. I should be elated. My biggest dream has come true. But I feel as if I just made the biggest mistake of my life.

And it was nothing like I thought it would be. It was terrible. I was terrible. I wasn't just tight. I was *uptight.* Now I'm mad at myself. And I miss him. I want to be in his arms. I want to just lie next to him and have him tell me I'm making a big deal over nothing and that everything is fine. We're fine.

I take off my pajamas and put on the sexiest negligée a girl without a sex life owns. It's a light-blue baby doll with black lace trimming. I glance in the full-length mirror, then walk quietly towards his room. The mere thought of seeing him makes the emptiness disappear.

But just as I'm about to knock, I hear it. That snore. Just a normal snore. From a normal guy on a normal night. He's sleeping, snoring, like a normal male animal after mating. Normal. It's all very normal. And that's the opposite of how I feel.

Chapter 17

The lasts of everything were upon us.

A warm, but drizzly March Thursday was our last first day of spring in Iran.

"Persian New Year is the most accurate New Year in the world," Dad was explaining to Cyrus and me. "It wasn't randomly picked off the calendar. It starts right at spring equinox, at the exact second that spring does." He stared at our bored faces. "When all the seasons have passed and Mother Nature starts fresh all over again."

He was trying to anchor us firmly to our roots before we were pulled from them. In the past month, he had taken Cyrus and me to museums throughout Tehran, played classic Persian music during dinner, and read us poetry by Hafez, Khayyam and Rumi, not a word of which we understood. He kept reminding us that Iran has one of the richest and oldest histories in the world. And he was trying to cram that seemingly billion-year history into our psyches in one month.

The more patriotic Dad became, the more I wondered why he was moving us to America, a country he believed lacked culture.

The doorbell rang just as Dad was explaining that Iran and its New Year's tradition had outlived invasions by Greeks, Arabs, Turks and Mongols. I nodded, but kept my eye on the door. I peered over Mom's head to see who the last-minute guests were.

You could tell a lot about the kind of *eidi* (New Year's present for kids) a person would give just by looking at them. The elderly, grandmother-types usually gave money — and lots of it. Mom's snobby friends would get us clothes. "Made in France," they would boast. ("Aren't there any toys that are made in France?" I once asked to Mom's chagrin.) Aunts, uncles and people who bothered to keep up with our whims gave the best gifts: Barbies and Atari game cartridges.

Ari and his mom walked through our open door with a potted purple hyacinth, a small blue suitcase and a box from Noble Pastry balancing on Soraya's flat palm. She and Mom kissed cheeks as Ari's eyes scraped our muddy welcome mat.

"What's with the suitcase?" I asked as I walked towards Ari.

He didn't answer.

"Soraya joon is going to Esfehan for a week to visit her sister," Mom said. "Ari's going to be staying with us so he can get to know us better. Before we leave for America."

My eyes lit up and I smiled excitedly. I grabbed the suitcase from Ari and took it up to Cyrus' room.

I liked Ari. But there was something strange about him. Every time we saw each other, he acted as if we had just met. It would take him hours to warm up to me and just when we would start having fun, it would be time for us to part.

I came back down and joined them in the living room, where Ari sat next to his mom and studied the designs of the Persian carpet under his feet. I sat across him and stared at him with a frozen smile, hoping he would hurry and warm up to me so we wouldn't waste any valuable Barbie time.

But he wouldn't budge. Not even when I opened my *eidi* from my parents and excitedly waved my new Barbie Corvette at him. He just smiled, as if to say, "That's nice."

He didn't say a word to anyone the whole night. And after his mom left, he wasted the remaining three hours before our bedtime by being on the verge of tears and completely unapproachable for anything fun.

When I woke up the next day, he was in my room quietly playing with my Barbies. I jolted out of bed excitedly and grabbed Party Barbie. Ari got startled and dropped half-naked Beach Barbie.

"I'm sorry," he said, turning red. "I didn't mean to wake you."

"Why *didn't* you wake me?" I asked. "We could've been playing all morning."

He shook his head as if he hadn't heard me.

"I'm sorry," he said. "I shouldn't have touched your toys."

He got up and ran out of my room.

"What's wrong with that boy?" I asked Mom later.

"What do you mean?"

I told her about the Barbie incident and waited for her to tell me that maybe he doesn't remember me.

She smiled.

"Poor kid," she said. "His mom probably told him to be on his best behavior. He's probably watching his every move, making sure he's not a nuisance."

"Well, he *is* being a nuisance," I said, walking out.

I found Ari sitting alone in the den, watching a badly dubbed Bruce Lee movie with the volume turned low. He saw me walk in and sat up straight.

"Look, if you're going to be living with us in America, you're gonna have to be less polite," I said with my hand on my hip. "I already have one brother who barely talks and I have a baby brother who doesn't even know *how* to talk. So you better start talking and being goofy and playing with me or this is just not gonna work."

He stared at me, his almond-shaped eyes widening until they looked round. I suddenly got scared that he'd start crying. I was on guard, ready to run to Mom for help, when he finally smiled.

That boy knew his Barbies. And unlike Cyrus, he didn't think he was too good for anything but Ken. He actually liked to play with my toys better than with Cyrus'. Per Mom's orders, we tried to include Cyrus in our games, but he was too immature. All he wanted to do was pull off Barbie's arms and legs. Ari and I were much closer in age and had always had more of a connection than he and Cyrus did.

Ari had no qualms about changing pretend baby diapers, brushing Barbie's hair or dusting my three-story Barbie house.

But there was only so much eating, sleeping and driving Barbie and Ken could do together and still manage to amuse us. So we moved our game up a notch.

Off came their clothes and smack went their plastic bodies. We giggled and rubbed their anatomically incorrect bodies together while making kissing sounds. When Mom walked in with heaping bowls of vanilla ice cream once, we quickly threw Barbie in her bathtub and put a blanket over Ken.

From then on, every time Ken and Barbie were in the same room, they couldn't keep their hands off each other. And every time, I'd get a strange sensation, almost like I had to pee. But when I'd go to the bathroom, nothing would come out. I wasn't sure what I was feeling, but I had a hunch that I shouldn't tell anyone about it. Not even Ari.

By the time Ari's stay was over, we had grown inseparable. When Soraya picked him up, we held onto each other in tears.

"You'll see each other in a week and then you'll have all the time in the world together," Soraya said, intrigued by how much we had bonded.

As Ari pouted and walked out the door, I told them to wait and ran upstairs.

"Here," I said as I bounced back down the stairs and handed Ken to Ari. "You take him. If we can't be together, they shouldn't be either. We'll reunite them in America and they can pick up where they left off."

Chapter 18

I'm grieving the one-week anniversary of Grandmother's death, as well as the anniversary of my own personal doomsday.

At 3:30 on the morning we made love, when I could no longer play the memories over, I went to the medicine cabinet. The closest thing to a sleeping pill was NyQuil. I downed almost half the bottle with an orange-juice chaser and fell into a groggy sleep an hour later. I woke up soon after with my heart beating, not knowing where I was. I had dreamed that Grandmother was dressed up in a witch's costume giving me poison, which looked like the NyQuil. Suddenly, Ari appeared looking like Grandfather. He had tried to kiss me and I had shrieked that it was incest.

I tried to stay awake after I startled out of the dream, but the NyQuil knocked me back down like an out-of-shape boxer in the ring. Finally, after a dream of cats clawing at me, I gave up on sleep and woke up to face a bloody Sunday. Literally.

I've always hated Sundays. There's a depressing quiet aura to a Sunday, as if it's the last day on Earth and only the most lost souls dare to roam the streets before Armageddon comes crashing on their heads. The silence of Sundays sounds like the world's collective sigh, a whisper that there's something missing on Earth. And then you remember. That on the seventh day, He rested.

That's why people go to church on Sundays. They go to His home, where they know He's resting again and beg Him to come back out.

I climbed out of bed at 6 a.m., earlier than anybody in the house, earlier than God Himself. The calm of the dawn swept gently inside me, blanketing the night's fears. I walked to the window and looked out onto the horizon, where the sun was crawling out from under the cover of clouds, slowly stretching its rays towards the sky. The quiet had a sound to it; the air had a taste to it. I watched the blades of grass on our front lawn dance to the rhythm of the raining sprinklers. The empty street smelled like water on hot pavement. I felt the same quiet peace as on the days Grandmother and I used to pray together at dawn. I had a strange sense that she was with me, that she had woken me up from the beyond to once again have us share the morning's quiet with God.

I knelt down by my open window and looked up at the sky. I no longer know how to pray in Arabic, so I simply closed my eyes and felt Grandmother's peaceful presence, as if listening to her pray for the both of us.

I knew that last night, she had entered the heavens and told the angels to give me Ari. She had tried to ease my sorrow by giving me something to rejoice over. She had looked down over my night with Ari and blushed away only after the angels showed her a glimpse of my wish ripening to fruition.

I felt the morning breeze caress my skin like thousands of angels breathing down from the heavens, whispering comfort into my soul.

I walked out of my room softly, as if my feet, too, were whispering with every step. But when I opened my door, my body jolted back into its usual stiff mode, pushing the calm out through my awakened pores. I saw Ari walking hurriedly towards his bedroom with a pile of sheets.

My heart pounded harder with each step I took in his direction.

"Good morning," I said.

"Shit, Miryam," he said, holding his chest. "You scared me."

"What are you doing?" I asked.

"What does it look like I'm doing?"

It looked like he was changing his sheets.

"Do you need help?" I asked as I walked towards his bed.

"No," he said without looking at me. "Just make sure the boys don't wake up and come in here."

"What's the big deal? So, you're changing sheets."

"The big deal is this," he said, pointing to a bloodstain on the sheet.

"I'll wash that," I said.

"I said don't worry about it. I just don't understand why you bled so much. You should've told me so I could've brought a towel or something."

His tone felt more brusque than his thrust inside me the night before. His sheet was more important than the fact that there was enough of my blood on it for Dracula to have a field day.

He crumpled the sheets in a pile on the floor and flattened a new dark-blue one onto his bed. I sat on the leather chair by his desk and tightened my robe.

"What's wrong with you?" I asked.

"Nothing," he said with a frown. "Why are you up so early?"

"I had nightmares all night."

He stared at me.

"About my grandmother," I quickly added.

He looked away.

"Yeah, it was pretty bad," I said. "I wish I had slept with you after all."

"Well, if I had known you'd wake up so early today, I guess you could've. But I didn't want to risk them finding you in here at 3 in the afternoon."

Because you couldn't have just woken me up and told me to go back to my own bed early in the morning, asshole?

I got up from the chair and sat on his bed after he finished making it. He looked at me strangely.

"Don't worry," I said. "I'm not bleeding anymore."

He looked away and walked to his closet.

"Actually, I am still bleeding," I said. "But it won't leak or anything."

"What do you mean you're still bleeding?" he asked with an almost angry frown.

"I had to use a pad last night and I just checked. I'm still bleeding."

"Is that normal?"

"I don't know. I've never lost my virginity before."

"Well, make sure you ask someone if it's normal or not. And go to the doctor or something if it's not."

"No thanks," I said. "I didn't have a very good experience at the gynecologist last time when I had to explain the fact that I was a virgin at the age of 20. If I had just said I'm Iranian at the get-go, it would've spared me the half hour of concerned questions."

"Well, it obviously won't be an issue this time," he said matter of factly.

"I'm sure it's fine. I'm not in pain or anything. But I'm peeing a lot of blood, too."

"Ah, Miryam, please," he said, making a face. "Can we stop talking about blood?"

I remember the first time I told Ari I had gotten my period. It was when he was going through a phase of acting grown-up and macho, calling me a baby all the time. So I wanted to let him know that I was as womanly as he was manly. But no 14-year-old boy wants to hear the word "period" coming out of a woman's mouth unless she's an English teacher giving a lesson on punctuation. Ari was no exception. My strategy backfired and he kept his distance from me for months. He no longer treated me like a baby, but it was no better that he acted like I was an alien.

"Sorry," I said, focusing back on the clean sheets smoothed across his bed. "What did you want to talk about?"

"Nothing," he said. "I just don't want any more details about your blood."

"Why are you being such a jerk?"

He gave me an annoyed sigh and sat on the chair I had been sitting on.

"Listen, Miryam. I'm not being a jerk. It's early. We both had a rough night. I'm still worried about Nader and Cyrus being upset about their grandmother. You just came in here, caught me off guard and you're giving me the third degree. I haven't really had a chance to get my thoughts together yet."

"Third degree? What third degree?"

"I'm sorry," he said with the same frustrated tone. "You're right. I'm a jerk. Can we just deal with this later?"

"Fine!" I said loudly and stomped out.

"We'll talk later!" he called out after me.

But as morning turned to afternoon to night, he continued to ignore me. And he topped my first cherry-less Sunday with a cherry when he went to bed without saying goodnight to me for the first time ever.

I spent another sleepless night in my lonely bed.

Ari had shattered the image I used to have of the day after I lost my virginity to him. Countless times I had imagined us making love. Each fantasy ended differently. In one, he would wake me up the next day by whispering, "Good morning, Mrs. Tabaii." Another would have me waking up to rose petals scattered on my pillow. But not a single fantasy depicted a morning when he was colder than the now-empty side of his bed that I had briefly lain on the night before.

A week later, as I watch Ari take some plates into the kitchen, we still haven't approached "later." Not only have we not talked about that night, we haven't talked period. As in, we haven't talked at all, not just about my period. He hasn't even consoled me about my grandmother the way he has Nader and Cyrus.

A few of my parents' friends are over to pay us their respects about my grandmother. I endure the formalities and play hostess for as long as I can. But when Ari asks me to bring out another round of tea, my patience runs out. And so do I. Out the living room and into my room in tears. Everybody probably thinks I'm just upset about my grandmother. But I don't really care what they think. I'm just glad none of the guests runs after me to try to console me.

I look at the chaos in my room, at all the reminders of my night with him, when I had come in here and thrown off my clothes haphazardly. My room is as messy as my mind as my life.

My shoes are still sitting by the door, my bra is hanging off the chair and Snoopy's head on my underwear is poking out from under the bed. If Ari sees this mess, he'll shake his head and call me a slob. He'll never understand that I haven't cleaned up on purpose, that as long as everything looks like it did then, the night will continue to live.

I pick up the skirt I was wearing that night and bring it to my cheek. I close my eyes and cushion my face against the silk. I well up with tears. My shock at Ari ignoring our night, my pleadings with God and my anger at them both have slowly turned into a desperate acceptance that he and I did not share the same experience.

I hear a faint knock. I drop my skirt to the ground and turn my back quickly to the door. I wipe my eyes with my sleeve and look in the mirror at Ari walking in.

"The guests are gone," he says. "They didn't want to bother you so they told me to say 'bye' on their behalf."

I nod, relieved that they're gone and that Ari doesn't tell me I was rude for running out on the guests. He's probably actually grateful that that's why they finally left.

"Miryam, I need to talk to you."

"About what?"

"Something important."

"Can we do it later?" I ask without turning around.

"No, Miryam. It's important."

"What is it?"
"I'm moving out."

Chapter 19

THURSDAYS in Iran were blue. Not a depressing blue, but a warm, tranquil blue like the sky after a long-overdue storm. The later in the day it got, the prettier the blue grew. It started out as a blue almost too light to discern. It grew darker and more pronounced until nighttime, when it turned into my favorite color: a deep, velvety blue just a shade shy of violet.

Even school was fun on Thursdays. We were only an art and an independent-reading class away from the weekend, which in Iran are Thursday afternoons and Fridays.

The stretch of time between the last school bell at noon and the first one on Saturday morning seemed like eternity. Anything could happen in the interim. Our teacher could completely forget about the homework she had assigned. Or she could quit and be replaced by a teacher who deemed art the only subject worth learning. Or the government could re-think the concept of school entirely and decide that kids would be better off staying home and learning all they needed from cartoons.

As soon as I'd get home on Thursdays, I'd pack my overnight bag for Grandmother's house. I'd stuff the books I needed to do my homework with at the very bottom so I wouldn't even see them until the absolute last minute on Friday night.

Cyrus and I would hardly give Dad a chance to take off his tie when he got home from work. We'd be waiting by the door, bags in tow, ready to jump in the car and head towards Grandmother's.

The drive to her house always seemed longer than the drive back home on Friday nights. On the way there, I would peer out the car window at a city that looked more alive than on the other six days of the week. Everyone on the streets seemed to be returning my smile, every song on the radio sounded upbeat and the fumes coughing out of the back of buses smelled delicious.

I wouldn't let myself think of the drive back the following night, when that same route would look dreary and dismal. The streets would be empty and all the stores that on Thursday had been open and bustling with customers would be anchored shut with black iron bars that only let through the inside darkness.

I could smell the sadness in the street and see it on the faces of the people on the same buses that on Thursday had looked so full of life. They, too, seemed disappointed at the false promise of eternity.

We would reach Grandmother's house right before sunset, when Fatima, Grandmother's servant would hear our car's engine and run down the long, pebbled driveway to open the rusty iron gate.

Everything at Grandmother's house was better. Even the rain fell differently. As if in slow motion, so you could see each drop from behind a stained-glass window. The cherry trees had more branches, more fruit than the ones in our garden. The rooms were warmer in the winter, cooler in the summer. You could smell the roses, geraniums and gardenias all the way indoors.

And the candy tasted much sweeter. I waited all week for the four pieces that Grandmother would hand me and Cyrus as soon as we arrived. Even before we got to her house, I could almost see Grandmother taking the key out of her pocket. I could hear it turning in the lock to the tall, wooden closet in the TV room and the door whining open to the gush of sweet scents flowing from the plastic-lined shelf where the candies sat winking at me.

"Can I have more?" I would always ask.

She would smile, but shake her head.

"Why not?" I would ask with a pout.

"You got your four. Next week, as usual, you'll get another four. That's the rule."

Grandmother's house was exceptionally old, even older than Grandmother herself. Everything from the paint on the walls to the trees outside had been complaining of neglect for years. Grandmother and Fatima no longer had the energy to do anything but the bare minimum upkeep of the six bedrooms and the vast gardens both downstairs and upstairs. Dad had tried to talk Grandmother into selling the house and moving into a smaller place after Grandfather died. I was relieved when she had refused and said she couldn't live anywhere else. It was her only home and my only remaining haven.

If my parents had asked me back then if I'd rather spend a day at Disneyland or at Grandmother's, I would've faced a serious dilemma.

We always had the same meal on Thursday nights: chicken soup, spaghetti Bolognese, and chocolate ice cream for dessert. Mom and Dad would join us for dinner before going home and leaving me and Cyrus to stay overnight. After dinner, the adults would talk over tea while Cyrus and I climbed into our pajamas and waited for Grandmother in the room we shared on the weekends.

"We're all alone now, kiddies," she would say in a scary voice after Mom and Dad had left. "No parents here to protect you from the ghosts!"

She would turn off the bedroom lights and we'd scream with mock-horror and delight. We would snuggle under our covers listening to Grandmother's made-up scary stories.

In the summer, we held our ritual out on the veranda, where we slept in *pasheh bands*, beds with nets to ward off mosquitoes. We would lie in the dark, looking up at the sky and listening to the sound of crickets and the howl of wolves in the nearby mountains. I never knew if the goose bumps dotting my skin were from the cool summer breeze or the thrill of Grandmother's spooky stories.

I would hug my blanket, waiting for her to begin. "*Yeki bood, yeki nabood,*" the Farsi version of "Once upon a time."

Even after three or four stories, I would beg her for "just one more." She never told us more than five. But that seemed to be the magic number and I'd drift off to sleep with her hoarse voice still echoing softly in my head.

I tried to wake up early on Friday mornings, so I could watch Grandmother bending and kneeling during dawn prayers.

I was glad Grandmother prayed. She was one less person I had to worry would go to hell. Ever since religion had become part of our school curriculum, I had discovered that I was surrounded by sinners. My parents didn't pray, didn't fast during the holy month of Ramadan or obey any other of God's orders. They did everything wrong, including drink alcohol and eat pork.

I vowed that when I turned 9, when a girl is considered of age in Islam, I would be a practicing Muslim and set a good example for my parents. But when the time came, not only did they not change their ways, but they also scolded me for what they called my "religious fanaticism." Dad stopped finding it cute when I would hide the alcohol, Mom force-fed me during Ramadan and they both forbade me to wake up at dawn to pray.

"Don't listen to that garbage they're brainwashing you with at school," Mom kept saying. "They're just trying to scare you with that nonsense about going to hell."

I'd go to school and learn all about sin. Then I'd come home and see my parents saying and doing the very things I was told were sins. I'd learn that God wanted me to obey my parents. But He also wanted me to avoid sinners. So what was I to do when my parents were sinners?

Watching Grandmother pray on Friday mornings gave me hope. There was faith somewhere in my family and I didn't come from a long line of sinners after all. But I was still confused as to why my parents respected Grandmother's faith while they chided mine.

I finally asked Grandmother about it one morning after she finished praying.

"Do my parents hate God?" I asked as I watched her fold her white chador.

She looked at me with a deep, curious frown.

"Of course not," she said.

"Then why do they tell me to stop talking nonsense when I tell them they'll go to hell for not being religious? And why don't they pray like you?"

She smiled. "You don't have to pray to believe in God. It's better if you do, but you can still be a good person and believe in God without praying."

I looked down and nodded slowly. Grandmother gazed at me and sensed my continuing confusion.

"You can't teach someone to believe in God. It has to come from your heart."

"But I do believe in God," I said.

Her smile widened. "I'm very glad to hear that."

"But I'm scared to pray or be religious because Mom and Dad don't like it."

She chuckled and shook her head slowly. "People all through history have had to struggle to practice their faith," she said. She looked at my frown and smiled. "The point is that you should do what feels right for you. Your parents are probably just scared that you might take it too far or that they're scaring you at school."

I nodded quickly, excited that she was right on both counts.

"Your parents will respect your faith as long as it's coming from your heart and not because they're scaring you about hell in school," she said. "You shouldn't fear God, Miryam. Think of Him like a much higher version of your father. Loving and understanding. So, don't listen to the things they tell you in school if it doesn't feel right in your heart. You don't have to pray five times a day if you can't. God would much rather have you be a good person who helps others without praying than to have you pray ten times a day but hurt others. Doesn't that just make more sense?"

I nodded again.

"You just believe in God the way you do and be a good person," she said. "That's all that matters. And your parents will be fine with it if they know it's not out of fear and if you don't take it too far. You shouldn't take anything too far in life. Too much of anything is bad. It's all about balance."

For the first time since the revolution, I wasn't religiously confused. I wasn't scared for my parents or torn about what I was taught at school. Grandmother had helped me avoid the wrath of both God and my parents. She had instantly shown me how to belong in God's kingdom as well as in my modern family.

"So there's nothing wrong with me that I don't want to cover my head all the time, but I do want to pray?" I asked excitedly.

"Of course not. That's exactly what I'm talking about: balance. And it's wonderful that you want to pray."

"Can I pray with you?" I asked.

"Of course you can," she said with a smile. "Don't you remember how I would have you pray with me when you were little?"

I nodded and smiled, embarrassed about how much I used to dread it.

"I haven't asked you to pray in a long time because I sensed that you didn't want to. Like I said, you can't force it on anyone."

I blushed. "I want to pray with you now."

That evening, Grandmother gave me a chador and an extra prayer mat and we stood next to each other facing Mecca. She asked me to recite the Arabic prayer out loud for the both of us.

"God is very proud of you," she said when we were finished. "And so am I."

I beamed. No one had ever been proud of me before. Or at least, no one had ever told me so.

My bond with Grandmother solidified after that day. I decided that I wanted to be a wise and balanced woman just like her. And I wanted to make her proud more often.

I'd follow her everywhere, paying attention to how she threaded a needle, how much turmeric she pinched into her *khoreshteh gheimeh* and how she smiled despite obvious loneliness.

One day, I decided to surprise her by cleaning the only unkempt room in her house. Just a week before, she had talked to me about the importance of a clean house.

"When your surroundings are clear, you mind is clear," she had said.

Except for one small room behind the kitchen, her entire house reflected this clarity. That room was Grandmother's private sanctuary, where she said she used to go to for some alone time back when Grandfather was alive. I had never really been in the room before and only caught glimpses of how messy it was. A sanctuary, I decided, should be free of clutter. And I wanted to clear the room so as to free Grandmother's mind of clutter.

I waited until she went to the garden to plant her new tomato seeds before I walked into the dusty, mold-scented room. I looked around at the books and old newspapers stacked along the scratched walls, the clothes piled beneath the giant sewing machine, and the scattered plastic bags overflowing with junk. Among the dozen black plastic bags, there was a see-through one stuffed with what looked like candy. I walked forward skeptically, as if floating in slow motion towards a mirage. When I stood above it, I covered my smiling mouth with my hand. *It really was candy.* All kinds of candy and gum and lollipops. The chewing gum with the picture of the rooster on it, the chocolate eggs with the prize in the plastic yolk, the liquid-filled bubble gum, the chocolate-centered lollipops — they were all there.

I had always pictured Grandmother going to the store every Thursday morning and buying exactly eight pieces of candy for Cyrus and me. I had never imagined that she had a huge bagful that she simply reached into before we came over every week.

I dug my hand deep into the bag and felt the various-shaped candies wiggle through my fingers. I brought out handfuls and watched them rain back down, laughing like a beggar stumbling upon a pot of gold.

"Miryam!"

I hadn't even heard the door open. I turned quickly around, my eyes widening at the sight of Grandmother in plastic green gardening shoes and matching gloves.

"I…I was just cleaning," I stuttered.

She didn't look at me. She continued to glance around with a frown, as if to make sure everything was as it had been.

"You found the candy, huh?" she finally said, turning towards me with a weak smile.

I nodded and giggled, relieved that she wasn't angry.

"Look at it all!" I sang and picked up another fistful.

Her smile widened.

"Can I have some?" I asked.

Still smiling, she shook her head.

"Why not?" I asked.

"Four pieces, Miryam," she said. "And you got your four yesterday."

"But you have so much in here."

"That's not the point."

"But why? Why only four? Mom lets us have as much as we want at home."

"Well, she shouldn't. And I'm not your mom."

She was quiet for a while as she watched me stare down into the bag.

"Remember what I told you about balance," she said.

"What does this have to do with balance?" I asked with a frown. "It's just candy."

"You'll enjoy it more if you only get a little at a time."

"No, no. I'll enjoy it more if I have more. Please?"

She shook her head.

The more I persisted, the more Grandmother's face changed from its usual softness. Her smile disappeared, replaced instead with a frown that increasingly deepened.

"That's enough, Miryam!" she snapped. "Come on out. You shouldn't even be in here. What are you doing in here anyway?"

"I was cleaning," I said. "To surprise you."

She looked around at the mess, then back at me.

"I was just about to start," I said.

She raised her eyebrows.

"I swear," I said.

"Don't swear, Miryam!"

"But it's true."

"Come on out," she said with a hint of frustration in her voice. "You shouldn't go through peoples' private things without permission."

That night, when my parents came to pick us up, I overheard Grandmother talking to Mom.

"I think you're spoiling Miryam," she said.

"Why?" Mom asked, sounding like she was frowning.

"She says you give her all the candy she wants. And she thinks I should too. She doesn't seem to understand that she can't just have whatever she wants whenever she wants. You're giving her the wrong message."

"Oh please, Soodabeh!" Mom said, chuckling and uncharacteristically calling Grandmother by her first name. "We're talking about *candy*."

"That's how it starts. And it's not just the candy. I've sensed it in her for a while now. She always just wants more. Of everything. And she acts as if she's entitled to it. She even went into my private room looking for more candy today."

"That doesn't sound at all like Miryam," Mom said.

"Well, that's what happened. She's your daughter, but if I were you, I'd start setting limits for her. If she continues thinking she should get whatever she wants, she's going to have a very hard time in life."

Mom laughed. "I really think you're making a big deal out of this. Miryam is a perfectly sensible girl and she is not the least bit spoiled."

Grandmother ignored Mom and said, "When you don't appreciate what you have, you'll always want more. But no matter how much more you get, it'll never be enough. Because you're always going to want just one more of something. And you end up confusing wanting with needing."

"Oh, you do exaggerate, Soodabeh," Mom said. "Talking philosophically about a little girl wanting a couple of extra pieces of candy."

Mom obviously took Grandmother's "philosophy" as a personal affront to her parenting. And I took it as an attack on me personally.

I never told Grandmother or Mom that I had overheard their conversation. And I tried to act as if nothing had happened. But everything had changed. I never asked Grandmother for anything again. Not "just one more" story, scoop of ice cream or piece of candy. The only reason I even accepted my usual four pieces was so she wouldn't think I was acting strange.

I thought Grandmother hated me. I was nothing but a spoiled nuisance and she was only pretending to care about me. I was hurt that she thought I had been snooping, that I had gone looking for the candy and that she hadn't believed me about being in her room to clean.

Maybe if we had stayed in Iran longer, I would've eventually realized why she had said what she did. Maybe years later, I would've understood that it was for my own good and that it really wasn't about candy. But it was only a month before we moved to America and I spent the last four times at her house doing my homework, waiting for Friday night, so I could go home.

Her house had always been my favorite place in the world, better than home on a snowy day, safer than Mom's arms during a storm.

But after the candy incident, her house became no different from school, Shomal or anywhere else I had once loved. It became yet another place where I no longer belonged.

Chapter 20

I stare at Ari in shock. The blood sinks from my face and drains into my clogged throat. I follow him to the living room and sit across from him on the sofa. He watches my hands shake as I take out a cigarette. He takes my lighter off the table and tries to light my cigarette. I grab it from him and do it myself.

I take a long drag.

"What...what do you mean move out?" I stutter as the smoke puffs out of my mouth.

"I have to, Miryam. We can't continue living together after what happened."

"Nothing happened," I say.

Suddenly I want him to ignore what I've been angry at him for ignoring.

"Come on, Miryam," he says, tilting his head.

"But I don't understand why you have to move out."

"Miryam," he says and clears his throat. "I never told you this, but I think under the circumstances, it might make sense why I'm so messed up over this."

My heart pounds so hard it feels like my ribcage is going to crack. I want to scream at him to hurry up and tell me, but he stares at the ground, as if the right words are crawling out of the carpet one at a time.

"When we first moved here from Iran, your dad sat me down one day and made it very clear to me that I am to look at you and treat you as my sister. That you may not be aware of your actions, but as someone older, I should understand the dynamics of living in the same house with you and make sure I watch how close we get. Stuff about our hormones and family values and trust. You name it, he talked about it. But that's the gist of it. And then, when your parents first moved back to Iran and left me in charge, they took it one step further. They rehashed all that stuff about you and me, then added that you're not allowed to go out with *any* guys period. That the most important thing they expect from me is to keep an eye on you and make sure you don't, to use their words, go astray."

He looks for my non-existent reaction.

"So all these years, I was watching you like a hawk," he continues. "Making sure you didn't date. I know you went out with a few guys here and there, but thank God, you never went out with anyone long enough for me to worry. You know, that it would lead to sex. It was easy. You weren't like other girls; you weren't boy crazy. And then after all these years, when I thought I had done such a good job, I, of all people, end up being the guy you have sex with. That is beyond messed up. Do you have any idea how that makes me feel that you lost your virginity to me?"

"I take it not flattered?" I mumble.

"I feel like scum, Miryam!" he practically yells. "I can't ever look at your parents again. They trusted me. You're like my sister."

I shake my head. I look down feeling embarrassed, angry and betrayed.

"I didn't think you shared their old-fashioned opinion that I should stay a virgin till I got married."

"It's not a matter of my opinion. I was just following their orders. They trusted me."

"The spy who loved me," I say in an angry, sing-song tone. "Is that why you would take me out with you all the time? To keep an eye on me? Our whole friendship was fake? You were just a spy?"

"Oh come on, Miryam," he says. "Of course not. Don't exaggerate. I just meant that they trusted me like your brother, and I betrayed their trust."

"What about betraying *my* trust?" I say with a choked-up voice. "I trusted you too. I thought you were my friend."

"I am. Of course I am. Please, Miryam. Don't twist it around like that."

"Forget all that," I say and shake my head as if trying to make his words fall out. "Just tell me this, Ari. Why did you do it? Why did you have sex with me then?"

He swallows. "I don't know. I got caught up in the moment."

"That's it? Just got caught up in the moment?"

"Well, yes. I got carried away. And I was wrong. It was wrong."

I want to scream that it was the opposite of wrong. That nothing could've been more right. That it was the most logical thing we've ever done instead of lapsing in judgment. But a pride stronger than I ever knew I had stops me from begging him to agree.

No one understands instant gratification and the power of the moment more than an addict. But even as I suck madly on my cigarette, I can't grasp how guys can forget the pleasure of the moment once it's gone.

In the moment of passion, guys live in the present, girls think of a beautiful future. When the moment is over, girls live in the past, guys think of a bleak future.

"I was wrong," Ari continues to mumble. "And I couldn't stop you. I didn't want to stop you. But I should've."

"Like I raped you?"

"Of course not," he says with frustration. "I wanted to- too. Do it, I mean. But where you were concerned, what happened between us that night was very normal. Under the circumstances, I mean. Sex is the antidote to death. It's the celebration of life. It's the act of creating life. And considering you had just found out about your grandmother's death, it was a very natural reaction for you to want to make love. You wanted to be close to someone."

"Oh cut the psychobabble, Ari! Don't justify it like that. And anyway, that was my reason according to your textbook brain. What about you? I don't believe in that caught-in-the-moment bullshit. Why did *you* do it?"

"I don't know," he says and rubs his temples. "All I know is that I feel like shit because of your parents."

"So it's all about my parents, huh? It doesn't matter how I feel or how you feel. It's all about them and your guilt."

"I just...I just can't continue living here after what happened, Miryam. I've broken our number-one house rule."

"What is this, *Three's Company*?"

"Come on, Miryam. You know I'm right."

"No, I don't. But it doesn't matter. Somehow, you're always right. No one knows anything except the great Ari. So go ahead and do the right thing. Or what *you* think is the right thing. Do what you gotta do. Bail out."

"Bail out of what, Miryam? That's not fair. I've stuck around for everything in this family. What happened between us aside, I need to start living my own life. I can't babysit for the rest of my life."

"Oh, so after all *we've* done for you, this is what it boils down to? You have to start living your own life?"

"You're not being fair, Miryam. You're making no sense and you're putting words in my mouth."

I know I am. But putting words in his mouth is a lot more civilized than putting my fist in it, pulling out my hair and breaking dishes over his head.

And what else is there to do when a guy tells you he's having a midlife crisis and he's leaving you to raise the kids so he can go sow his wild oats?

"How am I gonna handle things on my own?" I ask, suddenly bursting into tears.

"You can do it, Miryam," he says softly. "You're strong."

"No, I'm not!"

"It's not like I'm disappearing out of your lives," he says and holds my hand. "I'm moving three streets down."

"What?" I say, yanking my hand away. "You mean you've already found a place?"

He looks down and nods slowly.

"Well then," I say and get up in a flush. "Why are we even having this conversation? It's a done deal."

I start to walk away, but he grabs my arms and pulls me back.

"Angel, please don't be this way."

"Don't call me angel!" I snap.

"Don't call me stupid!" he says with a smile. "What movie?"

"That's not funny."

He stops smiling and looks down.

"Come on, Miryam. I'm trying to be mature about this. Why can't you be? This isn't easy for me either, but trust me, it's for the best."

Each time I heard the screech of packing tape being torn off and slapped on a giant brown box, it sounded and felt like he was sawing off my body parts and stuffing them in the crates. By midnight last night, all that remained were my wailing mouth and watering eyes stranded in his empty room.

But I didn't let him see me cry. Even when he walked towards me with outstretched arms before leaving last night, I simply returned his smile and let him hold my stiff body. I stayed in his arms just long enough for his shirt to soak up my perfume. I pulled away and walked to my room just before he could see the tears that had started to fall.

I watched him leave through my window. He sped off in the U-Haul without looking back, as if he had just been a tenant at our house.

He took everything but his bed. He said it was time he bought a new bed anyway and that my parents could now use his bed whenever they visited. I stared at the bare mattress, hurt that it wasn't special enough for him to keep. Or did he leave it as a memento for the only person who thought it special?

I stopped myself from crawling on the mattress and sniffing every inch of it. I closed his door and slipped back into my room.

How was I going to handle the boys on my own? Who would bring stability into our lives? Who would help me bring in the groceries and lift the enormous bottled waters?

Why hadn't Mom and Dad stopped him? Why did they have to start being understanding now all of a sudden? Why had they just thanked him for all his years of help and let him disappear? Why do they think I'm strong enough to be fine without him?

I cried all night as I mocked the weak, dreary November rain for its lethargy.

Chapter 21

Mom and Soraya were deeply absorbed in a conversation of no interest to Cyrus, Ari and me. But what *was* of interest to us was that they seemed unaware of the time. It was 11:30 p.m., just half an hour away from the citywide curfew that the government had imposed because of the war with Iraq. And we certainly weren't going to bring it to their attention. The closer it got to midnight, the more we giggled with excitement.

At the stroke of midnight, the three of us jumped up and down victoriously and pointed to our plastic watches. Mom and Soraya stared at us with identical-looking frowns. Then Mom suddenly shrieked and sprang up. But it was too late. We laughed at Mom as she held her hand in front of her mouth to conceal her embarrassed smile. She called Dad to tell him that we had missed curfew and would be spending the night at Soraya's.

Mom went to check on Nader, already asleep in Soraya's room, while I helped Soraya lay the non-matching sheets and pillows on Ari's bedroom floor. Ari tried to convince either Cyrus or me to trade places with him and sleep on his "oh so comfortable" bed. But neither of us fell for it. So he started begging his mom to let him join us on the floor.

It was obvious by Soraya's smile that she would give in. But she watched him clasp his hands and plead for a while before she finally nodded with apparent amusement at our gaiety.

By the time we lay the three sets of sheets down, every inch of the white carpet was covered.

Our moms weren't making a fuss over bedtime. They seemed to be as giddy about the spontaneous slumber party as we were. They took turns giggling their way into the kitchen and returning with all kinds of inappropriate midnight snacks for us all to share. The five of us huddled on Soraya's big bed, digging into the container of chocolate ice cream and crunching on potato chips.

Cyrus was the first to fall asleep. When Mom returned from carrying him to Ari's room, I avoided looking at her, afraid that she'd be wearing her "It's bedtime" face: eyebrows raised, tilted head nodding slowly, and lips pressed together in a mock sad smile. But when I peered over at her from the corner of my eye, she smiled knowingly.

"OK," she said. "You can stay up as late as you want. But go on into Ari's room and play quietly so Soraya and I can talk in private."

Ari looked up innocently at Soraya until she, too, nodded in defeat.

We raised our tight fists in the air victoriously, then quickly jumped off the bed and ran out of the room, afraid that even a second's delay would make them change their minds.

Everything seemed exciting that night. Even having to whisper and play quietly gave me the butterflies. Every sound made me giggle. Every time Ari would almost trip over Cyrus's legs, I would bend down in hysterics.

"I brought a Barbie," I whispered to Ari when he asked what we should do. "It's in my mom's bag. I'll get it and you get Ken."

Ari's eyes lit up and he nodded excitedly. Then he gasped.

"Oh no! I packed him already." He pointed to the stuffed open suitcase in the corner of his room. "I have no idea where he is in there."

"We'll dig him out."

Ari shook his head adamantly. "No. My mom will kill me if I mess up the suitcase."

We looked around the bare room and pouted.

"Hey, we don't need them," I said after a while. "We can still play. I'll be Barbie and you be Ken."

Ari frowned. I smiled and nodded.

It wasn't as easy, or as much fun, as I had thought. But pretending to take a shower, eat, drive to the hair salon and cook for Ken was better than sleeping. We played like mimes for almost an hour, coming up with as many things to do with air as possible. The more boring the game got, the more I wondered if Ari was thinking what I was.

I figured he was because even though he looked exhausted and bored, he kept postponing putting "Ken and Barbie" to bed.

Finally, I yawned. Ken put down his imaginary newspaper and turned off the lights. We lay quietly next to each other on the floor for a while. I thought Ari had fallen asleep. So my heart pounded when I heard his whisper.

"Do you think the kids are asleep, Barbie?"

I smiled in the dark. He called me Barbie. We were still playing.

I peered over at Cyrus. He had his back to us.

"I think so, Ken."

Another long silence ensued.

"Ari?" I whispered. "You up?"

"Yeah. But how are we going to do this?"

"What do you mean?"

"I mean we can't really kiss each other."

"Oh."

"Wait," he said just when I was getting discouraged. "I know."

I felt his hand over my mouth. He moved closer until his body was touching mine. He loosened his hand over my mouth so I could breathe, then he put his lips on his hand. He kissed the back of his hand, while I kissed his palm. We slowly rubbed bodies.

I started to get that funny feeling again. It was much more than when the real Ken and Barbie would kiss. It felt uncomfortable. For a while, I forgot to kiss Ari's palm and just tried to rub against him. Then he pulled away a little. We kissed his hand for a while longer, until Ken whispered, "Good night, Miryam."

I suddenly felt embarrassed and wondered if he knew about my funny feeling. Did boys feel it too?

It seemed forever before Ari fell asleep. I lay on my stomach and rubbed myself on the hard floor, moving as little and slowly as possible so the sheets wouldn't rustle. The longer I did it, the more uncomfortable, but kind of good, I felt down there. Then the sensation went away completely and left me with the same feeling as when you finally pee after having held it for a long time.

When Mom woke me the next morning, Ari was already awake and in the kitchen with Cyrus. I smiled shyly at him with my head slightly bowed, waiting to see how he would react towards me. I was relieved when he waved good morning and smiled back warmly with a mouthful of milk.

I wondered if Ari and I would do that every night when we lived together in America. I wondered if he had liked it as much as I did.

But once in America, not only did Ari and Miryam never do that again, neither did Ken and Barbie. And we've never talked about either couple since.

It's not the kind of thing you ever forget. But Ari so convincingly acted like we never did those things that to this day, I wonder if he even remembers.

Chapter 22

All I know is I need more wine.

Busboy is filling up water glasses, like anyone needs water for survival on a night like this. Waitress is concerned about who wants/doesn't want fresh goddamn ground pepper on their salads. But all I want is more wine.

We're at a French restaurant for Ari's 25th birthday. The kind of quaint, dark restaurant that Ari and I should be sitting in alone, at a table so small that there's barely room for food, feeding each other bites in between meaningful looks. Instead, there's a Caesar salad in front of all 12 of us as we sit around the long, rectangular table. They're dining; I'm whining.

Munch munch and salad is over. Twelve people in the world got their vegetable intake for the day because of this very occasion. Cheers to that! Let's have some wine!

Everyone is whining. *My steak is over-cooked. I asked for fries, not mashed potatoes. I'm sooo sorry to bother you, but is this really cod because it tastes a lot like halibut? I wanted my salad as an entrée, not an appetizer. Can I get some mustard, some A-1 sauce* (at which the waitress snickers, like why isn't *au jus* good enough for this *au peasant*), *some mayo, some ketchup?*

But I'm just whining for wine.

The waitress doesn't look happy with us. As if it's not bad enough that everyone is nagging, we're complaining about things that have nothing to do with her. The chef should be hearing most of this, not her. Maybe I'm just really sympathetic because I was a waitress for about five seconds when I was 19. I interviewed, started, served and quit within one shift. So the minute a server glances in my direction, I order right off the menu, no questions, no substitutions, with everything from appetizer to dessert rehearsed. All with a big, sympathetic smile and lots of 'thank you's.'

But I digress. The main course of this rant is that I need more wine.

The big surprise tonight wasn't Ari's face when we all yelled "happy birthday" as he walked into the restaurant. It was my face when I saw Brooke clasped to his arm. I recognized her immediately, even though she's dyed her hair black since high school.

More than being upset that he has a date, I'm stunned that his date is someone so shallow and not even pretty. I'm almost insulted that he finds her attractive when he obviously also thought me attractive, even if only for 20 minutes one long-ago night.

Brooke herself was never mean to me in high school. But the clique she was in taunted my "Eye-ranian" ass for four years. And here she is five years later, stealing my guy the way she and her friends used to steal my confidence.

Ari, sitting at the other end of the table, looks relaxed and at peace. I want to look like him. I want to feel like him. I want some more wine.

Paige has been staring at me pitifully all night. Her eyes sank in — well, pity — the second she saw Brooke on Ari's arms. By now, her head is in a perpetual tilt and eyes are scraping the floor. I smile at her and she says, "Aw, Miryam. You're so strong."

I smile wider, stretching my lips forcefully, as if showing that strength. I'm glad Bee couldn't make it tonight. She would've insisted that I play games with Ari. And I'd either have to obey her and make a fool out of myself or I'd get corny on her and say something like, "But I'd be playing a game of Solitaire, not Hearts." And then Paige would say, "Aw" again and I would scream for more wine.

Bee gets it, but she isn't very sympathetic. She actually thinks I can do better than Ari. She thinks he's too square. "He's so corny he should come with dental floss," she says about him.

"You see how he is with me?" I ask Paige. "As if nothing happened between us."

"Guys are scum," she says. "Having sex for them is like peeing. It's just a release. Then they flush the toilet like it never happened. All you can do is hope that whenever they feel the urge to pee, they're in your house so they use your toilet."

"Great," I say. "So I'm just a toilet. And when I opened my legs, I was basically just putting the toilet seat up for him."

She throws her head back and laughs. When she sees that I'm not laughing, she pouts and tilts her head. To Paige, this is probably not a big deal. She gets dumped a lot. I once told her that her vagina is the real Bermuda Triangle. Once men come, they disappear.

I look at Ari from the corner of my eye and watch him throw calamari into his mouth. I stare at his lips as he chews, remembering the feel of his tongue, the warmth of his breath. I was once you, calamari. I've been in there, too. But you're in there now and I hope you appreciate it. And you, wine, you go inside his mouth to intoxicate him, but you yourself get drunk just by being in that mouth. Stop snickering at me, wine. Stop giving me that superior look, calamari. I already envy you both enough.

Half a bottle of wine later, I muster enough courage to go to Ari. I put my black high heels right in front of each other as I walk towards him, just like Bee taught Paige and me that that's how models strut on the runway. I trip on the imaginary catwalk and save face by pretending to pick up something I dropped. I get back up and resume my normal, slouched composure. By the time I reach Ari, it feels as if I've gone on a mile-long walk for a hopeless charity.

My butt grabs the corner of the empty seat next to him, as though winning a game of musical chairs at the last second. Ari touches my knee to acknowledge that I'm there, but that he's still talking to Brooke. We smile at each other as if nothing else has ever happened between our stretched lips. He turns away and relaxes next to a babbling Brooke. I sit patiently like a chess piece at the hands of an amateur player.

I close my eyes, not caring who's looking at me, as long as I know Ari isn't. I whiff him, feel his presence and soak up his aura. He's wearing his Cartier cologne. I feel a twinge of superiority towards Brooke. She may be his date, but she doesn't know him well enough to know which colognes he wears, how often and when. Then I feel a twinge of inferiority when I remember that he wears the Cartier one on special occasions — and that he doesn't consider his birthday a special occasion.

I tell myself to capture the feel of his presence so I can savor it when I'm once again greeted by his absence. But instead, I wish I were alone in my room, imagining his face in the dark. Because I miss him more right now than when I'm away from him. Right now, with his face next to mine, I can no longer lie to myself and say that I just want to see him. I wish I wasn't staring at him, so I could continue believing that my pain will disappear once I see him.

Finally, he turns to me.

"What's up, angel?"

I shrug, blush and smile, scrambling for something to say. Nothing comes out. When he looks back at Brooke, I panic and turn him around.

"Ari, I stepped on some glass last night," I say. "If the glass actually got into my foot, it's not gonna like travel up through my bloodstream and kill me or something, is it?"

"What a strange question," he says with a frown. He thinks about it, then says, "No, I don't think so."

"Good," I say.

We both sigh with relief and leave it at that. Because a man will always be relieved when a woman doesn't say something like, "Can we talk about us?" And a drunk will always be relieved when someone doesn't ask something like, "How did you get glass in your foot?"

Just when I finally feel comfortable sitting next to him, he springs up and says he has to go. The pride I had tried to act through all night gets up and beats him to the door.

"No, no," I whimper. "Ari, please don't leave. Please. Um, they haven't even brought out a cake for you or anything."

"I know," he says with a smile. "That's why I'm leaving."

"But Ari, we didn't even really talk."

"I know, but I'm really tired. I gotta get some sleep. I'll call you tomorrow and we'll catch up."

I nod sadly.

He looks at me for exactly three seconds, then asks, "Miryam, are you mad at me?"

I pick my eyes off the floor and land them on his. I scramble for the perfect words, words that will make him understand everything. Words that will convey power, confidence and strength. I wish I could find those words. I wish I *were* those words.

I come up instead with just one pathetic word, just one syllable, one lie. But at least I put everything I've got into that "no."

"Good," he says.

He strokes my head with a smile and walks away.

I wonder if he's really just going to sleep. Or if Brooke is waiting for him by the door so they can go to his place to do all those things couples do before sleep.

She waves at me as he walks towards her. I wave back and envy the door he opens for her. She straightens the Prada bag on her shoulder and whispers something to Ari. He laughs.

I swallow hard and watch them fade slowly into the night.

The waitress taps me on the shoulder.

"Would you like some more wine?"

Chapter 23

EVEN a 10-year-old has a tough time packing up a lifetime. Suddenly, having so many toys was a bad thing. Mom said I was only allowed to bring one suitcase. How exactly was I supposed to fit my four-story dollhouse in one suitcase?

"I'll buy you all new toys when we get to America," she said. "Anything you want. Even though you are getting a little too old to be playing with toys."

The Barbies had to come. Twelve Barbies, different names. And I couldn't just take one Barbie and all the outfits, 'cause then Ski Barbie, Beach Barbie, Ballerina Barbie, Black Barbie, "Cindy," "Famosa," "Amanda" and the rest would once again be upstaged by Queen Barbie.

Thank God Barbies were so thin. Society is concerned about girls idealizing skinny Barbies. Society doesn't understand that you can't fit fat Barbies into a suitcase's corner pocket.

The monkey playing the drums was too big, though. The decoration dolls would also have to stay behind. So would *Shazdeh Khanoum*, the princess, in her ruffled pink gown. And the black doll in the white dress, with her two little girls in diapers, sitting on top of my armoire. I couldn't break up a family. And crybaby in her stroller, Big Teddy and his grandkids around him on the floor, the barking dog, the wagging-his-tail-if-he-had-fresh-batteries dog, the giant ladybug, the…

I was having my first anxiety attack. How could I just leave them after all these years? I had pounded my fists for them in toy stores and now I was abandoning them?

I had to appeal to Mom's maternal instincts.

"Would you be able to move to America if someone said you couldn't take me, Cyrus and Nader?" I asked her.

"Of course not, my baby," she said. "You kids are the *reason* we're moving to America. So you can have a better life."

Good answer. Just what I was hoping for.

She sat down to prepare for a meaningful talk.

"Well, then how can you expect *me* to move there and leave all my dolls?"

"Is this what this is about, Miryam?" She got up and went back to her closet. "I don't have time for this nonsense. We're leaving in a week and I have a million things to do. Now go and pack. Not one more word about this. We're giving up our lives and all you can think about are your toys? One suitcase and that's final."

I stomped out the room. Who asked for a better life!

The next few nights, I lay awake long after the light coming from under my parents' door flicked off. I followed the dolls' sad eyes around my room.

Please take me, Miryam. Remember the time we played after school? See how pretty I make your room look? Remember all those nights you felt alone and I cuddled with you till you fell asleep?

I had made peace with leaving behind the inanimate objects like the Barbie salon and the tea set, but the dolls just wouldn't understand. Every time I'd put one in the suitcase, another would scream.

Two days before we left, my room looked like a war zone. Dad had taken down my suitcase, with all the finalists packed.

I looked at the casualties. *Now what?*

I went into Cyrus' room. He was shooting spitballs from his Bic pen onto the street. He glanced back at me but didn't say anything. I opened his empty closets and looked around as if checking out a vacant apartment. I ran to my room and brought the leftover dolls into Cyrus' room for exile. I introduced the dolls and animals that until then had lived far across the room from each other. They were very friendly towards one another. This was truly a relief. They even joked around.

"You too, huh?" "Yeah, I was too big." "I was a decoration doll." "My dress was bigger than all her clothes put together."

I mixed and matched to create perfect homes. Some families had lots of pets; others had too many children to handle pets; and some didn't have kids but had always wanted them. I took all this into consideration. Then I put the Barbie salon, tea set and comic books on the lower shelf. That way, they would have a town center complete with a beauty salon, a tea parlor and a library. I finished it off by putting in the blankets that Mom was planning to throw away. Making it cozy was crucial.

The night before we left, I sat in front of the closet and talked to the dolls. I explained everything and I was impressed by their maturity. They said they couldn't complain and that all was well, considering there had been a revolution. I later observed them through a crack in the closet door without them noticing me. I was thrilled that they all got along and united in this trying time.

Cyrus hadn't said anything to me throughout the dolls' move. He had watched without complaining about my being in his room. But on that last night, he walked slowly towards the closet holding his favorite toy, a huge green tank.

"Could you put this in there, too?" he asked.

"Yes!" I said. "They'll need a car for going to town!"

I locked the closet, put the key in my pocket and brought my index finger to my nose. "Shhh."

Cyrus beamed. We had our own little secret from my parents.

Chapter 24

The definition of abnormality is panicking at 3 a.m. that you only have one pack of cigarettes left to carry you through the night.

And the definition of addiction is those cigarettes having you shackled in chains so tight that you give new meaning to the term chain smoking; you don't need to find your lighter because it's easier to just light each new cigarette using the flame of the previous one.

"It's OK," I console myself. "You didn't smoke that much. Everyone was bumming them off you tonight."

People haven't really quit smoking. They've just quit paying for their own cigarettes.

I rip open the new pack, tearing into the room's silence. I suck on the cigarette and watch the fire at the tip glow in the darkness like a sudden bolt of lightning in a black sky.

I feel scared, petrified of something I can't point to in my artificial blindness. I feel as if there is no one outside my empty room, no one beyond the deserted streets.

I panic and turn on my bedside lamp. I bring out the wine bottle and the crystal glass from under my bed.

Just one sip later, my blood grows warm, my muscles relax and the pain crawls away, hiding, but not disappearing. It will come back later. But I'll deal with later later. I will handle the pain one day at a time. Perhaps one sip at a time.

But this is no ordinary pain. It has learned to swim. I pour the wine on it, but still it rises, crawling past the current of butterflies swarming in my gut.

I imagine Ari and Brooke making love. I hear him moaning the same moan in her undeserving ear. I shiver at the warmth they create with their intertwined bodies. When they reach orgasm, I wail.

The light starts to pierce the shades, mocking the weak glow from the lamp.

I slip in the cassette and push the play button.

Sing, Elton, sing. Your voice goes with this depressing atmosphere like nuts with beer. And you're drowning out the sound of the hovering helicopters circling above the pre-dawn traffic, snickering about my abnormality.

I close my eyes and lip-sync to Elton John's "Sorry Seems to Be the Hardest Word," a song so painfully poignant and melodically maudlin that even someone not in love would cry.

"*What have I got to do to make you love me, what have I got to do to make you care...*"

Memories of the night we made love rush back to me like blood in a drunken head. I relive the night over and over, as if my mind is a boom box rewinding my favorite song until the cassette ribbon unravels.

I want the night back, so this time I can scream out his name in pleasure. Instead, I sit here night after night silenced by this agony, struggling to say his name with weak lungs from too many cigarettes puffed, thinking of too-few memories. Every night, the wine makes me seesaw between mirth and misery. I smile and cry respectively at the bliss of fresh love and the pain of its inevitable end.

Gloria Steinem, cover your ears; even my own naked body reminds me of him. I wish he had gotten me pregnant. So I could've shown something for what he thought was nothing. So I could've looked into our child's eyes as proof that he had loved me once, that what had happened between us was as significant as life itself.

I turn on the television, hoping the images will blanket my thoughts. The 4 a.m. commercials indicate that I am a sex-starved, lonely, alcoholic man seeking inpatient rehab, horny conversations and a glimpse of a better future from voice-activated tarot cards. Score for the concept of a target audience.

I hear a knock on the door and cough out the cigarette smoke. I grab the bottle and the glass, shove them under the bed and wipe my face with my sleeve.

Cyrus walks in dressed in sweats.

"What are you doing up?" I ask with a frown.

"Getting ready to kill Elton John," he says.

"Sorry," I mumble.

I click off the cassette.

"I didn't realize how loud it was," I say. "Go back to bed. Sorry."

"Sorry doesn't seem to be the hardest word," he says.

I frown. "Huh?"

"Never mind," he says with a chuckle.

He stands by the door and stares at me.

"Miryam, what is it?"

"What is what?"

"What's going on with you?"

Well there's a switch. Usually, I'm asking him that question.

"I miss Ari," I say, before quickly adding, "Don't you?"

"We just saw him last night. Or in your case, tonight."

"No, I mean..."

"Yeah. I know."

"I just can't handle things without him," I say.

"Handle what?" he asks as he closes the door and bends down to sit across from me. "Everything's fine."

I look at his eyes, surprised that they're staring directly into mine instead of bowed to the ground.

I nod. "How're your shrink sessions going?"

He shrugs. "I'm a little depressed."

"About what?"

"My depression."

How much have I drank that that actually made sense?

"What about AA?" I ask. "I didn't want to get on your case, but I know you haven't been going to too many meetings."

"I can't go to AA. It was making me worse."

"Cyrus..."

"I just can't. I can't buy into their philosophy. I told you how they think alcoholism is a disease and that if you have it, there is nothing you can do other than go to meetings to be fine. But I can't accept that I have no control over my life. I can't live the rest of my life thinking I have a disease."

Is this disease contagious, perhaps?

"You're an adult, Cyrus. I can't tell you what to do. It's your life. But if you really believe you have control over your life, then act like it. Control every aspect of your life and don't ruin it by being stupid."

"I know what I'm doing, Miryam. I'm not saying I never drink. But I'm not going to be an idiot about it."

"That's all I'm saying. Just be in control. Everything in moderation, like they say."

Neither of us talks for a while. Cyrus picks lint off his sweats as I blow my nose over and over.

"In that case," he says, "can I have some?"

He smiles.

"Some what?" I ask.

"Wine."

"What wine?"

"Come on, Miryam. You think I'm stupid? You reek of it and I can see the bottle under your bed. It's cool. We'll just have a couple of glasses together and talk. We haven't talked since, well, in a while."

I start to lie about the wine. But there's no hiding what he's already seen.

"I just hid it so you wouldn't be tempted," I say.

"A glass of wine is not a big deal."

I don't know if he's talking about himself or me. I hesitate. Cyrus and I had a falling-out a few months ago, before Ari moved out. Things at home got pretty ugly, as did his partying. He was dating Bee's roommate, Sophie. To say she and I didn't get along is an understatement. She was a bitch and a racist. She flattered Cyrus by saying she had made an exception to dating an Eye-ranian. She and Cyrus disappeared for a few days, partying it up in Mexico, "hooking up" with random people, doing all kinds of drugs.

All of a sudden, Cyrus was Mr. Popular and his ego soared in proportion to his drug use. I once told Sophie that she shouldn't smoke so much pot around Sushi and Sake (her two Yorkies) and she called me a "hypocritical bitch" because I smoke cigarettes in front of my little brother. She hated me for "mothering"

Cyrus and finally broke up with him, citing me as the reason. It bonded Ari and me intensely at the time, but caused a huge rift between Cyrus and me. I was so desperate to make peace with Cyrus that I even went to Bee's place unannounced to talk to Sophie about getting back together with Cyrus. Half an hour after I got there, she walked in with Rick, a tall blond hunk. I politely asked if I could have a word with her. She sighed and told Rick to wait for her in the kitchen.

Before broaching the subject of her and Cyrus, I asked, "Um, you and Rick, are you guys…I mean, are you a couple?"

"Not that it's any of your business," she said, "but if you must know, you could say we're a couple. We've fucked *a couple* of times."

And on that note, I abandoned the whole idea and didn't even bring up Cyrus.

He's barely talked to me since the Sophie saga. So right now, I feel desperate to gain back his trust and bond with him.

I carefully pull the bottle out from under the bed and fill my crystal wine glass. I down it while Cyrus runs out of the room. He comes back, sets a regular glass on the carpet and watches me fill it. I shake the bottle, frown exaggeratedly and before I have a chance to speak, Cyrus disappears again, returning with a full bottle.

We're both quiet until our third glass. I'm feeling completely numb, as if my body has shut down. I startle when Cyrus clears his throat.

He circles his finger around the rim of his glass and without looking up at me, says, "Miryam, I know about you and Ari."

My body switches on, full throttle. My blood races, my heart pounds and every sound echoes through my head as if trapped in a tunnel.

I'm not sure how much time passes before I actually say the words out loud. "What…what are you talking about?"

"I know you're in love with him," he says as if in slow motion.

"What? That's ridi…"

I stare at his raised eyebrows and stop mid-sentence. I should've known Cyrus knew. Quiet people are very perceptive. Instead of polluting the air with useless words, they pick up the floating cues and nuances that the rest of us bury with our banal banter.

"How do you know?" I ask, blushing.

"I've known all along. You're not very subtle. But don't worry. I don't think he knows. And if it's any consolation, I know he has feelings for you, too."

"What?" I say, sitting up. "How do you know?"

"Same way I know you have feelings for him."

"Did he ever say anything to you?" I ask.

"No. But I can just tell. I think that may even be why he moved out. Maybe he felt guilty about his feelings."

Realizing that Cyrus obviously doesn't know the full story about Ari and me, I shake my head. "No, it's not that. He just wanted to move on with his life. It had nothing to do with me."

"Do you feel the same way?" he asks.

"About Ari? Huh? What?"

"No. I mean, do you want to move out and get on with your life, too?"

"Of course I do. It has nothing to do with you or Nader. I'm just getting old, you know?"

"Old? Gimmie a break!"

He throws the last few drops of wine down his throat.

"You know what I realized the other day?" I say as I fill up his glass. "I can never be a ballerina."

"What the hell?" he says, squinting.

"I mean, I'm so old that if I wanted to be a ballerina, it would be too late."

"Ballerina?" He throws his head back and laughs. "You can't dance worth shit!"

"The point is that even if I had all the talent in the world, I'm too old to be a ballerina. Don't you see?"

"No, I don't see," he says. "I hear…the wine talking."

"Work with me here, Cyrus. I'm getting old and I have nothing to show for my life."

"Who the hell does, man? You'll be saying the same shit when you're 60 and you'll wanna kick yourself that you said it when you were 23."

"That's not true. Bee and Paige don't say this kind of stuff. But that's because they're going somewhere in life. I'm not. Growing up, I always thought I'd be somewhere by now. But I have nothing to show for my life. Nothing. I don't know how I ended up such a loser."

"You're not a loser," he says. "You just think too much. *Way* too much."

"Don't you think about this stuff?"

"Sometimes," he says. "But I try not to. There's no point in thinking about things too much, especially about things you can't control. It's like…it's like pissing your pants. 'Oh, why did I piss my pants?' You don't sit in your piss and think about why. You just change your pants and move on instead of thinking about why. Shit happens. Are you gonna clean it up and move on or sit in it and analyze it?"

"Interesting analogies," I say with a frown. "Piss and shit."

"That's right," he says with a smirk that I know is because he's amused by himself.

"But I think it's healthy to think about the whys sometimes," I say.

"Wrong," he says. "It's the most dangerous thing to do. Leave the whys for when you die. You'll meet God and ask Him about the whys all you want."

"I intend to," I say with a smile. "You know, I read somewhere that 'why' is the most common question people have. About things that happen in life, I mean. Or maybe I thought it. I don't remember."

"Do you always think this much?" he asks.

"Sometimes. Why?"

"Because you're gonna drive yourself crazy."

"Oh, I got there a long time ago. I drove there in a Ferrari."

"That's funny," he says.

"How come you always do that?" I ask.

"Do what?"

"You always say, 'that's funny' instead of actually laughing."

He frowns. "Huh. That's funny. I don't know."

"You did it again," I say, laughing.

He chuckles. I pull out a cigarette and offer him one. He shakes his head.

"You want some more wine?" he asks.

"You might as well start growing a vineyard in our backyard."

"That's funny," he says. "Oh my God, I really do do that!"

I laugh and watch him fill my glass.

"You don't want any more?" I ask when he doesn't refill his.

"No," he says, holding his stomach. "I feel sick. I think I need to eat something."

"There's some leftover chicken in the fridge."

"Thanks, but I'd rather have something edible."

"What's that supposed to mean?"

"It means you make a bland chicken," he says.

"Thanks a lot," I say with a crooked smile. "So what are you gonna eat?"

He pushes himself off the ground, groaning like an old man. "Don't worry. I'll figure something out. Are you gonna be OK?"

I nod.

"OK then," he says. "Get some sleep."

"Hey, Cyrus," I say before he walks out.

He looks at me. I point to the wine. "Shhh."

Chapter 25

I watched the dead, rusty leaves fall to the ground as the season dictates. Dad had woken me up half an hour earlier and told me to hurry. It was going to be crazy at the airport and we didn't want to miss our flight, did we?

It was late autumn and still dark outside. The bliss kissing the air was the same as on the days we would get up early to go skiing. The sky's crimson peered into my room. A draft squeezed in through the window's ledge. The air was crisp and smelled like Mom's cheeks on winter days.

I turned on the lights and looked at the clothes Mom had laid out: brown corduroy pants, my beige sweater with the white cows on it, white socks and my newly cleaned sneakers. I got dressed quickly and went to brush my teeth. I smiled at Dad in the hallway on his way to wake up Cyrus.

"Good girl," Mom said as I came out of the bathroom. "You're ready."

She was dressed, too, in all black. She followed me to my room and glanced around.

"Looks good," she said. "I'm so proud of you giving all your leftover toys to the orphanage I donated your and Cyrus' old clothes to. I'll buy you whatever you want when we get to America."

Her usually honed motherly intuition was clouded by her own worries or else she would've detected that I was guilty of something when I said she didn't need to buy me anything.

I started to make my bed, but Mom said to leave it. She stripped off the sheets and walked out with them crumpled in her hands.

I grabbed my Snoopy handbag and walked towards the door. But I couldn't step out. I leaned against the wall and stared at my empty room with a sudden lump in my throat. There wasn't even anything left to say goodbye to except a bare mattress, those orange-and-green drapes that I hated, the green Persian carpet dotted with my Magic-Marker stains, and stacks of empty shelves.

I walked to the drapes and pinched their rough fabric. Never again would I draw them open to beam at snow covering the streets, run downstairs to hear Mom say school was closed for the day, then slide in jubilation across the kitchen floor in my thick socks.

I squinted at the sun hiding behind the trees. I took a final glance at the emptiness, but told myself not to cry. So what if it doesn't snow in Los Angeles? It's still a better place, the place where Little Lulu and Richie Rich come from.

Be strong. What kind of an example would you set for the dolls if you cried?

I went to Cyrus' room to say goodbye to the dolls. But Dad was still in there. So I just waved at the closet and smiled at the puzzled look on his face. My last memory of our upstairs is Cyrus' voice screaming about wanting to wear his "other" shoes. Dad sounded impatient when he explained that they were already in the suitcase.

A hard-boiled egg and a glass of milk awaited me in the kitchen. Zohreh was burning incense on the stove. Her shirt was stained as usual. She walked towards me through the fog and circled the incense around my head while praying under her breath.

Dad came in and waved the smoke away from his face.

"You've stunk up this place again?" he said to Zohreh in Farsi. "Put that stuff out and stop with this nonsense superstition!"

"*Agha safar darid. Sheytanat ra ba khodetoon nabarid,*" Zohreh said, explaining that we had to get rid of evil energy before our trip.

She hurriedly circled some smoke around his head before throwing the blackened incense into the sink. Mom walked in, cradling Nader in her arms. Cyrus trailed behind her with a pout. My parents drank their tea in silence and took turns feeding Cyrus his runny eggs and wiping his runny nose.

The taxi came just in time for Mom to get up from the table and for me to throw my cold, untouched egg in the trashcan. I grabbed some raisin cookies from the cupboard and stuffed them into my mouth without bothering to pick out the raisins like I usually did.

Dad helped the driver put all five of our suitcases into the trunk of his beat-up *Peykan* and explained that we would follow him to the airport in another taxi.

Mom tied my scarf, making sure all my hair was covered.

"Now don't mess with that, Miryam," she said. "They're very strict at the airport and we don't want to give them any excuses for not letting us leave."

I nodded and didn't touch the too-tight scarf.

"*Zood bashid. Berim digeh,*" Dad said, telling us to hurry.

Mom and Zohreh were crying and hugging each other. It suddenly hit me that Zohreh wasn't coming with us. I couldn't even stand the emptiness in the house on the rare days she would take off. I would have a hollow feeling in my stomach until she returned. How was I going to survive every day being her day off?

My aunt and her husband were going to come stay at our house after we left, then sell it and wire us the money. So Zohreh would be staying and working for them in the interim.

I reluctantly left her tight embrace and passed under the Koran in her hand. I walked out of our house for the last time as if I were stepping into the sea in Shomal: getting my feet wet first, then slowly moving forward an inch at a time, until the water finally engulfed me.

Agha Mashadi, our street sweeper, who was the only person on the street at that hour, was raking the dead leaves. He saw us and walked towards the taxi. Dad opened his window.

"*Be salamat Agha. Khoda be hamrahetoon,*" Agha Mashadi said, wishing us a safe trip.

I started crying at the thought of not seeing him sweep the street as I walked to school every day. The old, round, raggedy-looking man who was missing most of his teeth, always smiled proudly and waved at me and the other neighborhood kids as we dragged ourselves away from home every morning. It cheered me up knowing he awoke earlier than I did and that he was busy sweeping the streets as I sat in class. The thought of someone else working in misery made my days go by faster. Whereas the other girls in my class had written "John Travolta" inside their notebooks, I had scribbled "Agha Mashadi" in the corner of mine. His name reminded me that he, too, was working, and it calmed my racing heart the way John Travolta's name sped up my friends' pulse.

I stared at Agha Mashadi's toothless grin and pictured him standing on this street every day, raking leaves or shoveling snow as the seasons passed without me there to see them. Or him.

Mom shushed me as I sobbed. Dad peeled off a wad of money and gave it to Agha Mashadi.

"*Zendeh bashid, Agha,*" he said to Dad, grateful for the money.

He walked towards Zohreh, and they stood next to each other like Popeye and Olive Oyl. I always told Zohreh she looked like Olive Oyl, but she never knew what I was talking about. Then one day, I excitedly dragged her to the television and pointed to Popeye's wife on the screen. She got insulted and said that thinness was a sign of poverty and disease. But Zohreh never did eat. Her only association with food was cooking it. More food found its way onto her clothes than into her mouth.

I missed her even as I watched her splash rosewater behind our taxi, then walk back to Agha Mashadi. I could see their lips moving as they waved. I wondered what they were saying. Did they envy us for going to that magical land called America? Or were they grateful that they were too poor for such opportunities?

Dread suddenly replaced any excitement I had had about moving to America. I wanted to run back into Zohreh's safe arms. I wanted to bury my face into the stains on her shirt. I wanted to *be* Zohreh, in her mismatched clothes, with her simple, familiar life in Tehran.

The car rattled as it dipped in and out of potholes. I stared back and watched Zohreh and Agha Mashadi getting smaller and smaller, until they vanished from my life. Soon, they were nothing but specks in the distance, and our home just another house.

Chapter 26

I smack my alarm clock on the head again, but still it ding-dings. I manage to drift off back to sleep, but when I dream that my clock is telling me to pick it up, I open my eyes and realize that it's the phone ringing. I fumble on my nightstand and grab the cordless.

"Hello?" I say, trying to sound awake.

"Miryam!" Ari screams. "Why the fuck aren't you picking up the phone?"

"What do you mean? I just did."

"About 12 hours too late. Were you fucking sleeping?"

"What's wrong with you?" I ask.

"What's wrong with *you*? Do you have any idea what's going on?"

"What do you mean?"

"He's fine and at my place now. But I had to bail Cyrus out of jail for drunk driving this morning. He got pulled over for driving too fast, then got arrested. Going to fucking Jack in the Box to get a hamburger, drunk off his ass, at 6 in the morning."

The phone slips from my ear.

"Miryam, are you there?" Ari shouts into the phone as Cyrus' words, "You make a bland chicken" echo in my heavy, hungover head.

Chapter 27

By the 10th hour of the flight from London to Los Angeles, the blonde stewardess who had given Cyrus, Nader, Ari and me our coloring books didn't look so pretty to me anymore.

We had met up with Ari and his mom at Tehran's then-international Mehrabad airport. My parents and Soraya squeezed one another's sweaty palms, knowing our lives depended on whether the bearded man behind the glass at passport control was in a good mood. Mom kept reassuring Soraya that there was no reason for them not to let Ari leave the country; he was just a child and had nothing to do with his father's position with the Shah.

Dad handed our passports to the man and whispered to Soraya to step aside. The man stared at our passports and faces intensely. Dad did all the talking, explaining that we were just an average family going to London on vacation. Since the hostage crisis, there were no longer any direct flights between Iran and the United States, so the man had no way of knowing that our real destination was the "evil country."

After studying Ari's passport, the guy walked away from the booth, leaving Soraya to practically faint in the corner. We had to stay put and ignore her presence, but my parents kept motioning for her to calm down. Dad's shirt was wet from his armpits to his navel. Mom kept fixing her scarf and checking to make sure my hair wasn't peeking out from under mine.

When the guy returned, he asked what Ari's relation was and why he was traveling with us. Dad said that Ari was going to visit his grandmother in London and we were just chaperoning him on the flight.

I kept smiling at the guy, hoping he'd think we were a nice family that would never desert their country. He didn't even notice, but when Mom saw my frozen smile, she poked me and whispered for me to look serious. Because the guy might misinterpret my smile, whatever that meant. It reminded me of when I had my picture taken in my black scarf for my post-revolutionary passport. The photographer had also told me not to smile. All my life, before every picture, I was told to smile. But suddenly, smiling had become taboo.

So I donned my sternest frown and tried to look miserable in the passport line. The guy took down Ari's grandmother's address in London before stamping our passports and shooing us away.

We walked slowly and quietly out of his sight before the adults hugged each other and repeated "*Khoda ro shokr*" (thank God) in unison. Dad told Soraya that he had given my aunt's address in London as Ari's grandmother's.

Soraya's gaiety disappeared when it was time for her to say goodbye to Ari. She was obviously fighting back tears and trying to stay strong for him. But when she kissed him for the last time and unwrapped her arms from his neck, she cried so violently that she struggled to breathe. My own tears poured down and my heart ached watching Ari hold onto Soraya's waist and refusing to let go. I turned away, but everywhere I looked, there were more families tearfully holding onto one another. It was obvious that half the people leaving the country would probably never return. I could no longer stand the pain and walked quickly ahead to the gate as Dad tried to detangle Ari from his mom.

Ari was still crying when we boarded the plane. I stroked his hand, but didn't know what to say. I ached for him and wished my parents would find a way to comfort him. But they were in their own world, whispering to each other and checking their watches every 10 seconds. It wasn't until the pilot said we were ready for takeoff that they sighed exaggeratedly, then kissed each other. On the mouth.

As the plane rolled down the runway, I saw on their faces a look that until then I hadn't even realized was missing. I hadn't seen them smile like that in so long. They were just...themselves again.

Mom held me tight.

"*Digeh tamoom shod* (it's finally over)," she said. "*Digeh raftim* (we've officially left.)"

She kissed Ari and tried to take his mind off his mom by asking him what toys he wanted when we got to America.

My parents' joy was contagious. Suddenly, all of us, even Ari, were smiling and talking about America, the land of paradise. All this happiness was because of us kids. But I was just happy that my parents were happy again.

I had never cared that I had to wear the *hijab* and cover myself in public. It didn't matter that religion and Koran classes had become more important at school than science and math. I was a kid and didn't have too much freedom to begin with. It was no different if my parents made me do something or if the government did. A 10-year-old lives to obey, no matter whom she's obeying. But if it made my parents feel better that I would soon be cramming for an algebra test instead of one on the Koran, I was happy for them.

Not that I was unhappy about going to America. Since the revolution, you couldn't find anything decent in Iran. No Snoopy stickers, no Walkmans, no English comic books. I was eager to go to a land where choices — of toys and junk food — abound.

My mouth had watered at an ad for a Slurpee, the "Coldest Drink in Town," in one of my *Richie Rich* comics. Finally, I could go to town in America and have a Slurpee. A blue one, just like in the ad.

I went berserk at Heathrow airport, buying chocolates, gummy bears and postcards I'd never send. But we only had a two-hour layover before our flight to L.A., so my parents curtailed my shopping spree. Cyrus was cranky, Nader was sleepy, and I should just wait until America.

America, America, everything America.

Straight from Iran and into the shops at Heathrow, I deduced that I had seen all of London. And I wanted to stay. Why couldn't we just live in London? Why did we have to get on another plane? Wasn't the whole point just leaving Iran?

I didn't get a chance to ask until after Pan Am cruised above the foggy London sky.

"Why do we have to go to America? They speak English in London."

My parents looked at each other, and as always, Dad answered.

"Don't you want to go to America?"

"Yes, but why America? Why not London or somewhere else where they speak English?"

"Because America is the only place where everyone is welcome," he said. "They accept everyone as their own. As long as we're leaving our country, we want to go somewhere where we'll feel at home. I never want my children to feel like foreigners, like they don't belong."

It was a much more elaborate answer than I had wanted. Nothing about how America had better toys or even better schools. But I trusted Dad. My parents had been all over the world and they probably knew where was best.

After 11 hours of silence interrupted only by the monotonous hum of the plane's engine, we finally hovered above the dark Los Angeles sky. Dad traded seats with me so I could look out the window.

Giant squares of orange-and-white lights glared up at me. *Down there is my new home*, I thought. *My new friends, teachers and school are all somewhere under those lights. My new life is waiting for me down there.* Excitement and fear once again grappled within me. I reached for Mom's hand and she squeezed my palm to assuage my nerves. We didn't talk, but we understood that though for different reasons, our trepidation was the same.

When Pan Am's wheels smoothly touched ground, the passengers broke into applause. I thought it was because they, too, were happy to finally be in America. Giddy in the fervor of the moment, I slammed my hands together like tiny cymbals until they turned bright red.

It felt like years since we had left Iran. I had already forgotten what our house looked like. I already missed Zohreh, Agha Mashadi and the familiar whisper of the air-conditioner in my room that would've lulled me to sleep by now.

Just when I thought the ordeal of travel was over, we stood behind seemingly hundreds of people in the passport line for non-U.S. citizens. Had I known the phrase déjà vu, I would have used it. Instead, I fidgeted in yet another line thinking, "Didn't we already go through this in Iran and in London?"

Getting an American visa was an almost impossible feat for Iranians at the time. Iranians had been welcomed to the United States before the revolution, and many more of us would flock here in the years to follow. But our timing, at the crux of the revolution and the hostage crisis, made our arrival a mini miracle. The blue stamp in our passports should've been in gold to aptly symbolize its value and beauty. It had taken Dad months of talking to the right people, or what Iranians call "*party bazi,*" to get these much-coveted visas.

But the man behind the podium didn't even open our passports to see the visas we were so proud of. Our brown passports spoke for themselves: we were shitty Iranians.

He escorted us into a small glass chamber, where a pale, skinny man frowned at us from behind a desk. We kids stood back with Mom while Dad explained that he had gotten a working visa as an architect. This proved to the man that we would be living in, not just visiting, his country.

"Why are you here, Sir?" he asked Dad.

"For my family," Dad said with a shaky voice. "For a better fate."

"Better fate," the guy repeated, chuckling sarcastically. "You think the Americans you took hostage didn't deserve a better fate?"

"Yes," Dad said. "But I —"

"Don't interrupt me, Sir. You think they didn't want to spend Christmas with their families? Do you even know what Christmas is? You think your family is above theirs? You think nothing at all has happened and you can just leave that country of yours and come here for a better fate after what your goddamn country has done?"

Dad hesitated. When he realized the man was actually waiting for an answer, he mumbled, "No."

"No? But you damn well did, didn't you?"

"Yes," Dad said, looking down.

I wanted to step in, tell the guy that I spoke English fluently, that I had gone to an American school, that I "do too know what Christmas is." Santa Claus had given me my Barbie salon last year. My parents had hated the revolution from day one. We weren't one of those people. We hated them, too. We were innocent; why wasn't Dad defending us?

The guy scribbled in our passports with a red marker, then threw them on the floor. My parents bent down to pick them up.

"Go to the red line!" the guy yelled, his face turning red.

"Yes, thank you," Dad said softly.

"DON'T THANK ME, SIR!"

I gasped at his tone, stared in shock at his narrowed eyes.

We left the chamber like lost souls looking for heaven, glancing over our shoulders for the devil's shadow. None of us spoke. And we avoided each others' eyes in shame. I didn't understand why the man had treated us that way, why my parents hadn't stood up to him and why they had lost that joyful look again.

"*Pedar sag* (son of a bitch)," Dad muttered as we walked to the red line.

I expected a long exchange of dialogue between my parents about the incident, but they just stood there quietly. They didn't even tell me to stop crying. Maybe they understood that it wasn't a child's usual cry. Maybe they felt my disappointment and knew that I may never again feel the same about them. That man was just a cruel stranger. It was my parents who had let me down. They hadn't protected me. They showed me for the first time that they didn't have all the answers.

I realized that our American visas came with no guarantees and we could still be banished back to Iran. Didn't sound too bad at that point. But for my parents' sake, I prayed silently for God's help. I promised Him that if He let us into America, I would do everything to make my parents proud.

At the front of the line, another extremely pale man grabbed our passports. *Why was everyone in this country so ghastly white?*

"Why are you in the red line?" he asked.

"I don't know," Dad said fake-laughing.

The man thumbed through our passports.

"Any political reason you're here?"

"No, no," Dad said. "I'm just here with my family."

He pointed to us like we were his trophies. I smiled. We were in America. It was OK to smile again.

It worked. The guy scribbled something in our passports and handed them to Dad.

"Welcome to the United States. Please stay to your right as you exit the passport-control area."

"Yes, thank you," Dad said, smiling so hard he was practically laughing. "Thank you, Sir."

The man smiled back, but motioned for us to move along.

"*Ajab agha bood in yeki* (what a gentleman this one was)," Dad said.

We followed him to the baggage-claim area, where our only mementos of Iran rolled off the carousel one suitcase at a time.

We sat quietly in the taxi as it sped through the dark, unfamiliar streets. I rolled down my window, but didn't smell the air of home. I didn't hear water swishing loudly through street canals the way it would on quiet, late nights in Tehran.

Starting fresh meant everything from finding a place to live to buying new glasses from which to drink foreign water. We owned nothing but those visas in our passports.

That night, exhaustion didn't help me pass out on the hard hotel bed. I lay awake staring at a full moon that shone on my fears like a giant magnifying glass. I subconsciously waited for Agha Sadeghi, our street's night watchman in Tehran. I listened for his footsteps, the blow of his whistle.

The sound of his whistle had a dual purpose: it reminded people sleeping in their homes that he was protecting them, while warning would-be burglars that he was on their lookout. He was an old-fashioned alarm system, equipped with eyes and veins instead of cameras and wires.

As the hotel room echoed only with the sound of my heartbeat, and the stars magnified the silhouette of the ominously black sky, I knew that the sound of that whistle was thousands of miles away, guarding an empty home whose safety I would never again feel.

I got out of bed and walked to my parents' connecting room. Maybe I could sleep next to them. Maybe they could remind me why America was such a wonderful place. But just as I started to knock, I heard the faint sound of sobs coming from inside. It wasn't Nader crying. And it wasn't a cry of joy. It was Mom, crying the cry of fear, uncertainty and loneliness. It was a cry that made me feel selfish. My parents were scared, too. I tried to listen to what they were saying, but their few spoken words were muffled through sobs and the thick door separating us.

I climbed back into bed and stared at Cyrus and Ari as they slept. I decided that on this night when we were starting everything anew, I was going to start being an adult.

Chapter 28

"Bee, what's the big deal?" I ask. "Just lend me some money and I'll pay you back when I get another job."

"It's not about the money," she says. "You need to tell your parents that you got fired. It's not a big deal. These things happen."

"It was humiliating telling them when I got *hired* as a receptionist, let alone getting fired. This is not significant enough to bother my parents with. I'll get another job real soon. I just need some money until then."

"I'm not lending you money, Miryam."

"Please, Bee. I can't tell my parents to send me money and I can't tell them I got fired, and you're not going to convince me."

"I'm not going to do it, Miryam. I refuse to be a part of all this lying to your parents. You didn't tell them about Cyrus getting arrested because you said you don't want to tell them about the *big* things. And now you don't want to tell them about your job because it's a *small* thing? Fuckin' A, Miryam!"

"Fuckin' Bee. What kind of a friend are you? I can't tell Ari that I got fired, either. Paige has no money of her own and I'd rather die than have her ask her parents. You're the only one I can turn to."

"Do you hear yourself? You're falling apart, Miryam. I am not doing anything for you until you talk to your parents. All you do is sit there and pine over Ari. You don't eat, you don't sleep, even though you're taking tranquilizers and sleeping pills left and right, which I'm not giving you anymore by the way. My dad's pharmacy isn't a buffet, you know. He can get into trouble for this."

"But I just..."

"You got fired because you were always late to work on the days you bothered showing up. You're probably actually happy that you got fired so you don't have to bother waking up at all anymore. You're just gonna sit there locked in your room and think of Ari all day. He's not there to pick up the slack. You can't even take care of yourself anymore, let alone your brothers. Wasn't it enough of a wake-up call that Cyrus got arrested for drunk driving? You act like that never even happened. And I refuse to watch all this anymore. I don't care if you hate me or never talk to me again. I'm not lending you money. I'm not doing anything so that maybe you can stop pretending everything is fine. Maybe if you..."

I hang up without letting her finish. I thumb through the Yellow Pages and jot down the addresses of the first three pawnshops listed. I ransack my jewelry box like a rushed robber and kiss the diamond necklace my grandmother gave me to remember her by before we left Iran. I run out of the house praying the stores are still open.

Chapter 29

An 11-year-old who has witnessed a war and a revolution could never stay in the warm cocoon of childhood, no matter that I still watched cartoons and played with toys. I was simply making up for lost time by playing with the better toys and watching the more elaborate cartoons that I hadn't had access to in Iran.

Everything I had dealt with after the revolution forced me to grow up too fast. Starting a new school in a new country was no exception. At my first day of school in America, to all my teachers, it was a subject of vocal relief that I spoke fluent English despite being from Iran. But to the other students, I was the equally vocal subject of ridicule as the new "Eye-ranian" girl.

The lesson I picked up on my first day wasn't the subject-verb agreement Mr. Oats was teaching in English class, but rather the prejudice my peers were attacking me with at recess. It started with them saying, "Hello Persian Kitty" in reference to my Hello Kitty backpack and escalated from there. I was more confused than hurt. I had gone to an American school, spoke perfect English, knew all about the American culture; I was just a normal, awkward pre-teen with a few pimples heralding puberty, no different from any of them. But the entire sixth-grade class disagreed from the second Mr. Oats introduced me as "Miryam from Iran."

I had never known about the concept of prejudice before, let alone experienced it. If I didn't like someone, it was because of something personal, not a generalization. I was an equal-opportunity hater. So being taunted by people who didn't even know me, for something as impersonal as where I was from, made no sense. They even called me an "alien," which puzzled me even more. I distinctly remembered learning the word "alien" in the third grade, when we were studying the solar system in science. Aliens, if they existed at all, were from another planet, not another country.

For the next few months, instead of concentrating on my schoolwork, I tried hard to shed my identity as an Iranian. I erased all my childhood memories, spoke English at home despite my parents' objections and trained my ear to pick up American slang.

It was easier to teach myself to hate Iran and agree with the hostility my peers had towards my country than to separate their made-up facts from fiction or hurt my parents by telling them the truth: that I was fitting in at school as well as a vegan in a slaughterhouse.

For those who hadn't yet heard the news that I was Iranian, I would make up different countries of origin (France, Germany, Slovakia) and read about them at the library, preparing to justify my false heritage of the week. And sometimes, I would tell people that I was only *half* Iranian, so only half of me would go under attack.

By mid-semester, most everyone had gotten bored of making fun of my nationality. They had even stopped singing the Flock of Seagulls' song "And I ran; I ran back to Eye-ran."

So when Principal Kennedy asked to discuss my progress with Mom, I panicked that if the kids heard her thick Iranian accent, they would once again break into song. When I could no longer put off the meeting, I made up some lame excuse and told Principal Kennedy that Mom could only meet with him at 11:15 a.m., when all the kids were in P.E. and away from the main building.

Mom looked hurt when I pushed her hand away just as Megan, the coolest girl in school, passed by us on her way to get her gym clothes out of her locker.

She looked Mom up and down and snickered at what I assume was Mom's overdone makeup. Mom didn't understand that I needed to hold her hand more than ever, but that it would mean another month of teasing from Megan and the cool crowd. So I pretended not to know the strange dressed-up woman and sprinted three feet ahead of her to the principal's office.

The kids called Mr. Kennedy "Dick Face" behind his back. I've never understood all those Richards who choose to go by the nickname "Dick." And when you're a junior high school principal and insist on pre-teen students calling you by your first name, you're just plain asking for it. He was also quite a large man, so some of the kids, and even teachers, called him "Big Dick."

Dick sat up firmly in his large, leather chair, the kind of chair they probably only sell to people who can prove their authority status, the kind of chair that intimidates anyone who sits across from it.

As he told Mom that my math skills were exceptional compared to my peers, I silently cursed Dad's new boss for not giving him the morning off so he could come to this meeting instead of Mom. Dad spoke fluent English, sans accent.

Mom nodded and smiled as Mr. Kennedy raved about my survival skills, aptly describing what felt like fending for myself in a jungle. Mom looked at me proudly and I turned away.

"Yes, Sir," she said. "She's good girl too. She always doing her homevork vhen she come home from eskool, *before* she vatching da cartoons."

I lowered my head to hide my blush.

Even the principal is gonna think I'm a dork. MTV, Mom, MTV. Not *cartoons.*

Mr. Kennedy smiled. "Good for you, Miryam."

"She means school," I said.

"Excuse me?" he said.

"My mom. She means school, not eskool."

Mom gave me a dirty look, but I didn't care. It was enough that Mr. Kennedy smiled and said he had understood her.

I still don't understand why Iranians have to add an "e" in front of an English word that starts with an "s." Plenty of words in Farsi that start with an "s" and Iranians have no trouble pronouncing them correctly. They don't pronounce *sib* (apple) "esib." So why would spaghetti be "espaghetti?"

Mom once introduced Nader to a girl named Estella and he referred to her as "Stella" for months, until I told him that her name was indeed Estella and sometimes there actually is an "e" in front of an "s" word, even if it's a word Mom is using.

I think it's a vowel thing. Because they only do that with "s" words that have a consonant as their second letter. So they like to buy a vowel and add an "e" at the beginning. Wow. I just figured that out. They should never go on *Wheel of Fortune*. They'd go bankrupt. But I digress.

Mr. Kennedy heralded the end of the meeting by standing up and extending his hand. I pushed Mom out of the door before she had a chance to shake his hand.

"*Chikar mikoni, Maryam*?" Mom asked loudly, wondering why I had done that.

"Shhh. Shhh," I whispered. "Don't speak Farsi."

"*Zadeh be saret, bacheh*?" (Have you lost your mind, child?)

No time to answer her. The kids are back in the building and I must get her out of here before they hear her talking Farsi to me. There are still a few kids who think I'm Hungarian. Come on, Mom, Iranian, go home.

I stood by the school's front gate, Mr. Kennedy guarding me as if to make sure I don't escape. I would've done anything, *anything*, to go home with Mom. But I just waved back lethargically as she made an illegal U-turn in front of the school.

"Come on, Miryam," Mr. Kennedy said. "I believe you have history now."

He tried to physically move me. But I made like there was glue under my new Reeboks and didn't budge until I saw our new black Honda turn the corner. I fought hard not to cry. Or to tell Mr. Kennedy that there was no point in me going to class because I wanted to be a housewife like Mom when I grew up. So it was more important that I go home and have her teach me how to scrub toilets.

But instead, I sat in history class and caught only snippets of Ms. Foster's lecture on women's rights and all that other useless junk you learn in school that you'll never apply in the real world.

Chapter 30

I guess you can go home again.

When I ask Dad whether they're coming for their yearly visit in July or August, he rebuffs the cliché.

"Neither," he says. "You kids are coming here for a visit."

"What?"

"That's right," he says cheerfully. "Your mother and I were discussing when to come there and then we realized, why don't *you* guys come instead? The boys are on summer break, we're getting tired of making the long trip over there and it's about time you guys come back to Iran after all these years."

"What about my job?" I ask, pinching my nose like a paranoid Pinocchio.

"Oh, don't worry about that," Dad says. "I'm not thrilled about you working as a receptionist anyway. You're too good for that. Come here, get a break and when you go back, you can look for a more suitable job for someone with a college education."

Silence.

"So," Dad says after my long pause. "What do you think of coming back home after all these years?"

"I think it's a great idea, Dad."

I can "quit" my job and Cyrus doesn't have an Iranian driver's license. Besides, I'm running out of jewelry.

"Of course it's a great idea," he says with a laugh. "Oh, and Ari is coming too."

"He is?"

"Yup. Soraya said he has a lot of vacation days he hasn't used up at work and I convinced her that it would be perfectly safe for him to come to Iran after all these years. The government is much more lenient now."

"What do you mean?"

"Oh, she was worried that they would give Ari problems because of his dad," he says. "But that's ridiculous. It's not that bad anymore here. Anyway, the point is that he's coming too. So, book your tickets right away. Talk to Ari and make sure you're on the same flight. It'll make the long trip easier if you're all together. I just wired some money into the bank account for your plane tickets."

"Thanks, Dad," I say. "I'm so excited. I don't know why we never thought of doing this before."

"You always insisted on taking summer school when you were in college. So there was never an opportunity before."

"Right," I say. "But that aside, it just never occurred to me that we could ever come back to Iran."

"Of course you can come back. You're not fugitives."

"I know. I just never thought of it before."

"Well, that's what daddies are for," he says, sounding like he's smiling wide enough to fit across the trans-Atlantic telephone poles.

I hang up and light a cigarette. More intense than the nicotine head rush is how vividly the images of my old room, our house and our street rush to my head. Like a terminally ill patient pondering death, senses of both peace and fear fight within me at the thought of going back where I came from.

I flick the ash from my cigarette into the ashtray and smooth it into dust. I repeat after each puff until the flame dies, heaping the ashes to ashes, piling dust onto dust.

Chapter 31

It always annoyed Ari when I would stop in front of the house with the red door on our way home from school every afternoon.

For the two blocks until we reached that house, we were still in school zone. I could still hear the high-pitched voices that would tease me every day, still hear kids laugh together after school and be reminded that I wasn't one of them, still see friends lingering about talking, as I walked quickly away from everything to which I didn't belong.

With each house we passed by, all the signs would slowly disappear. No more actual signs of "School Zone," no more cars with soccer moms racing to pick up their kids, no more kids walking close to us to their homes.

Finally, we'd turn the corner, pass by the Chevron station and see the house with the red door. Every step, every house, after that would take us closer to home. So I'd make Ari stand there and linger in my neutral zone, exactly halfway between school and home, between loneliness and fear, the middle ground of peace between the end spectrums of pain.

I told him it was because I loved that house. I said the dog-shaped mailbox made me laugh and the pretty red door reminded me of Christmas.

But he'd never let me stand there for more than a few minutes, some days not at all. I never had enough time to listen to the quiet and know that no matter how loud they shouted, the voices of the kids at school would never reach that house. Neither would the whimper of Mom's sobs or the melodrama of Dad's speeches.

I never got a chance to peer through the French windows, past the sheer white drapes and see the inside. I never got to imagine living in a house that was a stranger to Mom's disheveled hair, droopy eyes and stained grey sweats.

If only I could look inside, I would have proof that in that house with the pretty red door, there was no dad who had quit his job and was hungover every day, barely having woken up at 3 p.m., when my day was half over. There was no mom whose eyes matched the color of that door. If I opened the door, the mom wouldn't don a fake smile and rip my heart up more than if she had just continued crying. She would ask me how school was and actually listen instead of smiling distantly when I mumbled, "Horrible as usual."

The dad in the red house wouldn't scold me for staying up 10 minutes past my bedtime only because I was postponing the start of his nightly drinking binge. The parents in that house wouldn't treat me like I was an ignorant child by telling me nothing was wrong.

Maybe the walls in that house could talk. They would tell happy, maybe even funny, stories. And on the nights the dad couldn't wait until we went to bed to start drinking, I could sit at the dinner table and listen to the walls instead of to him. I wouldn't have to listen to him talk yet again about how he had designed the most renowned buildings in Tehran, that he was too good to have to work with third-rate architects in America for too-little money.

Maybe the dining table was made of soundproof glass so the kids wouldn't jump in their chairs when the dad banged on it and said, "No, you may not be excused. Dinner may be over, but I'm still talking. This isn't just dinnertime; it's family time."

Time would pass quickly in that house; it wouldn't take the dad an hour to eat his dinner, one grain of rice at a time, while he reminded the kids again that they were the reason he had given up all he had in Iran.

The wines in that house would be down in the cellar, aging and improving, waiting to be opened on special occasions. They wouldn't be "cheap, but tolerable," replaced every night. They would come from the finest vineyards, not from a store that had special deals for those who bought wine in bulk.

When the dad in that house would tell the daughter he loved her most, he wouldn't only say it when the bottle was empty, when she loved him least.

The walls, too, would be soundproof, so she couldn't hear the parents fighting over everything. And maybe then she could share her problems with the mom because she wouldn't have overheard the mom telling her sister on the phone, "Well, at least the kids are happy. That's all that matters."

No one could have depression in the house with the red door; no one could be bored; no one could feel guilty. Not even my mom, not even my dad, not even me.

The house with the red door would be a happy home. And you can't be homesick when you *are* home.

But I wasn't even allowed to touch the red door, let alone open it and go inside. Ari would pace impatiently and tell me to hurry. I would take one last look at the house with the pretty red door, then take the first step towards our house, the one with the grungy green gate.

Chapter 32

I walk out the travel agency and clutch my purse tightly to my side. I pick up my pace and kick a pebble in my path. I watch it fly and hit the head of a homeless man sitting on the sidewalk, leaning against a graffiti-covered wall. I run to him and apologize, carefully digging in my purse for some money. He smiles and tells me that if I walk too fast, I'll never realize that life is rushing by me. I smile back and stare into his eyes, surprised by the sparkle twinkling in his black pupils. I hand him a $5-bill (extra generous for someone who just pawned her grandmother's heirloom), apologize again and walk away.

I hug myself from the night's chill as I wait to cross the street. I look at the homeless man and watch as he takes a gulp from a bottle peering out of a paper bag. He swallows, squirming at the bitter taste of it all.

I imagine the gush of liquid sliding down and hugging his insides from the chill. With each swig, he eases more into the hard ground. Soon, the voices in his head will slow to mere whispers. The voices of sobriety are in a racket of rock 'n' roll, those of drunkenness in a tango. But unlike the beauty and grace of a tango, the man is haggard, aged and dirty. And in no time, he'll stumble gracelessly on the cold streets.

A miniature white poodle jumps over the man's leg and barks at him. I smile and follow its leash up to the wrinkled hand of an elderly woman. She scolds Fifi, glances at the man with both pity and disgust, then looks quickly away.

The wind fights, but fails, to rustle her perfectly blow-dried grey hair. She clutches the leash tightly, her red fingernails glistening even from afar. Red lipstick matches her nails just as her ironed beige pants match her brown sweater and boots.

Even as I remain focused on her, I grow keenly aware of my plain jeans and T-shirt, my chipped nail polish and my greasy hair.

She bends down to pick up Fifi's poop with a plastic bag and walks to the giant trash bin. She dumps the dump inside and steps away when she sees the homeless man come behind her and throw his bottle of vodka in the bin with a thump.

I focus back on her elegance, remembering Grandfather on that early morning we walked to the bakery together, when he wore a suit just to pick up bread.

How does a woman her age care to look so good just to walk her dog? When did she decide life was worth all the effort? Who told her any of it even matters? What gives her the motivation to get out of bed, carefully choose what to wear, actually pick up lipstick and glide it over her wrinkled lips, when she knows she's got one well-pedicured foot in the grave? Where does she find the will to survive?

Who, what, when, where, how? And sometimes why.

Why do I envy the homeless man as much as I do her?

As I watch her give him a final glance of pity before turning the corner and walking towards the warmth awaiting her at home, I realize that it's because the homeless man already knows what those of us cushioned in the cocoon of our comforts never will: whether we'll survive the worst that life gets.

Chapter 33

"Persian New Year?" Mrs. Hyde, my seventh-grade science teacher, had said when one of the Iranian boys said he won't be in school on the day of the test. "Does this mean all the Iranians will be absent? Well, that's just too bad. I'm not rescheduling the test. I can't rearrange my syllabus for Persian New Year and Chinese New Year and whatever else nationality you kids are. *American* New Year is when you're all off legitimately."

But Dad wouldn't budge. He said that family unity was even more important now that we were out of Iran and we had to stay home from school and celebrate whether we liked it or not.

I grumbled to Mom as she watched me climb into the new dress she had bought me for the occasion.

"Don't argue with your father," she said. "You know how we feel about our traditions. This is the only Iranian holiday we celebrate and if you have to get an F on your test, so be it."

I looked in the mirror before following her to the living room. I was 13, but I looked 8 in the ruffled pink dress. But I didn't nag about it.

Who cares about the dress? Who cares about Persian New Year? Not me. Not anymore.

It was no longer my favorite time of year. Now that we were in America, it was just a Thursday.

I sat quietly on the sofa as Mom put the finishing touches on the Haft-Seen, the traditional table laid out on Iranian New Year. It didn't look the same here. She didn't look the same here. Nothing was the same. The sound of cars rushing by outside as people went to school or work reminded me that it was just another day, not the most festive holiday of the year. I missed the gentle lull of Iran's streets on this day, when everyone was nestled in their newly spring-cleaned homes, donning new clothes and waiting anxiously for the stroke of spring. I wanted to be in Shomal, where we had spent almost every New Year since I was born. I wanted to be back where even the birds smelled the sweetness in the air and chirped just a little louder, happier, for the last-minute guests arriving at our villa. Here, the celebration seemed pointless, as if we were clinging on to something that we knew was no longer there, like trying to revive a loved one who had already stopped breathing.

I dragged myself to the Haft-Seen table. Haft-Seen, which means seven "S's," refers to the seven symbolic objects beginning with the letter "S" in Farsi that are placed on the table for a happy forthcoming year. I've heard different interpretations of what the objects symbolize. Most people say that *sib* (apple) is a symbol of health; *sabzeh* (sprouts) signifies growth, while *sekeh (*coins) represents prosperity. The rest of the spread connotes such things as re-birth, sweetness and love. Not all the objects start with an "S," but are nonetheless important parts of the table. Candles, for instance, don't start with an "S" but are part of the spread and stand for inner light. Goldfish don't start with an "S," either, but are one of the most crucial elements in that they represent life. Mom always buys six goldfishes, one to personify each of us.

My favorite part of the table is the colored eggs. In Iran, I would always decorate each egg to represent each of my family members. That was the first year I didn't bother and just watched Mom dip them in pastel paint. The boring-looking eggs made the table look even more plain than the elegant, colorful tables she used to lay out in Shomal.

I poked my head into the crystal fishbowl. One of the goldfishes had already died. I whispered to the other five to just jump out and spare us the wait.

I wanted to ask everyone if they, too, were homesick, but I didn't want Dad to scold me for bringing gloom into the house on the first day of spring. I forced myself to smile for the pictures and to compliment Mom on the blah-looking Haft-Seen.

Dad put the TV on the Persian channel just as a bald man announced the dawn of spring. We all kissed each other and put candy into our mouths as a symbol of sweetness in the upcoming year.

In lieu of gifts, Dad opened up the Koran to give us kids crisp new money as our *eidis.* I stared at the $100-bills nestled in the Koran and felt a sharp pang of nostalgia. Even though it was much more money than I ever would've gotten in Iranian currency, it seemed odd that my *eidi* was in green dollars instead of colorful tomans.

When I brought the money to my nose, I smiled the only real smile of the day. It was new and crisp, almost warm. It smelled exactly like the fresh tomans I used to peel out of the Koran in Iran.

Mom and Dad sat together watching Persian television as I stood in the middle of the living room, staring around me exaggeratedly, as if to say, "That's it? It's over?"

The quiet, interrupted only by the man on TV throwing in random English words as he spoke an improper Farsi, told me that it was. And that Persian New Year would never be the same.

I sighed away to my room to read up on reptiles in case Mrs. Hyde changed her mind and let the absent Persian kids make up the test. My mind wandered as I stared blankly at the picture of a green snake shedding its skin.

It was the first time I had really thought of Iran since we had moved to America. I had been too busy adjusting to school, to a new country, and trying to shed my identity as an Iranian to think about how much I missed home. But that day, everything from the Haft-Seen table to the absence of my usual joy on Persian New Year made over a year's worth of pain come out at once.

I cried out of homesickness for hours. When the tears no longer felt good, I took my red pen and pressed it forcefully on a sheet of paper. "I hate school, I hate this place and I hate whatever made us leave Iran." Then I crumbled the paper and buried it at the bottom of my trashcan.

My hatred turned into envy when two years later, my parents decided to take a one-month trip back to Iran.

They left Ari in charge. He was 17 and old enough to watch over us. And I was 15, and old enough to understand all the gossip circulating in the Persian community about how improper it was for my parents to leave Ari alone with me for a whole month. As a matter of fact, it was pretty unthinkable of them to let Ari live under the same roof as their daughter in the first place.

I heard the gossip from my peers, who would bluntly tell me what their parents were saying about us. I never said anything to my parents because I didn't want them to kick Ari out. Surely my parents must've heard the gossip, too. But they couldn't go back on their word to Soraya. And they loved Ari like a son, a more polite, studious version of their own eldest son.

Nader, who was only 4 then, went back with my parents. And Cyrus, Ari and I lived so responsibly during that month that our daily lives were like episodes of *The Brady Bunch,* sans the perfect parents and housekeeper watching over us.

Ari drove us to and from school in Dad's car; we did our homework, defrosted one of the almost-30 meals Mom had cooked and stored in the freezer, and we went to sleep relatively close to our bedtimes. Every night at 9, my parents would call to check up on us.

Maybe if something had gone wrong during that month, everything would be different today. Maybe if there had been a fire or an earthquake, or if Cyrus had been kidnapped, our lives wouldn't be what they are today. Maybe if Ari had tried something with me instead of just waving me a goodnight every night, he would've been banished from my life.

But just like on *The Brady Bunch*, our episode ended in a perfectly wrapped-up cliché. Not a scratch on the faces my parents kissed a month later.

And that's why six months later, they decided to move back to Iran for good.

I didn't even get a chance to throw up with morning sickness. Most new mommies go through nine months of pregnancy, then go to the hospital, deliver and hold their 7-pound baby. All after having had sex.

With my hymen still intact, I was handed a bouncing 7-year-old boy to raise.

And he wasn't even mine.

Nader was born a couple of years before we moved to America. He went back to Iran with my parents and would visit us once or twice a year when they did. But when he was starting the first grade, my parents thought their usual, "Where can a child get a better education than in America?" and brought him to live with us. Ari and I were both licensed drivers by then and my parents left us plenty of money, and what else could a 7-year-old possibly need other than a ride to and from school, a roof over his head and some food?

Ari and I accepted the responsibility and took Nader in like he was a stray dog. We were actually excited about having him around because he was a loud, lively child. My parents never bothered to formally make Ari or me Nader's legal guardian. And I didn't bother wondering where Child Protective Services was when my parents were making these breezy decisions. There was nothing wrong with what they were doing. We all believed that. They just wanted what was best for their kids. After the revolution, even child neglect was in the name of sacrifice. In my parents' opinion, three people who were hardly considered responsible adults by the U.S. laws looking after Nader was better than him living in Iran without freedom. As if a 7-year-old needs "freedom" in order to enjoy eating the boogers out of his nose.

Latchkey kids were normal in the '80s. (Latchkey kids were young children who were left alone or with older siblings after school because their parents were at work.) But latchkey kids would see their parents at the end of the day, not the end of the year. I grew up bonding with the ridiculously perfect families that defined the '80s-sitcom genre. My parental figures were the Huxtables, the Keatons and the Seavers. I actually believed that all normal families lived that way, and that all problems could really be solved in 22 minutes, which made my family seem not just abnormal, but non-existent.

Petrified of debt, my parents had long ago paid for our house in full and used up the rest of their savings living here the first four years. They provided us with everything. And I mean everything. I didn't realize we weren't rich anymore until I was 16.

When my parents went back to Iran that first time when I was 15, I thought it was just because they were homesick. They didn't tell us till much later that the government in Iran had threatened to confiscate all their assets and properties if they didn't move back and fight for them. My aunt and her husband couldn't even sell our house and had just left it barren. All the laws of a normal country had gone into exile with the Shah and if you didn't comply with the whims of the new government, you paid the price. Literally.

So it wasn't that my parents were these heartless, selfish people who just left their kids in God's hands. The government took away anything they had as collateral, the value of the Iranian currency plummeted, and supporting a family of six in America without both my parents earning income became less and less feasible. Dad's pride and the barely average salary he earned made him quit soon after he started working as an architect in America. Mom was too depressed to work. And no matter how much money they could've earned if they both worked here, it still wouldn't have been anything close to what their properties in Iran were worth. They decided that fighting to get them back from the government was a better use of their time and energy and a much wiser economic decision. So they figured that with them out of the financial picture here, with Dad once again earning money as a renowned architect in Iran, and by getting back their properties and liquidating them for cash, we kids would be better off financially in America.

Every three months, they would send us enough money to cover all our expenses. They even bought me a brand-new Toyota when I graduated high school.

Ari's mom was grateful enough to my parents for giving Ari a new, better life in America that she didn't want them to spend a penny out of pocket for him. She sent money to cover his "rent" and personal expenses, but my parents drew the line and refused to accept money from her for his share of utilities, gasoline or grocery bills. "He's part of our family," my parents would constantly remind her.

And we kids were constantly reminded that we were blessed. My parents and Soraya had sacrificed everything for us. The three of them lived lonely lives, sending money to faces they never saw, just to know that their children were safe and free. According to them, we had nothing to complain about.

Ari never did complain. He was born to lead and nurture. At least I was taking care of my brothers. But sometimes I'd think Ari would snap and say my parents had no right to expect him to raise their kids. But he never did. I sometimes wondered if he loved Cyrus and Nader more than I did. Nobody would've believed he wasn't really family.

If there were a national poll on which one of us would break down, Ari would've won hands down. But I never once heard him complain, talk about his dad or say he missed his mom. And he wasn't one of these clichés waiting to happen either. He wasn't this optimistic rock who would someday bomb the Empire State Building and have people say, "Well, he was just the last person you'd think could do such a thing." He was a genuinely happy kid who accepted and tolerated every adversity that came along. And once he turned 16, he always had a summer job, whether it was selling popcorn at the movies or delivering pizza.

He made it impossible for me to ever nag to my parents, because they'd always compare me to him.

But nag I did. Especially because I was the only girl. My parents thought that just because I had my own room, I should have no complaints about living with three boys. My main complaint wasn't how messy all the boys were. It was that Ari was so clean and Nader and Cyrus were so messy (and I was somewhere in between) (of course) that Ari and I constantly argued about the neatness of the house. I thought that as long as there wasn't mold growing in the kitchen sink and I was doing the boys' laundry often enough that they could change their underwear every day, we were fine. But Ari wanted me to be Martha Stewart. And God bless his little male heart, he was, after all, an Iranian man and thought it was my job, as woman of the house, to do all the cooking and cleaning, and to teach the boys about neatness.

Everyday living challenges aside, I knew that our lives just weren't normal and that instead of the teenage blues, I had Supermom burnout at the age of 17. My parents weren't yelling at me to finish my spinach; I was yelling at my brothers to finish theirs. I knew it wasn't typical for a 17-year-old girl to say things like, "If I let you starve for three days, you'll stop making these gag faces when I put your dinner on the table."

"Thank your sister," Ari would say. "She was cooking for two hours after school today."

On a typical day once Nader arrived, I'd make breakfast at 7 a.m. I'd shower and get dressed for school, screaming intermittently for Cyrus to get out of bed. Ari would get Nader ready. We'd eat breakfast in silence and leave the kitchen a mess. Ari would drop Nader and Cyrus off at their schools before the two of us carpooled to ours.

In the afternoons, depending on how much homework I had, I'd either cook dinner or we'd order in. We'd do our homework, eat dinner in front of the TV or in our rooms, I'd get stuck cleaning the kitchen and sometimes help Nader with his homework. Every night, I would get in a fight with Ari and Cyrus about whose turn it was to take out the trash.

Even if I'd had any friends, I wouldn't have had time for a social life. I spent my weekends doing laundry, grocery shopping, cleaning the house, going over the budget and catching up on sleep. Ari helped with the housework, but I usually did the bulk of it. His main duties were to drop off Nader at soccer practice, spend time with him and Cyrus and basically, be their father figure. He and I hardly spoke of anything but the boys. And for years, Cyrus, Nader and I hardly spoke period. They'd grunt a "thank you" after dinner, yell if I hadn't bought their favorite junk foods, and I'd scream at them for being so messy and spoiled. It wasn't until recently that we started speaking full sentences to each other.

I stopped talking to my parents about my problems because Dad had the same basic speech prepared for every dilemma I threw his way.

"Dad, I'm tired of taking care of these two."

"Honey, our country saw a revolution. People died. People lost everything. We're very lucky. Your mother and I sacrificed everything to take you to America. Surely, you can sacrifice a little for your family."

"Dad, I need money."

"Honey, our country saw a revolution. Some people lost all their money. The richest men from before the revolution are now cabdrivers. You're telling me you can't survive even though you have a free house and your own car?"

"Dad, I'm having trouble in calculus."

"Honey, our country saw a revolution. Your mother and I sacrificed everything to take our children to America for a better education. You can try a little harder to get good grades and show us our sacrifice was worthwhile."

And that became my mind's mantra and my life's motto: sacrifice.

Part II

Chapter 1

"Iran Air, Gate B62, 19:35" finally flashes on the large-screen monitor at Frankfurt Main's International Airport. After the 11-hour flight from Los Angeles, we had a five-hour layover in Germany before the next leg of our trip to Tehran. Even though boarding doesn't start for another hour, we gather our belongings and drudge towards the gate, our bodies heavier than our cramped carry-ons. The men around us look disheveled, with shirts busting out of their pants and 4 o'clock shadows silhouetting their haggard faces. The women don't look a whole lot better. Some of them are already wearing their Islamic uniforms. I'm about to comment on how messy they all look when I realize that I probably look just as bad.

Kids are screaming, women are yelling at them to shut up, and the men are discussing the latest political developments in Iran.

Two German and three Iranian stewardesses are standing in the check-in area. The Iranian stewardesses are covered from head to toe in dark blue, their faces plain as vanilla ice cream. The Germans with their blonde hair combed neatly into buns, lips painted pink and eyes sparkling blue, look like strawberry ice cream topped with whipped cream.

One of the German stewardesses frowns and motions with her hands for a group of men talking loudly to keep it down. I stare at the men and blush as their voices continue to rise despite the warning. I glance at the German stewardess, hoping she'll notice me so I can smile at her. But she's shaking her head and whispering to her colleague. About what? How uncivilized we are? How she can't wait to apply for a job at American Airlines?

It's not that I'm necessarily ashamed of being Iranian. It's just that Iranians are so loud. They talk loudly, they dress loudly, they listen to music loudly, they force their opinions down your throat loudly, they even drive loudly. Anytime I hear a car's engine go "vroom vroom" before the light has even turned green, I instinctively know it's an Iranian guy indirectly telling everyone he has a small dick.

"Ari, I can't stand here for another hour," I say. "I'm going for a walk."

"Don't be late."

I find a small bar and gulp three glasses of red wine in a row. I get up to the perfect head rush and jog to our gate in time for boarding. All the women are fully covered. Ari hands me my get-up. I button my beige raincoat and toss my scarf loosely on my head.

"Wear it," he says, watching me.

"Why? We're not on the plane yet. We're still in German territory."

He sighs exaggeratedly. "Would it kill you to just tie the damn thing?"

I take out my makeup case without answering him. I dab on some powder and a fresh coat of lipstick.

"What the hell are you doing?" Ari yells. "Everyone is taking their makeup off and you're putting yours *on*?"

I don't answer. Gotta look good for the German stewardesses.

Just my luck, when we get to the front of the line, an Iranian stewardess takes my boarding pass. The German one isn't even looking at me.

Look at me, please. See that we're not all Islamic and some of us hate this get-up. Look how I refuse to cover my head until the last minute. Please look at my burgundy lipstick as proof that I don't support the government of the country this plane is flying to.

But she's just tearing across the dotted line of some old lady's boarding pass, telling her in English that her carry-on is too big. The old woman frowns and asks the nearby passengers to translate. She frowns more with each word and tells the stewardess in Farsi that her carry-on is *not* too big and the stewardess doesn't know what she's talking about.

"Just let her take it. Is OK," one of the men says to the stewardess.

"Sir, it's against policy," the stewardess says. "She has to check it."

"No, is OK. She's old. Let her take it. Is not problem."

"Sir, it *is* a problem," the stewardess says, losing her forced smile.

The old woman tells everyone that her son said it would be OK, so the stewardess *must* be wrong. I'm about to intervene and do something civilized, when Ari tells me to move forward. The Iranian stewardess asks me to kindly put on my scarf completely before getting on the plane. Ari gives me a dirty look as I tighten my scarf.

A bearded steward greets us warmly and points us to our middle-row seats. I shove in a pair of ear plugs, nestle the little white pillow that smells like a dentist's office onto Nader's armrest and close my eyes. He shoves me away.

As soon as I'm allowed to, I unbuckle my seatbelt, climb over Nader and run to the bathroom. I throw up and flood the toilet with red wine. Flush. Gargle. Splash water on face. Limp back to seat. Pass out.

Chapter 2

Ari wakes me after we land.

Thank God Iranians aren't very by the rules. The stewardess had actually let me sleep without my seatbelt during the landing. She hadn't even said anything when my scarf had slipped off.

We walk to the front of the plane and climb down a narrow staircase onto the runway. The slightly humid air hits my face and I smile at the forgotten scent of home.

We get on a bus and wait until the last passenger squeezes in. I sit on my carry-on bag and stare out the window at the night's blackness.

The bus drops us off in front of the main terminal and we run towards the large hallway, only because everyone else does. But we don't run as fast as the other passengers and get stuck at the end of the passport-control line.

The bare, white hall is decorated only with a picture of Khomeini and another guy in a turban. The only sound that echoes is the periodic loud stamp that sounds like a boom punching onto a passport. Silence, boom, silence, silence, boom, boom. No one talks or even smiles, emphasizing the palpable silence jolted by the booms.

Ari hands me my passport without looking at me.

We get to the window, and a bearded man in an army-green uniform grabs our passports. I look at Ari to see if he's worried about the guy giving him any problems. I stare at Ari's pale, sweaty face and forget all about my nausea, my fatigue and my foul mood. Not once during this almost two-day journey have I thought about his feelings. How in a matter of minutes, he'll be seeing his mother for the first time in more than a decade. How it's his return to the country and the government that killed his father. How one tap into the computer in front of that man in the window could…I don't know what it could do. I feel selfish that all I've been thinking about is myself. I reach over to touch Ari's hand. Then I remember that he's not blood-related and I can't touch him in public.

"What is your relation to her?" the man asks Ari while pointing at me.

See, Ari, even the government wants you to clarify our relationship.

We've had sex, Ari says. But just once. I was consoling her after her grandmother died. But you know it was more than that, right man? Wink, high five.

When I see how scared Ari looks, I climb out of my head and into reality.

"He's a friend of the family's," I say. "He was..."

"I wasn't talking to you," the man says without looking at me.

I want to slide my hand through the slot, yank his beard and have that angry tuck talk for me. But I just look at Ari.

"She's a friend of the family's," Ari stutters in broken Farsi. "I've been keeping an eye on her little brothers during the trip here."

The man looks at me, at my passport picture, then back at me. No reaction on his filthy face. Nothing to indicate if we're about to be taken to jail for reasons only he could rationalize. My heart pounds louder and I pray that I don't throw up again. If I do, it'll be the wine again. Can they arrest you for the contents of your vomit? Could they collect samples from it and bring it to court for the judge to sniff? Would the evidence hold up in court even though said wine was allegedly consumed in non-Muslim territory?

I jump at the bang of the stamp. The man makes eye contact and actually chuckles at me. But he immediately gets back in character and stamps the rest of our passports with a stern face. He throws them under the crack in the window and shoos us away as if we're a swarm of mosquitoes.

It's fascinating how someone who probably doesn't have a fifth-grade education feels so superior just because hostility and an ability to instill fear are considered strong attributes when working for this government. Job qualifications: heightened sense of ego, sadism, and an ability to take frequent power trips.

My hands shake as I grab all the passports and hand Ari his before tucking the other three carefully in my purse.

"Go!" the man yells at me. "No need to hold up the line organizing your handbag."

"What?" I say with a frown. "*I'm* holding up the line? We've been standing here for..."

But Cyrus pulls me away from the window while Ari grabs our carry-ons.

"Don't fucking argue with him," Cyrus mumbles in English. "You forgetting where you are?"

The baggage-claim area is as loud as passport control was quiet. As if everyone is purging the sounds they had suppressed earlier.

We pull our suitcases from the screeching carousel as five old men in orange uniforms race their carts towards us. They start fighting over which of their frail bodies gets to lift our heavy luggage. While four of them argue about who got there first and whose cart has better wheels, a fifth one quietly lifts our bags onto his cart.

Then I see my parents and Soraya, who's running so fast towards Ari that her checkered black-and-white scarf slips off. By the time she grabs Ari in her arms, tears are streaming down her face. For a moment, I forget about my own parents and focus only on Ari and his mom crying audibly, hugging each other so tightly that I can feel the tonic of pain and pleasure.

It gets harder and harder to swallow the lump in my throat. I land in Dad's embrace. Mom hugs Nader and Cyrus simultaneously, crying and whispering, "My babies, my babies are home."

I notice that people nearby are smiling at us. I wipe my eyes with the edge of my scarf. It's barely 4 a.m. My parents and Soraya probably didn't even bother sleeping last night and left for the airport soon after midnight. And yet, even at this hour, Dad stands out from the raggedy-looking men in his dark-blue suit and tie; Mom looks so neat with her matching beige pants, coat and scarf. Soraya looks like she belongs at one of the royal luncheons she used to attend. She looks regal in her Ferragamo pumps, with her manicured, colorless nails and her silk scarf. Her slim, but feminine body draws attention even through her roomy Burberry raincoat.

"Let me look at you, Miryam," Mom says.

She grabs my shoulders and turns me around so I face her. She eyes me and just smiles, probably not wanting to ruin the moment with comments about how messy, tired and pale I look.

Cyrus and Nader both look shy and uncomfortable. Nader clutches Mom's coat the way he used to tug at her skirt when he was little. He doesn't talk. And Cyrus pretends to be guarding our carry-ons so he can avoid more displays of affection.

Soraya walks over to me. I reach out to shake her hand. She laughs and looks at Mom.

"A little too polite, isn't she?" Soraya says.

She kisses my cheeks. "I'm not that much of a stranger to you, am I?" she asks with a smile.

"Of course not," I say. "I'm sorry. I didn't mean to..."

But she's moved onto Cyrus and Nader, who learned from my mistake and immediately proceed to kiss her.

I look over at Ari. He's got a dazed expression as he watches his mom talk to Nader.

"Come on everyone," Dad says. "Let's get out of here. Where's your luggage?"

I point to the guy leaning against a cart with our suitcases piled on, smoking a cigarette. His four colleagues notice Dad approaching the man and run to him, yelling.

"Slow down," Dad says. "One at a time. What's the problem?"

They point to the guy with our luggage and complain to Dad in unison like kids tattling to their father.

"He took all the luggage, but I got here first," one of them says.

"Look, Sir," another one says. "Look at my wheels. My cart can handle the luggage better."

Dad motions with his hands for them to calm down and peels some money from a wad in his back pocket. He divides it among the five of them for their troubles.

"Did you see that honey?" Dad says to me as we walk away. "All that was for less than 5 cents."

The men race their carts back to the carousel. I watch Soraya and Ari walk arm in arm, as Mom takes my hand and smiles. "Welcome home."

Chapter 3

I open my eyes at 5 a.m. and squint at the grayish hues swimming around my childhood room. The darkness dilutes slightly under the glow of streetlamps peering through the curtains. I reach across the wall next to my bed and feel for the switch. I haven't touched this light switch, the one I used to hate turning off at nights, in more than a decade. Yet it's still here. It's been sitting dutifully on this same wall. It still has the same pointy shape, the same smooth texture. And with one flick, I'll be home again.

On our way to our house from the airport, I had gazed out Dad's car window as my childhood winked back at me. We passed by Charlie's toy store, the bookstore where I used to buy my comics, and the kabob restaurant where we'd have dinner once a month. The places remained anchored to the ground despite the time that had slipped away. The past hovered like a low fog nestled in my head. I could almost smell the memories. I held back tears that wanted to fall to the rhythmic flow of water in the *joobs,* the ubiquitous canals lining Tehran's streets.

I had expected our house to look smaller than I had remembered it as a child because that's what people always say about seeing their childhood homes as adults. But it didn't. It looked the same, only older. It still proudly showed off to the smaller houses on the block, but bowed its head slightly, ashamed of the peeling white paint on its front bars.

Once inside, I went straight to my bedroom in a haze.

"Don't you want to see the rest of the house?" Mom had asked.

"Not tonight."

It was already too much. I didn't have the energy to kiss every piece of furniture, hug all the trees in the garden and smile at the empty closet where I had hidden my dolls 13 years ago. I just went to bed and passed out.

I inhale the smell of dust mixed with the humid air humming out of the old-fashioned air-conditioner. The familiar scents from when I used to lie in this same bed at nights, dreading going to school the next day, mix in the air and take me back in time.

I finally flick on the light and my childhood room comes to life: the yellow-green flowery wallpaper that wasn't even nice in the '70s, the greenish Persian carpet, the drapes that mimic the color of the leaves they overlook in autumn.

It was never a childlike room. And now it looks even less so; it looks dirty and decrepit. I know Mom has cleaned it immaculately and that it only looks dirty. The kind of dirty you can't wash off any more than you can erase wrinkles on an old face.

I hear a faint knock, then the door opens. Both my parents do that; knock as they open the door. It defeats the whole purpose of knocking and usually annoys me. But right now, Mom's smile looks so inviting that I wish she had barged in sooner.

"What are you doing up?" she asks in a half whisper.

"Jet lag, I guess. What about you?"

"I couldn't sleep," she says. "Too much excitement. I was going to get something to eat and saw your light on. Are you OK? Do you need me turn off the AC?"

"No, I'm fine."

"Do you need another blanket?"

"No, I'm fine."

"We have lots of blankets."

I smile. "I'm sure you do."

"Maybe you're too hot. Should I turn *up* the AC?"

"The temperature is fine."

"Are you hungry?" she asks.

"Mom, just come and sit here."

Her long, white nightgown scrapes the floor as she walks towards me.

"I missed you," I say, watching her sit on my bed.

"Me too."

I take her hand and stare into her palm like a fortuneteller. I look up at her face, at the wrinkles sitting stubbornly around her eyes. It's as if the lines have crawled up from her palm and spread across her face to prove that they are no longer symbols of her future, but stamps of a life gone by.

"I've aged a lot since last year, no?" she says.

"Not at all," I lie.

I press her hand tightly and take a mental picture of her. The last remnants of a stubborn waterproof mascara smeared around the corner of her eyes, hair sticking up slightly, skin shining from the over-application of Clarins night cream.

It's better than any picture from a camera. Because I also capture the smell of her Clarins, the goose bumps on my skin and the sounds of dawn breaking outside my childhood home.

I inch closer and hold her. I smell her face, her disheveled hair and her soft neck. She pets me on the head and strokes my arm.

"Oh my God. You *are* cold. Look at these goose bumps." She breaks away from me. "No wonder you couldn't sleep. Let me go turn it off."

"Mom, leave it," I say. "I can't even feel the air."

"How about another blanket then?"

Chapter 4

I fall back asleep and wake up a few hours later to the sound of a man singing, "Salt, come and get your salt!"

I fly out of bed and peer out my window. I see an old man pushing a small wagon piled with salt down the street. Just as I wonder if anyone actually buys salt from a mobile salesman, a gaggle of housewives fastening scarves around their heads run out their doors towards him. I miss Iran's old-fashioned charm even as I'm looking down on it.

I try to breathe in the dusty Tehran air. But instead, a sudden, strong scent of incense swims through my nostrils. I smile at the delicious-smelling superstition, knowing that Mom and Roya, our maid, are burning incense because of our arrival. People have probably been calling, sending flowers and all those things that in Persian culture mean something bad is bound to happen. So we have to burn incense to get rid of jealousy and evil eyes.

Zohreh, our old maid, was no longer our maid. (Nor did she turn into an old maid like she had always feared. She got married and moved to her husband's province a few years after we moved to America.) Roya has been my parents' housekeeper since they moved back to Iran. She attacks me with incense when I walk into the kitchen. She circles it all around me, chants prayers in my ears, then hugs and kisses me. She smells like soap from a gas station bathroom.

"Did you see my beautiful girl?" Mom asks, a smile embedded in her voice.

"Yes, yes, beautiful girl," Roya says. "May she live to be a hundred."

"God forbid," I mumble in English.

The fast-talking maid practically bowing before me stands up to my shoulders with wide hips and a hunchback. Her welcoming smile consists of three brown-black teeth, bare gums and another two crooked teeth peering in from the back. Strands of black hair poke out the edges of her green scarf. She looks as if someone put a blindfold on her, sent her to her closet and made her wear whatever she touched: thick black stockings; white nurse shoes; a long, green skirt over brown pants; and an oversized, purple men's shirt. She's topped it all with a grey chador that keeps sliding off her head.

The innocence in her eyes softens the wrinkles around them, making it hard to tell how old she is.

"Do you take tea or coffee for breakfast?" she asks.

"Oh, just water," I say. "Thank you."

"Water?" she says with a horrified look. "You need something to warm your stomach in the morning. I'll bring you some tea. Your breakfast is on the table."

I thank her and slip out into the living room. Cyrus and Nader are sitting at the long, oval dining table, eating silently. There's more food on the table than what's in our fridge in the States in a month: eggs, boiled, scrambled and poached; a basket of bread; sour-cherry jam; cold cuts; sausages; milk; orange juice, and Persian and Swiss cheese.

Mom sits next to Nader and piles more Persian cheese on his plate. He stuffs some *Sangak* bread into his mouth and wipes the jam dribbling off his chin with his sleeve. Mom yanks out a tissue and dabs the corner of her eyes.

"What's the matter?" I ask.

"Nothing, nothing," she says. "I just can't believe all of you are here. All my babies. Back home. It's like a dream."

"Nightmare," Cyrus mumbles.

I look at Mom to make sure she didn't hear him. I give him a dirty look that I know he caught even though he doesn't acknowledge it.

Roya wobbles in with my tea. "She's been crying all morning. Every single person that calls, she cries. You better appreciate how much she loves you."

She looks right at me, as if waiting for an answer. I nod and smile.

"You're burning that damn stuff again?" Dad yells as he bounces down the stairs.

"Sir, it's the children's first day here," Roya says. "We can't risk anything,"

"You women and your superstition. Open the windows. I can't breathe."

He's wearing the same suit he wore to the airport last night. You don't see many men wearing suits on Tehran's streets, but Dad is always impeccably dressed. I love that about him. I can just picture him standing on a pile of dirt in front of one of the buildings he designed, drawing the respect of his haggard-looking crew. I think that's one of the reasons Dad never liked living in America. He wasn't used to being a nobody. Here, everybody from the local butcher to the mayor knows and respects Dad. He has a presence about him, an aura and a charm that makes others notice him. He also intimidates people despite being short and small-framed. Maybe it's because he looks stern even when he's genuinely smiling.

Dad is a very proud man. Proud of his work, his family and himself. He never saw it as a good thing that every man is treated equal in America. To him, there's a difference — a big difference — between employer and employee, prince and pauper, even man and woman.

"I didn't work hard my whole life and gain a reputation as one of the best architects in Iran to have some punk address me as 'Yo, man' on the streets," he once said when we first moved to the States.

Dad adores me. He makes it known that I'm his favorite. Sometimes, he's subtle about it; other times, he comes right out and says it, even in front of Cyrus and Nader. Knowing this, I always strive to please him. I want him to be as proud of me as he is of himself. I never talk back to him the way I do to Mom. Not that I don't respect Mom, but she and I have a casual relationship. I even joke around with her and say things like, "shut up," and get a smile back instead of a scolding. But with Dad, I'm nothing but polite and respectful. He thinks a man's wife and children should obey and respect him, not treat him like a friend.

He kisses Cyrus and Nader on the cheek, me on the forehead. He calls out to Roya for his tea.

"Coming, coming," Roya mumbles as she limps out of the kitchen with the tea. "You told me to open the windows. How many hands do I have?"

Actually, she might as well just have one. She's constantly pulling her chador back on her head with the other. She notices me smiling and squints her eyes kindly in response. I look away shyly.

After breakfast, I'm climbing over the pile of clothes scattered in my room, mumbling about the lack of closet space, when Mom walks in.

"You can use the downstairs closet too, if you want," she says. "And I hope you brought some appropriate clothes."

"Appropriate for what?"

"Parties," she says, twirling. "Lots of parties. Starting tomorrow night at our house."

She trips over my shoes and plops down on my bed.

"We're having a party?" I ask. "For what?"

She frowns. "What do you mean for what?"

Chapter 5

"It's burning hot outside and I'll be going to a few different stores," Mom says. "Don't you want to just stay home and relax so you'll be fresh for tonight?"

I continue buttoning my coat. "No. I want to see Tehran."

"I'm going grocery shopping, for God's sake," she says and throws on her black scarf.

"I wanna come too," Nader whines.

"Fine," Mom says with a sigh. "Come on. It's going to be easy showing you two a good time in Iran."

Mom's car is in the shop (again, she says) so we climb into the white Peykan taxi. The bearded driver and Mom greet each other warmly and by name, before Mom tells him where to go.

I turn on my camcorder and stick my head out the back window. We dip in and out of a dozen potholes before blending in with the hundreds of old, dirty, worn out cars on the Modaress Expressway. Drivers ignore the faint, white lines marking the lanes and use up every possible inch of road, even the edge of the sidewalks.

The only way I know we're on a freeway is because the sign says so. Pedestrians dart in front of vehicles, trucks drive backwards, and bicycles zoom by faster than cars. And surely a baby car seat must seem highly unnecessary when even a helmet is overkill and you can just sit behind your husband on a motorcycle and stuff your newborn under your chador, which is dragging on the ground.

Some cars have six or seven people piled inside. I zoom in on a motorcycle holding a family of four alongside a six-seater SUV with a lone teenager talking on her cell phone. Mom tells me that the rich drive SUVS, the bigger, the better, to intimidate the smaller cars and motorcycles, and get the right of way. In a place void of laws, size really does matter.

Graffiti covers the street walls. Murals proudly depict anti-Shah slogans and poems about the revolution amidst drawings of knives, guns and blood.

Beads of sweat drip from under my black scarf and coat. But I don't dare say anything to Mom about how any human is expected to wear such a getup in this heat. She told me so. I look at Nader, at the cabdriver, at all the men on the street, and envy them for being in T-shirts. Their only restriction is that they can't wear shorts, while women can't even wear sandals because their freakin' toes might show. I look at Mom's shoes and notice that she's wearing a pair of flats without stockings.

"Mom, your ankles are showing!"

"Oh, Miryam, you do exaggerate," she says. "Honestly, it's not that bad. They're not that strict anymore. Is this why you have your scarf on so tight?"

She reaches over an annoyed Nader and loosens the knot in my scarf. "People will think you're a peasant if you wear your scarf like this."

The cabdriver peeks at us from his rearview mirror and chuckles. I nudge Mom to be quiet, scared that he'll take us straight to the *Komiteh* (Islamic police) if he hears her. Iran has regular police officers like other countries; the Komiteh are the revolutionary guards who are more of a morality police.

"Agha Ahmadi is one of us," she says.

I nudge her again, but she ignores me.

"My daughter just came from America. She's a little paranoid."

"May she live a hundred years," he says, looking back at me. "Don't worry, Miss. I don't even remember the last time I saw a Komiteh anywhere. Those days are gone. Everything is just a formality."

"He means that there's no reason to be so cautious," Mom says. "Look around you. Look at all the chic women. Don't pay any attention to the *kalagh siahs.*"

The cabbie laughs.

"The what?" Nader asks.

"Kalagh Siahs (black crows)," Mom says again, laughing with the cabbie at Nader. "It means those fanatic religious women in the black chadors who only show their faces."

I scan the passengers in the nearby cars and notice the chic women who look as if they just stepped out of something like *Scarf Style* magazine. They wear their bright, patterned scarves loosely around their heads as though they're in fashion and not national law. The hair peering out of their scarves is dyed, sprayed and teased. Some of them haven't even knotted their scarves; they've just sort of thrown them over their shoulders.

I try to comb through my hair with my hand and tie my scarf loosely, but it keeps slipping off. The cabdriver continues to smile at me from the rearview mirror. Amateur, he's probably thinking.

"Much better," he says, catching my eye.

He looks back down and fiddles with a cassette until the Persian singer Googoosh's voice blasts out of his fuzzy speakers. Women aren't allowed to sing in Iran, let alone an exiled female singer who embodied Western chic before the revolution. He's gonna get us killed in this pursuit to prove that Iran isn't so bad. Then to top it off, Mom starts flailing her arms and wiggling in her seat in an attempt to dance. I quickly roll up my window. Paranoia never killed anybody, but dancing to Googoosh in a strange man's car in Iran could.

The cabbie triple-parks on Jordan Street and says he'll wait for us. Cars maneuver around the cab without even honking, as if it's parked in a perfectly appropriate space.

Mom grabs our hands and yanks us across the street.

"I forgot that they drive like maniacs here," I say. "Don't you get scared?"

"Jungle law," she says. "You'll get the hang of it."

"She won't have any problems," Nader says. "She's already half baboon."

I think he's talking about how hairy I am, but I'm not sure.

But I am sure that he's acting childish around Mom again. It's not just him though; Cyrus and I are just as guilty. Whenever we're around our parents, we instantly regress in age. I abandon all responsibility, not just for my brothers, but in general. Cyrus turns into a teenager torn between rebelling and pleasing, and Nader turns into a baby starved for attention.

I follow Mom into the *baghali*, a small general store. She introduces me to the old man behind the counter with my official new name: "My daughter from America."

I smile with my head slightly bowed. I ask him if I can videotape his store. He nods repeatedly and with obvious pride. I'm not sure why or whom I'm even filming for, but it's as if I'm making a documentary to prove that Iran isn't so bad after all.

Mom stands by the counter and reads her shopping list out to a young Afghan boy. He scurries to find the items on her list and races them back to the counter as if he's on an Easter egg hunt. In five minutes, Mom is done without having taken a single step. I brag into the camera about the convenience of shopping in Iran.

The grocer hears me and looks into the camera. He waves and points proudly to the display of toilet paper behind him.

Mom turns her head and frowns into the camera. "Vat is dis junk you are filming, Miryam?" she says in English. "Vhy you don't save da film for da party tonight?"

"Film," the grocer says, repeating the only word he understood. "Film, I have."

So do I. More than I need. But he seems so excited that he "communicated" with us in English that I don't want to ruin his moment. So I just thank him when he tells the Afghan boy to hurry and bring me some camcorder film.

The grocer punches madly on a pocket calculator and tallies up Mom's purchases.

"How much?" Mom asks when he's finished.

"It's nothing, Mrs. Mirashti. You're welcome to it."

"No, please," Mom says with an I-don't-have-time-for-this-game tone. "How much?"

"Really, don't worry about it."

Mom sighs. "Please."

"Thirty-five thousand tomans," he finally says, looking down.

Mom opens her large purse and brings out more money than an IRS worker sees after tax day. She divides it into three tall piles and tells the grocer to count it out. He smacks the three piles into one, stacks it in his left palm and peels back the bills quickly with his right thumb. He counts out loud, but Mom isn't even listening. She's helping the Afghan boy bag the groceries.

"And seven," the grocer says, handing back the extra money to Mom.

"He could've taken whatever he wanted," I say to Mom in English. "You weren't even watching him."

"Very honest people Iranians," she says, almost insulted that I would insinuate that he would rip her off.

"I guess people don't have much use for a wallet here," Nader says, watching Mom stuff the rest of the money into her purse.

Mom motions for the Afghan boy carrying the bags to follow us. "I don't think they even sell wallets in Iran," she says as we walk out the store. "You need a briefcase for carrying cash just to run errands. What I just paid 35 *thousand* tomans for would've been about 35 tomans before the revolution."

The value of the Iranian currency is so low that what used to buy you a Barbie house before the revolution won't even buy you a pack of cigarettes now.

Next, we go to the fruit stand in Niavaran. We hop out of the taxi as Agha Ahmadi lights a cigarette, turns up the volume on his stereo and leans back in his seat.

Open crates displaying colorful fruits run outside the store and along the sidewalk. The owner sees me admiring his cucumbers as Mom introduces him to Nader and me. I reach out to shake his hand. But he "tsk tsks" me and reminds me that men and women can't shake hands in public.

Sorry. How very sexually forward of me.

Instead of his hand, he puts a plum in my palm.

"Try this," he says with a smile. "Tell me if you can find fruit like this in America."

I bite into it, and its sweet juices flood my mouth.

"This is absolutely delicious," I say.

Mom smiles proudly, as if she personally planted the tree that grew the plum. To tell her she didn't exactly plant the tree would offend her. To say it tasted as sweet as Ari did on the night we kissed would offend her, the grocer, the farmer, and possibly land me in jail.

When Mom is done, the cabbie scurries to put the grocery bags in the trunk. He sits in his seat and pulls away from the curb, cutting off four other cars and sending a herd of black crows (the human kind) squirming for their lives.

When we stop at another baghali, I tell Mom that I'll just stay in the car. You've seen one baghali, you've seen them all.

"How quickly they get bored," Mom mumbles to no one in particular as she gets out of the car. "Two hours ago, this was her idea of Disneyland."

Not sure how old she thinks I am, but she'd have a point if she had said "two hours ago, this was her idea of Sunset Strip on a Saturday night."

Even the cabbie is sweating through his green T-shirt by the time Mom is done with all her shopping. He tells us he'll get us home in no time by taking a shortcut that'll have us home in just one hour of traffic instead of two.

"I don't like driving on the main streets anyway," he says. "Just last week, two men got out of their cars in the middle of the road and started beating each other up. People are turning into animals in this country."

Oh, it's not that bad. It's just road rage. And here in Iran, everything has just stayed traditional; they use their fists instead of semi-automatics.

"Everyone is just so frustrated in this country," Agha Ahmadi says. "They're looking for any excuse to let out their anger. I don't know what's going to become of this place."

You mean this isn't it?

"How much, Agha Ahamadi?" Mom asks when we reach our house.

"It's OK, Mrs. Mirashti," he says. "Don't worry about it."

"No, please," Mom says.

"It's quite all right," he says.

"Thank you, but please tell me," Mom says. "I don't have time."

"Whatever you think is fair," he says.

Mom peels five green bills and hands them to him. He looks down.

"Is this OK?" Mom asks, watching his face closely.

"Well, we did go to quite a few places. And...and the traffic."

"How much do you want?" Mom asks.

"Oh, no, it's fine," he says. "Really. I'm so sorry."

Mom looks impatient as she hands him two more green bills. "Is this OK?"

"You're too generous," he says, grabbing the money. "Really, you didn't even need to pay me. I'm so embarrassed."

It's easy to read subtext in Iran. *You don't need to pay me; it was my pleasure. But as long as you insist, can you* over-pay *me?*

Chapter 6

When I get out of the shower, I find Mom rummaging through my closet.

"What is all this junk you brought?" she asks. "Women here are very chic. They wear evening gowns to parties, not these frilly little dresses you brought. Don't you have something nice and elegant?"

"Whatever I have is right here," I say like a salesgirl in a boutique.

Mom shakes her head. "I have neglected you, haven't I? Well, I guess it's too late to do anything for tonight. But we're going to the tailor's first thing next week and getting you some appropriate dresses."

She throws my favorite little black dress on the bed. "This will have to do for tonight. God, I'm going to be mortified in front of all my friends. My daughter from America and her dress doesn't have a single rhinestone on it."

The guests won't be here for another five hours, so I put on a little summer dress and go down to the kitchen to help.

"Nothing for you to do, lady," Roya says, shooing me out. "This party is in your honor and I will not have you lifting a finger."

I peek at the three huge trays of hors d'oeuvres they're working on.

"Is that caviar?" I ask.

"You want some?" Mom asks excitedly.

I smile. Mom hands me a full container of caviar and a spoon.

I put a heaping teaspoon of the little black eggs into my mouth and bite down, wondering if I'll even like it still. But I smile as each little dot bursts into my mouth like a mini orgasm.

"Aren't you glad you came to Iran now?" Mom asks. "You'd have caviar everyday if you lived here."

"It's not *that* cheap, is it?" I ask as I roll the spoon on my tongue.

"No, but it's a lot cheaper than it is there. And this is the finest Iranian caviar. Americans pay $400 for what you just ate in two seconds. See the life we have here? Now you go back to America and work 12 hours a day just so you can afford a Big Mac."

I look at Roya as she silently chops celery stalks and offer her some.

"No, no, never," she says. "You enjoy, my lady. Fortunately, I never liked the stuff. I prefer full-grown fish."

I offer Mom some.

She makes a face. "I'm so sick of caviar."

Sick of caviar. A very high-class problem, I must say.

"If you lived here, you could have caviar every day," Mom says. Again. "God, how I wish you lived here."

I'm starting to think that this isn't just about caviar.

"Mom, if you're so against us living in the States, why did you ever take us there? It's not like we cared where we lived at the time."

She shakes her head. "Not a day goes by that I don't think about that. I panicked about what you kids would go through after the revolution. But I look at all the girls your age that grew up here. They're perfectly normal and well adjusted."

I raise an eyebrow. "So how come you had Nader come and live with us? You must've known better then?"

"I didn't want him to feel deprived thinking his brother and sister grew up in America but he didn't. I wanted all of you to have the same upbringing. You'll understand when you're a mother."

"But you're saying that you regret having moved there in the first place?" I ask.

She dries her hands with a rag and picks up a bowl of water. She motions for Roya to drop in the chopped celery. "I did what I thought was best at the time. But yes, if you must know, I wish I had my family all in one place, in a country where the morals aren't skewed."

"You think the morals everywhere are skewed," I say.

"Well, I do know that unlike American mothers, we don't just hand birth-control pills to our 12-year-old daughters and send them out on a date."

"My Lord, Ma'am, do they *really*?" Roya asks, mouth open exaggeratedly.

How this must sound to a woman who yesterday called the pregnant cockroach she found in the kitchen a whore.

"Oh, they do not," I say, trying not to laugh at Roya's horrified expression. "My mom's been watching too much television."

"Have I?" Mom says. "How many of your American friends are on the pill?

"Mom, I'm not 12."

Besides, Paige prefers the sponge.

"All I know is that Americans are too liberal. Girls here don't have ten abortions before they're married. Or guzzle alcohol before they even reach puberty."

"Did you by any chance hang up that 'Death to America' banner down the street?" I ask.

"I don't hate America," she says with a frown. She never could take a joke. "I've been all over the world. Americans are the kindest, most loving people. Intelligent people who…"

Roya cuts her off. "I'm 56 years old and I've never touched alcohol in my life. People everywhere would do well to fear God. That's what's wrong with the world today. No one is afraid of God anymore. People are too spoiled."

"That's right," Mom says.

I snort-laugh. Mom barely even knows what branch of Islam she was born into.

"Just because I'm not religious doesn't mean I don't believe in God," Mom says. "And it's true. People *are* too spoiled. Now take your caviar and go get ready for the party. You're distracting us."

I'm lying on my bed a few hours later when Nader barges in.

"Your highness' presence is requested downstairs," he says with a bow. "A bunch of old farts are here and Mom says they want to see your ugly face."

I get up with a sigh and slide my feet into the flats sitting by my bed.

"You look like a Troll," Nader says as he stares at my poofy hair.

I do look like a Troll. I brush my hair, put on dark-red lipstick and straighten what I'm sure is my too-simple-for-Mom necklace.

I follow Nader down the staircase, feeling more pairs of eyes stare at me with each step. All the men are in suits and the women look like they're at the Oscars. Beaded gowns, almost all black, sweep across our giant colorful Persian carpet. Sparkling necklaces drape the women's wrinkled or tight-from-plastic-surgery necks. And, unlike most of the faces, these jewels aren't fake. You can see the sparkle and the gleam that have replaced those in their owners' eyes. The women all look bored, smiling artificially.

"There she is," Mom says, pulling me down the remaining two steps.

A bunch of women I've never seen before goo-goo and gaga over me like I'm a newborn. Mom introduces me to her friends, most of whom have shortened their names to something appropriate for a 2-year-old. Or a dog. Fifi, Sisi, Mimi, Shoo Shoo.

They gush about how pretty I am, how they've been dying to meet me and how happy they are that I'm in Iran. Mom beams at all the attention I'm getting.

"Yes," she says. "She is pretty, isn't she? Don't mind her dress through. I told her to bring some of her gowns, but she didn't listen to me. She'll learn, I suppose."

She pretends to stroke my hair while actually smoothing down the puff.

"And she looks a little pale," Mom continues. "She's still jet lagged. It's only been a couple of days since she got here."

And then she sees them. Mom glares at my flat shoes as if she's possessed by the devil and I'm wearing crosses on my feet. Her head almost spins exorcist-style. But she catches herself and immediately smiles for no reason at her friends. Only I know that her smile means she'll deal with me later.

"Leave her alone," Ni Ni says. "Kids from abroad are all like that. They have their own idea of fashion. They probably think we're overdressed."

She laughs loudly and the rest of the women follow suit.

Dad's friends are slightly more tolerable than Mom's. They don't talk about my non-existent beauty, but focus instead on my non-existent career. Dad embellishes a tad by giving me a vocation as a junior advertising executive. I think this is in reference to an interview I had for a receptionist position at an ad agency last year. I didn't get the job. But in Dad's mind, I got it and went from receptionist to executive in six months.

I play along, ignoring Nader's smirks. He's getting his own share of the third-degree from another group of guests. Cyrus is away from the crowd, talking to a tall bald man. I feel sorry for him that no one is lip-syncing his praises. There must be *something* they can make up about him too.

And our Cyrus here has exquisite taste in booze. He'll only get sloshed on the finest of scotches.

"Would you please excuse me?" I say to the group of smiling men encircling Dad and me. "I think my mom is calling me."

They nod in unison. Dad pinches my cheek and picks up his glass of scotch.

I'm looking for Ari when a man in a tux bows before me.

"What can I get you to drink?" he asks.

"Oh, are you the bartender?" I ask without waiting for an answer. "Vodka... with something sour."

He bows again and I follow him towards a long table at the corner stacked with crystal pitchers of colorful drinks. He hands me a bright-green drink and apologizes for I don't know what. People are always apologizing here. I fit right in.

I go to Cyrus to ask if Ari's here yet, and I notice that he's drinking the same thing I am. I apologize to the bald man for interrupting their conversation and pull Cyrus away.

"Are you crazy?" I whisper. "You're drinking again?"

"It's just one drink, Miryam."

"You know what? You're not my problem anymore. Where's Ari?"

"You're gonna go tattle on me to Ari now?" he asks with a smirk.

"No, the world actually *doesn't* revolve around you despite what you've been led to believe. I just wanna know where Ari is."

He points towards the dining table and walks back to the bald guy.

I push and shove my way through the crowd towards Ari as if I'm in a rock concert fighting to touch the lead singer. He waves when I get close enough for him to see me. My heart sinks as if the rock star just threw me his sweaty bandana.

I stare at his face. I had forgotten what he looks like. Bee always says that whenever she's in love, she forgets what the guy looks like when she doesn't see him for a few days. She swears that it's a tested theory for knowing when you're in love. And I've officially passed the test.

I glance away and try not to stare directly at him the way I do when he looks exceptionally good. I had forgotten how handsome he looks in a suit. I don't know much about ties, but the thin, colorful one hanging from his neck makes him stand out from the other men. His hair looks extra wavy and his skin has taken a bronze hue from the blazing Tehran sun.

"I've been looking for you," he says, kissing me on both cheeks.

"You have?" I ask with a flirtatious twist to my voice.

"Yeah, my mom wants to see you."

Oh.

He taps his mom on the shoulder and she turns around. She's skinny as a Virginia Slims cigarette, with a firm butt rounding out of her long, red dress.

"There's my love," she says, swallowing a large shrimp and throwing its tail on a plate.

She kisses and hugs me tight.

"Soraya joon, I can't believe how amazing you look," I say.

"And why not?" she says with a wink.

"No, I mean, you haven't changed at all. I didn't get a chance to really see you at the airport. And now, well, you just look great."

"Thank you, honey," she continues in perfect English. "But I tell you, seeing Ari took 10 years off my face. I didn't look this young last week."

He squeezes her shoulder and smiles. I can't believe he has a mother.

"You and I have a lot of catching up to do," Soraya says to me. "But not here. Come over for lunch on Friday, just you, and we'll talk till our tongues fall off."

"OK," I say, feeling a little shy all of a sudden.

What does she want to talk about? Could Ari have told her about us?

I look at him and he's just smiling at her like he's in love with her.

"What do you want me to cook for you?" she asks.

She cooks, too?

"Oh, I don't really care. Anything is fine."

"What a little angel she is," Soraya says, smiling motherly at me.

I blush and wait for Ari to say that that's his nickname for me. But he doesn't.

"OK, you guys will have to excuse me," Soraya says, looking at me. "Your mom will kill me if I don't mingle."

She pats my back and slithers towards a group of women huddled together.

"She's so cool," I say to Ari.

"Yeah, she's something else."

"God, you must be so happy. What's it been like seeing her after all this time?"

"Unreal," he says. "I don't know if I'm ever gonna wake up thinking it's not a dream. Is it just me or is she not the most beautiful woman you've ever seen?"

I smile. "Aw, that's so sweet."

He smiles and looks in her direction.

"Listen, did you bring me the stuff?" I ask when he turns back to me.

He rolls his eyes. "Yes, little girl, I brought you your cancer candy."

"Gimmie!" I say.

"Here?"

"No. Just come with me..."

...upstairs to the bedroom where we used to play Barbie, tear off my inappropriate dress, yank at my poofy hair, smear my not-enough makeup with your kisses and make love to me till I'm limp as the stuffed animals that used to decorate the bed.

I take him to our garden through the little entrance behind the dining room. He follows me behind the cherry tree all the way in the back. I stand under it and let its leaves hang over me like an oversized wig. He bends his head and crawls under.

"The things I do for you," he says.

He reaches into his jacket and hands me a pack of Marlboro Lights. I tear off the wrapping, yank one out and wait for Ari to light it with the blue Bic in his hand. I suck on the filter and swallow the smoke like an asthma patient sucking on an inhaler. I take a large sip of my drink and take another drag of the cigarette to wash out the taste.

"This alcohol tastes like gasoline," I say, making a face.

"Yeah, that's why I'm not drinking it," he says. "I hear you can go blind from it."

I take another gulp. "Really?"

"Yeah. It's bad shit. It's homemade and they actually bring it to your house in a gasoline container."

"Who's they?"

"Assyrians?" he says with a frown. "No, no, Armenians. It's legal for them to drink because they're Christian."

"Oh well," I say, downing the drink. "It's better than nothing."

We stand quietly under the tree as I smoke. Every so often, I shift in my stance and crunch the dead leaves under my feet. I get a chill down my spine, not from the cold, but from some excitement I can't describe. I feel like Ari looks: peaceful. He's leaning against the trunk, staring up at the sky and I'm aiming my ashes inside a hallowed leaf. I'm the rebel kid sneaking a smoke and he's the innocent lookout. Our silence is accentuated by the sound of crickets and an occasional roll of laughter from inside. I bury the cigarette into the ground and throw some leaves over it.

I'm making my way around the dining table when the music suddenly goes dead. I look up and see Roya wobbling out of the kitchen in a green chador. Women run to the coat closet and scramble to find their Islamic uniforms while waiters hurriedly hide as many drinks as they can behind curtains and under sofas. The guests scurry to the garden in a frenzy.

"Relax, everyone!" Dad yells. "He's a local."

I hear a collected sigh of relief as the Persian music comes back on and drinks find their way back to the guests' hands, as if God quickly pressed rewind after accidentally pushing fast-forward earlier.

"What happened?" I ask.

Mom points to a bearded man in all-black attire, sitting by himself drinking a glass of whiskey.

"He's from the Komiteh," she whispers, as if he can hear her through all this noise. "But your father knows him, so no worries."

Mom proceeds to calm every guest personally, bragging that parties at our house are always safe. I stand in the corner and watch the guy sipping scotch and observing the party. I even catch him winking at a young girl in a black mini-skirt.

Dad brushes past me carrying a briefcase. He walks quickly towards the guy and opens the briefcase to reveal the stash of 1000-toman notes. The man takes a large swig of his drink and gets up. He pats Dad on the back and walks past me towards the kitchen door.

"Very generous of you, Mr. Mirashti," he says, clutching the briefcase. "You shouldn't have, really."

He walks into the night and Dad bolts the door behind him.

Dad grabs my arm and walks me back to the living room.

"No, really Dad, you shouldn't have," I say. "But it's a good thing you were so generous with your bribe or you'd all be sliced to pieces. Is that what he meant?"

Dad lets out a loud laugh. "Haven't been here three days and already you can read between the lines. That's my girl."

Chapter 7

"Who is it?" I ask Mom as I sit up in bed.

"Leila," she whispers.

I groan and drop my head back on the pillow.

"Get up and talk to her," she says.

She leaves the phone by my nightstand and walks out. I feel around the table and grab the cordless. I mumble to Leila that I'll call her back later.

"When?" she asks.

When I remember who the hell you are.

I hang up and put the phone to my forehead. Its cold metal feels good against the throb. I fall on my pillow in mass dizziness. My mouth is as dry as a chardonnay, my head is spinning like a blender mixing margaritas, and my eyes are probably red as Bloody Mary's.

Sheer fear shoots me out of bed. I'm still in my dress from last night. I pull it off and tighten a pink bathrobe around me.

"Hi Mommy," I say softly, waiting for her reaction.

"What did Leila want?" she asks, smoothing down my hair.

"Oh, nothing."

"What would you like to eat? It's too late for breakfast, but we have a ton of leftovers for lunch. Go sit at the dining table. I'll bring you a little bit of everything."

"Well good morning, sunshine!" Nader yells extra loudly as I sit down.

"Where's the water?" I ask.

I gulp straight from the bottle he points to.

"How are you feeling?" Cyrus asks.

"Like shit. You?"

"I'm not the one who drank enough to fill our pool," he says.

"Shhh," I whisper. "Not so loud. What happened?"

"Your highness was shit-faced," Nader says.

"Nader, shut *up*. Cyrus, what happened?"

"You came up to me and told me you were gonna throw up. I took you upstairs, you puked all over me, then passed out in your bed. The end."

"What did Mom and Dad say?" I ask, looking around for them.

"Nothing. They didn't notice. I told them you had jet lag and had gone to bed."

"Good boy," I say quickly. "What about Ari? What did he say?"

"I don't think he knew how drunk you were. But he did come up to me when he was leaving and told me not to let you smoke all over the place. He said you were smoking like two inches from Mom and Dad at one point."

"Shit. Shit." I slam my fist on my thigh.

"Don't worry," Cyrus says. "No one knows anything. All you have to do is buy me a new Armani suit and that's the end of it."

"Sorry," I say, looking into his eyes.

"It's cool."

"You're cool. I really appreciate it."

"It's cool."

"Now I, on the other hand, could use this for a bribe or two," Nader says.

"I told you to shut up," I say and grab the water again. "Cyrus, who's Leila?"

He cracks up. "Are you kidding? You only told her your life story for 10 hours before you started feeling sick. You don't remember? Tall chick, short hair, black mini-skirt."

"Oh yeah," I say with a frown. "She moved back here after growing up in Paris or somewhere."

An hour nap and a gallon of water later, I find Mom in her bedroom walking with a stack of books on her head.

"Mom, you're like a ruler you walk so straight now. You're still doing that?"

"I have scoliosis," we say in unison.

She glares at me as I laugh.

"What do you want?" she asks. "I need to concentrate."

"I need Leila's phone number. If your phone book is on your head, I'll just grab it."

I smile.

"You kids think this is so amusing, don't you?"

"I have scoliosis," we say together again.

She drops the books, hands me her phone book from her bedside drawer and tells me to find Mrs. Shahbani's number.

I dial the number on the cordless phone before walking into my room and closing the door.

"Sorry about before, Leila," I say as I flop down on my unmade bed. "I wasn't feeling too well."

"I'm sure," she says with a laugh. "That's one of the reasons I called...to see how you're doing. You looked green when I last saw you. I know it's a bad hangover. We've all been there with the *aragh sagi*."

"The what?"

"*Aragh sagi* (dog sweat)," she repeats. "That's what they call the vodka here. It takes some getting used to. But believe me, in no time, your body will think it's the second coming of Absolut."

I like her. She's very down to earth and easy to talk to. Already, I can tell she's different from the Persian girls in L.A.

"Are you too hungover to come over tonight?" she asks.

"Come over? To your place?"

"Yeah. I'm having some people over. Some young people, not like last night."

"What's the occasion?" I ask.

"Occasion?" She laughs. "It's nighttime."

Mom thinks it's a fantastic idea for us to go to Leila's and make some friends.

"Just one thing, Miryam," she says. "Leila is my friend's daughter. These are classy people. Don't let Cyrus drink and embarrass me, OK?"

"Why do you suddenly care if Cyrus drinks? It never bothered you before."

She hesitates. "This is Iran."

"What does that mean?"

"Just...just keep an eye on him," she says.

"He wasn't drunk last night, was he?"

"Well, no. But he wouldn't be stupid enough to get drunk under our nose."

"Right," I say, nodding slowly. "That would be very stupid."

Chapter 8

The blast of techno music guides us towards Leila's front door. She opens it and shrieks when she sees us. Just how close did we get last night? Are we like best friends forever and ever now?

She kisses Cyrus and takes my scarf and coat. She hangs them up with a dozen others and I wonder how anyone can keep track of all these Islamic uniforms at the end of the night. They all look alike. Hence the word uniform, I guess.

"You know, you can hear the music all the way outside," I say.

"Yeah?" she says with a frown.

"Well, isn't it dangerous? Won't the Komiteh come?"

"Aw, newcomer," she says, pinching my cheek. "Don't worry. You've heard too many horror stories. It's not that bad."

We walk towards a small den-like area with about 20 people sitting in a circle.

"Everyone, I'd like you to meet Miryam and Cyrus," Leila says, pointing at us. "They're Iran virgins."

They all look us up and down with outbursts of ooh and aah.

Cyrus and I are each lighting a cigarette when Leila calls us over. We walk towards her and she points to the rainbow of drinks on the bar.

"I see you've prepared for my arrival," I say with a laugh.

She cracks up.

Gotta make them laugh with *you sober, so they won't laugh* at *you drunk.*

Leila motions for a man at the end of the room to hurry over. I do a double take when I see the bartender from last night scurrying towards us.

"Miss Miryam," he says, bowing. "What can I get you?"

"Oh hi," I say. "Nice to see you again."

"Oh, you'll be seeing Agha Azari a lot," Leila says. "He's the best bartender in Tehran. Everyone asks him to come for parties. Right, Agha Azari?"

"At your service, Miss Leila," he says with a half-bow. "You're too kind."

"Give Miryam your hangover special," Leila says.

"No, no," I say. "I can't."

"Miss Miryam, it's the best cure," Agha Azari says before looking towards Cyrus.

"Nothing for me," Cyrus says.

"Why not?" Agha Azari asks, almost offended.

Peer pressure from a bartender.

"I'm allergic to alcohol," Cyrus says.

"Really?" Agha Azari says with an I've-been-a-bartender-my-whole-life-and-I've-never-heard-of-that-before look. "What happens when you drink?"

"I get drunk," Cyrus says and walks away.

Agha Azari and Leila look at me blankly as I laugh hysterically. Agha Azari smiles and turns back to the bar.

"You brought a bartender for 20 people?" I ask Leila.

"We were actually out of alcohol," she says. "So I asked him to come because he's the only bartender who can also get you alcohol."

"Is it hard to get alcohol?"

"Nah. I mean, you do have to know people. But everyone has at least one liquor connect. I tell you, it's getting so good that I actually know people who can get you beer and gin now. Can you believe that?"

Not sure why I wouldn't, but I just raise my eyebrows, trying to look impressed.

Chapter 9

"Again?" I ask when Mom says I have to dress up and sit pretty for visitors.

For the past week, I've had to sit in the living room like one of Mom's antique statues and smile for aunts, uncles, third cousins, neighbors, Dad's co-workers, Mom's bridge partners and aunt's husband's stepdaughter's cousins twice removed. People whom Cyrus, Nader and I have never seen before have been coming over and flooding our house with flowers, pastries, pistachios and artistic books on Iran, as if our arrival has been a national event.

"Fine," I say. "But I'm going out to dinner with some friends at 8 o'clock."

"To a restaurant?" Mom asks, scrunching her face.

"Yeah. What's wrong with that?"

"It's so pointless," she says. "What's a girl who's been to the best restaurants in L.A. going to get out of sitting in a restaurant here in an Islamic uniform?"

After I model three of my most respectable outfits for Mom and she calls them revealing, ugly and dull respectively, I respectfully ask her to just pick out whatever she deems appropriate. She chooses a beige skirt and a loose-fitting brown top that subtly accentuates my breasts. I wear them with a pair of blown suede pumps and clear nylons, straighten my hair just the way she likes it and plop down on the living room sofa.

"How come Nader and Cyrus don't have to be here?" I ask, wondering why they're not back from playing soccer with our cousins.

"These people are coming to see you," Mom says. "Now smile!"

Half-an-hour later than late, a couple my parents' age walks in with their 20-something-year-old son. They hand me a huge bouquet of flowers.

"Maryam flowers for Maryam, the flower," the father says with a wide grin.

We create a perfect circle around the living room and stare at each other with fake smiles that disappear in relief when Roya wobbles in with a tray of teas. Even she's dressed up. She's actually wearing all one color and her skirt has rhinestones on it.

"So, tell me about yourself," the man says to me. "What did you study in school?"

"She studied communications," Mom says, smoothing down my hair.

I return the man's smile, then look away towards Dad. He's wearing his best suit and has his few remaining strands of hair gelled back. He's sitting very straight and poised. He yawns and I follow suit.

"Miryam?" Mom snaps.

"Huh?"

"Mr. Mostofi asked you a question," she says, giving me a dirty look.

"And you didn't answer him?" I whisper.

"Painting," Mom says. "Her main hobby is painting. She's a very talented artist. You should see some of her work. It's partly why she's doing so well at her job."

"That's very impressive," he says. "I can't draw a straight line with a ruler."

He looks at his wife and the two laugh loudly.

I gulp down my extra-hot tea. The burn feels good on my tongue and it's a little less obvious than beating myself.

"My son here is a good drawer though," Mr. Mostofi says.

I smile at the son and he looks away. He hasn't said a word since he got here.

"You'd get along great with my brother, Cyrus," I tell him when he looks back at me.

Dad chuckles, then bites his lip to stop himself. Mom gives us both dirty looks. The parents stare at us.

"What do you do?" Mrs. Mostofi asks.

"She works at an advertising agency," Mom says quickly. "Advertising is very big in America. Very big."

"Yes," I say. "It's very big of us to convince people that they need things that they don't need and can't afford."

The woman frowns and smiles at the same time, not sure if I'm serious. But Mom is sure...that regardless of what I just said, my tone was inappropriate. She widens her eyes at me and forces a smile.

"I'm just using the communications skills I studied to talk about the industry I work in," I say with a shrug.

I'm just indirectly indicating that I'm sick of this bullshit Iranian pretense.

After a few minutes of silence, Mom and the woman make small talk while I peer over at Dad, wondering why he's not talking. Politics, architecture, the usual. *Does he even know these people?* He's brushing imaginary lint off his pants. He looks up and picks up a dish of pistachios. He searches through it, digs out the empty shells and piles them on the table next to him. Then he examines the stitching on his chair. I watch him amuse himself until I hear Mom clear her throat. Dad and I both jump out of our slouches and look at her. She gives Dad a dirty look and bends her neck towards the family, as in, "Say something."

But after another few minutes of silence, it's obvious that Dad can't think of anything to say.

"Well, we've got to get going," the man says. "It was delightful meeting you."

Dad springs up. "Thank you for coming," he says, leading the way to the door.

When they walk out after a typical Iranian goodbye of seemingly hours, I slam the door and yell at Mom, "Who the hell were they?"

"God, they were boring," Dad says, loosening his tie.

"Don't encourage her, Dariush," Mom says.

"What?" I say, looking at Mom. "You found them interesting?"

"The boy was nice, no?" she says.

"There was a boy here?" I ask. "I didn't notice."

Dad laughs and throws his tie on the couch.

"He was a little shy, but he was nice," Mom says, giving Dad a dirty look before turning back to me. "And not bad looking, huh?"

I stare at her with a frown. She smiles.

"Oh my God!" I scream. "Oh my God! Is that what this was all about? You were trying to set me up? With *him*?"

"He comes from a very high-class family!" Mom snaps.

"I don't want to hear anymore," I say, covering my ears. "Don't *ever* try to do that to me again. I refuse to be part of this barbaric, stone-age tradition."

"Just give him a chance," Mom says.

"But if I marry him, I'll have to live in Iran," I say. "What'll happen to my promising future as an advertising executive? Or does he not believe in da vomen vorking?"

I climb into a pair of jeans and pull a T-shirt over my head. I admit that I'm really going to miss the Islamic uniform when I leave. It's nice not having to fix my hair or care what I wear underneath the long coat. I go out in my pajamas on a regular basis. I've heard that during heat waves, some women are even naked under their trench coats.

Leila picks me up in her Nissan SUV and drives like a maniac towards the Chinese restaurant on Pahlavi Street, which was renamed "Vali Asr" after the revolution. All the streets and monuments, anything that bore the Shah's or the Pahlavi dynasty's name, was changed after the revolution, usually to something bearing the name of an Islamic prophet or a mullah.

We walk into the restaurant and see Kassra, or as the girls calls him, "Tehran's playboy," waving us over from a large rectangular table. While we wait for our group of 12 to trickle in, I tell Leila and Yasmine (my second cousin that I got drunk with that first time in Shomal) about the incident with the awkward boy. They crack up laughing and hum the Persian wedding song.

"You didn't actually think they were gonna let you leave Iran without doing their damnedest to marry you off, did you?" Leila asks.

"And live here?" I say.

"So naïve, so naïve," Leila says, shaking her head. "That's your parents' dream come true. Half the young girls who live here now after growing up abroad were tricked into coming here just so they could be married off."

"Don't frighten her," Kassra says, scooting his chair next to mine.

"Hey, I want some too," Yasmine says when he takes my glass under the table.

"Shhh," he says. "Newcomers first."

"What are you guys talking about?" I ask.

Kassra reaches into a paper bag, takes out a large thermos and pours its contents into my glass. He brings the glass back up and tops it off with Coke.

"Oh my God," I say, bringing the glass to my nose. "Is that what I think it is?"

"Nothing for you to freak out about, my lovely," Kassra says. "Watch this."

He calls over the waiter.

"Ali Agha, we need a kettle for our Russian tea," Kassra tells him.

The waiter nods and bows with a smile. Kassra pours what's left in the thermos into the kettle that the waiter hands him.

"Thank you," he says to the waiter.

"At your service," the waiter says. "The coast is clear tonight. Enjoy."

Kassra winks at me. "Now isn't this more fun than an open bar?"

When I stumble home two hours later, Mom gives me a funny look. But I don't think she suspects that I'd be coming home drunk from a Chinese restaurant in Iran.

"How was it?" she asks. "Stupid, no?"

"Actually, it was quite interesting," I say.

"What was so interesting?" she asks with a frown. "The Chinese food that tasted more like Persian food or the waiter telling you to pull up your scarf every two minutes?"

"Oh, it wasn't so bad."

Chapter 10

THE taxi takes me 20 minutes south of downtown, where the smog is exceptionally bad. It's so hard to breathe that some people are actually wearing oxygen masks.

Before the driver can start his whole, "No please, it's OK" charade, I peel five 1000-toman notes and hand them to him. He thanks me profusely and knowing that I've definitely overpaid, I feel proud that I'm finally getting the hang of things in Tehran.

Soraya opens the door and yanks off my scarf before kissing my over-heated cheeks.

"Take this damn thing off," she says in English. "God, you must hate it."

"It's not so bad," I say. "You get used to it."

"Yes, unfortunately you do," she says. She shakes her head. "I feel sorry for the young people trapped here. Our generation, we already lived our youths. Good ones, too. But these poor young people. This oppression is all they've ever known."

"What about all the kids that grew up abroad and came back to live here?" I ask while I follow her towards the sofa at the end of the room.

"Well, they're just plain crazy."

She goes into the kitchen to bring us tea. I raise my voice so she can hear me. "I've met a lot of these young people. They seem to like it here."

"Oh, I don't buy that," she says. "They probably just prefer the luxury of life here. Luxury over freedom."

I nod, even though she can't see me. I plop down on the sofa that looks like a Kandinsky painting with the white base as its canvas; and the blue, red, green and yellow lines the haphazardly thrown-on paint. I trace the lines with my hand, and like a child who got caught smearing lipstick on the furniture, I jolt when Soraya walks out of the kitchen. She smiles and sets down the tray.

She sits on an armchair and pulls out a cigarette from a pack of Winston Lights. She holds the open box in front of me. I hesitate, hearing Mom's voice telling me not to embarrass her. I take one and look for Soraya's nonexistent reaction.

"Where's Ari?" I ask, trying to sound nonchalant.

"He's out with Bernard," she says.

I frown.

"That Austrian diplomat," she says. "Ari met him at your parents' party. Thank God for your mom and her social circle. At least maybe Ari will meet some people through you guys. I don't socialize much since Ari's father and I got divorced."

"That was a very long time ago," I say, blowing on my tea.

"Yes, but you know how it is. Divorced and widowed women aren't very accepted in this society. All the women are a little threatened. As if I'm looking to steal their men. And that was never a game I wanted to play. I'm quite happy in my little home with my books and my jewelry-design business."

She tells me that most of the women from our social class who work in Tehran either design jewelry or tailor haute couture replicas out of their homes.

I look around the dimly lit apartment as I go back and forth between blowing on my tea and taking drags of my cigarette. The apartment is about the size of our living room, with scarce and modest furniture: a few picture frames on small, round tables, and thick dusty drapes covering all the windows, as if to block the outside world. It instantly reminds me of Miss Havisham's lonely life in *Great Expectations.* I imagine Soraya bent over a small lamp in the wee hours of the night, designing a young, happy bride's wedding ring. I catch her eye and smile sympathetically.

The silence between us starts to get uncomfortable, so I tell her she must be very proud of Ari. That starts her rolling again.

"The past week has been so amazing that sometimes I wish he could stay here," she says. "But this is no place to live. He has his life there. I'm grateful his boss gave him a three-week vacation. After all these years of not seeing him, even that one extra week is priceless."

"I'm sure his boss would've given him even more than that," I say. "I don't think Ari's taken a single day off since he started working at that company. And he puts in a lot of overtime. All he does is work."

"That's fine, I suppose," Soraya says. "It's how it should be. I mean, that's partly why I sent him abroad. To get a good education and work hard at a good career."

She sighs. "Work. Work. Work. That's what America is all about."

Her tone is flat and I'm not sure if she thinks that's a good thing or not. Regardless, I feel embarrassed, wondering if she knows I'm unemployed. I scramble to change the subject.

"Balance is important," I say quickly. "I mean, working hard is great. But so is socializing. The right amount, I mean. I don't mean socializing is important ...I mean, it's important to balance work life with..."

I'm grateful that Soraya interrupts my obviously nervous rant.

"I know what you're saying," she says. "And you're right. He should socialize more." She looks down. "I really hope he marries a girl who appreciates him."

I shift on the couch and cross my legs.

"He's so good to me," she continues. "But he's not a mama's boy. I cut the apron strings a long time ago. I had no choice, really." She sets her empty tea glass down. I continue to blow on mine. "Usually a boy who treats his mother well will treat his wife well, too. It's the same basic relationship, except for the sexual aspect."

I blush, as if I'm the wife she's referring to. I mumble that the apartment is hot so she won't read into my blush. She gets up and turns up the air-conditioner

She grabs two picture frames on her way back to the sofa. She yanks out a tissue from a silver napkin holder and wipes the dust off the frames. One is of Ari's dad in his uniform at a royal luncheon. The other is of Ari and his parents in Rome in the early '70s. I actually wonder why she has a picture of her ex-husband who cheated on her framed in her living room, but I don't say anything.

"Wow," I say. "Ari looks just like his dad. Especially his eyes."

I quickly look at Soraya and hope it wasn't inappropriate to compare her son to his dead father. I'm relieved when she nods and smiles.

"It's as if they Xeroxed his father and put him in my womb," she says with a laugh.

I focus on Mr. Tabaii's face. How long after this picture was taken did he die? What would he think if he were to know when and how he would die? I give the man in the picture a voice and a glimpse of the future: "I will be killed because of this very uniform I'm wearing."

I do that sometimes with pictures of people who are now dead. I did it with my grandmother's picture at her wake. I stared in her young eyes for a long time, having her think that this is the picture her grandchildren would frame at her wake in Los Angeles. I imagined her on the day the picture was taken. She had probably just looked into the camera, smiled, and then gone about her day. She had thought it just another picture, not one that her grandchildren, who weren't even born then, would frame at her wake on the other side of the world, in a country she had never even seen, decades later.

As if Soraya isn't sitting next to me in person, I stare at her face in the picture. Could this proud-looking wife and mother have fathomed that she would spend her future without either of the two male figures by her side?

I smile and hand the frames back to her. She puts them on the coffee table and gets up excitedly. She runs to the bedroom and yells something I don't understand. I hear some rustling and mumbling, and I wonder if I'm supposed to follow her. I get up and pace self-consciously.

I look around the apartment, imagining Ari here as a child. He was here when he found out his father was killed. He was here when his mom told him he would have to go to America with a family he barely knew. I stare at the door and imagine him walking out for the last time and coming to meet us at the airport.

"Found it," Soraya says, walking out her bedroom and slapping the cover of a green photo album.

She flips quickly through the album, twitching her nose at the dust rising with each turning page.

"Look at that," she finally says, slamming her hand on a picture.

I look down at a 4-by-6 picture of Ari and me on the foyer of our villa in Shomal.

"Oh wow," I say, moving closer until my nose almost touches the page.

I'm about 5 years old, standing up to Ari's waist, and we have our arms around each other. I'm wearing an orange bikini bottom without a top and I'm grinning with my two front teeth missing. Ari is in tiny blue swim trunks, making a tough-guy face. I flip the page and see dozens more pictures of us.

"You know," Soraya says with a chuckle, "your mom and I used to joke all the time about how you two would get married someday."

The apartment gets hot again.

"Little did we know that you'd grow up as brother and sister."

The apartment cools back down.

Maybe I had overheard all these "jokes" about me and Ari getting married and when I hit puberty, my subconscious remembered them and thought we were destined for each other. Maybe my love for Ari is nothing more than a psychological glitch that any shrink can de-program.

Soraya puts the album on the floor and goes into the kitchen to check on the *khoreshteh fesenjoon.*

"The rice needs another ten minutes," she says when she returns. "Before we eat, I'd like to tell you why I wanted you to come over here today."

She sits down next to me and takes a deep breath as if she's about to take a dive. "I always feel guilty that you and I aren't closer, Miryam. You were just a little girl the last time I saw you. And I had no idea it would be so long before I saw you or Ari again. I can't begin to tell you how much he loves and respects you. You have been the closest person to him in my absence. More than anyone else in your family. You're like his sister."

I smile.

"I hope this stays between you and me, Miryam, but to tell you the truth, I was a little upset with your parents when they first moved back to Iran. I mean, having trusted them to take care of Ari for me."

She pauses and seems hesitant to go on. When she starts speaking again, her voice is softer. "I didn't think it was right for them to leave you kids all alone like that. But who was I to talk after handing my son to other people to raise? So I never brought it up. But I was so nervous that first year you kids were alone over there. And I was so proud of how you all handled it. Especially you, Miryam. You were the woman of the house. And I know how much you took care of Ari. I know how close you guys have grown over the years. I felt so close to you when I saw you at the airport."

I blush, thinking of when I had tried to shake her hand instead of kissing her at the airport.

"I always felt so guilty," she continues, "when I'd talk to you over the phone and you'd talk to me like a stranger. And then when you just wanted to shake my hand at the airport. I don't blame you, of course. I *was* a stranger to you. I *am* a stranger to you. But for all it's worth, I wanted to see you in private today and thank you for everything you've done for my son. Thank you for taking care of him and being a sister to him."

She grabs a wad of tissues from the box and hands me a few. I reach over and hold her. I close my eyes so my gathered tears can fall down my lids with ease. And so I don't see Soraya and can pretend that the soft hair I'm caressing is Mom's instead of Soraya's, that the woman crying out of gratitude and pride for me, the mother whose tight embrace I'm in, is actually my own.

Chapter 11

An hour after lunch, Soraya tells me her maid called in sick and she has a lot of cleaning to do. I wonder if that's her polite way of kicking me out. But I refuse to leave without seeing Ari, so I play dumb and insist on helping.

"No, no," she says with a chuckle. "That's not what I meant."

"But I don't mind. I love cleaning. It's very therapeutic for me."

"I can't believe I'm doing this," she says, handing me a pair of plastic gloves. "Please don't tell your mom that you paid me back for lunch by scrubbing my oven."

When I'm one inhale of oven-cleaner fumes closer to having smoked the equivalent of a carton of cigarettes, Ari finally comes home.

"Ah, my two favorite women, cleaning the house," he says.

I pull my head out the oven and smile sweetly at his sweaty face.

"Did you have a nice time?" Soraya asks.

"Yeah. He beat the shit out of me though."

"Language, language," she says.

"Who beat the shit out of you doing what?" I ask.

"Basketball. I was playing one on one with Bernard."

"Am I gonna meet this guy?" I ask.

"You did meet him," he says. "At your parents' party."

I get nervous, knowing I don't remember anything from that night.

"No, I mean, like hang out with him."

Good save.

"Actually, he's having a get-together at his house tonight. Wanna come?"

"Sure," I say, a little too eagerly.

"Oh wait," I groan. "I forgot. Dad said I can't go to any more parties."

Soraya and Ari both stare at me. What am I supposed to say? I've been getting a little too shit-faced?

"He's worried about the Komiteh," I lie.

"Oh that's ridiculous," Soraya says. "Your parents throw some of the biggest parties in the city. How can they be worried about you going to a little gathering?"

"Besides, Bernard is a diplomat," Ari says, stretching his back. "You can't be any safer than at his house. Diplomats can literally get away with murder."

"I'll talk to your dad," Soraya says. "Honestly, that's ridiculous."

"No, don't do that," I blurt. "I mean, he'll be upset that I told you anything. I'll just tell them I'm having dinner with you guys. So if you can just cover for me if he calls here, that would be great."

I can't believe I'm asking a grown woman to lie for me so I can sneak out to a party. An hour after her saying how proud she is of how I handled myself like a grown woman as a child.

"I guess I could do that," Soraya says with a slight frown.

"Come over here around 8 and we'll go together," Ari says. "And bring Cyrus."

"Oh. I can't do that. He might tell."

"What's with you?" Ari asks.

Are you trying to say Jim never vomits at home?

"If I go home, they won't let me come back," I say. "I'll just stay here till we go to the party."

Because of lunch with Soraya and assuming I would see Ari, I wore my favorite blue summer dress and made sure my hair and makeup looked good, so thankfully I don't need to go back home to get ready for the party.

"Yeah, I'll just tell my parents I'm having dinner here," I say again.

"I…I guess I could go along with that if they call," Soraya says.

She and Ari both stare at me. I smile and stick my head back in the oven.

"Fereshteh Street, please," Ari tells the cabbie on our way to Bernard's house.

The driver nods and speeds through the red light, then flies over a dead cat. He turns a corner at roller-coaster speed as I clutch Ari's hand. I feel him smiling as he squeezes my hand. My heart drops, exaggerating the rollercoaster feeling I already have. I let go of his hand, but he grabs it right back and caresses it. I'm grateful for the dark hiding my blush and the wind blowing through Ari's window cooling my body's rising heat.

I look out the window at the sun's last rays melting into oblivion. A familiar but forgotten sense of peace suddenly whispers through me.

"Did you know that *Fereshteh* means 'angel' in Farsi?" I ask Ari.

He nods and squeezes my hand harder.

I scream as the cabbie barely misses hitting a stray dog.

Ari laughs. "Brother, can you please slow down a little? She's digging her nails into my flesh back here!"

The driver screeches the brakes in front of a red light as we slam into the back seat. I roll down my window and fan myself.

A one-legged boy holding a crate of cigarette hops towards the car, pleading for us to buy a pack.

I fumble through my purse for money. Not enough to buy whatever junk Iranian brand he's selling, but I hand him whatever I have just as the light turns green and the cabbie speeds ahead. He lowers the volume on his radio and says, "You see what they've done to us? You see the poverty in this country? What was he? 12? 13? He probably supports his whole family doing that."

He doesn't give Ari or me a chance to respond and continues to let out his pent-up anger towards the government. He practically screams profanities at the mullahs. I quickly roll up my window.

"I would do anything to get out of this hell-hole," he says. "But I can barely afford living here, let alone in a different country. I work 16 hours a day and my family only gets to eat meat or chicken on special occasions. How are we supposed to survive when our incomes are in tomans, but the price of everything is in dollars?"

"How do they?" I ask.

He sits up in his seat. He stares at me through the rearview mirror, his eyes dancing with fervor at my question.

"Survive?" he asks. "Barely." His voice grows louder and more animated. "Do you know how rampant malnutrition is? Do you know that my family has to sleep in the cold during winter because I can't afford to pay for heat? Meanwhile these tyrants, these mullahs, are living it up. I hope God shreds their flesh into little pieces."

He says he can't forgive himself for being one of the anti-Shah demonstrators at the onset of the revolution.

"I thought I was demonstrating for a better regime," he practically screams. "To think. To *think* that I asked for *this!* Something worse than bad. Even that dictator was better than these mullahs. I was one of the people who handed my country to these tyrants? I played a part in my beautiful country being like a third-world country even though we have so many resources and our people have so much potential? Do you know how much influence we had in the world? We could've been a superpower. Oh, you kids were too young to remember. Iran was up there. *Way* up there. And now look at us. We're no different from Bangladesh."

He smacks his hand on his head.

"Do you think things will ever change?" Ari asks.

He nods. "I pray for it every day. Maybe my children, God bless their hearts, maybe they'll see that day. Because things can't go on like this. Maybe next year, maybe in 30 years. But there's bound to be another revolution. Every day, the rich get richer and the poor get poorer. There is no middle class. Same problem as before the revolution. The same thing that caused the revolution in the first place is happening all over again."

"Yes," Ari says. "Still no middle class. The only difference is that the people who are rich now are part of the government that kicked out the Shah and vowed to fix the social structure that they blamed him for creating."

"Exactly," the cabbie says, slamming his hands on the steering wheel. "Exactly. And at least back then, we didn't have to deal with this inflation. Seven dollars. The toman was seven dollars before the revolution. It's close to nine *thousand* now."

Ari shakes his head. "Unbelievable."

"Meanwhile the mullah's kids are living it up," the cabbie says. "There are Iranians starving to death, and yet I've seen the kids of these supposed religious fanatics who are anti-West and anti-materialism, driving their Ferraris and Maserati's in the poverty-stricken slums of Tehran. Their arrogance…"

"You're kidding," Ari says.

"Oh, the hypocrisy is as unbelievable as it is ludicrous," the cabbie says. "I've seen guys…right around your age…supposedly from these ultra-religious families, with tattoos on their bodies, which obviously goes against Islam, but the tattoos…" He shakes his head and laughs before he continues. "The tattoos say 'Allah' or 'Ali' (a prophet) or something like that, so that makes it OK, I suppose."

Ari throw his head back and laughs.

"Private jets," the cabbie says. "Parties more lavish than anything you've seen. They flaunt their money…"

"Blood money," Ari says.

"So you do know what I'm talking about," the cabbie says. "Yes, blood money. That they took from innocent rich people to supposedly help the poor…"

"All too well," Ari says matter of factly. "All too well."

"Lifestyles of the rich and fanatic," he says to me in English and laughs.

I shake my head in agreed disbelief. I look away and stare out the window. I don't understand how Ari can talk so nonchalantly about "blood money," about the government that killed his father and confiscated all his mom's property and money even though she inherited it from her father, who had no political ties and had earned his wealth legally and legitimately. Ari's dad did work for the Shah, but none of Soraya's money came from her husband.

Most people in our social class, including my family, lost everything they owned after the revolution, and for no reason other than the whims of the government. But few lost as much as Ari's mom. A few years ago, Mom told me that she once asked Soraya how she managed not to be bitter and to stay so humble, and Soraya had said, "Our country had one king and they kicked him out with his tail between his legs. The king, with all his wealth and power, was replaceable, so the rest of us should really shut up, know our places and not brag about who we used to be or how much we used to have." She didn't even bother fighting the government to get back all her properties the way my parents and so many others did. She sold the few pieces of land the government didn't confiscate and said the money was just enough for her to live modestly and to send Ari until he could support himself.

She doesn't know it, but Ari told me that even though Soraya has enough tucked away for her old age, since he got his first "real job" after college, he's been putting a little bit of every paycheck into a savings account for her.

I squeeze his hand and smile. He looks at me and smiles back, even though he doesn't know why I'm smiling.

Then he turns back to the cabbie, who's still talking. Cabdrivers in Iran are some of the best conversationalists. It reminds me of when Dad says that some of the richest men from before the revolution are now cabdrivers. I've tried to strike up conversations with the countless cabdrivers sitting with me in Tehran's notorious traffic, not just to pass the time, but also because there's no better way to learn about the undercurrents of a country than from these men, who meet all kinds of people, then sit for hours, alone and bored, with nothing to occupy them but their thoughts. But this well-versed driver is among the most particularly pent-up, politically opinionated and outspoken ones I have encountered.

"The truth is that countries like America, no offense, have us right where they want," the cabbie says. "Oh, America complains about Iran's regime, but they know damn well that they created it. They have blood on their hands because they don't want Iran to be powerful again. We were too powerful for their good. That's why that bastard Carter helped overthrow the Shah in the first place."

"Well, to be fair," Ari says, "Iranians did start the uprising. The demonstrations..."

"Sure, the Iranian people didn't want a dictatorship anymore," the cabbie says. "But you think they could've overthrown the Shah if Carter and that bitch Margaret Thatcher hadn't turned their backs on him and secretly supported Khomeini? The Shah wasn't letting the world take advantage of Iran anymore. He was hiking up the price of oil for what it was really worth, and the West saw the domestic unrest as the perfect opportunity to overthrow him for their own economic interests. They had their own agenda. They didn't care about the people, just oil, just money. It's always about money."

I think he's upset when we reach Bernard's house. He wasn't quite through with his monologue about the evils of Jimmy Carter and Margaret Thatcher, and how they "did this to us," and yet their countries have the nerve to call *us* the bad guys.

Ari pats the guy on the shoulder and tells him to take it easy. I really want to give the cabbie a hug, but I just smile at him through the mirror and scoot out.

"Have tomorrow night be a special occasion for your family," Ari says, handing him a large wad of money. "Get your kids some meat or chicken for dinner."

He shakes his head and pushes Ari's hand away.

"No, no," he says. "I was just making conversation. I didn't mean anything by it. I can't accept this. It's too much."

I'm about to tell Ari in English that maybe we're offending him, but Ari stuffs the money into the guy's shirt pocket and walks away.

"God bless you," the cabbie yells after us. "God bless you and your woman."

Chapter 12

"Nice to see you again, Miryam," Bernard says, taking my scarf. "What a lovely time I had at your parents' house that night. Such an elegant party."

"Thank you," I say, oddly proud of my parents for a party.

I catch myself staring at Bernard and quickly look away. I must've been really drunk to forget a face like his. Other than his blue eyes, there's nothing spectacular about his features, but his well-defined jawline and cheekbones give him a rugged handsomeness. He's also tall, built and the epitome of charming. He's already made me blush three times by winking and flashing a sexy smile my way.

I watch him walk down a hallway with my coat and scarf as I follow Ari to the living room. The house is bigger than it looks from the outside. The floors are white marble, and the furniture is ultra-modern. An intricate chandelier is the only antique-looking piece, dropping from the high ceiling over a baby-grand piano in the spacious living room.

"Do you play?" I ask when Bernard walks back to us.

"No," he says, following my gaze to the piano. "None of this is mine actually. I'm renting the place during my post in Tehran. It belongs to a family living in Belgium at the moment."

"You must've been upset that your post was in Tehran," I say.

Here I go again. The first non-Iranian I've seen since the States and I'm back to saying derogatory things about Iran.

"I didn't think one way or the other when it was first assigned to me," he says. "But now that I'm here, I quite love it actually. I'm enjoying myself a bit too much maybe. I don't want to be re-assigned a different post when the time comes."

"Looks like we're early," Ari says, glancing around.

"Actually, everyone is here," Bernard says. "We're sitting in the garden tonight. It's such a nice night for it and I don't take advantage of the beautiful garden enough."

We follow him outside to a small, but well-kept garden. A curvy row of stepstones protrudes out of the grass and leads us to a tiled area where the guests sit on wicker chairs with white cushions. A square wicker table with a glass top holds dozens of colorful drinks in crystal glasses.

Bernard introduces me to everyone after they joke with Ari about "long time no see."

Except for one couple, the rest of the dozen or so guests are not Iranian. After only 10 days in Iran, people with blond hair and blue eyes suddenly look alien and exotic. As I walk slowly towards them, I grow increasingly ashamed that they have to deal with life in Iran.

"Hello, I'm Susan."

"Miryam. Nice to meet you."

I'm so sorry that you have to wear a scarf in my damn country.

"I'm Jack. This is my wife, Nancy."

So sorry you guys can't kiss in public.

"Matthew."

You must really miss eating ham. I'm so sorry about that.

"Michael. I'm an American journalist here on a story."

I will personally go and tear up the "Death to America" banners around the city.

"I'm Timothy. And this is my dog, Buddy."

I'm so sorry the Koran says dogs are dirty.

Ari grabs the seat next to a petite blonde in a yellow summer dress and asks how her foot is. Somehow she finds this incredibly amusing and throws herself on him, laughing. I look at her feet, at her perfectly pedicured pink toes in beige sandals, and fail to see anything handicapped — or humorous — about them.

I fidget and look around for a place to sit. To no avail. I look at Ari, but he's talking softly to the girl. No, she's not pretty, I decide. And she's short. And she shows too much of her gums when she smiles. Or rather laughs like a hyena.

"Oh, darling, let me get you a seat," Bernard says, noticing me on his way back inside. "And what would you like to drink? I've made a splendid pitcher of margarita."

I hesitate. I don't want to risk going home drunk. But I also can't picture myself in this serene garden with Ari, the hum of music swimming through my ears, the cocktails on the table winking at me, with a Pepsi in my hand. That's a picture a tad out of focus. A focused one would be of me gulping margaritas until I can no longer focus.

"A margarita would be great."

I pick at the food laid out on the table. Stuffed grape leaves, an assortment of cheeses, pasta salad and three kinds of chicken.

Bernard still hasn't come out with my chair, so I walk around touching trees and smelling flowers like they're part of a magical land I've stumbled upon. I smile and caress a pink rose, then frown exaggeratedly when its thorn pricks my ring finger, as if everyone is watching me and I have to act as if the only reason I'm not sitting with them is because I've been deprived of nature for years. I walk slowly from plant to plant, trying hard not to have my clinking short heels draw any attention. I hide behind a fern and watch Ari and the blonde talking and laughing. And when he takes her hand and caresses it, I grab the fern's blade and poke its sharp point into my palm until it practically bleeds.

Buddy walks towards me and pees next to the fern. He barks at me when he's done. I shoo him away before he can draw any more attention in my direction.

Bernard finally walks out and slams a folding chair onto the ground. The kind you make kids sit on during Thanksgiving dinner.

"Where did she go?" he asks no one in particular.

"Who?" the journalist asks.

"Oh, that girl?" the petite, not-pretty, hyena-like blonde says. "I think she's over there."

She points towards the fern.

I walk-run towards Bernard, feeling 20 pair of eyes pierce through me. My cheeks grow hot. I smile at no one in particular. And just when I tell myself that I'm only imagining all their stares, my heel catches the strap of someone's handbag and I fall head-first onto some guy, knocking the margarita out of his hand.

He shrieks and jumps out of the chair, pulling me up with him. Buddy circles around us and skids on the puddle of margarita. Trickles of laughter and outbursts of, "Are you OK?" blend with Buddy's boisterous barks.

I don't answer because I'm not sure if they're asking the guy or me.

"I'm so sorry."

At last count, I said it 12 times…to the guy, to Bernard, to Ari, to the other guests, to the dog, to the chair, to the purse.

I look at Ari and mouth another "sorry." He smiles and shakes his head.

The actual commotion ends about half an hour before it does in my head. I sit and sip, that is, gulp, my margarita and replay the incident over and over. I imagine that that's what everyone is discussing and that every smile I get from anyone glancing in my direction is one of pity. I blush every time Ari looks at me.

I keep checking my watch to see how much closer it is to my midnight curfew and how long it's been since I've spoken. The more time passes, the more noticeable my silence feels. The longer I wait, the more attention anything I say will get. So I decide to make like Cyrus and just stay mute. It's just me, myself and an eye trying to avoid contact.

At 11: 03, Bernard comes and kneels next to me.

"I'm being such a bad host," he says. "I do apologize if you're not enjoying yourself."

"Don't be silly," I blurt. "I am enjoying myself."

He smiles the way you would at a 6-year-old. Just when I had stopped blushing, I feel my face turn an ugly shade of red.

"I mean, I'm just in a quiet mood and really, it's just a nice night and really, it's fine," I say, trying to catch my breath to my words.

"I'm afraid I don't know how to throw the kind of bashes your parents do," he says. "That's probably what you're accustomed to."

"Don't be silly. This is great, really."

He smiles again. And I swear, I think he stops himself from pinching my cheeks.

"Let me at least refresh your drink," he says, grabbing my glass.

Oh, please don't leave me!

He walks away and I watch him like a little girl whose daddy just dropped her off at pre-school for the first time.

The short, ugly blonde with the gummy smile and handicapped foot suddenly springs up.

"I have to get going," she says, throwing air kisses towards everyone. "I have a personal yogi coming to my house at 7 in the morning and I have to save my energy so I can channel it properly."

Everyone laughs. But she frowns and mumbles that she's serious.

I look at Ari to see if he's upset that she's leaving. He's staring right at me.

"What?" I mouth, my heart beating.

"Come here," he mouths back.

I smile. My heart starts running so fast with trepidation that it trips over my lungs. But at least my feet don't trip this time. I make it to his side like a proud toddler who reaches her father's outstretched arms without falling.

"Hi," I say.

"Hi," he says, imitating my voice.

"What?" I say.

"Why are sitting there all by yourself like a hermit?"

I shrug. "I'm just observing."

"Oh, you are, are you? And what interesting observations have you made?"

"Stop," I say like a little girl.

"Sit."

I'm about to take the vacant chair when he pulls me down on his lap.

"Ari," I say, trying to wiggle away from his grip.

"Just sit on your brother's lap like a good girl," he says in a baby voice.

"What's wrong with you? Are you drunk?"

"Me? Never!" He laughs. "Do you mind relaxing your muscles so I don't bruise? Or get a hard-on?"

"Who *are* you?" I ask.

Jim never vomits at home.

He looks relaxed. Too relaxed. His smile is strange and his cheeks are bright red. His gestures are almost in slow motion, his speech choppy. I've only seen him like this twice before. I love it when he's drunk.

Bernard finds me and hands me my drink.

"Looks like you got her to join in nicely," he says to Ari.

How mortifying.

I suddenly wonder if Ari is only paying attention to me now that the other girl is gone. I feel like the end piece of bread in a packaged loaf. That slice with the different texture on one side that you never eat, but keep putting back in the package just in case. The one that you'll either eat in desperation or eventually throw out. The one you constantly tease and take for granted that it'll always be there.

So if ever you reach for that slice, it'll be so excited that it'll say, "Ari, I'm having such a good time. I wish I didn't have to go home soon."

"Why don't you just tell your dad you're spending the night at our house?" he says.

"On what grounds?" I ask, my face flushing.

"On the grounds that I miss you."

I stare at him with a smile so wide that it borders on a laugh.

"Tell him you're sick," Ari says.

"No, no, he'll freak. He'll think I'm drunk."

"What's the big deal anyway?" he asks with a frown.

"You don't understand, Ari. All the little fucked up categories of my life are turning into one huge fuck and I need to watch it."

He nods his head exaggeratedly. "Hmmm. In other words, all the separate categories of your life are like an ongoing foreplay. And you need to put an end to it before you get majorly fucked?"

"OK, I don't know who you are and what you've done with Ari, but if you find him, tell him to come up with a good excuse. Otherwise, I'm outta here."

"Seriously, what's so fucked up?"

"My staying out late, partying…"

Bernard walks over with a tray of shot glasses.

"None for me," I say.

"Come on, Miryam," he says. "You can't find tequila like this in Iran. One of the perks of being a diplomat."

"You can't find tequila in Iran period," the journalist says.

Everyone roars with laughter.

"But I can't go home drunk," I whine.

I knew mid-sentence that I shouldn't say it, but it's too late. Everyone looks at me like "awww, how cute, little girl can't drink."

What's so "awww" about it? Haven't you people ever heard of Cinderella? So, I've modernized it a bit. I gotta stop drinking and go home before I puke at the stroke of midnight.

"Come on, angel," Ari says. "Just one."

Four shots later, my eyes bug out at Ari coming out of the kitchen and giving me a thumbs up.

"Are you serious?" I shriek. "You talked to my dad? He said OK?"

"I told him that my mom wants to take us to a museum early tomorrow morning and it would be easier if you just spent the night at our place because the museum is closer to our house. And I called my mom and told her to cover for you in case your dad calls."

"Oh my God! I've created a monster!"

He chuckles.

"My dad bought all that?"

"Apparently. I mean, I'm sure you'll be in deep shit when you go home tomorrow, but at least you won't get fucked tonight." Pause. "By your parents anyway."

"Darling, why don't you relax and have another drink?" Bernard says as I walk into the kitchen carrying a few dirty dishes. "Leave this stuff. I've got the maid coming tomorrow."

"It's the least I could do," I say. "I've definitely overstayed my welcome."

He mumbles something I don't hear. So I just smile and walk back into the garden, where Ari is sitting by himself.

The night suddenly sounds so quiet. All the chairs are vacant, half-empty glasses are scattered on the table and the distant sound of crickets and soft music has replaced people's chatter.

"Do you miss being in America and cleaning the house all day long?" Ari asks.

"Huh?"

"I come home today and you're scrubbing my mom's oven and now you're cleaning Bernard's house..."

"I'm just trying to help. It's a mess out here."

"Not from where I'm sitting."

Only Ari could make me smile at that corny cliché. My mouth freezes in a half-smile and I swallow hard. I turn my back to him and grab some empty glasses and wads of crumpled napkins. My hands start shaking. I'm gonna drop all these glasses and make an idiot out of myself again. I carefully put them back on the table and grab my almost-empty drink instead. Ari jumps up and grabs me from behind.

"Come on, Martha Stewart."

He takes my hand and walks me inside. My entire body is shaking and I'm having trouble walking straight. So I'm glad when Ari leads me to the sofa. He lets go of my hand and sits. I almost drop my glass before it lands at the edge of the table. I fall into the sofa and Ari pulls me to him. He tugs at my hair and stares into my eyes. I look away nervously. He tilts my head roughly and puts his mouth on my ear. "I want you."

My eyes dive into his, then drown with fear. He pulls me up with him, holds me close and tangos with me to the barely audible music coming from the garden. I hear Bernard humming in the kitchen. For some reason, his voice soothes me.

Just when I'm relaxed enough to put my head on Ari's shoulder, he lifts me up and carries me across the hall to Bernard's room.

He throws me on the bed. I bounce on the mattress and watch him kick the door shut. I inhale deeply and realize that even my breath is shaking. I startle at the sound of a flick. Ari looks almost stern as he lights the four candles around Bernard's bed.

My heart's pounding echoes throughout my body. He's trying to create a soft mood with candles, but my body is as stiff as the candlesticks. I feel dizzy, almost nauseated. I stare down at the black carpet showing its blue hues through the glow rising from the candles. Ari sits on the bed and leans me down with him. I crawl back to the edge of the bed and kick off my shoes.

"Come here, Barbie," he whispers.

He pulls me on top of him. My heart sinks; I look down nervously. He smiles and laughs softly. I start to talk about the first time we had Ken and Barbie kiss, but his smile vanishes and he slowly puts his lips onto mine. I close my eyes and concentrate on the feel of his lips. I hold him tight. I squeeze him with what little strength I have. I tug at his hair as if an orgasm is about to explode out my fingertips. My insides are going to burst with happiness and come out of my eyes as tears.

I pull away suddenly and switch positions. I lie on the bed and hold onto his face above mine. I stare into his eyes. He stares back. But even with his intense gaze, he can't see my eyes as clearly as I see them reflected in his. He can't see the sheer joy in my eyes. He doesn't see in them a party where my dreams, prayers and wishes have finally gathered to celebrate reality.

I suck his lips and feel a gush that tastes like sweet cherries. He graces my lips gently, then gives me French kisses more pungent and perfect than grapes in a French vineyard.

He moans softly a few times. I watch his face as we rub bodies. His eyes are shut tight and he's frowning slightly. He reaches under my dress and puts his hand inside my underwear. He slides it down and penetrates me with his middle finger. It hurts and I groan in a way that he could interpret as either pleasure or pain. But he can sense how tight I am and tells me to relax my muscles. It's like the first time all over again. I tell myself not to ruin it like I did that time. I spread my legs wider and try to loosen my muscles. He gently slides his finger in and out of me while rubbing the outside.

"You're burning hot," he says as if his finger is a thermometer inside me.

I breathe harder, louder.

"Feels good, angel?"

"Mmmm...yes, Ari."

My legs part wider, my body screaming for more, much more. My mind and body are in sync this time. I'm relaxed and ready to recreate our first time, to finally relish what I've been waiting and yearning for.

I'm about the slide my zipper-less dress off and help him unbutton his pants when he moans loudly and collapses on top of me.

"Shit!" he says.

"What is it?"

"Shit, Miryam," he says again.

"Should I take it personally that that's always the first thing you say when you're with me?"

"Miryam, I just came."

"What? Are you kidding? In your pants?"

He laughs nervously. "Yeah. I'm so sorry."

I fake-laugh to hide my disappointment.

"What are you, 12?" I ask, my body's frustration obvious in my tone.

He throws his head back and laughs.

"Just like when I really was 12," he says.

"Huh?"

"Remember that curfew night when we played Ken and Barbie at my house?"

"You came?" I shriek.

He nods and laughs again. He rolls to his side and looks at me. "So, you wanna masturbate now like you did that night?"

My cheeks get hot and my smile vanishes. "What are you talking about?"

He gives me a sly smile. "Oh come on. You know you did. I saw you!"

I squeeze my eyes shut and bite my upper lip. "Shit! I thought you were asleep."

"I know you did," he says, laughing.

"Wow," I say after a while. "Do we have a history together or what?"

He smiles and looks at me for a long time. My insides churn.

"I'm serious though," he says. "Do you want to? Or do you want me to…"

The thought of anything easing my sexual frustration and bringing me to orgasm when I know he already came feels more embarrassing than fulfilling.

"No, I'm good," I say.

"Sorry," he says.

"It's OK."

I want to say, "next time," but I stop myself, hoping he'll say it.

But he just smiles. I stroke his cheek softly and brush my fingers across his stretched lips. He kisses my fingertips, then grabs my hand and pulls me back to him. He puts my head on his chest and intertwines our fingers. I close my eyes and listen to him breathe, slower and slower until I can no longer hear anything. His body goes limp under mine and his fingers loosen their grip. I slide next to him, cradling myself around him like a cat.

The candles stand like knife handles crying under blades of fire. I follow their flame up to the ceiling and watch them dance around the silhouette of our shadow, our slow breaths their rhythm. I watch them burn for hours until the sun shames their light into oblivion.

Some of the candles cry so much, they die before their time. The others shed only a few tears and stand tall when the night draws to a close.

I envy the tall white candles. I empathize with the shrunken blue ones.

Chapter 13

Cinderella turns into Pinocchio.

I feel a gentle nudge. I open my eyes and look at Bernard, first with a frown, then with a shriek.

"What is it?" I ask, sitting up.

"Shhh," he says and points at Ari sleeping next to me. "Come outside."

I look down at myself, relieved that I'm fully clothed. I follow Bernard into the living room and cringe at the sunlight flooding the room.

"I'm really sorry," I say. "I mean, we didn't mean to take over your bedroom. We just fell asleep. We were really…"

"That's not a problem," he says, waving his hand in front of me. "I passed out on the sofa anyway. But Ari's mother called and said that your father is looking for you. He's uh…he's rather upset. She said she told him you're on your way home from a museum. In a taxi."

I look at my watch.

"Oh my God!" I yell. "It's 3 o'clock! Why didn't you wake me up sooner?"

"I just woke up myself," he says. "My cleaning lady rang the doorbell."

He motions towards the kitchen and I suddenly notice a scarved woman eyeing me as she sweeps the floor. I turn quickly around.

She thinks I'm a whore. Still in my clothes from last night, makeup smeared all over my face. Oh no, then she'll see Ari walking out of the bedroom and…

"I guess we were all rather drunk," Bernard says, smiling. "How do you say in America? 'Wasted?'"

I move away from the cleaning lady's view and start pacing. "Oh my God! Call me a cab quick!"

"I already did, darling," he says, taking my hand. "It'll be here any minute. Just relax. You're a big girl."

He stares down at my boobs.

I ask the cabbie to tell me all about the most famous museum in Tehran.

But Dad doesn't even ask which museum we went to.

I sit across from him in the family room and trace the designs on the Persian carpet with the pointy tip of my shoe. I feel him glaring at me.

"What in the world has gotten into you, Miryam?"

"I'm sorry, Baba joon," I say without looking up. "I told her it was a bad idea for me to spend the night. But she insisted. You know how I hate arguing."

He gets quiet, magnifying the clatter of pots and pans from the kitchen, where Mom and Roya are making dinner. The stench of *khoreshteh bademjoon* shoots upstairs. The meat sizzling in a pan of chopped onions feels like it's searing on my cottony tongue. And the more eggplants, tomato sauce and sour grapes they dump in, the stronger it smells, as if it's all churning in my stomach instead of in the pot.

I see Dad shaking his head from the corner of my eye. "You used to spend hours just by yourself, reading, painting, listening to classical music. What happened?"

I take off my shoes and dig my bare heels into the carpet until I get rug burn.

"It's as if you have no substance anymore," he says.

Sure I do. Alcohol, pills, tobacco.

He frowns and puckers his lips the way he does whenever he's worried.

"I don't read because I don't know how to read in Farsi," I say. "I don't know where to find English books here. I've read your copy of *Les Misérables* in English three times already."

"Don't be so literal!" he snaps. "You know what I mean." He lowers his voice. "You're just not my little Miryam anymore."

He waits for a response, maybe a *goo* or a *ga*. But I continue to stare down.

"The phone rings all day long," he says. "And it's always for you. Girls, guys. Different guys."

"Who?" I ask a little too enthusiastically, as if he's giving me my messages.

He shakes his head and stares at me with disbelief.

He starts to say something, but I interrupt him. "I didn't know. About the phone calls. Have you guys not been giving me my messages on purpose? Because..."

"You just don't get it, do you?" he says. "This is Iran. Word gets around. Before you know it, you'll have a bad reputation. Is that what you want?"

"Bad reputation for what? I'm not doing anything any other girl in this city isn't doing."

"I didn't raise you to be like all the other girls in this city!" he yells.

I swallow hard. I don't remember Dad ever yelling at me like this before.

"What's wrong with them?" I ask softly.

"I'm just not crazy about the group of people you're associating with," he says, trying to soften his tone. "You're above them. You're educated, intelligent, talented. You've got a lot going for you. These people have nothing to do but party every night until the day they die. They have no goals or ambitions. I don't want you picking up that mentality."

"But Dad, there's nothing to do in this country except to go out and party. That's all *you guys* do."

"I work six days a week," he snaps. "And your mother spends almost all her free time at different charities."

I can't argue with that.

"Besides," he says. "We're older."

"What does that mean?" I ask a little too loudly.

"It means that your mother and I are married. You're a young, single girl who's going to get a bad reputation if you keep this up. You know how much talk there is in this city. I wouldn't want you getting a bad reputation when deep down, you're such a good, clean girl."

"Well, if you know that, then why do you care what other people think? You're the one who always told me to be my own person and not care what people think."

"I meant that you shouldn't be fooled by men or be pressured by your friends into doing things you didn't want to do. I didn't mean you shouldn't care what society thinks of you. It matters what other people think. We live in a world with other people. We're social animals."

"Some of us are a little more evolved," I say under my breath. "Fine. So just ground me and forbid me to go out anymore."

I shake my head at the irony that growing up, I was never grounded, not because I never did anything wrong, but because there was never anyone there to ground me. Not just irony, but also a double entendre in there.

"I'm not going to ground you," he says, rolling his eyes. "I was hoping you yourself would realize that this isn't you. Wouldn't you rather use your first time in Iran after all these years to spend some time with your family and get to know your culture instead of…"

"But I *am* trying to get to know my culture. I was at a museum."

He glares at me. "You think I'm stupid?"

I bow my head and dig my nails into the sofa's rough, potato-sac-like fabric. "I'm so tired of you guys caring so much what society thinks," I whisper.

"That's just how it is," he says as he leans back in the armchair. "You're of marrying age and I don't want your name out there as a party girl. And it's not just society. I personally don't approve of your behavior."

He gets quiet, but in a way that's obvious he's not finished. When he doesn't say anything for a while, I look up at him. He immediately looks down and shifts his body in the chair. He clears his throat and says, "This is not easy for me to say, Miryam. You and I have never talked openly about men and sex. I never…"

"Who's talking about sex?" I ask, putting my hands on my knees.

"I always figured you were too much of a lady for me to have to worry," he says as if he didn't hear me. "But now, it seems…I'm not saying you're not a lady. You are. But try to act more like it."

I start to argue, but then I realize that I'm really not a lady. At least not what Dad would consider one. If Dad knew I wasn't a virgin, he would…he would … I don't know what he would do, but it's frightening enough to stop me from thinking about it.

I look up at him. He's staring blankly at the muted television. I imagine the disappointment in his face if he knew. I imagine telling him right now. The guilt is unbearable.

I stand up with my head bowed. I walk over and gently kiss his forehead. He cups his hand around the back of my head to keep me there. I make the kiss linger while I savor the smell of his cologne. I run my hand across his head and brush a few strands of hair over his bald spot. He takes my hand and smacks it gently on his head. We both smile as a gesture of truce.

Five minutes later, Leila calls to say there's a "kick-ass" party at some guy's house tonight.

"Oh what perfect timing," I say before I rehash my conversation with Dad.

"So, like what?" she says. "You're never leaving the house again?"

"I better lay low for a while. Maybe they'll ease up if I…"

"It's a lost cause, babe," she says. "They'll never fall for that misery routine."

"Oh, but you underestimate how miserable I can be."

Chapter 14

It's one thing when you're stuck at home in the States. You've got a million TV channels, at least one of which will have Jack, Janet and Chrissy keeping you company. But the only things that change on the two existing channels in Iran are the mullahs who preach about the evils of the Westernized world.

We do have an illegal satellite dish, but it only carries channels from India, Japan and Israel. The Israeli channel shows recent American movies in Hebrew every night. Every night, my parents sit and watch these movies. In Hebrew.

Dad, who's in a good mood that I'm actually home and spending time with them, boasts about how much Hebrew he's learned from that channel. He counts to 10 looking at me like a little boy reciting the ABC's to his mom.

We all laugh.

I start feeling guilty that I'm the reason Dad has been so cranky lately. I decide to enjoy my whole family bearing the entire showing of the Steve Martin version of *Father of the Bride*. In Hebrew.

Nader falls asleep after 10 minutes and Cyrus springs up from the sofa.

"This looks like a father-daughter movie," he says as he limps to his room. "You guys enjoy!"

Just as Steve Martin is struggling to fit into his old tuxedo, our phone rings. It's almost 11 o'clock. My parents glare at me. Dad picks up the phone and hands it to me without even talking to the person at the other end.

"What are you doing home?" Leila shrieks on the other end. "I thought for sure you'd be here."

"I told you I can't come out for a while," I whisper. "Where's here anyway?"

"Oh my God, Reza's house. Everyone's here. Come on."

"No, I can't."

"Come on, Miryam," she says. "I'll come pick you up."

Yasmine screams into the phone that I have to come.

"Seriously, stop it you guys. I told you I can't."

"OK," Leila says. "But you're missing out. Bye."

I hand the phone back to Dad.

"Party?" he asks.

"Yeah," I say softly.

"You can go if you want," Mom says as she looks at Dad's once-again stern face.

"It's OK," I say.

"No, go," Mom says. "Your friends want you there."

"She said she doesn't want to go," Dad says. "Leave her alone."

We continue watching the movie in silence as I grow increasingly restless at what a good, wholesome girl "Annie" is. Fuck, even her name is wholesome. I'm sure Dad is comparing me to her. Her only outburst is over getting a blender as a gift from her fiancé.

At which point, Mom says in English, "What her problem is? Is good gift."

"It's a feminist thing, Mom. She thinks the gift is implying that she should stay in the kitchen once they're married."

Mom shakes her head. "Ridiculous nonsense this feminism."

"Does this mean you've decided not to be the ERA's spokeswoman, after all?" I ask.

She gives me a dirty look because of the sarcasm in my voice, not because she understood a word of what I said.

Annie and her fiancé patch things up, thanks to her dad's help. The tension between Dad and me rises proportionately to the touchy-feely moments between Annie and her father.

I stare at the phone, then check the clock on my nightstand. 12:23 a.m. It's not that late. I can still call Ari. He's probably up. Maybe he's tried to call me but our line's been busy. And now he thinks it's too late to call. Maybe he's even waiting for me to call. Yeah, that's it.

But first, I need a drink to calm me down. I climb out of bed, turn off my lights and tiptoe towards my parents' bedroom. I listen for Dad's snore. It's faint, but definitely audible. I hear Mom clear her throat. I should probably wait a while longer, but I can't waste any more time.

I walk slowly downstairs in the dark, counting the 12 steps that lead to the living room. I used to count everything when I was little, especially stairs. But I never imagined that it would actually come in handy someday when I'd have to climb down the stairs in the dark to sneak up alcohol.

I tiptoe to the mahogany china cabinet behind the dining table. I immediately see the giant vodka jug. I grab its handle and close the cabinet door. I don't want to turn on the kitchen lights, so I grab the jug's handle and run upstairs with a pounding heart.

I wash the glass holding the toothbrushes by the bathroom sink and bring it to my room. I pour the vodka and gasp at the gasoline-like smell. I fill the glass and put it in my closet before retracing my steps and putting the plastic bottle back in its place downstairs. I really should cut up some lime, but I can't exactly pass off limes as a midnight snack if my parents come downstairs. This drink is for medicinal purposes; no time to make a pretty cocktail out of it.

Back upstairs, I open my bedroom window to get the smell of the vodka out. I light a cigarette, sit on top of the radiator and put my drink on the narrow sill outside the window. I bring the glass to my lips three times before I finally get the courage to take a sip. It burns my throat and I spit most of it out. It's bad enough with orange juice in it, but this is downright torture. It tastes exactly like I imagine rubbing alcohol would. I think of Kitty Dukakis.

Come on, Miryam, follow in the footsteps of a powerful woman for a change.

I grab the vanilla wafers Mom put on my nightstand yesterday. I take a large gulp of vodka and stuff the wafers into my mouth, chewing like a squirrel on speed. I gag twice and stick my head out the window, in case I have to throw up.

When I've finished half the drink and feel comfortably numb, as my favorite band says, I grab the cordless phone and dial. Soraya picks up on the second ring. I instinctively hang up.

Shit. Shit. Shit.

Ari probably knows it was me. And if I don't call back, it'll be worse. I press redial and bite my lower lip hard. This time, Ari picks up on the second ring.

"Did you just call and hang up?" he asks after he hears my voice.

"Yeah, but it was an accident. My face hit the off button."

"Oh." He doesn't sound like he believes me.

"What are you doing?" I ask.

"Uh, *sleeping*," he says.

"Oh, sorry."

"It's 1a.m."

"Really? I'm sorry. I thought it was only 12:30."

He laughs. "*Only?*"

My lips quiver as I take another large swig of vodka.

"What's up, Miryam?"

"Nothing. I just, I couldn't sleep."

"This is new for you?"

OK, Miryam. Buckle down. You didn't just inhale a pint of gasoline for small talk and sarcasm.

"Well, if you must know, I called to talk to you about the other night."

Silence.

"Hello? Did you hear me?"

"Yes, I heard you," he says. "But do you really think this is the best time to talk about it? I'm half asleep and my mom is in the next room."

"Well then wake up and whisper," I say, trying to sound bitchy. "And maybe this wouldn't be an issue if you had called me earlier."

I wait for him to say that he did call, that his was one of the messages I had accused Dad of not giving me.

When he doesn't, I say, "If we don't talk about it now, you're just gonna blow it off again."

"What do you mean *again*? We talked after last time."

"Yeah, a week later," I say. "And you didn't even call to see if I got home OK yesterday or if everything was fine with my parents. And you didn't call all day today. If I hadn't called right now, you probably wouldn't..."

"Alright, alright. Let's talk."

"Why do you keep doing this, Ari? Why did you tell me last time was a mistake, then went ahead and did it again? Is there something going on here or am I just some chick who happens to be next to you when your hormones are out of whack?"

"I was drunk, Miryam," he says.

"Oh great," I say. "So last time, it was just because my grandmother had died and this time was just because you were drunk. So there's always some excuse. Some bullshit excuse. It's never because you feel anything."

He's quiet.

"You were not even that drunk," I say. "You knew what you were doing."

"I mean my inhibitions were lowered."

"Oh here we go again with the psychobabble," I groan.

"It's not psychobabble," he whispers. "I didn't have my guards up."

"No, you had something *else* up," I say.

"Miryam..." he says with a surprised chuckle.

I know it's not like me to say something so brazenly sexual to him. Out loud, anyway. The alcohol must be kicking in and my "guards" must be down.

"I know," I say. "Jim never vomits at home."

He laughs. "I was just about to say that."

I smile, then remember what we were talking about and get serious again.

"Actually," I say, taking a drag of my cigarette, "if your inhibitions were lowered, as you say, that means that you were being the real you. You know, in vino veritas."

"In what?"

"In vino veritas," I repeat. "Don't you know? It's Latin for 'in wine, there is truth.'"

"I didn't have wine," he says with a laugh. "Maybe it doesn't apply to tequila."

"Ari! Be serious!"

"Sorry," he says, a hint of humor still in his voice.

"Because your inhibitions were lowered," I say, "you could let your guards down and do what felt natural without any filters." I put out my cigarette and frown. "Or was it the opposite? Was the rational part of your brain not working? Or was I just the girl who happened to be there when the opposite of your guard was up?"

"I don't know, Miryam," he says quickly, as if he immediately understood and analyzed everything I just said.

"How lovely. Thanks for putting so much thought into that."

"No, listen to me," he says. "You're not just some girl. I obviously love you as a person. And maybe sometimes that line gets a little skewed. I'm sorry."

"So that night was another mistake that we should just ignore?"

He's quiet for a long time, giving me a chance to take two more gulps of my drink.

"I don't know," he finally says. "We obviously feel something for each other, but maybe it's not what we think it is. Or it shouldn't be. We could ruin our friendship if we get involved. Think of everything that's at stake. It could get really messy."

"We've been over this," I say. "That's what you said last time. So why do you keep doing this, then acting like a jerk afterwards?"

"I'm sorry. I know I've been a jerk. I..."

"Yes, you have. Don't you even care what I think or does my input not count?"

"Of course I do, Miryam. I want to know what you think. But I was waiting until we could talk in person." He pauses before saying, "What *do* you think?"

"I don't know what I think," I say.

Focus, Miryam, focus. Don't lose this opportunity.

The phone is low on battery and suddenly starts beeping. Each beep pierces through my ear and pounds into my skull, as if reminding me to think.

I take a deep breath and clear my throat.

"I have feelings for you and I don't think it would be such a bad idea if we moved our relationship to the next level," I say.

I shut my eyes tight and bite hard on my lip.

Please say something. Anything. Please just break the silence.

"You're willing to take that risk?" he finally asks.

"What *risk*? Why is it such a big deal?"

"Because it is. It's not that simple."

"It can be if we both want it badly enough. But you don't."

"It's not that, Miryam. It's just not that simple." He sighs. "Let me just clear my head a little, OK? Give me a couple of days and we'll talk then."

"You've had days to think about this. You've had *years* to think about this. This has nothing to do with thinking. You either feel it or you don't."

"I *do* feel it, Miryam." He sighs. "I swear I do. But I'm a little confused right now. I just need some time. I swear that's all it is."

"In other words, you need me to sit here and wait while you decide if you have the guts to be more than my friend."

"Miryam, I wish I could be more like you. You're always sure about what you want. I admire that about you. I'm not like that. I have to analyze everything, even something like this. *Especially* something like this. Our friendship means the world to me. I have to make sure that I can handle taking it to another level. I know that makes no sense to you. But please just trust me on this. Please just bear with me and I swear I'll do the right thing."

That's what I'm afraid of.

I light another cigarette and empty the drink down my throat. I don't even flinch. My taste buds must be numb. Or I've acquired a taste for gasoline. I put the glass down on the floor and hold on to the edge of the bed to keep from falling off. I steady myself and close my eyes to stop the spinning. I breathe hard and grit my teeth. I feel like I'm falling off a high-rise with no ground in sight. The phone slips from my ear.

"God, help me please," I mumble repeatedly into my pillow.

I hear Ari's voice coming from the floor.

"Hold on, you fell," I say too softly for him to hear.

I sit up slowly, trying to breathe. I reach for the phone and fall on the floor.

"Miryam, what's going on?" he yells into the telephone.

I pick it up, moaning. "Nothing. I'm fine."

"Miryam, what the hell just happened?"

"Listen to me," I slur. "Just calm down. Just calm down and stay on the line. Your call will be answered in the order it was received."

I wobble to my door and squint towards my parents' room. As far as I can tell, their door is still closed. I stumble across the hall to the bathroom and accidentally slam the door on the back wall.

"Shhh," I whisper to the door.

I splash some cold water on my face. I kneel in front of the toilet and poke my index finger down my throat, praying that I throw up. With each thrust of my finger, my stomach gurgles louder and louder, like a freezer when it's making ice cubes. But nothing comes out. Beads of sweat run down my throbbing forehead until they meet wads of spit at the corners of my mouth. I try to gag as quietly as I can, but the closer I get to actually vomiting, the louder the gags get. Finally, a torrent of clear liquid, with specks of chewed-up vanilla wafers, gushes into the toilet bowl. I rest my drenched head on the toilet seat in exhaustion, like a woman who just gave birth. I panic when I realize that the bathroom door was open the whole time. But I squint and realize that no one's lights are on.

Ari is still there when I pick up the phone.

"Miryam, if you don't tell me what the fuck is going on, I'm gonna take a cab and come there right now. Do you hear me? You're scaring me."

"No, don't do that," I say, trying not to slur. "I'm fine. I'm fine."

"You're not fine," he says in a loud whisper.

"I'm fine," I say, standing up and squinting into the mirror. "See? Sooo fine." I smile at my reflection. "Sooo fine." I laugh and drop on my bed, my breaths getting more and more shallow.

"But not all fine," I say with my eyes closed. "See, I love you so much, Ari. I am so in love with you. So so madly in love with you. You don't know. You just don't know. How can you not know…how beautiful we are together? How can you not? Know?"

I moan before settling into a steady, silent sob. It sounds so sad that I start feeling sorry for myself and cry even harder. He listens without saying a word until my batteries die.

Chapter 15

"Yo, Sissy, get up!"

I open my eyes and look up at Nader hovering over me in grey sweatpants and a white T-shirt. I groan and roll off my numb arm.

"Look around you, Sissy Space Cadet."

I squint and stare at the remnants from last night. The empty glass is sitting on its side next to my bed, the window is still open and cigarette ashes are scattered everywhere, even on my blanket, which is crumpled at the foot of the bed. The phone is buried under my pillow with its antenna sticking out. And the alcohol that must've spilled on the cover of *Les Miserables* on my nightstand is making the black ink bleed onto the pages. Unlike the characters it depicts, the book's cover has practically no spine left.

Nader bends down and whispers, "What the hell were you doing last night? Were you drunk?"

I squint at the giant red digits on my alarm clock. 6:12 a.m.

"Nader, what are doing up so early?" I groan.

"I got up to go to the bathroom and saw your lights on. I thought you were still up from last night. Then I saw the mess in here. You really should clean up before Mom and Dad see all this."

"Leave me alone," I mumble.

"Is this your way of admiring Cyrus?"

Groan. Pull covers over throbbing head. Pass out.

I wake up a couple of hours later to a spotless room, with all the damning evidence gone.

I lock the bathroom door and run soapy water under the sticky glass I drank from last night until it runs clear. I stick the toothbrushes back into it and dab some toothpaste on the outside edges. It's not like anyone would accuse me of drinking just because the toothbrush glass isn't the right kind of dirty, but when you need to hide evidence, you learn to cover your tracks beyond a shadow of a doubt.

I fish around the clutter on my vanity table for my bottle of Advil. When I finally manage to flip off the childproof cap, all the pills explode onto the floor.

Bee once told me that if you take two Advils, then sleep, your hangover will be gone by the time you wake up. I throw eight into my mouth and take a sip of the ash-drenched water on my nightstand.

I stare into the mirror and cringe at my ghastly sight. My face is puffed up with actual morsels of salt around the edges of my narrowed eyes. I pick at a piece and taste it. I've cried a lot in my day, but never to the point of actually creating salt.

I wipe the salt and goo from around my eyes and sit on the window ledge to get some fresh air. I half-inhale, half-gag on the cigarette dangling from my chapped lips as I stare at the beautiful day. The sky is clear, the sun not yet too hot and the gentle breeze feels like a hard slap in the face.

Three girls around 9 years old stand talking on the street. They're sporting their Islamic uniforms and backpacks that look heavier than they are. They're complaining about how much homework their teacher gives. One of them suddenly shrieks and tells her friends that she forgot to do part of last night's assignment. She asks her friend if she can quickly copy hers.

The panic on her face reminds me of when I was her age and thought that adults couldn't possibly have any problems because they didn't have school. I would frown at worried-looking adults and wonder, "How difficult can life be when you don't have school or homework?"

A dusty blue bus turns into the narrow street and the girls climb in methodically like little toy soldiers. I watch them with envy. Even the one who's probably going to get slapped for not having finished her homework will have forgotten about it by tonight. But I'll still feel the throb of this headache and the shame of what caused it.

The school bus disappears, leaving only a torrent of exhaust in its trail. I close the window and yank the curtains to block the bright day.

I climb into bed and pull the covers over my shivering body. Snippets of my words from last night and the echo of sobs still trapped in me reverberate in my head like a fuzzy AM radio reception. I try to tune them out, focus instead on the sound of my chattering teeth like a mantra. But all the sounds just mesh together into a concerto of chaos.

Chapter 16

"It's time for dinner for God's sake," Mom screams. "Wake up!"

I squint at the light and motion for her to turn them back off. She yanks the blanket off of me and opens the window.

"It's nighttime," she says. "Do you realize that? It's nighttime. How are you gonna sleep tonight? What am I saying? I'm worried about you *sleeping*? You're driving me crazy, Miryam."

I sit up and rub my forehead. Mom picks up a pile of my clothes from the floor, then piles them a few inches further.

"Messy, messy," she mutters, skimming through the news that Ari has called "50 times."

I don't say anything about Ari even though that's all I'm thinking about. I half-listen to her scold me about how I ruined the one day that Dad doesn't have work and wanted to spend time with me.

"Why didn't you just wake me up if I caused so much trouble?" I ask.

"I'm cursed with loving you too much. I actually felt bad waking you up. Your father almost came to wake you up three times and I stopped him. 'She must need the rest if she's sleeping,' I kept telling him. 'No one needs this much sleep,' he said. Then Cyrus kept saying to leave you alone. Why that boy defends you so much is beyond me."

I close my eyes and yawn.

"What?" Mom asks with a dirty look. "You're still tired?"

"Mom, I'm up. Can you just leave so I can get dressed?"

"Don't bother getting dressed. It's almost bedtime. Just put on your robe and come and eat something. And call Ari. And tell him to stop calling."

I put on my bathrobe, avoiding the mirror. I walk down the hall and smile shyly as I pass by the family room, where Dad is reading the paper with his legs stretched out on the coffee table. He smiles and shakes his head.

"Sorry," I say, poking my head through the door. "I couldn't fall asleep last night."

"You're a big girl," he says without looking up from the paper. "I can't exactly send you to bed at 9 p.m. But this isn't healthy, honey."

Why is he being so sweet? Jim never…

"I'm sorry," I say and walk quietly downstairs, afraid to draw any further attention to myself.

I cover my ears to drown out Mom yelling at Nader for eating watermelon without using a plate. He wipes his wet mouth with his sleeve and practically screams, "Good morning" when he sees me.

"Your food is on the dining table," Mom says to me. "Go! Go before it gets any colder!"

I pull out a chair and look around the table hoping to see something besides the plate of runny eggs that's making me gag. I push the plate away and take a sip of diet Coke. Mom walks in with some bread and the telephone.

"Here," she says, handing me the phone. "Call Ari. But eat first."

"Mom, I can't eat this."

She sighs. "*Now* what's the matter?"

"I hate eggs. You know that."

She tilts her head back and groans. "I forgot. I completely forgot. All you kids and your picky eating habits. I can't keep it all straight."

"Eggs are the only thing I can't eat."

"Well we don't have anything else. Just force yourself to eat it."

"I can't. I'll just have some bread and cheese. I'm not that hungry anyway."

"You haven't eaten in 24 hours. Bread and cheese isn't food. You call that boy back and I'll go and see what I can fix you."

"It's OK, Mom. Really, I'm fine."

"Don't argue with me!" she snaps. "Honestly, I don't know how you kids live in America. I'm surprised you're not skin and bones. All of you."

She passes by Nader on her way back to the kitchen and yells, "And you! Enough watermelon! You're going to get diarrhea. I have to force one kid to eat and the other one to stop eating. Honestly, you're all driving me to the madhouse."

I smile at Nader when he sits down next to me.

"Bad girl," he says.

"Thanks for before Nader," I whisper.

He starts to say something, but stops when he sees Cyrus walking towards us.

"What?" I say when I notice Cyrus glaring at me.

"Are you OK?" he asks.

"I'm fine. Jeez, I slept a lot one day. Why is everyone treating me like a leper?"

"I heard you crying last night," he whispers.

"Me too," Nader says.

I take a sip of diet Coke and look down.

"Who were you talking to?" Cyrus asks.

"None of your business," I mumble.

"I'm trying to be nice here, Miryam," he says.

"Cyrus, please. Thanks for your concern, but this really doesn't *concern* you. I'm fine."

"Are you like in love or something?" Nader asks.

I blush and peer over at Cyrus. But he's just blowing on his tea.

"Just because I was crying you assume I'm in love?"

"No," Nader says. "Just because you were crying on the phone to someone at 2 in the morning I assume you're in love."

"If you must know, I was talking to Paige. I just miss her, that's all."

"Oh, so you're a *lesbian*!" Nader says.

"Nader," I say, rolling my eyes. "If you're concerned, you have no reason to be. And if you're trying to be a pest, go do it elsewhere."

"OK. But consider yourself warned. Next time, I'm listening at your door."

He gets up and walks away without pushing in his chair.

"Miryam..."

"Cyrus, please," I say. "Not you too. First Mom, then Nader, and now you. I'm drained. I feel like I've already had a full day."

I get up and walk lethargically up the stairs, as if each one is a mountain. I sit on my bed and catch my breath. I stare at the phone collecting sweat in my hand. I once read in *Cosmo* that the most attractive thing to a man is a woman who's in love with him.

Let's test out that crock of shit.

"Were you at a party last night?" Ari asks.

"Huh? We talked last night. What are you talking about?"

"I mean before you called me. Were you at a party?"

"No. Why?"

"Why were you drunk then?" he asks sternly.

I don't answer.

"You drank at home?" he asks. "By yourself?"

"Um, yeah. Just a little though."

"A little? You could hardly talk. You were OK at the beginning. I couldn't even tell at first, but it was pretty obvious at the end."

"I'm really sorry, Ari."

"About what? About being drunk or putting me in that position or what?"

"Everything, I guess. Are you mad?"

"I'm not mad," he says with a sigh. "I'm just, I don't know, worried. And a little shocked. I don't want to sound like an ass, but how much of what you were saying was because you were drunk? Do you even remember what you were saying?"

"I remember everything," I say quickly. "I'm just sorry it had to come out like that. And I'm not sure what you're so shocked about. I mean, I lost my virginity to you. Didn't that tip you off that I may I have feelings for you?"

He doesn't say anything...along the lines of feelings are one thing, sooo madly in love is another.

Mom walks in with a turkey sandwich and french fries. Suddenly, I feel famished and I mouth a "thank you" to her. She smiles. I want to drop the phone, hug my mommy and never let go.

"Hang up and eat!" she says.

"Who's that?" Ari asks.

"My mom. I gotta go."

"Oh Jesus. I've been trying to get a hold of you all day and now you have to go?"

Role reversal at its finest. But I'm not doing it to show him how I felt all those times I wanted to talk, but he couldn't. I'm simply exhausted and hungry. And I need some time to digest the words and ensuing embarrassment from last night's conversation.

"I'll talk to you later," I say.

He sighs exaggeratedly and hangs up.

Even though I'm starved, I have to force the food down with the help of diet Coke.

Mom beams when I walk into the kitchen holding my empty plate.

"That's my good girl," she says. "You like turkey? I'll make you a turkey sandwich every day."

No, that's not right. You're supposed to yell at me. You're supposed to call me a good-for-nothing lush. You're supposed to slap me.

I walk upstairs to the bathroom and turn on the shower. I sit on the toilet, bury my heavy head in my hands and sob silently in the thick fog.

Chapter 17

"But Ari's sick, Mom," I say. "I need to go and see him."

"Are you forgetting that you yourself told us that you want to go to your grandmother's grave today?" she asks. "And now you want to go to Ari's house? Your father is going to be home any minute now so he can take you to the cemetery."

I look down and bite my lip. I *had* forgotten. But Ari's leaving for Esfahan tomorrow and this is the only day he's alone at home so we can talk in private.

"Can't you call Dad and tell him I can't go today?" I ask. "It's too hot to go to the cemetery today anyway. We'll go when we get back from Shomal."

"You're the one who wanted to go," she says again.

"I know, but Ari's sick."

"So, what's that got to do with you?" she asks with a frown. "What are you, his mother?"

I follow her into the bathroom and watch her through the mirror.

"Besides, we don't need you catching a cold and staying in bed the rest of the time you're here," she says as she grabs a bottle of Windex from under the sink.

"No, he doesn't have a cold. It's a stomach bug or something."

"Do whatever you want," she says, throwing a dusty rag in the sink. "Honestly, why do I even bother? It's not like I have any control over what you do when you're in America. It's so stupid for me to think I actually have a say in your life just because you're here for a few weeks."

"Right," I say.

"Excuse me?" she says, glaring at me with raised eyebrows.

"Well, you're right," I say. "It feels weird to have to ask your permission about every little thing. I'm not used to it. I'm a grown woman with my own life in America."

"I wouldn't exactly say you're a grown woman," she says.

She means I'm still a virgin.

"Well, can I go or not?"

"I said do whatever you want. I give up."

"God, you're acting like I'm asking to go shoot heroin at a male strip joint," I say.

She shoots me a dirty look. "Where did you learn this sarcasm?"

"Why do you act like I'm such a horrible daughter?"

"Miryam, I'm not in the mood for this, OK? I said you can go. Now leave me alone. I have a lot of cleaning to do. I have to follow Roya around and do a second round of cleaning after she's done. She's too old for this, honestly. She has no energy."

She imitates Roya's dusting by donning a gloomy face and sweeping her hand lethargically on the door. I guess it's Roya's turn to be on the shit list. She's a bad, bad girl, too.

I follow Mom as she roams around cleaning the bedroom. When she pays me no attention, I walk out. Maybe I should bring up a plate of food and shove it down my throat in front of her. Honestly, she acts like I'm such a disappointment just because I'm lying to sneak out of the house to see the guy I slept with, then got drunk and confessed my love to.

Talk about believing your lies. When Ari opens the door, I'm about to say that he doesn't look sick. We awkwardly kiss cheeks before he leads the way to the living room. As if I was gonna go to his bedroom and he had to make sure I'd just sit on the living room sofa.

"You want something to drink? Water or something?"

As opposed to vodka?

"I'll take a diet Coke," I say.

"Diet Pepsi OK?"

"Yeah, whatever."

Jesus, I'm sitting here with my heart in my throat and he thinks I care whether I wash it down with Coke or Pepsi.

I watch him go into the kitchen and take note of how he's dressed. He's wearing dark-blue sweatpants, a white T-shirt and white socks. It's as if he made a point of letting me know I'm not important enough for him to look good for.

Must be nice to be a guy. It took me an hour to decide what to wear so I'd look good, but not too good. I finally settled for jeans and a red tank top. Red as in power and boldness, not passion and bloodshed. You know, because he's really going to sit there and analyze the symbolism of my tank top.

I pour the diet Pepsi into the glass and watch the foam rise, then settle.

"OK, Miryam," he says. He sits down with a sigh. "Let's not beat around the bush. Let's just be honest and get this over with."

"I don't know what you want to get over with, but I don't think I, for one, can be any more honest if I tried."

"You mean if you drank any more."

He laughs and pats me on the knee. Well, at least he's in a good mood.

"Is this going to be a habit for you?" he asks.

"No, of course not."

"You're acting like Cyrus. I don't need to worry about *two* of you, you know."

"You certainly don't need to worry about *me*," I say. "You're not my keeper. Or my babysitter. You did enough watching over me per my parents' order when you lived with us."

He shakes his head. "I see you've stopped twisting my words around and aren't the least bit hung up on the conversation we had in L.A. that I'll regret till my dying day."

He moves farther away from me on the sofa and I hate myself for ruining his good mood and acting like a bitch. I take his hand.

"Sorry," I say. "I…I don't know why I said that. I know what you meant about worrying about me. I know it's because you care. Sorry."

He sighs. "I more than just care about you. I love you more than anything else in this world."

"I know."

"Do you?" he asks.

"Yes. I really do."

"Good," he says. "Because I do."

I well up with tears.

"But…" he says. "But I…I just…"

"But you love me as a friend and you don't wanna jeopardize our friendship," I say.

"Well, I don't. How can you not understand that? How can you not see that a friendship like ours happens once in a lifetime? How can I risk losing the most important person in the world to me? I don't want to lose anymore people that I love."

"But why do you just assume you would lose me if we get into a relationship?"

"I don't just assume it," he says with obvious frustration. "But if there's even a slight possibility, I just can't…I can't risk it."

I take a huge sip of my drink to help swallow the lump in my throat. And if he sees my hand shaking as I hold the glass, he can just assume it's delirium tremens from alcohol withdrawal.

"I just don't know what to do," he says with a sigh.

I wait for him to continue, but he just stares into space. I look down and even I get surprised when my eyes can no longer keep the tears trapped in and they fall uncontrollably down my cheeks. The more I try to stop them, the more stubbornly they roll down.

"Don't be like that, Miryam," he says with a frustrated sigh. "We're having a mature conversation here."

"No we're not," I wail. "We're going back and forth and getting nowhere. I know you think it was just because I was drunk, but it was still hard for me, Ari. I bared my soul to you and you can't even decide what you want to do."

He takes my hand and squeezes it.

"You're going to Shomal and I'm going to Esfehan tomorrow. Let's just both take this time to clear our heads and we'll talk when we get back, OK?"

"There's nothing for me to think about," I say, pulling my hand away from his. "I don't even know why you dragged me all over here to talk in person when you're not saying anything you didn't already say over the phone. I can't believe I didn't go to my grandmother's gravesite today to come and talk to you in person when you're just rehashing everything you already said. It's obvious that the ball is in your court. So you do your thinking and I'll just wait for your *responsible* decision."

Chapter 18

I sleep through most of the five-hour drive to Shomal. I wake up about half an hour before we arrive and squint through the sun's blare. My family is outside posing for pictures. I clutch my stomach and wonder where I can pee. All I see are mountains and an empty stretch of road.

I slowly open the door on my side of the car and squat down. Just when I'm feeling relaxed and enjoying the gush of flowing pee, a car filled with boys zooms by and pushes the fumes from the exhaust in my face. One of the boys sticks his head out the window and looks right at me.

"Whore!" he yells as the other boys roar with laughter.

"Miryam, is that you?" Dad asks. "Come over here and get in the pictures."

Midnight at the Caspian Sea. But it's too dark for me to see it. All I see are the dim lights below the veranda, seemingly too many for this hour.

Everyone is asleep now and I'm alone in this cozy living room, with the only light coming from the dying fireplace.

I walk slowly around the villa, each step jolting me back in time. The floors creak, complaining that they don't remember me being so heavy; the walls have cracked, heartbroken from years of loneliness; and the doors whine when opened, disturbed from their decade-long sleep.

I smile at the caricature-like paintings hanging on the aged walls. My favorite old man is still mooning the stuffy old lady. He's still bending down after all these years, exposed even through the many winter rains and humid summers that have passed. And though no one was here to laugh at his gesture, he dutifully stood in this position, waiting for someone to pass by and chuckle.

My feet trace the cracks in the tiles on the veranda until they find the spot where Ari and I had stood arm in arm posing for the pictures I saw in Soraya's album. I wish he were here, if only so we could recapture the photo with our grown-up bodies.

I walk through the trail of bushes until I reach the gardener's shack. I peek in the window and see his little girl sleeping on the floor, clutching a raggedy blanket too short to cover her dirty bare feet.

When I had stepped out of the car, she had smiled shyly at me, the "lady" arriving on her land for only two days. She bowed with respect as she eyed my attire. Look at everyone tending to her, look at her camcorder, her jeans. Look at her, period.

She'll never know that as she dreams of my designer sneakers, I'll stay awake, envying the simplicity of her life, thinking of her plain white scarf and her little bare feet.

Chapter 19

The next day, Yasmine, Kassra, Leila and Ali arrive at our villa around noon. They climb out fanning themselves with their hands. The girls quickly strip out of their uniforms before following me inside.

When Yasmine starts unpacking, I stare back and forth between her and the bikini she takes out.

"You're planning on wearing that here?" I ask.

"Yeah," she says matter of factly as she takes the tags off the bottoms. "Waterskiing."

"Here?" I ask. "Are you out of your mind?"

"Oh, here we go again," she says. "Would you relax, Miryam? Honestly, what have they been feeding your mind about this place in the States? It's not that bad."

"Yeah, but waterskiing for crying out loud?" I say.

"It's cool," she says. "We've got Agha Reza."

"What in God's name is an Agha Reza?" I ask.

"He's our boat guy. We called him from Ali's car phone. He's probably waiting for us already. He takes us all the way to the middle of the sea in his boat and we strip down to our bathing suits and waterski. He's cool."

Yasmine and Leila don their bikinis, then pull black chadors over them. When they walk out, Mom laughs hysterically and insists on taking a picture of their getup. They wrap their chadors tightly around their heads and stretch their bare legs out the front and give the camera sexy glares.

"Khomeini would roll in his grave if he saw this one," Mom says.

But her gaiety vanishes when I tell her about "their Agha Reza" and the waterskiing. She "tsk tsks" me and says that I can ride on the boat with them, but I can't waterski in my bathing suit.

"Please, Miryam," she says. "These girls are pros when it comes to doing this kind of stuff in Iran. You're not like them, so just play it safe so we can get you back to America in one piece."

I was hoping she'd say that. Because speaking of one piece, I wouldn't be caught dead wearing even a one-piece in front of Kassra and Ali. I have five pounds of stomach fat and 20 pounds of body hair to shed.

I throw a long coat over my khaki capri pants and green tank top. Nader stays back because he gets seasick in small boats. But Cyrus pulls on a pair of shorts and follows us to the shore. We climb into Agha Reza's old, beat-up little boat.

"The sea is smooth today my friends," he says. "You'll have a great run."

The balding, bearded Agha Reza starts the engine. We pick up speed across the deserted sea as the boat slaps the waves and the afternoon sun glares on us. I close my eyes and feel the warmth and cool overlap onto my body as I pretend Ari is sitting next to me. Agha Reza does some tricks with the boat as if doing aerobatics in a plane. The boat jumps high, turns fast and dives into the sea with its tip. I pretend that my screams, like everyone else's, are from sheer pleasure instead of fear.

When we get three feet to the left of bumble-fuck, Agha Reza stops the engine and Kassra jumps in the water. He skis for 15 minutes straight. As in, nonstop. His skiing actually has a few twists and turns to it.

I cup my hands around the cigarette I'm trying to light and listen to the girls cheer Kassra on. Suddenly, I feel a pang of envy. I don't even know how to waterski, let alone have my own "Agha Reza" at my beck and call. These people just pick up and go to Shomal, waterski in the summer, snow ski in Shemshak in the winter, spend their nights at party after party with hundreds of friends and never worry about money. As a vacation from their vacation-like lives, they hop over to Europe, buy the most fashionable clothes and come back to show them off at another round of parties. They change guys probably more often than they do their underwear.

What do I do? I'm an unpaid housewife and mother without a husband or children and I'm still struggling to find a job that pays $8 an hour. And every once in a while, I join the only two friends I have at a club, where we pay $800 for a few drinks, get drunk, then I come home and cry because the one guy I love thinks being with me is a cardinal sin.

Oh, but I'm so blessed because I live in Los Angeles. That magical land whose very name hints at a haven hovered by angels.

Kassra climbs back onto the boat and shakes his head like a wet dog. Yasmine jumps in and shrieks from the cold water. The guys imitate her girlish squeals and splash water her way. She finally stands up on the skis without falling and I watch her with a smile.

"Hey Kassra," I say. "Can I give it a try? I mean, even though I'm not wearing a bathing suit?"

"Sure. Just take off your coat and you should be light enough."

Just two minutes into Yasmine's skiing, Agha Reza screams at her to duck under the water.

"*Boro zireh ab*!" he yells before he turns to me and Leila. "*Shoma do ta ham beparid too ab!*"

"What's he talking about?" I ask Leila.

He throws the guys their shirts and motions for me to hurry up and jump in the water.

"Holy shit!" Kassra screams.

"What's going on?" Cyrus asks.

"Komiteh!" Leila says, panicking.

I squint at a small boat in the distance speeding towards us.

"How do you know that's a Komiteh?" I ask.

"Just trust us!" Ali says. "Get into the water! Now!"

"I can't hold my breath under the water!" I scream.

"Just do it!" he yells.

Cyrus and I look at each other. He takes my hand and tells me to relax.

Kassra looks at us and screams, "This is no time for mushiness. Get the fuck off the boat!"

Leila and I button our coats and jump into the freezing sea and swim under the boat. Our coats float above the water like failed parachutes. After about 10 seconds, she pokes me and we come up for air.

She whispers, "Help me hold the boat up a little so we can breathe."

We push up as hard as we can, but it's too heavy. We swim towards the boat's tip and bring only our lips above water. Agha Reza sees our heads bob up and whispers for us to get back under.

I duck back in and hear the roar of a boat engine drawing closer. I come up for a breath and hear one of the Komiteh guys yell, "You think we're stupid? Get them out of the water!"

I actually feel relieved. I'm going to die, but at least it won't be by drowning.

Leila and I climb onto the boat just as one of the men yanks Yasmine's arm.

"Get out of there, you whore!" he yells.

"Don't talk to me like that!" she yells back.

"Shut up!" Kassra tells her in English.

"Who the fuck does this guy think he is?" she says in English.

"Someone who can kill you with his bare hands," Kassra says. "Now shut the fuck up!"

Leila starts crying as she watches Agha Reza step onto the Komiteh's boat and they yell for the rest of us to follow suit.

"*Zood bash, zood bash,*" one of them says, yelling at me to hurry as I grab my sandals.

He turns to Yasmine and says, "Next time you want to seem inconspicuous, you might want to wear something besides a red bikini, you little whore."

We speed towards shore without pausing for any boat tricks.

When the Komiteh ask where we live, the gang looks at Cyrus and me. I know they're thinking that if Mom and Dad and all the adults at our villa get involved, we might not be as severely punished. In other words, they don't have too much cash on them, but my parents do.

I look down. But Cyrus quickly says, "Miryam's Meadows."

My heart beats so fast that if it were to replace the boat's engine, we'd get to shore in about two seconds.

Our villa is well known in town because of its size, so the Komiteh head right for it without asking us for directions. As they park their boat in front of our villa, for the first time, I don't feel proud of "my" meadows.

We climb out and march into the villa with our heads bowed, the Komiteh following closely behind. Dad sees us and runs out looking terrified. The women quickly throw on anything that can pass as a scarf. My aunt grabs the tablecloth and throws it on her head.

"Go into your rooms and cover yourselves!" Dad yells. "Hurry!"

We run into the girls' room and shut the door.

"Shhh," I say to a wailing Leila. "I can't hear what's going on out there."

"Look at Miryam," Yasmine says to Leila. "You've been here all these years and this little Iran virgin is handling her first bust like a pro. You should be ashamed."

She yanks off her bikini top and struts out her boobs. "What do you suppose they'd do if I went out like this and told them I'm innocent?" she says with a chuckle.

I laugh. Leila glares at us.

"This isn't funny," she says, crying louder. "We're dead."

"Oh relax," Yasmine says.

"Relax? We were in our bikinis, on a boat with three men."

"Oh, worse comes to worse, they'll make us marry the guys," Yasmine says. "Cyrus is blood-related to Miryam, so no problem there. So that leaves Kassra and Ali. Which one do you want, Leila? Kassra or Ali? Or how about Agha Reza?" She laughs. "Yeah, Miryam will get Kassra, I'll get Ali and you can have Agha Reza."

An hour later, Dad walks in without knocking. Yasmine screams and rolls herself around the drapes.

Dad ignores her. He plops down on the bed and sighs exaggeratedly.

"You're lucky they accepted the bribe," he says. "But next time they catch any of you, you're going straight to jail."

"Oh, Mr. Mirashti!" Leila yelps and throws her arms around him.

Dad pats her head like a dog's and smiles.

"Don't worry about it, Leila joon. I just don't know what you were all thinking." He looks at me. "I can't believe your mother let you guys do this. She knows the Komiteh in Shomal are so much stricter than the ones in Tehran. They don't mess around."

"Sorry Dad," I say with a smile that I'm hoping tells him how proud I am of him. Bailing his little girl's ass out of jail. Proud father-daughter moment.

He shakes his head and sighs again.

"Bastards," he says as he gets up and walks towards the door. "I feel so sorry for you young people. What are you supposed to do for fun?"

He closes the door behind him. I smile at the girls with pity.

Leila starts to say something, but then notices that Yasmine is still draped in the curtains, chewing on the fabric.

"Would you put some damn clothes on?"

Chapter 20

"Why don't we all go for a long walk instead," Kassra says when I whisper if any of them will join me for an after-dinner smoke. "It's such a nice night."

"Good idea," Yasmine says and grabs her purse.

"Don't bother with that," I whisper. "I have a pack in my pocket. If my mom sees your purse, she'll get suspicious."

"I need my purse."

She looks at Leila and they giggle.

"Something smells fishy," I say with a frown.

"Is not fish," Mom says in English as she passes by on her way to the kitchen. "Is shrimp for tomorrow lunch."

Ten minutes and two cigarettes into our stroll, Kassra jumps over a shrub and squats down on a patch of grass. The rest of us follow suit.

"Why are we sitting here?" I ask.

Yasmine unzips her fake Fendi purse and takes out a small plastic bag.

"Hello?" I say.

"Anyone bring anything to cut with?" Ali asks.

"Shit, no," Yasmine says as she empties some white powder onto a hand-held mirror.

"I have my keys on me," Kassra says. "They won't be perfect lines, but it'll do."

I realize my mouth is open as I peer at the mirror from the corner of my eye.

Yasmine grabs Kassra's keys and cuts a line. She sticks a rolled-up 1000-toman note up her right nostril and snorts. She rubs her nose and hands the mirror to Leila.

"Miryam?" Leila asks.

I shake my head.

I watch her stick the rolled-up bill into her nose. If only Khomeini could see them using the 1000-toman note with his face on it to snort drugs. They've made him roll in his grave twice today. I hug my knees and rock myself to the rhythm of the cool breeze.

"Do you guys do this a lot?" I ask.

"Of course not," Leila says. "We're not druggies. Not like some kids. You wouldn't believe how popular coke has become in our crowd. It's scary."

"Really?" I ask.

"What else are we gonna do, right?" Yasmine says after she snorts. "I mean how much can a person drink?"

I watch her rub her nose. I realize that this is the first time I've ever seen cocaine. And in Iran no less.

You never think about the "normal," random things going on around the world. You never imagine an orgy taking place in Timbuktu, or that a bunch of Iranian kids are snorting cocaine in the middle of Shomal. I want to take a picture of them, show it to random people on the streets of Los Angeles and say, "See how normal we are? We do coke, too. We have drug problems, too."

"You guys, are you sure you should be doing this?" I ask.

"Probably not," Leila says, smiling. "But it's a little too dark to play hide and seek."

"No," I say. "I mean, after what happened today. You guys have a lot of nerve."

"No sweat," Yasmine says. "We'll hear if your parents or someone comes around. They won't look for us; they'll be shit-faced on booze themselves. And we're in a private place, not in the middle of the sea."

Yeah, private place. My place. I go from scared to intrigued to angry. I know I'm not exactly clean-cut, but I do draw the line somewhere.

"Another line?" Ali asks Yasmine.

"Yeah, but let me cut. You don't cut clean."

I toss and turn in bed. I can't decide if I'm more angry at Leila and Yasmine for doing coke in my childhood retreat or scared that they do coke period. Wine is fine; coke is not.

I close my eyes and crawl into Ari's invisible arms. But it doesn't work. It hasn't worked in a long time, not since the night I felt his real arms around me.

Now, as I lie in the dark, hugging the emptiness, all the shadows of the night take on the shape of his face and create a tangible void inside me. My fear grows and I feel insecure and shaky, as if I've lost my emotional equilibrium.

Everything has changed. And I want the old days back. I want back the days I thought boys were icky, the days when drinking wine with Yasmine was a one-time thrill instead of a habitual necessity, when I could eat up the joys of childhood without feeling guilty that my parents' souls were fed with sorrow.

I want to go back to when being an adult meant getting to order a Big Mac instead of a Happy Meal.

Chapter 21

"Why don't we walk along the beach the rest of the way?" Mom says when we're halfway to the town center. "You always loved that when you were little."

We cross the street and Mom tightens her grip on my hand, not to avoid cars, but the donkeys, cows, chicken and roosters mingling along the road.

A street sign with a cow's picture warns drivers to watch for crossing bovine. A large brown cow walks slowly towards the sign and stands casually under it.

I laugh and take a picture of her. The cow stares at me, almost with a frown, as if asking, "What's so amusing about a cow waiting for a bus?"

"Paige is gonna die laughing when she sees this picture," I say.

Mom gives me a weak smile.

"Do you miss her?" she asks.

"Paige? Yeah. But it's no big deal. I'll see her soon. Why?"

She shrugs without meeting my curious eyes.

When we get to the beach, we take off our shoes, pull up our pants to our knees and stroll along the edge of the shore. Mom's old, but-still-soft hands caress my young ones. Our palms touch, the lines of our lives crossing paths.

The waves scream, soar, slap the sand, then recede softly back into the sea. Only the intermittent sound of seagulls lulls the roar of the waves. The sand is dark and smooth like an ink pad. We stamp our feet into it, leaving a trail of prints behind us. The sun is starting to set. The last rays of dusk dip into the sea. The seashells of all sizes scattered along the sand look like slices of fish ears, listening to all the secrets of the shore, then sharing them with the curious sea when the waves draw them back into the water.

I try to imagine that I'm wearing a flowery sundress, my head topped with a straw hat and ignore the sweat dripping inside my trench coat and along the corners of my scarf. Mom looks at me.

"Is the heat bothering you?" she asks.

I don't want to ruin the moment, so I just smile and shake my head.

Mom points out the remains of all the villas that have been swept under the sea. The water level of the Caspian Sea has fluctuated over the years, rising and swallowing the acres of land that used to lie before it. So many people's homes were swept under the sea. It's as if property owners in Iran just can't get a break. What the government didn't confiscate, nature stole.

"Miryam," Mom says, clearing her throat. "Have you enjoyed your stay in Iran so far?"

"Yes," I say. "I really have."

She smiles. "Would you ever consider moving back here?"

I frown and look up at her. "No. It's nice for a visit, but it's no place to live. For me, I mean."

"Why?" she asks softly.

"What do you mean why? As it is, I barely have a say in my own life. I don't need the government controlling me on top of everyone else."

I wait for a reaction from her, possibly a dirty look about my sarcasm, definitely sarcasm of her own. But she continues to stare down quietly. I can't read what's behind her silence, but I know there's something more to it than an end to our conversation.

Chapter 22

After the drive back from Shomal, I'm in dire need of a cigarette and some alone time. I take a quick shower, making sure to get out in time to call Ari before it gets too late. I'm sitting on my bed staring at the phone in my hand when Mom walks in without knocking.

"Are you out of the shower?" she asks.

I look around and above me exaggeratedly. "Apparently."

"Good," she says. "Your father wants to have a word with you."

I drop the phone on my bed and follow her into the family room. Dad is sitting on his armchair, staring down. Mom scans the hallway before closing the door and walking in. I watch her with a frown. We never close the family-room door. As in, Jim never vomits at home. But Mom avoids my eyes and eases onto the couch.

"Miryam," Dad says clearing his throat. "We want to talk to you before we talk to your brothers. And don't interrupt me until I finish please. You can have a chance to defend yourself when I'm through."

"Defend myself about what?" I ask.

"If you'll allow me please," he says, raising his eyebrows. "Miryam, I'm going to get right to the point. We've decided that you are not going back to America. None of you. You're going to live here with us."

I look at Mom. She nods without looking at me. My heart pounds louder with each passing second of silence. Because I realize they're serious.

"We know everything," Dad says.

He looks at me as if waiting for a response. I hesitate, then say, "What's…"

"I said don't interrupt me till I finish," he says.

I wait for him to continue, but he stares blankly ahead.

"Well," I say, trying to hide my annoyance. "Go on then."

"We know about Cyrus' drinking, about his arrest, about…" He sighs. "Everything. Do I have to spell it all out? Everything."

I swallow hard. "How? I mean…"

"Bee's mom called us. Before you came here. She told us everything. We know he's in therapy and in that AA thing for alcoholic people. And we know about you, too, Miryam. We know you got fired."

I look down, suddenly feeling dizzy and weak.

"So you tricked us into coming here and staying?"

"No!" Dad snaps. "Unlike you, we don't lie. This was a little vacation, just like I said it would be. I wanted to see everything with my own eyes. And I saw Cyrus drinking, I saw you drinking, and I decided just last week that the best option was to keep you all here so I can keep an eye on you."

"But I…I didn't do anything wrong. I'll get another job."

"And we know you smoke," Dad continues. "Both of you."

I blush. All these years I thought I had so cleverly fooled them. But I suppose when it comes to parents, children's trickery skills are like those of an amateur magician.

"You're making me stay here because I smoke?"

"Let me finish," Dad says. "We know you've had trouble being in charge since Ari moved out. It's not your fault. We should never have put you in that situation in the first place. But that's beside the point."

I'm so tempted to *make* "that situation" a point. But I stop myself and just raise my eyebrows, snickering.

"You haven't answered my question," I say.

"Why do you have to stay?" Dad says in a rhetorical tone. "Because you don't have a job there. We haven't been thrilled with your behavior in Iran so far. All you do is party. And because there is no way that Cyrus and Nader are going back, and no daughter of mine is going to live by herself in America while she's single. There's enough talk about this family as it is. Do you have *any* idea what it's like, how embarrassing it is, to get a phone call from Behnaz's mother saying *my* children are going down the wrong path? Her daughter has been dating since she was 14 and I hardly wanted you to be friends with her because of that. And now *her* mother tells me that *my* children are bad?"

His eyes squint into slits. Mom shakes her head disappointedly.

"So, like what?" I say. "I spent all these years in school so I could just end up back here and get married? And what about Cyrus? He hasn't even graduated."

"From what we hear, he was hardly going to school," Dad says

"Now that's not fair!" I yell. "How would Bee's mom even know that?"

"It's not important," Dad says. "He's staying here and that's final. He's coming to work for me starting next week. I don't require a college diploma. I'll teach him everything he needs to know. As for you, you didn't earn a college degree so you could get fired from a receptionist's position. And we can't afford to support you anymore. I have not been killing myself working over here, selling all my properties so you three can do whatever the hell you please over there. I did not, did *not,* take my children to America so they could pick up on immoral mentality. I took you there so you could study and become successful and upstanding citizens. And I'm not financially supporting you anymore!"

"I'm not asking you to! Just give me a chance to find another job. I've barely just gotten out of school."

Mom looks at Dad and shakes her head again.

"No, Miryam," Dad says without noticing her. "I'm sorry. Freedom comes with a price. And we can't afford to pay the price anymore."

"And he means that literally *and* metaphorically," Mom says, making sure I knew that *she* got the metaphor.

"But Dad, if you know Cyrus is in AA, don't you think he needs to go back so he can continue to get some help?"

"No. I don't. I think he needs to stay right here where we can keep an eye on him and make sure he doesn't humiliate this family any further."

Even Al-Anon would kick these parents out.

"OK fine. So Cyrus and I are trapped here. What about Nader? Why does he deserve this? What's going to happen to him here?"

"He'll go to school here just like any other kid his age. The education system in Iran is 10 times better than America's anyway."

"Oh really? Is that why you ran us out of this place like mad in the first place?"

"That was a mistake. We panicked. And we're not going to make the same mistake twice."

Mom nods like a puppet at the hands of an epileptic.

"He barely knows how to speak Farsi," I say. "How can he go to the ninth grade in an Iranian school?"

"We've already enrolled him in a special school that has a program for kids just like him. You don't worry about Nader. We're his parents."

"Is that so?" I yell.

Dad rubs his temples and shifts in his seat, looking powerful and in control.

"Yes, it is. And watch your tone, young lady."

"Dad, please. You're being so unfair."

"I am not being unfair. You have been unfair. By lying to us all these years. Telling us things were fine when they weren't. I don't trust you anymore. And this is all you have to say for yourself? That I'm being unfair? You should be apologizing. You should be thanking me for giving you a chance to redeem yourself. You have failed me and you're saying *I'm* being unfair?" He raises his voice another octave. "You're an ingrate and a liar!"

I stare into his narrowed eyes in shock. I look down and whisper, "I was just trying to protect you. I was doing the best I could."

"We didn't need you to protect us. We needed the truth. But you don't have to worry about any of that anymore."

"And God knows what you kids have been eating there all these years," Mom says, shaking her head sadly.

Dad and I stare at her with identical frowns.

"Niloofar, don't interrupt me please," Dad says.

"This is so unfair!" I scream. "This has nothing to do with smoking or lying. You're making me stay here just because I'm a girl! Because I won't have my brothers living with me and people might talk. But I don't need to save face in front of anyone! I'm an adult! And I don't care what people think!"

"You are an immature adult, which is worse than being a child. You were actually a very mature child, but you've turned into an immature adult. And even if you don't care what people think, you should care what *I* think. I am your father and until you get married, you live by *my* rules! Is that clear?"

I cup my face in my hands and start sobbing.

"I wish I had never taken you to America in the first place," he says with a sigh.

"I wish you hadn't either!" I scream with tears rolling down my face. "Then I wouldn't have learned that I have a say in my own life and that I don't have to get the short end of the stick just because I'm a girl." I shake my head. "Life, liberty and the pursuit of happiness. No, not for me, not for a girl! An Iranian girl, no less. No, God forbid! So I need to stay in this stupid country, where the motto is death, bondage and...the avoidance of misery. Ignorance is bliss. Well, I wish I had stayed ignorant. But I'm not ignorant. I know that you're taking my rights away!"

Dad chuckles. "Your *rights*? To do what? Make a mockery of this family? Ruin yourself? That's not a right! And stop throwing all these garbage women's rights stuff in my face. I was the first person to tell you to get an education and make something of yourself. But I am not having you throw your life away in the name of women's rights."

Mom takes my hand and caresses it. She wipes my tears and gives me a weak, worried smile. I look away.

"And we haven't spoken to your brothers yet," Dad says. "So don't go out of this room screaming and acting like a child. Let us talk to them. We especially need to talk to Cyrus privately, without you telling him what's going on beforehand. So please be mature and let us help your brother without you brainwashing him."

"Do whatever the hell you have to! They're both your problem now!"

I get up and stomp to the door.

"Where are you going?" Dad yells after me. "I'm not finished talking to you!"

"Yes you are!" I scream, storming out and slamming the door behind me.

Chapter 23

It's dark outside now. I can barely see the falling snow. I watched it for hours until dusk took over, when the specks of snow swimming across the night's landscape looked like a kaleidoscope of white dots twirling to the black of closed eyes.

The weather in Tehran is exactly how I feel: cold, bitterly cold, to the point of numbness. When the clouds gathered and blackened the blue sky, rain was overdue. The tears had frozen and fell to the ground as snow with no end in sight, covering everything in white. Not cleansing, but hiding all the dirt under a façade of purity and innocence.

My room is as spotless and fresh looking as the snow outside. Whenever my mind is in shambles, I organize, rearrange, clean and dust to the last invisible angle. And for a while, I feel like all is well with the world. But soon enough, I'll forget to put my mascara exactly eight inches away from my lipstick on the table, chaos will once again ensue, and I'll remember that I have real problems to deal with. One of these days, or years, I'll realize that clean house means going inside. Start with the master bedroom, the mind, and go down from there. Throw out the empty bottles, vacuum the bitter memories and dust the sleeping dreams.

I tiptoe across the room and bring out the skeletons in my closet. I fish for a full pack of cigarettes under my green sweater. I fill the glass with vodka before putting the flask back in the sleeve of my UCLA sweatshirt.

Just as I finish half my drink and contemplate filling it up, I hear it. The whistle. For the past four months, a fine young lad donning torn slippers, baggy black pants and the same white T-shirt with armpit stains whistles for me or throws rocks at my window. I talked to him once and asked what he wanted. He didn't beat around the bush. A kiss, he said. This isn't Romeo and Juliet, I said. Please, he said. Get lost, I said. But he finds his way back almost every night and I've learned to ignore him. I used to be scared that my parents would hear him. But that was way back when his crush on me was the only thing I had to hide from them.

I crouch on the floor and draw the drapes.

"Lady, lady, come down," he says in a loud whisper.

One time, I heard him moaning and when I peeked at him through a crack in the drapes, I saw that he was masturbating next to a shrub. At least he wasn't beating it around my bush. Where's the Komiteh when you need them?

The cold freezes the guy's whistles in mid-air and makes him give up sooner than usual. I watch as he hugs himself and walks away. I can't believe I actually feel a little sorry for him.

I'm about to close the window when I see the street sweeper shoveling the last of the snow off the road. He looks up and waves at me cheerfully as if he were waiting to see me before going home. I wave back with a smile.

We've never spoken. But every night, we make each other feel less lonely as he shovels snow or rakes dead leaves and I watch him while smoking another cigarette in my chain.

Some nights after he leaves and there's no one left to keep me company, I draw the drapes and imagine Ari slipping through my window like a ghost disguised in the mist of my smoke. Those are on the nights I sip homemade wine like a lady instead of chugging vodka like a Russian czar. And if I've actually shaved my legs, I sit on the bed, with my bare legs crossed, talking, flirting and giggling with him.

Oh yes, Ari, I'm so happy here. I live like a princess. The masseuse and manicurist tend to me every week. I eat caviar for breakfast. I even went skiing last week. Oh, and you've got competition. A prince living beneath my window is just waiting for my hair to grow long enough so he can use it to climb up to my room.

I leave out the part about not having anyone to show my painted hands and feet to. Or that the masseuse squeezes out my tears. And that I usually puke out the caviar after it mixes with the previous night's vodka. Or that I only got to ski for 10 minutes because there was a power outage that had everyone dangling on the chair lift for two hours. And that even if my hair does grow long enough, it's usually so oily that if the perverted pauper grabbed it, the grease would just make him slide right back down before he could rescue me from my dungeon.

I inevitably get too drunk at some point, even on wine, and that's when I stop my lady-like pretense and cry like a madwoman.

It's been over a year since Ari left. I didn't go to the airport to see him off. I sat home eating myself up instead, wishing I were on that plane heading to freedom, miserable that he wasn't actually a part of our family and under my parents' scrutiny. He was, after all, as much to blame for Cyrus as I was.

But my parents failed to parole me even when I pleaded my case extra obnoxiously on the days before Ari's flight.

The only way I've kept my sanity so far is by pretending Ari and I never spoke after he got back from Esfehan.

"This is all going to sound so stupid now," he said after I told him about the conversation with my parents and their ensuing decision to make us all live here. "But I did a lot of thinking in Esfehan. I realized that I felt so guilty about breaking your parents' trust that I wanted to pretend nothing had changed after we had sex. I was so wrapped up in my own guilt and confusion that I wasn't thinking about how what we did affected you. Or about how I felt about you. All I felt was guilt. But when I looked past that guilt, I realized that...that on some level, I've always loved you as more than just a friend. But I never acted on it because of, well, the guilt. And now that we've...we've..."

"Had sex," I said.

He chuckled nervously. "Now that we've had sex, we can't pretend it didn't happen."

"I never pretended it didn't happen," I said.

"I know," he said. "I...I can't pretend it didn't happen. Or that it didn't mean anything. I'm sorry I acted like you were just some random girl afterwards. And I'm sorry I was such a coward about everything. I was scared...about everything. But the scariest thing of all is the thought of losing you."

The lump in my throat made it impossible for me to talk and tell him he'd never lose me. I fought back tears as I listened to his chocked-up voice.

"I can't imagine my life without you, Miryam. I love you. And I want to be with you."

I felt a joy unlike any emotion I had ever felt before. I wanted to get up, twirl around the room in glee, then drop back down and raise my hands to the heavens. But then I remembered. And I banged my fists on the ground, cursed the heavens for the cruel joke, spit on reality for taking my dream away even as it finally rested in my hands.

"Would you have moved back in?" I asked. "I mean, if I were coming back."

"No," he said. "That wouldn't have been right. Not with the boys in the house. I would've lived at my place, but we'd be together. I don't know. I didn't think of the details. I figured we'd take it as it came. I thought we'd figure it all out together. But now..."

But now slapped me hard across the face. Now was the cruelest moment of my life. Now was worse than yesterday had ever been, worse than tomorrow could ever be.

Chapter 24

For the first two weeks, Cyrus went to work with Dad wearing a suit and a frown. He beautifully acted the part of the punished child forced to grow up too fast. But after those initial weeks, it was obvious that he actually liked working. Dad had found the button with which to un-mute Cyrus, whose mouth became a machine gun shooting words instead of bullets. He quickly picked up and talked incessantly in architectural lingo. He and Dad began boring the hell out of the rest of us talking about work during dinner. Mom, of course, beamed in between yawns.

It's obvious that Cyrus looks up to Dad and finally feels like part of the family we never were. He's like an orphan who was finally placed in a good foster home after years of neglect. I realize how much he needs Mom and Dad. How much he's always needed them. More than Nader or I ever did. He's regressed in age, acting not like a 19-year-old man, but like the 11-year-old kid he was when my parents first moved back to Iran. My parents, in turn, are proud of their model son.

And he's in love. Her name is Mitra. He picked her out of the seemingly hundreds of girls who were after him. The fact that he grew up in the States made his popularity soar like the price of gas in America after the Iranian Revolution. And Cyrus, who had always been ashamed to admit where he was from when he lived in the States, now lives to be asked where he's from so he can say, "America." The question he used to dread answering because it proved he didn't belong is now the very question that makes him feel accepted, even superior.

The only thing that matters in our social circle is that we grew up in America. We would be accepted even if we were bank robbers back there. In America, people always ask, "What do you do?" Here, no one cares what you do or even if you do anything. The only question they ask is, "Where did you grow up?"

And if your answer is anything other than "Iran," you're held in high regard. This is a place where it's easy for losers to garner superficial respect.

My parents love Mitra. She's the opposite of me. She's a perky, sweet little thing. She has changed Cyrus' life around completely. He's become hardworking, responsible, polite and cheerful. He spends all his free time at Mitra's, hasn't touched alcohol in months and never goes out partying.

Neither do I. But for different reasons. When I found out that doing coke is a regular pastime for most of the kids, including Leila and Yasmine, it grew increasingly difficult to just look at my scared face in the powdery mirror and pass it along without using my nose as a vacuum cleaner. But I even managed that for longer than I thought I could. It's when "e-parties" became popular that I became scarce. Not that I couldn't just as easily refuse to partake in ecstasy and dwell instead in my familiar misery, but Yasmine was concerned enough to tell me that our "friends" had no qualms about slipping the stuff in drinks. They considered it a favor. And God forbid I refuse a drink.

And when the young, hip Tehran crowd I knew started dropping acid, I dropped out of the party scene altogether. I have enough acid of my own lurking in what's left of my stomach, thank you very much.

I don't miss the parties. What's the point of going through the charade of getting dressed up and making small talk when you can just drink in your pajamas and have meaningful conversations with the walls?

And I don't miss my so-called friends either. Because now that I need comfort most, and my friends know it, the phone never rings. But the day after I threw "one of the best parties the city had ever seen," and 120 of my "friends" had a blast at my expense, the phone never stopped ringing.

Dad is happy that I'm not going out anymore. Aside from the fact that it wasn't appropriate behavior for a nice Iranian girl, he says, it was dangerous to risk the Komiteh busting any one of the parties I went to.

Little does he know that now, sitting in my room every night, I am in no less danger.

Because the most dangerous place in the world for me is inside my own head. But at least I'm their good little girl again. I stay home (day after day), sleep (when Mom lets me), eat (by force), read (when we're not having a power outage), and cry (when I'm awake). And I take an average of four showers a day: to pass the time, to wash off the grime from the smog that crawls through my window and onto my skin, and to get extra clean in case there's no hot water in the days to come.

I am always alone, awake, in the frightening quiet of the night. I look out the window, at the empty street. I imagine standing all by myself in the middle, staring over my shoulder for the sight of another person, the sound of a single footstep. For a sign telling me where I am, which direction to go. But all I see are the snow-capped tree branches on either side, intertwining above me, cradling me from the cold like a caring, covert cave.

I want to crawl under the covers and pull them over me tight, like I did as a little girl, thinking that monsters would leave me alone if they couldn't see even an inch of my flesh. I was willing to suffocate just to feel safe.

But what I fear now isn't something I'm hiding from; it's something that's hiding from me. Something I can never identify, explain or grasp. It's the same fear as when I'm walking down the streets, then suddenly feel like the whole world is looking at me, reading my insane thoughts, then pointing and laughing. And I want to crawl behind one of those giant trashcans on the street corners until the feeling of not belonging in this world of normal people disappears.

The house is so quiet, big and lonely. I feel like the world's keeper, the city's night watchman. They all sleep, oblivious to all there is to feel. I feel it all for them and carry the burden of what day people, walking under the blinding sun, will never see or feel. They will never feel the loneliness of the night and think, even for an instant, that this loneliness is very real. That if tomorrow, the sun doesn't come out and no one wakes up, this loneliness, this quiet, will be all there is to life.

People always say, "Things will look better in the morning." Of course they will. The sun's shine sugar coats everything. All the senses, real and raw, can only exist in the quiet and dark of night.

I feel what the old, unloved man feels. I hear the insomniac's blinks. I see what the alcoholic sees. I hear those voices, too. I'm scared, too.

Chapter 25

In the morning, I'm about to close my window when I see Nader standing in the street waiting for his school bus. He's kicking rocks with his beat-up sneakers.

I don't call out to him. I sit on the windowsill and watch him, wondering what's going through his mind. He looks lonely on the deserted street, hugging himself from the chill of the late-November wind. I imagine him in class, sitting on the hard wooden chair, his classmates laughing at his American accent instead of his jokes.

The sun is low in the sky, barely creeping from behind the mountain tips. The street looks different than it does at night. It looks cleaner, newer, almost innocent. The silence of morning is deafening to ears accustomed only to the sounds of night.

Maybe I've always been a night owl because the cool morning air still reminds me of my early school days, when sun and haze would fight for the sky's attention, when the streets were so quiet you could hear children's sorrows, when I would hug Mom extra tightly as we said goodbye.

Or maybe I never trust the sun's wink at dusk, when it promises me that it will rise again tomorrow, that I, too, will wake up from the echo of death and see that the world did not end at sunset.

The school bus honks at a stray cat and jolts me. I watch Nader climb onto the blue bus bustling with boys. The doors close behind him. I close my window, draw the curtains and fall asleep knowing everyone is awake for the day.

Chapter 26

I was born an addict.

God stamped my forehead with the same warning label slapped on the bottle of tranquilizers Bee gave me: May be addictive.

As early as the third grade, I managed to turn even oxygen into a drug. I showed all the girls in my class that they could get a head rush by inhaling deeply ten times in a row.

From then on, I went as far as I could with substances as long as I stayed in the realm of the legal. Because illegal drugs, real drugs, scared me. As long as it was legal, sold in stores, given to me by doctors, it wasn't really a drug.

Until two years ago, thoughts of Ari had been my real drug. Like a mad search for heroin's high, I chased the dragon until it landed back in my arms and blew its hot breath into my mouth. Unlike a heroin addict, I succeeded in recapturing the perfection of the first time. But just when I thought I had the dragon by the tail, it vanished like a magic trick and left me in a puff of smoke.

So I clutch the bottle like a life raft. I hold onto it hoping it will help me drift across the ocean and back into his arms. Or at least help me survive.

In this city, in this family, in this body, all I can do is survive. Those of us who have been burned know that people will weigh you down until you sink, but bottles will help you stay afloat.

It's a simple act of defiance, a way to show power where there is none. It's the only way I can prove my independence. No one can yank the bottle from my hand every night because no one knows it's there. It's the one area of my life where I can still pretend to have control, even as I stumble into a coma at dawn. I'm making a statement, even if I'm slurring all my unspoken words.

But tomorrow, come noon, they'll once again gather around the lunch table and shake their heads as to how much I sleep. Then I'll wake up, she'll stuff some food down my throat, and I'll slam another door.

I'll wait until they slam the last of the doors before I reach into my closet and grab my life raft.

Chapter 27

"You are a miserable, good-for-nothing mess," Mom said to me yesterday. "And you expect us to let you go back to America? What for? So you can waste our money and waste your life away? You have nothing to show for your life and you're not doing anything to change it. What's wrong with you? What are you so depressed about? People in this country are living in poverty. You have a roof over your head, you're with your family, in your country, and all you can do is whine and cry and feel sorry for yourself. Come with me to one of the orphanages or the women's shelters I visit and see what real problems are, what real pain is. So what if you're not in your precious America anymore? We can't let you live alone over there. People will talk. And you're here for your brother's sake. Can't you make some sacrifices for your family for once instead of just thinking about yourself? You lied to us all these years and turned your brother into a mess because of it. So now that he's finally in decent shape, you can't just be happy and let us be a normal family?"

I chuckle. At the audacity of the word "normal family" coming out of her mouth.

And yesterday was exactly like the day before. Just like today was exactly like yesterday. And this second was exactly like the second before it.

This second was exactly like the second before it.

Each day is different only in that Mom is just a little more sarcastic, her age-old lecture is slightly shorter, and I smoke a few more cigarettes.

She doesn't understand that even if I do nothing productive, I am a time bomb of thought, feeling and depth. I'm not like others. I never have been. Productive people are so busy with hectic routines hailed commendable in a workaholic world that they don't have time to realize their souls are dying. My soul, however, is not dying. I am killing it. It is a personal, active act. Dying is passive, suicide active.

And I am an activist.

Chapter 28

After four glasses of vodka last night, I actually did figure out the meaning of life. I knew I would forget it if I didn't write it down immediately. I wobbled to Dad's computer in the den and typed with mad inspiration. I wrote without pause, my eyes barely focused on the screen as I pounded on the keys. The words looked jumbled in my drunken haze, but I knew my brilliance was coming through clearly.

I woke up today and ran to the computer to read the secret I would soon share with the world. I stared at my words:

"[rtdpms; js[[omrdd od yjr [pomy pg ;ogr/ og rsvj [rtdpm od js[[u. yjrm yjru eo;; fp hppf smf hppfmrdd od ejsy ,slrd yjr ept;f hp tpimf/ yjrtr/ yjrtrd D ,ptr niy o vsm ;lakdj fu oiau iukadj ;j ;aljuiea kmerj;oij ‘ dr'tr slll honns fir snyesy dmf yjsy[d trs;;u yjr pm;u yjomh er s;}}

It really was brilliant. I swear. And I could've proven it, if only I had put my hands in the correct position on the keyboard.

Chapter 29

Some people are gluttons. And gluttony is one of the seven deadly sins. Get a taste of pleasure and instincts surpass their intended simplicity. In some people, a taste of love, wine, food, excitement, joy – just one taste – and chaos ensues.

Or is it just me?

Doesn't everybody pop four tranquilizers and a sleeping pill after having three drinks for no reason whatsoever?

It all started last night with a sip of wine. Soon, my body turned into a toxic waste dump. As if I need any help from all this poison to rot. Merely waking up these days invisibly rots my insides just as time inevitably ages the visible façade that is my outer shell.

I'm turning into such a pessimist. That can't be good for anyone.

I try to be cheerful, but when someone figuratively slaps me every time I smile, you see my stoned face, my drugged body at midnight. Any drug that'll make me go into a 10-hour coma, so I won't even dream, will do. Then I wake up and face another day in Tehran: smile, slap, smile, slap, slap, slap, slam, sedatives, stone, sleep.

The sky is black, carpeting everything below it in dirt. The city's colorful landscape is painted over by pollution, potholes filled with putrid water, chipped graffiti-plagued walls. All the cars are black – the white ones, the red ones, the green ones – they're all black, muddy and dusty. The sun's rays spin the specks of dirt into a vertigo of blackness. Black sky, black chadors, clothes, beards, cars, walls, eyes.

People on the streets all look alike. Everyone blends in, not by the uniforms on their bodies, but by the sadness on their faces, the distant look in their eyes. Their mouths are expressionless, almost forbidden from smiling, laughing and especially questioning. Their souls wear clothes in dire need of airing, dusting, changing.

What I first thought was paradise is actually the land of paradox.

Sorrow is celebrated, celebrations shunned. The poor swallow pride, the decadently wealthy complain about the price of luxury. People have learned to accept the unacceptable and abide by laws that at their very core are unjust. Narrow-mindedness is widely accepted, individuality collectively denied. Under this government, the blind swear by the beauty of madness, the vigilant play deaf to the madness of the blind.

It's a religious government under which even the truly pious are terrorized in the name of God. Women are told they are weak, men that they are the controllers. But it is women who have to take control where men have none: It is women who must cover their bodies so as not to tempt men's weaknesses.

The city sucks you in, makes you believe it's a new and exciting world at first. Then, quite simply, you drown. And you scream with all your might for someone to grab your hand and pull you out. But your hand just blends in the darkness with all the rest. The city streets are home to the ailing, for whom suffering is a way of life.

Nestled in one of these streets is home itself. A home that's never sweet, but bitter as regret. In this home live a hysterical mother, a miserable father and children who learned everything from them.

Whether on the streets or at home, I am doomed. My sole sanctuary is within the confinements of my mind. There, I am a lone castaway, the sole survivor of a ship wrecked from suffering. And like a ship in a bottle, I trap myself within my mind, escaping the outside world. I flood my mind in wine, drown my thoughts from reality, so I can blind myself to the blackness inside.

Because to see that blackness, to admit that real doom is actually in my mind, is to sin against the very instinct of survival.

Chapter 30

BEE always says that there are three distinct ways of having intercourse: making love, having sex and fucking. But let's stick to a subject I actually have a clue about. There are three distinct ways that I refer to my mom: Mommy, Mom and The Mother.

The Mother takes one of my cigarettes and inhales it like Puff the Magic Dragon as she proceeds to tell me again that I am the devil's child for smoking. She started smoking again last month after having quit for 16 years. It's her way of proving that I'm killing her.

"Miryam, what's wrong with you? You've become so quiet. And so serious. All you do is read."

"Some of us have to actually read books instead of hoping the words will seep in while we walk with them on our head."

Actually, I wish it really worked that way. Then maybe I could stack some feminist books on her head and pray that osmosis would cure her mental scoliosis. But then again, where would I find a book on feminism in this house? Or in this country for that matter?

"Is this your way of punishing us for making you stay here?" she asks.

"No. I'm just trying to survive staying here."

"How? By sleeping the time away? Which, by the way, I know you've been stealing my sleeping pills. And my tranquilizers."

She shakes her head. "Where did you learn all this self-destructive behavior? Why are you being so difficult?"

"What do you want me to do?" I ask. "I can't find a job here, I'm done with school, you don't want me socializing. At least you didn't. And now you're begging me to. I don't know which it is." I sigh and look at her, but she doesn't say anything. "There isn't anything *to* do here, Mom. You tell me what you want me to do and I'll do it."

"I'd love for you to volunteer at some of the places I do. Maybe the hospital for the children with cancer. Or one of the orphanages or women's shelters."

I look down, ashamed to admit that I don't have the kind of strength and detachment it takes to be around all that pain, then walk helplessly away from it.

I shake my head.

"What do *you* want to do?"

"I want to leave."

She ignores my answer and says instead, "Miryam, I want you to tell me the truth. Are you taking happy pills?"

I frown, then chuckle. "What the hell is a happy pill?"

"I don't know. Happy pill. You know, happy pill."

"Why?" I ask. "Do I look too happy?"

I smile. "And even if I were, I certainly wouldn't be stealing *those* from you."

Mom stares at me, her nostrils quivering, her cheeks flushing. I watch her face getting almost distorted with anger as my heart starts beating faster and faster. Suddenly, she throws her cigarette in the ashtray and springs up.

She storms out of the room and slams the door. I swallow hard and hug the covers.

Her footsteps pound in the hallway. The walls actually shake.

"You're the reason I'm miserable!" she yells towards my room. "If I need happy pills, it's because of you, you basket case! You're miserable and you want to punish us by making sure everyone around you is miserable too. So just stay in that room and be miserable!"

I get up from my bed and walk slowly to my door. I crack it open quietly and peek out. Mom plops down on the sofa and watches Dad flinch after a swig of scotch.

"Let her rot in there!" he screams. "She's not worth it! This is the thanks we get after everything we've done. We're the ones who took you to America in the first place, young lady! You wouldn't know what an America even is if it weren't for us."

He grabs the bottle of scotch and refills his glass. I hear the ice cubes rattle. His hand shakes as he inhales the drink in one gulp.

"She thinks she's above living here!" he screams. "We can live here, but her highness can't. The hell with this family! The hell with all of you! First that bum of a son and now her. What the hell am I killing myself for with worry when all they care about is themselves? The hell with all of you!"

He bangs his fist on the glass table. It shatters. Mom gasps and covers her mouth with her hand. I start to whimper and shake as tears stream down my face.

Mom speaks softly, almost in a whisper. "Dariush, what's wrong with you?"

She stares at him as she slowly bends down to pick up the broken glasses.

"Come and let me wash your hand," she says softly.

"Leave it!" he screams.

The blood drips from his knuckles onto the green Persian carpet.

I suddenly notice Cyrus and Nader standing outside their bedroom doors, staring at Dad.

Nader's voice is shaky. "What's going on?"

"Get back in your room!" Dad screams.

Nader bites down on his lip and starts to cry. Cyrus grabs his shoulders, but Nader jerks forward and runs back into his room.

"Dad, what's your problem?" Cyrus says nonchalantly. "So she's depressed. She's the one suffering. Besides, you're the one who told her to stop going out. And..."

"Shut up!" Dad screams. "I wasn't talking to you! You're the one who created all this mess to begin with. You're just as bad!"

"Yeah, and you're not," Cyrus mumbles under his breath. "Drunk off your ass yelling at me for drinking or her being depressed? No hypocrisy there."

Dad gets up and lunges in Cyrus' direction. "What did you say?"

Mom grabs his shoulders. "Dariush, stop it! Don't you touch him!"

I run out of my room and push Cyrus out of Dad's way.

"It's OK, Mir," Cyrus says and holds me from behind. "Go back inside."

"Oh, now the other one is out of her dungeon," Dad says calmly. "What? You want a drink? Here you go!" He goes to the table and slides the bottle of scotch across the shattered glass. It skids to the edge, then falls onto the floor and shatters into a hundred shiny pieces. The brown liquid streams across the white marble like rusted tears.

Mom covers her mouth with her hands again and stares at the floor. I let go of Cyrus and run into the bathroom. I lock the door and slide behind it onto the cold tiles. I pull my knees to me and rock myself in the dark.

A door slams outside. I jump in place and wail into my cupped hands. I hear Dad screaming at Cyrus, but my own screams muffle out his words. When my sobs quiet down, I realize he's talking about me.

"And she was the good one!" he yells. "The one with the promise. She's the one I thought would amount to something. And now she thinks that superficial life she had over there is more important than being here with her family. Why don't you use your time here and volunteer at some charities like your mom does? I pay a thousand dollars a month so she can talk to her friends back there but I couldn't pay her enough to say two words to her family once in a while."

"Family?" I scream as I stand up to face the door. "You call this a family? This isn't a family. It's a joke." I rest my head against the door and continue to cry, first loudly, then in short, choppy spurts. A few shallow breaths wheeze out of me.

I scream again and struggle to breathe. "I'm miserable because I'm rotting here! You didn't bring me here because of me. You brought me back for yourselves. I was just getting my life started over there and you yanked me away from it and stuck me here and just expected me to be happy. What do I have to be happy about here? I didn't even get a chance to say goodbye to my friends. It wasn't bad enough that I spent half my life being a mother to Cyrus and Nader and taking care of things over there? This is the thanks I get for it? Telling me I did a rotten job and I get to be punished for it by being locked up in this house for the rest of my life? And now you talk about family? What family? I'm stuck in a house with strangers, locked in my room thinking about how my education went down the drain! My opportunities, down the drain! Freedom, down the drain! My love life, down the drain!"

"Your *what?*" Dad says loudly. "Your love life?"

"Oh, *that* you heard alright," I say.

"Yes," I yell. "My love life. You don't want any more lies? Well, how's this for honesty: Ari is my only family. And I...we...we're in love with each other. But now he's moving on with his life while I'm stuck here playing family charades."

My knees shake and drop me to the floor. I rest my head on the door listening to it rattle to the beat of my quivering body. I hear footsteps outside, then dead silence. I peek through the crack under the door and see only blackness.

Chapter 31

I wake up with a headache. I don't remember when I came out of the bathroom last night, when I fell into my bed and passed out. It's the first time I've blacked out sober.

I sit up in bed and stare ahead. My words from last night rush to me so fast that I can't even pretend for one second that I dreamed them. I hug my blanket and whisper, "Oh, my God" repeatedly.

I curl my toes so hard they crack. I look at the clock. 1:12 p.m. At least Dad's already at work. If he wasn't too hungover to make it.

But Mom. Mom's probably sitting at the kitchen table repeating my speech in her head for the 40th time.

It's windy outside. Every time my window rattles, I startle. Every sound is magnified. When the school down the street lets out and the mob of boys runs beneath my window, laughing, screaming and chattering, it feels like madness. But at the same time, their voices sound so soothing, so innocent, so oblivious to my pain. It's as if they're proof that the world didn't end after I humiliated myself last night. They're still happy that school is out, still eager to play soccer. It can't be that bad; life is still going on.

But just when I think my outburst wasn't so bad, "We're in love with each other" echoes through me, and I crawl back under the covers and bury my face into my pillow.

I'm even embarrassed to face Nader. From behind a thick, wooden door, I exposed more of myself to my family than if I had stripped naked in front of them.

I lie back down and watch the two large red dots on my clock flash for hours. Whenever my words from last night crawl to the forefront of my brain, I count the flashing seconds out loud, until I'm synchronized with the clock.

At 3:12, I can no longer hold in my pee. I climb out of bed and tiptoe towards the door. I put my ear against it. No sounds. I turn the knob as quietly as I can and slip through. I make it to the bathroom without anyone seeing me.

I'm about to walk back into my room when I hear Mom's footsteps coming up the stairs. I dash in and close the door, but I know she saw me. I get back into bed and lean against the headboard.

The door opens. She walks in and looks at me.

"How long have you been up?" she asks.

"A while," I say softly without looking up.

"I was just about to come wake you. Are you hungry?"

I shake my head.

She draws open the curtains, then sits on my bed. I pull up my legs and hug my knees extra tightly. I don't look at her. But I feel her stare. I swallow hard. My heart is beating so hard and fast that it actually hurts, like it wants about to scream, "I can't take it anymore," and explode.

I feel Mom's hand on mine. I force my eyes to look up. She smiles. I clasp her hand. I beg them not to, but the tears adamantly fall.

I look at her again. She closes her eyes gently and gives me another sweet smile.

"You have nothing to be embarrassed about," she says.

"Oh, Mom!"

I throw my arms around her and bury my face in her neck.

"I know," she whispers. "You let out a lot and you're scared."

I come up for air, then dive right back into her. The tighter she holds me, the louder I whimper. It's been a long time since she's held me. It's been a long time since anybody's held me. I had forgotten her smell, that soft whisper of lotion, hairspray and tea. I had forgotten how soothing that smell is, like that lotion is seeping into rough skin and that tea is hugging a sore stomach.

She pushes my body into hers, as if squeezing out my pain. I forget her hurtful words, her sarcasm, her dirty looks. That was someone else. This is my mommy and her arms are the warmest, safest place on Earth.

Only a mother can invoke love in an instant.

"I'm so sorry about last night," I say as I slowly pull away. "I didn't mean what I said about our family. I just meant that..."

She shakes her head. "Yes you did. You don't need to apologize. You're right. We're not the ideal family."

"No one's family is ideal," I say.

She looks down and squeezes her eyes shut. When she opens them, they look distant and pained. "It breaks my heart when I see you so sad all the time. It kills me inside. But Miryam, we didn't do any of this to punish you."

Just when my sobs die down, hers begin. I hold her hand and look down.

"You need to understand the position we were in, Miryam. We were petrified when we found out about Cyrus' drinking and getting arrested. And you smoking. And when you first got here, all you did was go out and party hard and ...it was shocking for us to see. You've got to understand that. We're parents. It felt like we had lost all control of our children. We were worried to death. But making you stay here wasn't entirely about that like you think. It's ironic that you said last night that this is how we rewarded you for taking care of your brothers all these years, by bringing you here. Because we actually did see it as a reward. It's all about perspective, I suppose. You see it as a jail sentence. Whereas we thought this would be good for you. After all these years of taking care of things, we thought it would be good for you to come here and be taken care of for a change, be with your family, not have to work, not have to worry about money or anything else. If I were you, I would've loved this."

She waits for me to say something, but I don't.

She nods knowingly. "But you're not me."

I look down.

"I know you're hurt and angry, Miryam," she continues. "But so am I. You feel like a stranger to me. You may not think of me as the perfect mother, but I am still your mother. And it kills me when I see that you don't talk to me, you don't share anything with me. All you do is make sarcastic remarks and stare at the wall when I talk to you. How do you think that makes me feel?"

I start to say something, but she raises her hand in the air and continues. "You expect me to be on your side, but you haven't done anything to help me understand your side and what's going on inside your head. I'm not a mind reader. We're different people. How am I supposed to know why you hate being here so much? You need to get in a state of hysterics to share your feelings with me? I was taking it personally...you talk to your friends, but never to me."

"Mom, I haven't talked to Bee or Paige in six months. I *haven't* been calling them. The phone bill is because of Ari. Not Bee and Paige. And I don't have any real friends here. I have no one *but* you here. That's why I've been resentful of you. Because you *can* be my friend, you can be someone I trust, but you're always so scared of Dad that you do whatever he says. Even if deep down, you know he's wrong."

She frowns. "What are you talking about? I am not scared of your father."

"Oh please, Mom! You're terrified of him. Everything he says goes. Just because he's Dad. Because he's a man. And I can't stand seeing you so weak with him. You never stand up for yourself and now you're not standing up for me. It's as if you don't have a mind of your own. What's the good of me talking to you and telling you what I think when all you do is say, 'Yeah, but your father thinks this' or 'Your father wants that.' What's the point?"

I stop talking just to see her reaction, but she's looking down expressionless.

"But you're assuming that I disagree with your father about you being here," she says after a while. "I don't disagree with him. I wanted you to stay here, too. I thought…"

"I'm talking about Ari, Mom," I say softly. I look down and bite my lip. My heart starts pounding. I feel at once thrilled and scared to be talking to her about Ari. "I didn't tell you about him because I knew you'd tell Dad and he wouldn't approve and…"

She frowns. "That's not true. Your father loves Ari."

"As a person, but not as my boyfriend. He would never let me go back to America just because of him. But I thought there would be a chance that you might understand about me and Ari, be happy about it even." I stop and watch her face. But it's blank. I take a deep breath and continue. "He's not just some guy I have a crush on. You know him, you know his mom, he comes from a high-class family, he's educated, all that stuff you guys care so much about. But I thought you would side with Dad and be angry, too."

"That's not true, Miryam. I love Ari."

"So you're not angry?" I ask. "About me and Ari, I mean?"

She shakes her head with a frown. "No, honey. Why would I be angry? A little surprised maybe." She laughs. "You know, Soraya and I used to joke about it all the time when you were kids. We'd always talk about how great it would be if you two got married someday."

"I know. She told me." I look down and swallow. "What about Dad? Is he mad?"

Mom shrugs and curls the edges of her lips. "I don't know. I didn't speak to him before he went to work this morning. And last night, he was too…I didn't want to talk to him about anything in that state. But I don't think he's mad…"

"But he always told Ari that he should treat me like a sister and not..."

"Oh, that was years ago," Mom says, waving her hand. "You were kids. Ari doesn't even live with you anymore. You're two mature adults."

She shakes her head. "Don't worry about your father. Even if he is upset about it, I'll straighten him out. Honestly, what more could he ask for? Ari is a perfect gentleman and he's everything we would want in a husband for you."

"Mom, stop with the husband stuff," I say. "We haven't even gone on a date together. Please. Don't ever say this stuff to him. Ari, I mean. He'll freak."

She frowns. "Don't you want to marry him?"

"Of course I do. But this is all very new. It's too soon to talk about that."

I watch her from the corner of my eye before asking, "Does this mean you'll let me go back?"

"To America? Oh, Miryam. Slow down here. This is all happening so fast. You tell me...well, just everything, all at once. I don't know how much I can do right now as far as..."

I fall back on my bed, defeated. Why did I even bother going full speed to tell her everything just to have her tell me to slow down.

"Shhh," she says, wiping my sudden tears of frustration. "Stop worrying so much. Everything will be fine. I promise. Just be patient and you'll get everything you want."

Chapter 32

I grab the crushed cockroach's wing and carry it to the den.

Mom shrieks. "Ah, what are you doing with that thing? Get it away from me!"

"There's three of them in my room," I say. "Can we please get an exterminator or are they paying us rent?"

"Dariush, go clean them up from her room," Mom says to Dad. "Miryam, come here. And throw that thing away!"

Dad tosses his newspaper on the table and pushes himself off the couch. He walks towards me and I wave the cockroach at him smiling, pretending I'm going to throw it at him. He grabs it from my hand without looking at me. My smile disappears as I watch him throw the roach in the trash and walk towards my bedroom.

It's been six days since that night. Dad and I haven't exchanged anything but a few grunts translating into "hello" and "goodnight" in as many days. I've stayed away from him as much as possible, afraid of his narrowed eyes and his still-foul mood. Every evening when I hear his car pull up into the garage, I shudder and escape to my room.

I swallow hard and look at Mom. She motions for me to go to her. I walk over and sit on the deflated couch cushion Dad had been sitting on.

"I have good news for you," Mom says lowering the volume on the TV. "I finally convinced your father to let you go back to America."

She smiles and watches my face closely. I stare at her for so long that her smile begins to turn into a curious frown. Then suddenly, I throw my arms around her.

"Oh, Mom, do you mean it?"

I pull away gently and kiss her cheeks audibly. "Thank you, Mom! Thank you so much! You don't know what this means to me."

Her smile widens as she motions for me to sit back down.

"What did you say to him?" I ask. "What did he say?"

"I'll tell you later. But right now, I want you to go and talk to your father. I want you to make the first move and apologize to him. Break the ice."

"Apologize for what?"

"Shhh," she whispers and looks towards my bedroom. "Didn't you just hear me? He's agreed to let you go back. He's giving you what you want. Now would it kill you to apologize to him?"

"Apologize for what?" I ask again. "What did I do? He should apologize to *me*."

"Oh come on, Miryam. Don't you know your father by now? He has too much pride to apologize. The longer he doesn't apologize, the more embarrassed it means he is by his behavior that night. He's not very good at this sort of thing. I know he was out of line. But he was drunk. And upset. And may I remind you that your behavior hasn't exactly been commendable? The nights *you'd* come home drunk?" She pauses and looks at me with raised eyebrows. "Now go talk to him. He's your father."

Dad walks out of my bedroom and walks past us down the stairs. Mom and I get quiet and look down.

"You didn't tell him I want to go back because of Ari, did you?" I ask when Dad is out of view.

"Miryam," Mom says, shaking her head, "I don't believe you. First you tell me I'm weak because I'm scared of your father and I don't stick up for you. Then when I do, you want me to do it by lying to him? Don't tell me I'm scared of him. *You're* the one who's so scared of him that you feel you need to lie."

I give her a crooked smile. "You're right."

She gets quiet and looks towards the staircase. I turn around and see Dad climbing up, holding a can of roach spray. He passes by us without looking again and walks back to my bedroom. Mom nudges me and moves her head in his direction.

I get up with a sigh. I walk slowly into my bedroom and sit on my bed. I cover my mouth and watch Dad crouch on the floor and spray the corner of my walls. When he's finished, he holds his lower back and stands up. He waves the fumes away from his face.

"Open the window," he says without looking at me.

I spring up and practically run to the window. I open it, then sit back down. I feel Dad's stare. I look up nervously. His face is stern, his frown deep, his lips pointing down almost exaggeratedly.

"You're on a waiting list for a flight in three weeks," he says. "The airlines are all booked. If that doesn't work out, you have a guaranteed ticket in a month. It's the best I could do."

He walks quickly towards the door. I swallow hard.

"Dad, wait."

He turns only his head. "What?"

He looks scary, scarier than when he had lunged at Cyrus. He sighs and glides his hand across his bald spot. He stands there and looks down. The longer he doesn't move, the harder my heart pounds. Finally, he closes the door and walks towards my bed. He looks me in the eyes before sitting down. I scoot a few inches away.

"What?" he says again after a long time.

"What, um, what made you change your mind?"

He snickers. "Change my mind? About you leaving? I haven't exactly changed my mind. But it seems you've brainwashed your mother somehow and that my word doesn't seem to have much pull anymore. She thinks we should give you another chance. And, well, I just don't have the energy anymore. I..."

He throws up his hands. "I give up, Miryam. I give up."

I swallow, then look up. "Give up on what, Dad? What have I done that you're so mad at me?"

"Hurt. Not mad, hurt. And it's killing me to watch you so sad all the time. At least if you're not here, I won't have to see what you do. I won't have to see you so miserable. You can't possibly spend the rest of your life sitting in your room, miserable. Go back to where you learned all this behavior in the first place and continue it over there, so at least we won't have to watch it. You're setting a bad example for your brothers."

"What?" I say. "*I'm* setting a bad example. For *them*?"

I want to remind him of his behavior, of Cyrus', but I know it's pointless.

"I don't even want to know anymore," he says, ignoring my remark. "That's the only reason I'm letting you and your mother have your way. I can't take this anymore."

"Don't you see that I'm depressed here? I wasn't like this over there. I was just getting into the swing of things when you…"

"The swing of things? You were a receptionist."

"That was just a temporary thing. I'm gonna pursue a career. Aren't you the one who wanted me to have a career and be my own person? How can you want me to stay here and get married?"

"I never said that!" he snaps. "That's not why I wanted you to stay here. I wanted you here because of your family. So we could be a family and you could get to know your country."

He frowns and waves his hand. "It doesn't matter. It's irrelevant now. Just go and do whatever you want. Your mother is responsible for your actions now. But this time, you're on your own. You can stay at the house for as long as you need to find your own apartment. Then, you will hire a broker and sell the house. We'll give you some of the money from that to get you started, but after that, you're completely on your own. We'll help you out here and there, but nothing like before. You want to live in America? Then you live the American way. You make it on your own. And you're not living alone. Or with Ari." He stares sternly into my eyes. "You need to find a nice, respectable roommate."

I blush. I look down and nod slowly.

"You think it's going to be easy?" he asks with a smirk.

"Are you doing this to prove that I can't do it? Because I can."

"This isn't a game, Miryam. This is as real as life gets. We're not trying to prove anything. We hope that *you'll* prove to us that you can make it. And if you don't, you're always welcome back here. This is your home. But as long as you live there, you're on your own. And that's not a punishment. We simply can't afford to pay for you over there anymore. And it's ridiculous for you to live alone in that house. Not to mention dangerous."

"That's fine, Dad. But I just want to say that it's not fair to expect me to do something you couldn't do."

His whole face, from his frown to his pressed lips, tightens up. "What's that supposed to mean?"

"You expected me to come back here after all these years and adjust to Iran and start a whole new life. Without any warning. That's exactly what you went through when you had to move to America after the revolution. And you couldn't make it. You can't just take someone out of their home and make them adapt to a new culture. It doesn't work. It didn't work for you and Mom over there, so how did you expect it to work for me over here?"

He relaxes his brow. "The difference is that this, *here*, Iran, is your home. You spent half your life here. You grew up here. Whereas your mother and I were middle-aged people who had to leave our home after *35 years* and go somewhere and start a whole new life. We had already established our lives here, whereas ..." He sighs with frustration. "What are we talking about here? What is the point of all this? You're going back. Isn't that what you wanted? You got what you wanted. You won. So what's the problem here? Why are you saying all this?"

"I'm saying all this," I say, my voice suddenly shaking, "because I'm not a robot. I want you to be happy for me that I'm leaving. I want you to understand. I want you to trust me and believe in me, not get rid of me. I'm sorry I've been difficult, but can't you even try to forgive me? You said that night that Iran is good enough for you to live in, but not for 'my highness.' But you chose to live here. I didn't choose to live here. I also didn't choose to live in America. You guys keep choosing where I should live and then think I'm difficult when I can't adjust to a new culture. Can't you..."

Dad and I both turn around and look at Mom standing by the door.

"Yes?" Dad says brusquely.

Mom fidgets. "Sorry. There's a phone call for Miryam."

"Can't you see we're talking?" Dad snaps. "Can't I have one minute alone with her without being interrupted?"

"But it's Ari," Mom says, looking at me.

"I don't care if it's the president," Dad says. "She can't talk now."

Mom nods quickly and closes the door behind her. Dad shakes his head and looks back at me. He frowns and goes in thought, obviously trying to figure out what he had been saying.

"Miryam, you're not who I thought you were," he says softly. "You've shown me a side of you that, frankly, scares me. I'm worried about you. You're going down the wrong path. And it's not a matter of forgiving you. It's a matter of you showing me that I have no reason to worry and that you will change your ways. You can be in Africa, for all I care. I want you to start taking responsibility for your life. I want..."

"I will, Dad. I promise you. I will. I'm going to go back and get a job and really focus on myself for a change. I won't have to worry about Nader and... well, I mean, I can concentrate on my own life now. I'll prove it to you."

He nods. He's quiet for a long time before saying, "You mean that?"

I nod vigorously. "Absolutely, Dad. I promise."

His face opens up like a dry sponge in water. I didn't realize just how tense he had been until I saw his muscles loosen.

"Then why don't you start now?" he says. "In the time you're here, I don't want to see you drinking. Cut down on smoking that garbage. Come out of your room, spend some time with us, let us see you smile. Can you do that for me so I can watch you leave without tearing up inside?"

"Of course."

Finally, a smile emerges from his lips. It's a weak one, but still, it manages to smooth over three weeks of frowns. The tension in the air softens. Even the bug spray suddenly smells pleasant.

I hesitate, then scoot closer and hug him. He holds me tight for a long time, then gently kisses my head.

"Miryam," he says as he pulls slowly away, "I'm not your enemy. Neither is your mother. We just want what's best for you. Even if it seems unfair to you. All we've ever wanted was your happiness. Nothing pains me more than seeing you sad. Nothing gives me more pleasure than seeing you smile. Nothing."

"I know, Dad. I know."

He gives me a pained smile. He slowly bats his eyes closed and strokes my hand. I watch him look down and feel as if he's about to say something, but he just pushes himself off the bed and walks away.

He's about to close my door behind him before he turns back around. "You promised."

I nod. But when he stands there staring at me instead of walking out, I frown.

"Oh, right," I say, suddenly understanding what he means. I spring up and prance to the door to watch whatever movie is playing in Hebrew on the family room TV.

"Grit your teeth and bear it," he says. "It's one month maximum. And really, we're not that bad."

Chapter 33

Hope springs eternal.

Another Persian New Year, another spring, another promise of hope.

The quiet of the city sounds like a huge sigh after last night's celebration, when everyone screamed away four seasons' worth of sorrow and smiled in a new beginning. So many resolutions, flowers, wise words, new clothes, clean bodies, crisp new money. So much hope.

But it's really just another day. It's just tomorrow. The words come out of the same tired mouths, the new clothes adorn the same dusty, bitter souls and the money exchanges the same greedy hands.

Or did the brown leaves really turn green overnight? Is there really hope for a spring beyond the fog so thick that it blankets the entire sleeping city?

All I have is hope. So I dab on the last of my favorite lipstick "Everything with Wine" and throw out the empty tube. I kiss the hope in the air and promise that into these lips will no longer go everything with wine.

My body has molded itself in the shape of a bottle, my head its spout. And if you unscrew my head and hold me upside down, wine will flow out of my neck instead of blood.

Now that the international war is over, I have to also end the domestic one. As a peace offering to my body, I'm going to make war restorations. I'm calling my plan "Building Rome." Because I know it won't be done in a day. It will take time to rebuild this drowning city on a foundation of bricks and cement instead of pills and drinks.

Bloody Mary, vodka, whisky, wine, tequila, screwdriver, champagne, beer, pina colada, martini, margarita, mojito, mimosa, kamikaze...these were a few of my favorite drinks.

Chapter 34

I grab the blue marker and as if stabbing time with a knife, cross out another one of the red lines in my notebook. Another day closer to my parole, another day closer to opening the doors of Rome. The days are dragging like a dagger in my flesh.

Twelve days since I've had a drink. I'm going bananas. And I'd love to crawl inside a blender, pour some rum over my head and whip myself into a nice banana daiquiri.

I walk into the kitchen and stare blankly into the fridge. I'm about to grab a bottle of grape juice when the phone rings. Roya's washing dishes, so I pick it up and hear the beep signaling that the call is from America.

"Hello?" Ari says.

"Ari!" I shriek.

Roya turns quickly around from behind the sink, then smiles seeing my face.

"Why are you calling during the day?" I ask

"Called to wish you guys a Happy New Year," he says.

"Happy New Year to you, too. No one's home though. Just me."

"Just the only person I really want to talk to," he says with a flirty tone.

I giggle. "I was gonna call you tonight actually. I have something to tell you."

"Me too," he says cheerfully. "I have good news."

"Me too. You go first."

"I'm coming for a visit," he says. "In a few weeks. For ten days."

He gets quiet and waits for my reaction.

"That's unbelievable," I say. "I was just going to tell you that my parents are letting me come back to America. So, I mean, it's really sweet of you, but you don't have to come anymore."

He laughs. "Well, I do want to see my mom."

I scrunch up my face and twirl the phone's chord tightly around my neck. I start hitting myself on the head. Roya stares at me and frowns. I wave my hand to let her know it's nothing.

"Your mom," I say into the phone. "Of course. No, I didn't mean you were coming for me. I meant, I mean..."

"Relax," he says and laughs again. "You were part of the reason. But I'm still gonna come because of my mom and my friends."

"Friends?"

"Well, friend, actually. You remember Bernard?"

"The diplomat?"

"Yeah. He came to L.A. for a while and we hung out a couple of times. He's been reassigned to Tehran for his post. So, I'll kill three birds with one stone."

"Oh."

"You don't sound very excited that I'm coming," he says.

"No, of course I am. It's just that I knew I'd see you soon anyway. I just thought it would be there instead of here. Actually, you don't sound too excited that *I'm* coming back. Or even surprised."

"I guess I'm still too excited about me coming there. Besides, I knew I'd be seeing you too. Same thing you said, the other way around." He laughs. "So, what happened? How come they changed their mind?"

I swallow and bite my lip. "Actually, that's what I wanted to talk to you about. I, um, now don't freak, OK? I told them about me and you."

He gets quiet for a while, then says, "You're joking, right?"

"No," I say with a nervous laugh. "I'm serious."

"What…what do you mean? What did you tell them?"

"Just that I…that I want to come back partly because of you. That you're more than my friend."

He gets quiet again. For a little too long.

"Hello? Ari?"

"You're being serious?" he asks.

"Yes, I'm being serious. Why?"

"I just didn't think you had it in you. To confront them. About anything. Let alone about us."

I feel nervous, defensive, and a little angry. Then I realize that it's because he's right. I don't have it in me. I didn't stand up to them because I'm strong. I just collapsed in front of them because I'm weak from all the weight. There's a difference.

"It just sort of came out of me," I mumble. "I lost it one night and went off. And somehow told them about us. And well, they finally said that I can come back there."

He mumbles, a little confused, a little nervous, a lot shocked. But he mumbles just incoherently enough not to flat out say anything to flatten my bubble.

We're both quiet, almost speechless, for a while.

"Go figure," he says with a nervous laugh. "You think you know people."

I don't know if he's talking about my parents or me. And I don't ask. I hear the front door open. I poke my head out the kitchen and see Dad walking in. I smile and wave before I step back into the kitchen.

"I gotta go," I whisper into the phone. "My dad's home. I'll talk to you later."

"Wait," he says. "Let me wish him a happy New Year."

I hand the phone to Dad. After they exchange pleasantries, I walk out and listen in from the stairway.

"Oh, really?" Dad says. "When?...hmm...well, I'm happy to hear that. I'd like to have a talk with you before Miryam comes back. I was actually going to call you closer to her departure, but this works out even better." Long pause. Then he laughs. "OK, son. I'll see you soon then."

I bolt up the stairs and into my room. He actually laughed. He called him "son."

I twirl around, then fall onto my bed. I smile at the ceiling. I zigzag my bare legs in the air. My life, my beautiful life, is about to begin. Finally.

Chapter 35

THEY'LL be home soon. All of them.

First, it'll be the big brother, the one who made the father scream in hysterics for hours. He'll come home, in a bad mood, and ask me to meddle. "Talk to *your* father," he'll say. "What's wrong with him anyway?"

Soon after, the mother will come home. She'll come to my room, ask for my help, call me selfish when I refuse to get involved. She'll cry some more, then pop a few sleeping pills and I'll envy her as she sleeps a drugged sleep.

After that, the innocent little brother will poke his head and ask if it's safe to come home. He'll tell me I'm the only one who speaks their language and to please make them stop fighting.

Then the father will come home. He'll be drunk. He'll come to my room, tell me that the mother is crazy, the big brother is arrogant, life is shit and he'll be dead soon.

"But don't you worry about it," he'll say as he pinches my cheeks. "You keep up the good work and don't act like him."

And I'll be the doorman, actually letting them all in.

I'm the only one who won't come home. I've been here all night, yet haven't been there in more than 10 years. I stayed home to embrace solitude after the last of them slammed the door.

Storm, then quiet. But never peace after war.

When the doctor yanked me out, the delivery room echoed with the sound of his voice: "Surprise, it's a punching bag!"

This time, it wasn't my fault. This time, it was Cyrus who came home drunk and made Dad shake with anger long after the walls stopped shaking from the echo of the slammed door.

I knew it was too good to be true. I should've known that Cyrus and Mitra would eventually break up and in turn break the fragile glass that shielded Cyrus' true self. And the longer you've been pretending to be perfect, the deeper your inner imperfections brew, the louder the explosion.

"Get the hell out of my face!" Dad yelled, shoving Cyrus against the wall. "Haven't we had enough drama in this house? Can't we have one goddamned day of peace?"

Mom started crying just hearing Dad's voice.

"I can't take this anymore," she said and ran out the door to my aunt's house.

I crawled into my room and heard the front door slam three more times. I sat beneath my window in the dark and peered out, first at Dad driving off, then at Cyrus being picked up by one of his friends, then at Nader taking advantage of the situation and leaving in a taxi even though he was grounded for something doubtless trivial.

I can't help any of them. Some people ease pain; others inflict it. And once again, I'm in the middle, struggling only to handle my own pain.

They beg for my help, but they don't really want it. They are adamant about their misery. These are people who would sit on a pile of gold and complain that their asses hurt.

I'm sorry, Rome. I'll do all I can for you, but there's more than one cliché attributed to you. I'm using one as inspiration to better myself. But the other one, "When in Rome, do as the Romans do," applies more right now. I'm still in Iran and I must do as the Iranians do: deal with the perpetual pain of this country any way possible.

Even if it means having a drink and popping three tranquilizers instead of my intended two.

Chapter 36

"You mean he never apologized to either of you?" Nader asks.

Cyrus chuckles. "Dad apologize? That's a laugh."

"He's just got too much pride," I say. "I think he was really embarrassed and didn't want to admit it."

"Give me a break, Miryam," Cyrus says. "Don't go soft on me just because he's letting you go back. What he did was fucked up and you know it, so don't defend him."

We're alone at home. Dad's at work, Mom's at the beauty parlor, and Roya is taking a nap in the basement. A cool midday breeze glides in and softens the sun's warmth. The sound of Nader's basketball bouncing off the wall seems like it's coming from the street below, where the neighborhood boys are playing soccer. There's a quiet lull in the air despite the sound of that ball, of the kids below arguing over the score, of cars honking at them to get out of the way.

They're the same sounds, the same quiet, that have drifted through these windows and every window in Tehran forever. They are the sounds that will never change, the Tehran that will never lose its innocence.

Everything about the moment reminds me of all the lazy Tehran afternoons of my childhood. I didn't know then that these sounds, these smells, these senses actually had a feel to them and that they were nestling themselves in my memory. At the time, they were just sounds of kids playing, cars honking. It was just dust in the air. It was just a breeze brushing against my skin. I didn't realize that they were unique sensations, that together, they captured the feel of a Tehran afternoon. Those same sounds, those same scents somewhere else, those same sensations not occurring simultaneously, wouldn't feel the same. Only together do they create the nostalgia of home.

But right now, all the senses have reunited. Like individual instruments in an orchestra combining to create harmony, all the elements are present, giving me the same feeling as when they were first imbedded in my psyche.

Sharing the moment with Cyrus and Nader only accentuates its intensity because they're part of the memory. Especially Cyrus. He used to be one of those boys playing soccer on the street. And I would sit on the curb and watch him, wishing that just once, he and his friends would let me join in.

Like the boys playing on the street outside right now, Cyrus and his friends used to attach so much importance to their games, oblivious that the tradition was as old as Iran itself and that countless generations of boys had kicked checkered black-and-white balls on these streets, believing they had been the first — or would be the last — to do so.

"Hey," Nader says, suddenly springing up. "Are you gonna shack up with Ari when you go back?"

Cyrus chuckles.

"Of course not," I say, giving them both a dirty look.

"So who're you gonna live with?" Nader asks.

I shrug.

"I still can't believe you and Ari are in loooove," Nader says, batting his eyelashes. "How was I not aware of this? Why was I not informed of this? Hey, have you guys done it?"

"Nader," I say, rolling my eyes.

"Tell me! I must know if there was kinky sex going on while I slept in the next room. I must know if my pseudo-parents were fucking every night."

"Shut the hell up!" I yell, trying not to laugh.

"Cyrus?" I say, ignoring Nader's smirk. "Are you gonna be OK?"

He shrugs and plays with his cigarette ashes. "What do you mean OK?"

"I mean…"

"She means are you gonna start getting sloshed with Dad every night?" Nader says.

"Nader, shut up!" Cyrus and I say at the same time.

A while passes before Cyrus answers me while lighting another cigarette. "I'll be fine if you are, Mir. At least I'll have them watching me like a hawk. But don't act like you're so different. Who's to say you're not gonna drink there every night by yourself."

"I'm just not," I say. "I'm not going back to fuck up my life. I'm going there to be with Ari and start my life. The only reason I drank over here was 'cause I was depressed."

"Wherever you go," Cyrus says, "there you are."

"What's that supposed to mean?" I say.

"It means that it doesn't work that way. You think you're never gonna be depressed about anything again as long as you live? Just because you'll be with Ari? And you'll never drink again? Geography is just that. Geography."

"That's not true," I say. "Necessarily. I know what you're saying, but geography also means environment and your environment can really affect you for better or worse."

"Whatever you say," he says without looking up.

I leave it at that, but deep inside, I'm petrified about how much I agree with him and with that phrase I've heard before. Wherever you go, there you are. The mind doesn't change, no matter where it is. Am I any different from my family that I said was defiant about their misery? Am I someone else's definition of someone who would sit on a pile of gold and complain that her ass hurts? Am I like them? Am I…even worse than them?

"Besides," I say more to myself than to Cyrus, "there's a big difference between having a few drinks here and there and drinking all the time."

"What an insightful conversation," Nader says. "You two are really inspirational. What wonderful role models I have. A brother, a sister and a father who fight over which one of them is the biggest boozer. And loser."

I laugh. The kind of laughter where it's so sad that the only thing you can do is cover it up with laughter.

"What I don't get though," Nader continues, "like I'm being totally serious here, is how can Dad come down so hard on you guys for doing the same thing he does?"

"Because he's a fucking hypocrite," Cyrus says.

"No, he is not," Mom says as she opens the door with a frown. "And watch your language."

I startle and sit up straight. Cyrus looks up at her, unfazed, and continues to smoke.

"You got a better word for it?" he asks.

"Put that out!" Mom snaps and waves the smoke away from her. "You shouldn't smoke around Nader."

She waits for Cyrus to put out the butt before she places the ashtray on the window ledge.

"Look," she says, sitting down next to me. "I don't want you kids disrespecting your father. The way he's been acting lately is…well, it's very unlike him. But he's had it. He loves you all very much and he's very upset that two of his children have gotten into drinking." She looks at Cyrus and me. "He rarely drinks."

"Please, Mom," Cyrus says, rolling his eyes. "We remember."

I look down.

"Remember what?" Nader asks, sitting up.

"That was a long time ago, Cyrus," Mom says. "And the fact that he stopped for so long should tell you how in control he usually is. He was going through a very rough time when we first moved to America. He was very depressed."

Cyrus looks at me. I turn away.

"Alcoholism runs in families, you know," Nader says.

"They are not alcoholics!" Mom snaps.

I peer over at Cyrus, but he's looking down.

When we first came to Iran, Cyrus told me that he sees so many alcoholics at the parties we go to. But that they blissfully "enjoy their disease" because they haven't answered AA's 20 questions. I wanted to ask him if he thought I was an alcoholic and if I would pass, or rather fail, AA's questionnaire. But I stopped myself. Partly because I knew that a question like that is its own answer.

"OK, drinkers," Nader says. "Whatever you wanna call it. It's hereditary."

"It's a bad habit," Mom says. "You don't inherit a bad habit."

"No, but you inherit the tendency to overdo something," Nader says. "Whatever that thing may be. Like Miryam, for example, has a tendency to want sex all the time."

Mom's eyes widen and she stares at me in shock. I scream at Nader to shut up. Cyrus bends over laughing.

"What is he talking about?" Mom says, still glaring at me.

"Nothing!" I yell. "Don't listen to him! He's just messing with you."

"I'm kidding," Nader says, seeing how seriously Mom is taking it. "Totally kidding. No, but seriously, don't you think there's a possibility that maybe these two inherited this from Dad?"

Mom frowns, then looks down in thought.

"I suppose," she says after a while. "Your father's mother, God rest her soul, was the same way."

"What do you mean?" I ask.

"She drank heavily," she says. "She really was an alcoholic."

"What?" I say, staring at her with a frown. "Grandmother?"

She nods. "And in those days no less. Do you know what a stigma was attached to a woman drinking in those days?" She pauses. "But she wouldn't do it in front of people. She would hide it and drink alone. But everyone knew."

Cyrus laughs and shakes his head. "We don't have a family tree. We have a family vine of fermented grapes."

I stare at him, then at Mom. Her words echo in my head in slow motion. I try to imagine Grandmother's kind, old face. I try to picture her sneaking a drink in the room she had called her sanctuary. But it doesn't fit. That wasn't her. She was candy, cookies and colorful stories.

Grandmother and alcoholic just don't belong in the same sentence.

Chapter 37

The rain sounds so enchanting.

Sitting next to Soraya as she drives to the airport, it's hard to believe we're in the same city as the one I was in earlier today. The bumper-to-bumper traffic has died down to reveal barren, dusty streets, barely lit by dim streetlamps.

The radio is tuned to a station playing maudlin classical Persian music. In between the guitar and piano overtures, a DJ who sounds like he's about to kill himself comes on and rambles about Islam.

Neither of us talks. Only the radio and the trucks slushing by in the rain interrupt my thoughts. Thoughts of Ari, of course. Nothing specific, just my usual fantasy, mixed with speculation and a hint of paranoia.

When Soraya's green Honda Civic inches towards the airport's entrance, I smile, knowing that in ten days, I'll be here again, with Ari, suitcases in tow, leaving forever.

We walk into the terminal, where 4 a.m. looks more like 4 p.m. It seems like all of Tehran is suddenly awake and under the airport's bright lights.

I'm sitting on a bench blowing away the smoke from my cigarette and rearranging the flowers I bought from the nearby kiosk when Soraya motions to me that Ari is here. I jump up and run towards her.

"Where?" I ask, letting out the lingering puff of smoke.

I'm sure she answers me. But I don't hear her.

His hair has gotten longer and he's lost weight. He shifts his khaki duffle bag on his right shoulder and steps onto the escalator. He looks around, but still doesn't see us. The tears well up quickly in my eyes and I realize that I've missed him more than I've ever missed anybody in my life. I look down and rub my eyes with the sleeve of my raincoat. When I look back up, he's staring right at me, first blankly, then with a smile.

I'm 13 years old in junior high and the boy I like just smiled at me from across the classroom. He squeezes past a family huddled together and dives into Soraya's arms. I watch them with a lump in my throat.

They greet each other for a slow-moving two minutes before he turns to me. He takes the flowers from me with a smile. Then he drops them on the floor and picks me up. He squeezes me tightly, tilting my head to the side. He pushes back the corner of my scarf and whispers in my ear, "I missed you."

I smile. And blush.

"I kept telling her not to come to the airport," Soraya says, looking at me. "But she insisted."

"Are you kidding?" Ari says, looking at his watch. "She's probably thrilled that she had something to do at this hour."

I continue to just smile.

We start walking out as Ari pulls two stems from the batch of roses I gave him and hands a red one to me and a yellow one to Soraya.

"Miryam, why don't you just spend the night at our place tonight?" Soraya says when we're in the car.

"No, no, I couldn't," I say.

"Sure you can," Ari says.

OK then, it's settled.

"But my parents…"

"Your parents will understand," Soraya says. "I'll tell them I didn't feel like driving you back home at this hour. It's kind of true anyway, honey. You live across town."

"Oh my God, I'm so sorry," I say. "I can take a taxi."

"No, no," she says. "Don't be ridiculous. You're missing my point. Let's just go back to our place, we'll sit and have a nice talk with Ari, get some sleep and I'll take you back home in the morning. Afternoon. Whenever you wake up."

I look at Ari from the back seat, but he's yawning and no longer paying attention.

"OK," I say.

"OK," Soraya says. "I'll call your parents when we get home. I'm sure they're waiting up for you anyway."

Ari and Soraya talk about her business as I sit quietly staring outside with a frozen smile. I feel like the city looks in its serene slumber under the gently falling rain. I'm already trying to remember the beauty of the moment as the drops dance outside my window.

I concentrate on the sound of Ari's breaths to reassure myself that he's really here, close enough to touch, to breathe the same air. His breathing sounds like singing, my drumming heart the background beat.

"It's so good to be back here," Ari says.

"Really?" I ask.

"Oh, absolutely," he says. "I've had a new appreciation for Iran since I left. There's so much good in our country. Maybe if we educate Americans about that, there won't be so much prejudice against Iran."

I start to argue with him, but for this moment, and maybe this moment only, I really can see the beauty of Iran.

No matter how the revolution has impacted Iran, one thing I have seen in Iranians is resiliency. Our culture has stayed rich in tradition and artistry, our people ripe with success. At some point, we have all tapped into our strengths and shown our malleability.

A sense of beauty and nobility have permeated and pulsated throughout our heritage, personifying Persia for millennia. Even in the midst of chaos, charm is always undeniably palpable in Iran.

I notice and smile at a "Darvish," an overly wrinkled, white-bearded man sitting next to a tiny lantern on a Persian-woven mat, smoking a hookah on a street corner, fortunetelling by reading Hafez's poetry.

I want to fly above the deserted streets and wake the sleeping city with the sound of my laughter bouncing off the ground and echoing into every home. How can people be asleep when there is so much joy to feel?

I smile at the graffiti-plagued walls and kiss the dust melting under the rain. I wave at the lone drivers inside the muddy trucks, wanting to blow my awakened bliss into their tired souls.

I want to kiss the ground. And I want to thank this city for being the host of the most beautiful night of my life. I love this country and everyone in it.

Maybe there are indeed pros to a religious government. People here fear God to the point that crime is minimal, limited mostly to car theft and house burglary. Even the poor would rather starve than steal. I've seen jewelry stores with their doors open, their owners taking a smoke break or going for a stroll far from the entrance without hesitation.

Lots of homes, too, have their doors open throughout the day to welcome neighbors, street workers, and stray cats alike for a meal and warm hospitality.

Crimes like murder and rape certainly do occur. But they're hush-hushed by the suppressed press. Largely because the most heinous of them are committed by the very people who silence the media.

I roll down my window and stick out my hand. The rain trickling off my palm feels like the sky is shedding tears of joy, celebrating the revival of my dormant devotion to the city it blankets.

We walk into the apartment and Ari immediately goes into his bedroom while Soraya calls my parents. I can tell from her expression that Mom is arguing with her, but in the end, Soraya nods at me with a smile.

I follow her to her bedroom, struggling to see even a glimmer of light peering through Ari's door. I wear the oversized T-shirt Soraya gives me and lie next to her in the queen-size bed. I wait for her to fall asleep before getting up and tiptoeing into the dark living room. I sit on the sofa, waiting and hoping for Ari to come out. Maybe if I pray hard enough, he'll come and sneak me into his bedroom.

Does God answer prayers about sex?

I notice the flowers I gave Ari sitting on the coffee table in their wrapping. I find a small vase, fill it with water and arrange the yellow and red roses in it. I crinkle the wrapping as loudly as I can. I bang the vase on the table.

But still he sleeps. I sigh and pick the dead leaves off the floor.

I crawl back into Soraya's bed, my heart pounding louder than if she were Ari. I close my eyes and inhale deeply. I am closer to Ari than I have been in years. But the fact that he's breathing the same Tehran smog as I am and he's within my physical reach, yet might as well be thousands of miles away, actually makes him feel farther away than ever.

Soraya hogs all the space as I hug the edge of the mattress. It's obvious she hasn't shared a bed with anyone in a long time. I suddenly miss my own bed, the familiar hue of darkness in my own room and the silence whispering through my own window. I rummage through my fear reservoir until I match the feeling inside me to the one I used to have on the nights before the first days of school. I clutch the blanket tightly and stare at the white dots behind my closed eyelids.

The rain sounds so foreboding.

Chapter 38

I walk into Leila's house and make like I'm Cinderella. It's the first party I've been to in more than a year, but since it's a goodbye party in my honor, my parents let me come after I promised not to drink.

I immediately go in search of my prince. He's laughing with Bernard and taking swigs of whiskey.

"Well hello, angel," he says.

"Hi Ari," I say, trying to sound cold.

"What's the matter?"

"Nothing," I say.

"You remember Bernard," Ari says.

"Of course. How are you?" I shake his outstretched hand.

"Wonderful," he says. "And how are your lovely parents?"

"Fine," I say. "I haven't seen you in a long time."

"Actually, I went back to Austria for a while and I was to be reassigned a new post in Sarajevo, but at the last minute, I was assigned to Tehran again."

"Lucky you," I say sarcastically.

"Oh, I do love it here. Such beautiful women." He winks at me.

"You're too kind," I say, trying to sound like a Bond girl. I notice that because Bernard always speaks so properly, I instinctively enunciate and talk more eloquently when I'm around him.

I turn back to Ari.

"And where have *you* been? Austria as well?"

"Sorry about not returning your calls, Miryam. I've been exhausted. Jet lag. I barely even made it tonight."

"Can I talk to you alone whenever you have a moment?" I ask him.

"Sure," he says. "Whenever you want."

"I'll leave you two alone," Bernard says. "I'll see you later, man."

He pats Ari's shoulder, smiles at me and walks away.

"What's up?" Ari asks.

"Can we sit?"

He follows me to some throw pillows on the floor in the corner of the living room and helps me down. My heart pounds louder than the music. It takes me three tries to speak.

"Ari, what's gonna happen with us when we leave on Monday?"

He smiles and starts to say something. But when he sees how serious I am, it's obvious that he stops himself from saying whatever sarcastic or funny thing he was going to. He gives me a different, more sincere smile.

"We'll take it as it comes, Miryam."

"What does that mean?" I say, trying to sound frustrated.

"We'll figure it out together."

"You haven't changed your mind about…I mean, do you still…"

He smiles. "Do I still love you?"

My heart drops. My eyes follow.

"Yes," he says. "I know I don't say it a lot, but…bear with me. I'm new at this. We'll make up for all the time we were away from each other." He takes my hand and kisses it.

There aren't enough drops of wine squeezed through all the grapes in all the vineyards in the world to induce the natural intoxication of requited love. Air tastes delicious; walking feels like dancing and every breath feels like the first one in life.

Life is wonderful. I look around to touch wood, but I can't find any. I down a shot to celebrate instead.

Gloria Gaynor's "I Will Survive," every girl's personal anthem, blasts through the speakers as Yasmine, Leila, three other girls and I sing out loud, dancing and laughing.

"*…I spent oh so many nights just feeling sorry for myself. I used to cry. But now I hold my head up high…*"

I sing louder when I notice Ari watching me. "*Weren't you the one who tried to break me with goodbye? Did you think I'd crumble? Did you think I'd lay down and die? Oh no, not I. I will survive…*"

When the song is over, I look back towards Ari, but he's gone. I roam the living room for a while, then give up. I go upstairs to a bathroom to put on a fresh coat of lipstick. Just as I'm blotting on a tissue, I hear shouts from downstairs. The music suddenly goes dead. I frown and listen to the downstairs commotion turn into a cacophony of chaos.

I make my way slowly down the staircase, holding onto the handrails. When I get halfway down, a guy motions for me to go back upstairs. He looks terrified.

"What's going on?" I ask in English, not even sure if he speaks it.

"*Bargard bala*," he says, telling me again to go upstairs.

"Why?" I ask in Farsi.

Before he can answer me, I see them. Six bearded Komiteh men, dressed in black, holding batons, rounding people up and yelling at them to get outside. I run upstairs. Halfway there, my shoe comes off and I roll backwards down the stairs and on my head.

"*Koja miri? Khanoum, koja fekr mikoni dari farar mikoni*?" One of the Komiteh men runs to me, asking where the hell I think I'm escaping to.

I feel his heavy hand grab the back of my dress and yank me up.

"*Velam kon*!" I scream for the guy to let go of me.

"*Ino bendaz root binam*," he yells, telling me to cover myself up with the chador he throws at me.

I look into his eyes, at the pure hatred and evil staring back at me. I clench the chador to me and follow him outside. I think of running away, but everywhere I look, those eyes stare back at me. Different eyes, same look.

One of the Komiteh men pushes the girls into a blue bus, while another one handcuffs the guys sprawled on the dust of a green bus. The word "God" is written in Arabic on the windshield of both buses.

I scan the scared faces along the green bus, but I don't see Ari's. I don't see anyone I recognize. We all turn around at the sound of a scream followed by running footsteps rising from the back of the house. But all we see are those black eyes trailing ours.

I climb onto the bus and see Leila sitting in the first seat, her hands buried in her face. Suddenly I remember that I'm the reason she threw this party, that I'm the cause of all these stoned faces and shaking bodies. Dozens of tear-filled eyes follow me as I walk to the back of the bus. I sink into an empty seat next to a girl I've never seen before.

She grabs my hand and presses it hard.

"What's gonna happen to us?" I whisper in Farsi.

"I don't know," she says.

A girl in front of us turns around.

"What do you mean you don't know?" she says. "We're all gonna die."

I look at the girl next to me, but she's staring out the window. I squeeze her hand.

As the bus rolls ahead, it passes by our street. I sob as I imagine Dad leaning back in his chair, watching Israeli television, yawning nonchalantly. Mom is peeling pomegranates, careful not to drop any of the seeds on the Persian carpet.

They don't know. They don't know anything. Yet.

But soon, they will. Dad's face will sag as the phone slips from his ear. Mom will scream at him to tell her what's happened. They'll blame each other for letting me go to such a big party when they're well aware that Leila's house is in a busy part of town and that any passerby hearing the roar of music and coed laughter could call the Komiteh.

The louder I cry, the louder the fat Komiteh guy tells me to shut up.

I silently thank God that Nader and Cyrus are sick with the flu and couldn't come to the party.

All the girls on the bus look the same, with their nyloned or bare legs inching out of oversized chadors, mascara smeared around their eyes, lipstick that was wiped off in a hurry bleeding onto their pale cheeks.

I wrap the chador tightly around me. My arms are dotted with goose bumps, but my face is soaked in sweat.

The wind gently blows the leaves off the tall trees lining Pahlavi Street. Just yesterday, I was sitting next to Mom as she drove down this same street. She had smiled when I told her that this is my favorite street in Tehran; that the top of the tree branches, creating a roof with their colorful leaves highlighted by the sun's halo of gold, makes it seem like we're driving through a rainbow. But now, Mom's smile isn't here to brighten the street where the same trees look like an arc over a black tunnel.

I plead with the angels to breathe and make the wind blow harder. I whisper to the wind to break the trees' branches, drop them on the bus. I stare at the trees, begging them to collapse on the bus and strand us. I tell them we need their help. But they sway nonchalantly.

The bus screeches in front of a large white building. I watch the girls slowly rise out of their seats and walk towards the door like soldiers marching towards enemy lines. The girl next to me nudges me to get up. I stare into the eyes of the Komiteh standing at the door and feel at once drunk and hungover.

I throw up. Everyone looks at me, not with disgust, but with pity. And as if I had yawned, suddenly vomit shoots out from every mouth on the bus. We glide to the door and drag our heels through the slush of throw up. We leave the bus smelling like pickled alcohol and fear.

Chapter 39

The Komiteh line us up in front of a cement wall. I'm staring straight ahead when I suddenly see a pair of hands holding a blindfold in front of me. I try to look behind me, but the hands force my head around and slap the blindfold on my eyes. It pulls, then tightens behind my head. My eyelashes feel squished; blinking hurts. I close my eyes. I hear soft whimpers next to me, heavy footsteps behind me.

I reach up and try to loosen the blindfold. I pull it down a little. It smells like gasoline. I start to gag, then pull it up as far away as I can from my nose. I poke my index finger inside to scratch my eye, then feel a hand grab my wrist and drag me along, first on pavement, then down some stairs. I hear a cacophony of cries and screams. I turn my head quickly from side to side, trying to figure out where the noises are coming from. But they're everywhere. It feels like madness.

"*Velam kon! Velam kon!*" I yell for the person holding me to let go.

"*Khafeh sho, jendeh!*"

I'm surprised to hear that it's a woman's voice saying, "Shut up, whore!"

She smells like three-day-old underarm sweat. I go limp as she drags my body at an angle like a wagon with broken wheels. She pushes me and I fall on the ground, hitting my head on the floor. My cries turn into wails. I feel her hands let go of me.

A foot kicks me and pushes me back against a wall. I hear more screams, more pleas for mercy, more shouts of, "Shut up, whore!"

I suddenly realize that my hands are free and I yank off the blindfold. I squint until my eyes adjust to the light. I stare at the thick black bars in front of me and pass out.

When I come to, Yasmine takes my hand and smiles weakly.

She moves closer and whispers, "You've peed all over yourself."

She hands me a Styrofoam cup of water. I take a small sip. I look at the girls in my cell, grateful that Leila isn't one of them. I open my mouth to ask Yasmine how long I was out, but nothing comes out but shallow breaths and incoherent noises.

"It's OK, Miryam," Yasmine says in English. "Don't panic. I've been in jail before. Our parents will bail us out soon."

When? Do they know we're here? Who called them? Why aren't they here yet?

But all I can do is grunt. Except for the bars, the jail cell looks like a regular room. The floor is covered in dirty white carpet, the walls are smeared with chipped yellow paint, and electrical sockets protrude out of corners. Yasmine notices me looking around and tells me that she's been in this exact "cell" before and that we're in the basement of an old mansion. Some of the other girls from the party are dispersed in the old wine cellar, the maid's room, anywhere in the house they could enclose with bars. The Komiteh confiscated the house from someone whose only crime was being rich. They executed him and turned his house, like so many others like it, into make-shift jails.

"It's not like we're in Evin or something," Yasmine says.

I nod weakly, remembering all the horror stories I've heard about the most notorious prison in Tehran, where they throw you into pitch-black solitary with nothing but a tin can to sit on.

We're all still wearing the clothes and shoes from the night of the party. We weren't stripped searched, didn't get fingerprinted, didn't have our mug shots taken, weren't given "prison clothes," pillows, blankets or adhere to the normal protocols of getting arrested in the United States. Or any other normal country, for that matter.

"Az Amrica miyay?"

I turn my head quickly towards the voice asking me if I come from America. I look at the bruise-faced young girl sitting at the far end of the cell. I nod. She smiles and continues to poke her finger through a cast on her arm.

Yasmine tells me in English that the girl and the other young one in our cell who aren't from our group were picked up for prostitution. My sore, stinging eyes widen as I stare at Yasmine nodding sadly. The barely teenaged girl looks at us, knowing we're talking about her. But she just smiles.

"*Hich karitoon nemikonand*," she says. *"Hich gohi nemitoonand bokhorand."* (They can't do shit to you.)

I try to smile at her, but it's as if my lips are crazy-glued together. I touch the dried blood on them and take a sip of water, letting it drip on my lips. I'm surprised that my voice is audible when I ask the girl how old she is.

"Nine," she says.

I cough out the water in shock. I thought that only happened in badly scripted movies. I wipe my mouth with my hand and continue to stare at her.

"What?" she asks with a smirk. "You don't have prostitutes in America?"

I turn away and close my eyes. I try to think happy thoughts, but everything horrific about humanity floods in front of my closed lids.

"Bastards took my watch," Yasmine says, rubbing her left wrist. "I don't even know what time it is."

Like it matters.

Chapter 40

"Does anyone have a cigarette?" Yasmine asks.

Sara, a tall, quiet girl from our group fishes into the pocket of her raincoat and throws a bunch of cigarettes across the room. I grab one, stick it in my mouth and wait for someone to light it.

I inhale and feel a warmth, a tingle, a deep-seated joy I thought I would never again experience. Better than the rush of nicotine is the thought that I'm subtracting seven minutes from my life.

If only I could subtract from the past instead of the future. Seven minutes comprised of agreeing to go the party, stepping into my dress, sliding red lipstick across my lips, slipping into my new high heels, calling the taxi, ringing Leila's doorbell, singing that I would not "lay down and die," that I'd survive, downing a drink instead of finding wood to knock on about my wonderful life.

"There's no smoking in here!" a woman from outside yells.

I put out my cigarette on the wall and hide the butt under a loose edge of carpet. The woman cranks open the door and yells at us to get out.

"Are we being released?" I whisper to Yasmine.

She shrugs and looks up at the woman.

I quickly slide my feet into my black heels. I push myself off the floor and run out.

"Slow down," the woman yells after me. "Where do you think you're going?"

I fidget and watch her round up the rest of the girls.

She leads the way up an old, narrow staircase and into a large room. She slams the door shut. I look around for my parents, for anyone but a Komiteh, but all I see are half a dozen beds with yellowing white sheets.

"Get undressed," a fat lady says to the dozen of us in the room. "Take off everything from the waist down."

"What's going on?" I ask in Farsi.

No one answers me. All the girls slowly take off their shoes and pull down their skirts or pants. I fold my arms across my chest and watch them with a frown.

The door swings open and four other Komiteh women, all large and stern looking, walk in.

"What's the matter with this one?" one of them asks, pointing at me. "Shy, are you? You don't have nothing I haven't seen before. Undress!"

The room echoes with the sounds of skirts, pants and dresses hitting the floor. When I finally pull my dress over my head, the other girls are watching me while hugging their naked bodies.

"Climb onto the beds," one of the women says. "One at a time."

Three girls march to the beds and climb up.

By the time it's my turn, the room reeks with the stench of vaginas that haven't been washed in days. I gag and walk towards an empty bed with crumpled sheets.

I lie down and stare at the ceiling. I stiffen my muscles and hold my breath.

I hear a snap. I lower my eyes and watch one of the women tighten a white plastic glove on her right hand. I look away again.

"Relax," she says. "It'll hurt less."

I try to loosen my muscles, but they stiffen right back up. I feel her finger at the opening of my vagina. She eases it in, then pokes at me twice. I let out a soft moan and look into her eyes. She stares back with surprising kindness. She slides out her finger.

She comes closer and whispers, "I'm sorry if I hurt you, sister. I'm just doing my job."

She gently wipes the sweat off my forehead with her other hand.

"*Geryeh nakon digeh,*" she says, telling me to stop crying. "*Tamoom shod.* (It's over.)"

I nod and wipe my tears. I slide off the bed and grab my clothes. I avoid looking at the two girls with their legs still sprawled on the beds.

I hear a scream and turn quickly around.

"Get your fucking hands off me, you whore!" one of the girls on the bed yells.

"You're the whore!" the woman examining her screams back.

"Far from a whore," the girl says. "I'm a virgin."

"*Khafeh sho binam!*" the woman says, telling her to shut up.

"I swear," the girl says. "When they raided the party, I jumped out the window and the pointy heel of my shoe rammed up my vagina."

The few girls who are still putting on their clothes snicker. The girl on the examining bed sits up.

"Shut up!" she yells in English. "Whose side are you on?"

She looks back at the woman and continues in Farsi. "It's true. I bled right there. If I wasn't wearing black underwear, you'd be able to see the blood."

"*Khafeh sho binam jendeyeh doroogh goo!*" the woman says. "*Fekr mikoni man kharam*?" (Shut up, you lying whore! You think I'm stupid?)

The girl slides off the bed and clutches her clothes to her. She stomps out of the room, yelling obscenities about the government.

"We'll deal with you like you won't believe!" the woman screams after her. "Thirty lashes isn't enough for you!"

I stare at her in shock. I call over the woman who had examined me.

"How many lashes am I going to get?" I whisper with a shaky voice.

"Oh, honey, none," she whispers back. "We don't give lashes to virgins."

I stare into her eyes trying to figure out if she's having mercy on me or if she really thinks I'm a virgin. But she just walks away.

Back in the cell, Yasmine strokes my head and says that she's not scared of the lashes.

"I hear they let you keep your shirt on," she says. "It's not that bad."

"I've gotten the lashes before," another girl says. "It really isn't that bad. The guys are the ones who have it really bad. We get beaten by the women. They're not that strong. Plus by law, they have to put a Koran under their arms while they whip us. They can't raise their arms up too high that way because the Koran isn't allowed to fall onto the floor."

"Because *that* would be wrong," I mumble.

All the girls, including the young prostitutes, smile and shake their heads in agreement.

"I'm not getting beaten," I say softly to Yasmine.

"What?" she says. "You're a virgin?"

I hesitate, then nod slowly.

Yasmine stops stroking my greasy hair and says, "Then what's the problem?"

"Is everyone getting lashed?" I ask.

One girl raises her hand.

"I'm not," she says. "I'm a virgin too."

I return her smile, then look down.

I guess the woman wasn't just trying to have mercy on me, or else she would've let others pass for virgins too. It's been so long since Ari and I had sex that maybe I'm back to being tight as a virgin.

I sit crouched over my knees, hugging myself and silently thanking God. I think of the night of my birthday when I thought my body had changed forever. I wonder if I'll bleed all over again the next time we make love.

Ari and I were supposed to leave for America today. Today is finally here, but I'm not there to see it. Today is when it was all supposed to end. Today is when it was all supposed to begin.

Chapter 41

I watch the girls walk out of the cell with their heads bowed. The fat lady shoves them forward, then slams the door. I look at Mojgan, the virgin, and smile shyly. I'm a phony. I shouldn't be sitting here with her. I should be up there getting lashed with the rest of the girls. Mojgan is the only one who deserves to be sitting here.

I fall asleep at some point and wake up to the sound of rattling keys. I sit up and watch the girls walk back into the cell on the heels of their feet. Mojgan and I help take their clothes off so their wounds can breathe. We're all quiet and avoid eye contact. I peel off Yasmine's dress and see the lash marks that travel from her neck down to the soles of her dirty feet. She lies down on her stomach and buries her face into the carpet.

It's not until a few hours later when someone finally speaks.

"For the first time in my life, I'm happy to be a girl," Sara says. "I caught a glimpse of the boys with their shirts off after they were beaten. The red lines on their backs were puffed out the size of my arm. Our wounds are like paper cuts compared to theirs."

"Were they all beaten?" I ask with a shaky voice.

"Every single one of them," Sara says. "Just for being at the party."

I close my eyes to get the image of Ari being beaten out of my head. But the harder I try not to picture it, the more vivid it becomes. I want to break out of the cell and run to him, blow on his wounds, kiss his burning skin and fall at his feet in mercy. I'm the reason he came to the party. I'm the reason for his misery. And no amount of pain I've gone through for him can compare to this.

Does he know the girls were checked for their virginity? Does he know that the non-virgins were beaten? Does he think I was beaten? Does he blame himself?

I want to scream out to him, tell him I'm fine and that he's the one I'm worried about. I want to beg for his forgiveness.

I pound my fist into the ground, then on my thighs. Yasmine wraps her bruised arm around me. I push her away. Another pair of arms grabs me from behind. I scream and wail until I pass out.

Yasmine wakes me up at some point and tells me we're being released. Our parents had appeared in front of a judge and paid the bribe.

"Miryam, I don't want you to leave Iran with a bad taste in your mouth," Yasmine says. "I've lived in Iran for almost six years now and this is the first time I've been in jail this long. And I've never been checked for my virginity. They usually just keep us overnight and our parents bail us out. But this time, they probably wanted to make scapegoats out of us and set an example for the rest of the young people. They do that sometimes. I'm sure the whole city knows about this by now. It was just bad luck, really. And I think we probably got assigned a bad judge at the start and he refused to let us get away with it. None of this would've happened if we had just gotten Judge Mostafa."

"As opposed to Judge Mental?"

She smiles.

The fat Komiteh lady clunks her way to our cell and opens the door halfway. She shoots us a dirty look.

"Next time I see any of your faces in here, I won't have mercy on you," she says. "Now that you're out of here, go and find God. Let Him into your souls and maybe He'll have some mercy on you and take the devil out. You whores!"

We walk out and wait for the woman to lead the way upstairs. She grabs one of the iron bars and slams the cell door shut. Two giant black cockroaches camouflaged by the black bars suddenly slide out the cell. I look at the young prostitutes. They catch my eye, then stare back down.

Chapter 42

THERE comes a point when your body no longer recognizes energy from lack thereof. When the hours all mesh into one, time loses all meaning and all you can do is wait for your body to faint.

That was four days ago.

Mom wakes me up by sobbing into my ear. When I finally open my eyes, I stare at her yellow, hollow face. She wipes her tears away and kisses my hand.

"Your father told me to wake you up," she says, sniffling. "You need to eat."

I close my eyes again, not letting go of her hand. I concentrate on the feel of her skin, the feel of the soft mattress cushioning my body. I sit up and throw myself into Mom's arms, smelling her neck and tugging at her hair. I look around my room.

"It's over, baby," she says. "You're home now."

The tears roll down my cheeks. She takes my face in her hands and kisses it.

"It's OK, my baby," she whispers. "I'm so sorry you had to go through that."

She kisses my head and gets up. Before leaving, she points to a pack of Marlboro Reds sitting on my nightstand.

"I only got you one pack," she says. "Because they were out of Marlboro Lights. I'll get you some when they have them back in stock."

I nod shyly and watch her walk away. I get out of bed slowly, my joints cracking like chunks of ice in warm water. It seems like hours before I reach the bathroom.

I look in the mirror at my gaunt, jaundiced face. The greasy strands of hair stuck to my head make me look almost bald. Yellow and red mix with the whites of my eyes, creating the crimson of the sun at dusk. I stare at the tears washing the dirt off my face.

I smoke two cigarettes in a row, gagging on every puff of the last one. I crouch under the shower, but the hot water makes my skin ache, as if each drop is a tiny blade cutting into my flesh. I wash myself as quickly as I can and climb out. I put on an old bathrobe and hold onto the handrail as I walk slowly down the stairs. The tiles feel cold to my bare feet, but I don't have the strength to go back up and put on socks or slippers.

Mom and Roya wipe their tears and stop whispering when they see me walk into the kitchen.

Roya throws herself on me and curses "them." She holds me tight and tells me that the Komiteh will die a painful death because God always answers her prayers.

She walks with me to the dining room and helps me ease into a chair. She strokes my hair with one hand and feeds me spoonfuls of kabob and rice with the other. My body shakes as I swallow the food, as if it just now realized what it's been missing.

Dad, Cyrus and Nader walk into the dining room. They sit down across the table and stare down in silence. They look sick, thin and pale. The three of them together don't add up to one healthy person.

When I finish the rice on my plate, Dad takes my hand and walks me slowly up the stairs. He moves towards my room, but I let go of his hand and walk towards the family room.

"Where are you going?" he asks.

"I have to call Ari," I say in a barely audible voice.

Mom leaps towards the phone.

"No," she practically yells. She flattens her palm on the phone. "Not yet, honey." She lowers her voice. "Get some rest first. You can call him when you feel better."

I shake my head. "No. I have to talk to him now. I have to make sure he's OK. They beat all the guys badly."

I try to grab the phone from her, but she clutches it firmly and backs away from me. She looks at Dad. Cyrus and Nader come up the stairs and lean against the wall. They stare back and forth between Mom and me.

"Mom," Cyrus says. "Let…"

"No, Cyrus!" Mom says, almost pleading.

Her high-pitched voice startles me. I stare at her. "What's wrong with you?"

"Dariush," Mom says, looking at Dad.

"What's going on?" I ask.

No one says anything.

"Come on, honey," Dad finally says, walking towards me. "Get some rest."

"I've had enough rest. I need to talk to Ari for just one second."

"You'll talk to him later," he says.

"Why can't I just talk to him now?"

They get quiet again.

"What's…what's going on?" I ask again, realizing no one will make eye contact with me.

Cyrus walks towards me and holds my hand. "Come on," he says. "Let's go to your room for a second."

Mom runs towards us. "Cyrus, no! Don't!"

Chapter 43

Maybe I'll change my name to Angela.

Kill two birds with one stone. Change my identity and be called something close to angel. Only something close to it. Because no one can ever call me "Angel" again.

Maybe Angela can learn to smile. Maybe Angela can allow herself to live.

Because Miryam can't. Miryam is blinking. She's breathing. But she doesn't exist anymore. He took her with him. She and everything she lived for. Her children, her grandchildren, her home with the white picket fence, her future, her identity.

Now she has to re-think her life. If she hadn't stopped believing in God that day, maybe she would become a nun. Maybe a spinster surrounded by cats. Maybe she'll even be able to marry. As long as she pretends he's Ari.

So what if she's being selfish? Why shouldn't she be? How much longer is she supposed to think of Ari? He was selfish for leaving her, so why shouldn't she be selfish? He, who had always been so cautious about everything, wasn't careful enough when it really mattered.

Didn't he know that there are no rules in this country? Didn't he know he could get killed? Didn't he know that when they find you in a room with a guy, they don't care what you're doing? That they will brand you a homosexual and stone you to death whether you were naked with him or just talking to him? Didn't he know that their suspicions or excuses are all the laws they need? How could he do that to Miryam? He's gone, free of pain, resting forever. He's not suffering anymore. So why should she feel sorry for him? She's the one left behind in this hell.

Ari, wherever you are, I hate you.

For years, I waited for you. Then your body told me that you loved me. Then your mind ignored what your body had said. So I waited for you some more.

Then I told you I loved you. And I waited for you to say it back. I waited forever. Then you told me you loved me too and wanted to be with me. Finally, the wait was over. But then, you left me forever.

I hate you, Ari. I hate that I wasted half my life for you only to have you take the other half with you before I even had a chance to waste it. Who do you think you are to have so much power over me that you could ruin my life like this? Why did you even come back to Iran? And what were you doing in that room with Bernard? *What were you doing with him?*

How could you leave me with all these questions? How could you make me wonder for the rest of my barren life who you really were? How could I have not known you at all? Did you have a secret life or is it all just a lie? Tell me, Ari. Come back and tell me. *You owe me, dammit; you owe me that much!*

Please, Ari, come back. Just for one minute. So I can see your face, kiss your mouth, tell you how much I miss you. You were the one I turned to when things went wrong in my life. How can you not be here for me to share the worst thing that's ever happened to me?

I love you, Ari.

Please come back. Please, Ari, come back. Come back so I can tell you I love you just one more time. Please Ari. Let me just say it. I won't even care if you say it back.

Chapter 44

Night falls. *Azan Maghreb* beckons.

Every night, the sound of a man chanting the prelude to the evening prayer over a loudspeaker echoes throughout the city. Every night, I close my window to muffle the sound of this maudlin call to prayer that heralds the end of another day.

But tonight, I leave the window open. I kneel beneath it and watch the sun sink into the sky as it pushes up the sounds of prayer like a seesaw.

The man's mournful voice spreads across the landscape and rises towards the mountains. *"Ash Hado Anna Mohammadan Rasool Allah."*

I listen to the man's melodic voice hover over the horizon, under the same peaceful sky that Ari lies. We're hearing the same sound. We are together, if only for this one moment.

I close my eyes and let the voice envelop me. The same voice that always saddened me now makes me serene and whole.

But too soon, the man chants the prayer's climactic refrain. His voice goes dead and I open my eyes to a black, starless sky. I draw the curtains and climb back into bed.

My room is just how I left it the night of the party. All the reminders of life before sit there as if nothing has happened, as if only a few hours have passed since. I stare at the makeup sitting on my vanity table. I frown, squint, then get up and throw them on the floor with force.

Mom checks on me before she goes to bed. I pretend to be asleep and dreaming, instead of awake and bombarded by memories. Even the good memories make me cry. Because they're nothing but preludes to pain.

I'm too tired to talk, listen or look at Mom's concerned eyes even one more time. There's nothing she can do for me.

I can no longer distinguish between being awake and asleep. Part of me is always awake, and on some level, I always know he's dead. But during the countless times throughout the day when the thought rises to the surface, it's as if I just found out.

I've only dreamt of him once. I wasn't even fully asleep. I was on that fuzzy edge between dream and reality.

He was kneeling by my bed, holding my hand. A joint dangled from his mouth. He took the joint out, held it up and said, "Miryam, you wanna get stoned with me?"

The smoke dripping from my cigarette burns my eyes until I see a fragment of the dream come alive. I see Ari's face. I hear his voice. My scream echoes in the maddeningly quiet room.

Mom quickly opens the door and runs to me.

"Are you OK?" she asks, wiping my sweaty face. "You had a nightmare, honey. You...you screamed Ari's name in your sleep."

I don't tell her that I wasn't sleeping. I just hold her tight.

I watch as they all trickle into my room. Dad, Cyrus, Nader, even Roya. They take turns holding me. I tell them that I'm too scared to sleep.

"Please don't leave me," I say quietly. "Please just don't leave me."

Except for Cyrus, who likes to be alone with his sorrow, they all stay.

No one tries to talk. We sit on the floor, me in Mom's lap, my face buried in her bosom. When she tries to get up, I clutch at her tightly.

"Just one second, honey," she says. "I'll be right back."

She returns with a glass of cognac. She hands it to me and tells me to drink it.

I look at Nader and offer him some, but he shakes his head. He's sitting so close to Mom he's practically in her lap. As if he wishes he weren't too young so he, too, could drink the cognac and not too old so he, too, could be cradled in her breasts.

"Niloofar," Dad says sternly in English. "What are you doing? This is inappropriate. Especially in front of the maid. Why are you giving her a drink?"

"I don't care," Mom says in English. "My daughter is sick. Vat I care vat da maid or anybody else tinks?"

"Alcohol is not medicine," Dad says.

"Is medicine for da soul," Mom says. "Der is no medicine doctor can give for da soul."

I sip my cognac and watch Roya pray. She stands in the corner, facing west, bowing, kneeling and looking up at the ceiling with her eyes closed.

The warm cognac coats my throat and travels down to my core, trying, but failing, to soothe the ache.

Suddenly, the lights go out.

"What happened?" Mom asks.

I hear Dad get up and go to my window.

"Power outage," he says.

But unlike during the many power outages we've had, no one complains. No one goes in search of flashlights or candles. Candles especially would make it look too much like a vigil. And there can be no vigil, because in a vigil, there is hope.

Dad sits back down. For hours, we sit in blackness, almost wondering why none of us thought to turn off the lights ourselves. We hide in the dark, grateful for the blindness, oblivious to whose sobs we're hearing, whose anguished face we're not seeing.

Once there's life on the streets and the silence is dead, I watch my family walk towards the faint light at my door like ghosts floating against a silhouette.

I get up and open my window. I hug the sun's rays like a warm blanket and fall asleep with the sound of people outside going about as if it's just another day.

Chapter 45

I gaze out at the window across the street from mine, at an old woman staring out. She looks right at me and smiles. My eyes walk into her tidy bedroom. I imagine standing where she is, looking into my room, thinking, "There are problems in that house."

Every time I exhale into the cool air, the cigarette smoke drifts back inside, hovering over my head like a halo. I throw out the butt, watch it waltz in the air and hit the ground.

The old woman draws her drapes. I stare ahead at the mountains in the distance. Traces of snow still rest on their caps like white-tipped spears cutting into the clouds. A hazy sun reflects off them and burns my eyes even from afar. I close the window and draw the yellow-and-green drapes.

I hug myself and shiver in the dark-blue sweater Ari gave me for my birthday four years ago. I used to wear it out to fancy restaurants and take it to the dry cleaner's saying, "Be careful. It's cashmere." Now I wear it around the house, sometimes even to bed.

I poke my pinky in the small burn hole from my cigarette and try to make it bigger. I play with the sweater's fuzz, thinking back to four years ago, three years ago, two years ago, last year. I try to think of anything but last week.

The reality is always at the forefront of my mind, even when I'm asleep. But sometimes, it's as if I just found out.

Every time the phone rings, my heart pounds. I wait for someone to pick it up and tell me it's Ari. That he's alive and safe in America. That he escaped from prison and went to America. That the story was just his cover-up. Or maybe it's the prison authorities calling to say it was all a mistake. He's not dead. He's still in jail and he'll be released soon.

But each time, it's just another person calling to fulfill their obligation, give us their condolences and be done with it. Mom or Dad say, "Thank you," and hang up.

Every time I hear them cradling the phone back in its place, my hope disappears. The pain starts and I die all over again.

I get up to grab another tissue, but quickly change directions and run outside my room and into the bathroom. I throw up for the fourth time today. That's once less than yesterday. But it's only 6 p.m.

I pass by Mom on my way back to my room. She's sitting on the easy chair in the family room, staring blankly ahead.

"How are you?" she asks.

I don't answer.

She gets up and follows me into my room. I want to tell her to leave me alone, but I don't have the energy. I sit on the floor, hugging my knees and chewing the oily hair that's perpetually stuck to my face.

"Miryam, please talk to me," Mom says, easing herself down on the floor.

I fart.

I look up at Mom. She lets out a giggle. I don't apologize. I don't even get embarrassed.

I let out another fart, one fainter than the last.

"Aftershock?" Mom asks with a smile.

I laugh. I laugh so hard, so loud that the room so used to silence covers its ears. Mom laughs a deep-seated laugh. But I continue long after she stops. I laugh, I laugh, and I laugh.

Mom's smile at my laughter looks sadder than her eyes ever did for my tears. Because she knows that I'm laughing the laugh of the sick, the insane. She tries to get me to stop. But the laughter takes on a mind of its own. Within seconds, I start crying, remnants of laughter echoing through my sobs.

I go to Mom and hold her. I clutch onto her body, trying for every inch of me to touch hers. I wiggle like a worm and put my head between her legs, as if fighting to crawl back inside her womb, turning into a baby, then a fetus, an egg, a sperm, and finally crumbling into nothingness, ceasing to exist.

Chapter 46

The only women who don't own enough black clothes are those in mourning. I yank the clothes out of my laundry hamper to piece together a black outfit that isn't too stained or foul-smelling.

I didn't go to Ari's burial, but Mom is making me go to Soraya's house for the funeral. She says it'll help me get closure and that I should pay my respects to his mother. Sometimes I forget that I wasn't the closest person to him, that someone else is suffering even more than I am.

I pull out my thickest pair of black tights from the hamper. I need to cover the bruise on my thigh, where I pounded myself for two hours while my family was at Ari's burial. I had to, after all, experience the pain of being there without actually watching them lower him into the ground.

I closed my window after I saw Dad's car turn the corner and roll towards the cemetery. I shut my door in case Roya passed by. I sat calmly on my bed and pounded, pinched and pricked myself in between taking drags of smoke. When I could no longer take the pain in my thigh, I searched the back of my right arm. I found it and jammed the cigarette into the root of the long, white stray hair that amused Ari so much. I watched it shrivel up, leaving in its place a burn mark.

I made sure that the shriveled-up hair stuck firmly to end of my cigarette before I added its ashes to the ashes already piled on the plate swimming with cigarette butts. I buried the hair among the debris and smoothed it all into dust.

Mom said she would take me to visit his grave whenever I was ready. I said that I would never visit his grave. He shouldn't even be buried at *Beheshteh Zahra*. They should've found room at the cemetery where his father rests and buried the father and son who suffered the same fate next to each other.

Or they should've flown his body to America so he wouldn't have to spend eternity in the country that had killed him. There, I may someday find the strength to visit him and say goodbye.

Mom walks into my room and asks if I'm ready to go to the funeral. I stop myself from asking, "Is anybody ever ready to go to a funeral?"

I nod and tell her I'll be down soon. I stop at the full-length mirror in our hallway. I look exactly the way the government wants me to look all the time: covered from head to toe in black, no nail polish, and misery decorating my face instead of makeup.

"You win, assholes," I whisper as I turn away. "You win."

Chapter 47

We walk into Soraya's apartment and blend quietly into the crowd of black. I find a seat close to the door and try to disappear from everyone's view. No one says condolences to me, as if I'm just another guest, here to get the formalities over with and go back to my normal life. If I were in the States, everyone would be coming to see me. But here, no one even knows me. No one knows who Ari was to me. Mine is nothing but another sad face in the crowd.

I look around for Soraya. When I see her walk out the bathroom, I have to look at Mom's shocked expression before trusting my own eyes.

She's dressed in red with red lips to match. The only indication that she's in pain is that her eyes are red to match her clothes, and her face looks aged, tired and pale. Her features are stretched disproportionately, almost crooked, like the result a botched facelift. Her lips are swollen and her eyes are puffed out and narrowed.

I walk extra slowly towards her. She holds me close and tugs at my hair so tightly I expect to see a fistful of hair in her hand when she finally lets go. Then abruptly, she walks away from me, almost shoving me aside as if she had mistaken me for someone else. Mom pats my empty seat and I return to it without acknowledging the stares from the other mourners. I hold Mom's hand again, tangling my fingers with hers, digging my unshapely, long nails into her palm.

My eyes trail the garden of flowers in the room before falling on the roses I had given Ari when he arrived. They're still here, in the same vase I had arranged them in that night. Their stems are bowed in sorrow, the few petals still alive touching those of white orchids in a nearby potted soil. Wilted flowers celebrating his presence mingling amidst fresh flowers lamenting his absence.

I look around the apartment. I see him everywhere: by the kitchen, holding a basketball; by the entrance, opening the door for me; by the bedroom with a suitcase in his hand.

Soraya hasn't moved from her chair since she sat down an hour ago. She stares almost resentfully at all the people who walk in and out of her apartment, kiss her hand and scramble to make room for the deluge of flowers.

But when one of the guests holds her hand and whispers something in her ear, she stands up in a flush.

"You want to know why I'm wearing red?" she screams. "Because I'm wearing the black inside." She points towards the window. "And I won't give them the satisfaction of seeing me wear black on the outside too."

"I didn't say anything about you wearing red," the woman says, looking around nervously.

"Yes, you did!" Soraya screams. "I heard you! You're all talking about me like I've gone insane just because I'm wearing red. Wouldn't *you* be insane, even if you were sane enough to wear black?"

A few people walk slowly towards her and hold her hands.

"Let go!" she screams. "Let go!"

She walks towards the window, flings it open and hollers into the street, "They think I've gone insane! What do they know? I went insane when you killed my husband. Now I'm past insanity. What's the point past insanity? Tell me! You must know! You've taken me there! What's next? You want to kill me too? Do it! Please do it! Come up here and take me too! Come up here, you bastards!"

She pulls off her red blouse and unhooks her black bra. She flings her bra to the side. "Is this enough? Is this wrong enough that you'll kill me for it?"

Her dangling breasts heave through her sobs. Mom runs to her and covers her with the blouse hanging off the window ledge.

I can't hear Mom's whisper, but I read her lips. "Soraya joon, come and let's put you to bed."

Soraya throws her bra onto the street and pushes Mom away.

"What else do you want from me?" she screams. "You took my husband; you took my son. Why are you so obsessed with me? Come up here, you bastards!"

Her shaking voice turns into coughs and wails until she becomes incoherent. The male guests lower their heads and walk out of the apartment. Mom comes back into the middle of living room and motions for the women to join them.

"I'll take care of her," Mom says. "Thank you for coming. I think she needs to be alone now."

"What do you want from me?" Soraya continues to scream, oblivious to what's going on in the background. "Come and kill me and put me out of my misery! What do I have to live for? Nothing! Come and kill me, too!"

Mom gives me a bottle of pills and a glass of water and tells me to take them to Soraya. I hesitate. Mom pushes me forward. I walk towards Soraya with apprehension, my heart beating faster with each step. I gently nudge her and hand her the glass.

"Look at this girl!" she yells, pointing at me. "She took care of my son when I had to let him go. She loved him like I did. And you took him away from her too. I'm old; I'm going to die soon. But what about her? Isn't she too young to see how cruel life is? Doesn't she deserve some time to live in fantasy before she sees what this world is really all about? Don't you have sons? Don't you know what it's like to lose a son? I would never have killed your sons! Why… why would you kill mine?" Her voice gets raspier and raspier until she needs to cough. Then she takes a deep breath and continues.

"That child slept in my arms for months after you killed his father. I would wipe the sweat from his face when he would wake up screaming his father's name. What did I do all that for? So you could one day take him away, too? You forced me to live alone, without my son. You forced me to send him away and live without him by my side. But that wasn't enough for you, was it? It wasn't enough that I didn't watch my son grow up. It wasn't enough that we lived on opposite sides of the world. You had to take him away from me completely."

"Soraya joon, please," I say with tears streaming down my face. "Please stop it! Please stop it!"

I put the glass on the windowsill and sit on the arm of a nearby sofa, burying my face in my hands.

"Please stop it," I whisper.

Mom comes and holds me. Soraya looks at us and walks away from the window. Mom hands her a pill from the bottle I put on the table. She swallows it dry. She walks past the remaining guests as they try to avoid looking at her dangling breasts. She goes into the bedroom, closes the door gently and screams.

I get up and look out the window. A small crowd is gathered below, staring up.

"What's happened?" a lady in a chador asks. "Who killed her son?"

You did. You and countless others like you. All of you who welcomed and supported this government did. Every single one of you killed her son.

I close the window and draw the curtains without answering her.

All the guests reluctantly leave. Mom tells us to go wait in the car. I ask to stay, but she shakes her head.

She picks up the bottle of pills. She empties half of it into her palm and hands me the bottle. "Take one of these when you get home, Miryam," she says. "Just one."

I stare at the bottle. Dad tries to yank it out of my hand, but I tighten my grip and pull it away from him.

"I'll try to convince Soraya to come and stay at our place so I can be with both of you," Mom says. "Just give me a few hours with her here."

I nod and watch her almost tiptoe into Soraya's room, closing the door gently behind her.

I stand there alone and stare at the bottle. I pop open the cap, empty the tiny white pills onto my palm and count.

Twelve. I don't even know what kind of pills they are. And I don't care.

Chapter 48

God, please don't let me die. I know I've overdosed, but I didn't do it to die. I didn't do it for attention either.

At last count, I'd taken seven of those pills. Maybe eight. I still don't know what's in them. But there's 30 mg. of "it" in each pill. 30x7=210.

My skin itches, as if the pills are itching to crawl out from under it. I hear my brain cracking inside my skull. Everything feels light: my head, my walk, my blood. Please God, let me wake up from it and for no one to know the unfathomable things I do. Please God, carry me as my feet walk on air.

I crawl out of bed and look in the mirror. My pupils are over-sized marbles swaying to a metronome. I'm keenly aware of everything, all the senses, but so numb to any feeling. The faintest sound makes me jolt like a leg jerking in early sleep. The water swishing in the street canal outside sounds like it's gushing inside my ear canal. I'm even blinking too loudly. All the sounds synthesize into a symphony of psychosis.

I look so thin and frail. One day, every cell in my body will retaliate like a fed-up soldier. They will revolt and kill the dictator that is my mind.

Are those cockroaches or my shoes?

According to my thermometer, I'm dead.

I'm thinking in fragments. I'm talking to myself in snippets.

I open the window to get some fresh air.

Is that Nader down there waiting for his bus?

I shiver under the sun, squint at the breeze. *Yes, it is Nader.* I can tell from the sadness on his face.

Just a few years ago, Ari drove him to school in America, where he was popular, energetic, fun-loving. Look at him now. Bent over from the weight of his bag like an old man who has seen too much of life. Everything that comprised his simple, happy life is gone. How cruel that he has to go to school right now. How can he do it? How could he get dressed, stand there, climb up the steps onto that bus? What's the point of school anyway? What's the hurry to cram in all the lessons that you will inevitably learn in life?

Come up here, Nader, and I'll teach you all you need to know. All the important things that they won't teach you in school.

Math: 30x7=210 mg=overdose.

Biology: Drugs destroy neurons that are essential to normal brain activity.

Health: Drugs kill.

Religion: Abusing one's body is a sin.

Chemistry: CO_2 kills, whereas O_2 is essential for the lungs.

French: Les drogues nuisent gravement à la santé.

Government: Federal law prohibits use of prescription drugs by anyone other than for whom it was prescribed.

Geometry: The shortest distance between the point of life and death is a long line of pills.

Philosophy: I think, therefore I am. Insane.

Physics: A body at rest will remain at rest. At best.

English Literature: A body in motion, collapsed by emotion, will ensue commotion.

Geography: Wherever you go, there you are.

History: Repeats itself.

Chapter 49

I'M cheating on my lover tonight. Whiskey instead of vodka.

Fear, anger and sorrow churn with the pills and alcohol like a cycle of chemicals and emotions traveling endlessly in two opposite directions of the same circle; soaking, washing, spinning, but never cleansing.

Even alcohol has abandoned me in my time of need. Even pills fail to numb me. They've turned their backs on me. They were there for the good times, winking at me from afar, kissing my lips and dancing in my blood. But now, like everyone else, they no longer want my company.

You thought you could live without us, they scream? *You abandoned us and now that you need us again, you come crawling back and expect us to be there?*

I beat myself, slam my head against the floor and cut myself with a knife. I wash the blood away with the vodka. It can no longer kill the pain, so I demand that it make it worse.

I watch the blood drain from me under the hot shower. So hot that it burns like the cigarettes I put out on my skin. I cover it all up in my black attire. I shock only myself when I undress in front of the bathroom mirror and stare at my 90-pound body adorned with tattoos of blood.

I wish I were still in jail. There, I couldn't see life on the streets. I wish I were still locked behind bars, physically trapped from leading even a mundane existence. But imprisoned only by my mind, I envy those I see walking free every day, those who don't struggle just to exist.

Shower now. The easiest of mundane tasks. There, under the flood, I belong.

Part III

Chapter 1

Depression is spreading through this house like a virus. Like a lingering flu that keeps getting passed back and forth. But they all blame it on me, because a symptom of depression in this family is a blindness that darkens all mirrors.

Mom says it's been over a year and I should be over him by now. Even Cyrus and Nader are better, she says. None of us will heal as long as I continue to remind them of what happened. It's over, she says. Time to move on, stop dwelling, stop wearing black even.

"We cannot bear to see you like this anymore," Mom says.

"So don't see me," I say. "Let me leave. I won't be fine until I'm out of this country."

"You can't leave just yet, Miryam," she says. "You can't take care of yourself yet. We found you a psychiatrist. We want you to go see him. We'll let you go back when he says you're ready."

The psychiatrist's waiting room smells like dust sprayed with disinfectant. I stare at the thin lips of a young patient talking to me about art. I frown at his questions. I don't remember Monet's work. I don't care about Manet's. He's talking too much, all nonsense. It's all mixing with the insanity already in my head. It's as if he's scribbling with crayons on a canvas that already has paint dribbling off it.

Cyrus' shrink's office in the States was designed in a way that you could never run into any other patients. But here, privacy doesn't matter. Schizophrenics, manic-depressives and psychopaths get to have their illnesses mingle before formally presenting them to the doctor.

Just when I let out a loud, exaggerated sigh aimed at the guy's incoherent jumble of a rant, the secretary leads me into an office that looks like a library from an old mystery movie. Or possibly where Professor Plum killed Miss Scarlet. With the candlestick.

I sit on a large brown armchair with rough yellow foam oozing out its peeling sleeve. The psychiatrist rises from his chair halfway, then sits back down with a nod. I immediately nickname him "Einstein" because of the resemblance. But only the physical one. I nod back and smile weakly at his wild white hair.

"I had a session with your parents a while ago," he says. "They filled me in on what's happened. You were still a little too sick to come see me back then. Nice to see you're doing better."

I frown.

"Are you still drinking?" he asks before I have a chance to ask if I look like his idea of someone who's doing "better."

I quickly look up at him. He raises his bushy white eyebrows.

"Miryam," he says. "I asked if you're still drinking."

"I'm trying to," I say. "But it's not working anymore."

He frowns, obvious that he doesn't understand why I would try to drink instead of to stop. But he doesn't say anything. He studies my blank face for a while and then says, "Why don't you tell me how you're feeling at this exact moment?"

I continue to stare down. Then I shift in my seat and take a deep breath. I look into his eyes and just when he thinks I'm about to open up my soul, I shrug.

Then I start crying softly. He watches me with a smile. When he realizes there's no end to my tears, but a definite end to our session, he starts talking. And never stops.

I take out and light a cigarette without asking for permission. I take a long drag and wait for him to tell me to put it out. But he doesn't. His glazed eyes stare out the window at a small patio with three dead plants. He's playing with a Bic pen and talking, very softly, about lucid dreaming. It's hard to hear him over the hum of the small electric fan that's blowing my smoke around in circles.

I look at my watch. Only 10 minutes left. I put my head on his desk with a slight bang. It works. He stops talking. I lift my head back up and look into his huge, stoned-looking eyes.

"How am I going to go on without him?" I ask.

"There's plenty of fish in the sea," he says in broken English, actually smiling at his inappropriate cliché.

"I lost my virginity to that fish."

"Aha," he says, raising his index finger. "Now we're getting somewhere. The first sexual experience. Very key in a young woman's life."

I wait for him to use that key, open a new dialogue and elaborate on his "aha" moment. But he doesn't. He stares at me with a frozen smile. It's obvious that we're not getting anywhere. How can I possibly explain my love for Ari to an old Iranian man who doesn't even know me, regardless that he's a psychiatrist? How would I explain my feelings to, say, our street sweeper?

"I was a virgin for 23 years," I say. "I was raised to be a virgin until I got married. And I gave it to him. That's how much he meant to me."

"Do your parents know? That you had sex with him?"

"No," I quickly say. "And please don't tell them."

"Of course not," he says with a frown. "I'm a professional. An open-minded professional." He shakes his head, obviously insulted that I would insinuate that he was anything but.

"So you're worried about your parents finding out?" he asks.

"A little," I say. "But I have bigger fish to fry."

"Aha," he says. "But you don't have a frying pan."

"Excuse me?"

"You say you have bigger fish to fry," he says with a smile. "But you don't even have a frying pan."

"I get the pun," I practically yell, angry at his smile and his lame jokes. "But other than it being *extremely* clever, what does that even mean?"

"It means you don't have the right tools," he says, not getting my sarcasm. "There are doctors who can sew your hymen back up if you're so concerned that you're not a virgin. I can refer you to someone. I know lots of doctors who specialize in it. One day of bedrest. If I'm not mistaken, it's an outpatient surgery. Very simple. I wouldn't even call it a surgery, more like a procedure. Like an abortion. Very common. Lots of girls here get it done."

I stare down at the ashtray cradling my cigarette butt. I pick it up and play with the ashes, brushing them all to one side. He watches me, probably analyzing it in some way. I think he's waiting for me to say something. But I don't. He flips through the Rolodex on his table, then jots something on a scrap piece of paper.

"Here's the number of a good one," he says and hands me the paper. "He specializes in sewing hymens."

I want to ask if he's a gynecologist or a plastic surgeon. Or maybe a tailor. But that would make him think it matters. I grab the paper and walk out of his office without so much as a thank you or even a goodbye. I crumple the paper and throw it in the street gutter, before hailing a taxi.

"Where to?" the driver asks.

"The hell out of here."

Chapter 2

I knew my parents wouldn't accept me saying I didn't want to see the psychiatrist anymore without an explanation or a barrage of questions. So I'm not surprised when an hour after I get home, Dad knocks, then walks into my bedroom, where I've climbed back into bed, propped against a pillow, staring into space, a cigarette dangling from my mouth.

"Dad, please don't make me to go back to him," I say, throwing my cigarette into a half-empty bottled water.

I already know his response, so when he starts to say something, I immediately plead, "And I don't want to try another shrink either. It's not going to help. Please, Dad. I don't want to see a therapist. I know everything they'll all say."

I think of Dr. Rubenstein, Cyrus' therapist in L.A. I almost resent him for his prophetic assessment that I might turn self-destructive because I lacked nurturing and attention growing up.

Dad sees the tired desperation on my face and walks towards my bed without saying anything.

"I know I need therapy," I say. "Lots of it. But I'm not ready. It's too overwhelming right now."

Dad sits at the edge of my bed and looks down.

"The sooner you start, the sooner you can get better," he says. "Start letting out everything that's built up in you. Everything going on in your head. It's not healthy to bottle it all up."

I grab my skull with both hands and shake my head, as if cradling the thoughts inside and trying to shake them out at the same time.

"Dad, please. The things in my head aren't even psychological at this point. They're philosophical. Existential."

I lean my head against the wall and sigh.

Dad nods slowly, seriously. Then he shrugs with a smile. "Try me."

I pull my knees to me and look back and forth between Dad's curious face and the pile of clothes on my floor.

Dad waits patiently until I finally take a deep breath and say, "Dad, I know you're not religious, but please don't say something like Islam is to blame. Tell me why God allowed them to kill Ari in His name?"

Dad frowns. "I'm not going to say that because I don't believe that. I don't believe Islam killed Ari. And I don't believe God killed him either."

I lower my head.

"God and religion are not the same thing," he says as he scoots closer to me. "In a country that has no democracy, they have to find a way to control people. They have to come up with their own justice system. Their particular way of scaring people into obeying laws. It could be through a dictatorship or fascism. Iran's government is supposedly a theocracy. But in reality, it's religious fanaticism. Fanaticism. *Interpreting* religion in their own way. It's nothing but politics. Don't get me started about the corruption in politics, here, or anywhere else in the world. But the government killed Ari. Not religion. Religion is the word they use for politics. And it's certainly not God because God would never condone killing anyone. For *anything.*"

"I try to tell myself that, Dad, but I just can't get the image of the word 'God' written on those buses that took us to jail that night out of my head."

Dad sighs and shakes his head. He gets quiet and his eyes take on that look of when he's trying to figure something out.

A few minutes pass before he says, "Miryam, name the worst person you can think of. In all of history, someone you think was the most heinous person in the world."

"Hitler," I say immediately.

"Perfect," he says, shifting his legs. "Perfect. Now think about this. God wouldn't even condone killing someone as bad as Hitler. God created Hitler and only He can decide Hitler's fate or judge Hitler. No man, no country, no religion, has the right to do that. That would be playing God. And God doesn't want man to play God."

"What if God decided that Ari's fate was for Islam to kill him?"

Dad shakes his head. "Ari's fate was his fate. But that doesn't mean that God would condone what happened to him. I repeat, God didn't kill Ari, honey. Neither did Islam. A bunch of ignorant people who think they know God killed him. Islam has a bad wrap. But when you think about it, all religions are the same. Religion is the biggest antidote to God. It is the work of the devil, if you ask me. Even worse; it's the devil impersonating God." His voice gets animated.

"Listen to that. Religion is the devil *impersonating* God. All religions. Religion broods on man's ego. And when a man is in ego, he is at the farthest point from God. Did you know that?

I shake my head, not even sure what he's talking about.

"What does ego have to do with..."

Dad interrupts me. "The ultimate layer that man needs to shed to get close to God is ego. Man has to sacrifice his ego. Which is impossible to do completely because man is by nature ego-driven."

He pauses. "By man, I mean people."

I nod.

"We're all driven by ego," he continues. "But we can control the degree to which we're attached to our egos. And the more we're in ego, the farther we are from God. So with that in mind, think of religion. Again, all religions. Every religion tells its followers that they are the best, that they are following God's right orders, that they are the chosen ones, that they are the ones who will go to heaven. Every religion thinks their holy book is God's final word. Now what can be more egotistical than that? To think that you're the chosen one but someone of another religion isn't because he doesn't follow your religion? To think that you're going to heaven because you follow the rules of a certain book but someone else will go to hell because they read a different book? It's comical when you think about it."

He smiles and watches my expressionless face.

"Ego is the antidote to God," Dad says. "And yet, religion soars your ego by telling you that you're better than another person because your religion is better than his. Even though that other person is also a human being that God created."

He stares at me. "Are you following me?"

I nod swiftly. "Yes, I...I actually am. I've never thought about it that way. It makes sense."

Dad gets excited at my interest. His voice gets louder. "How can you be close to God if you think you're better than someone else, which means you're in ego, and in the *name* of God no less?"

I nod again. "I get it, Dad. But how do you know this? About ego, I mean?"

"All religions have that in common," he says. "Humility. That's why I said I don't blame Islam specifically. All religions preach humility. Which is the opposite of ego."

He stares out the window and shakes his head. "It's hard for me to understand people who don't see this. Even if religion isn't man-made, it is definitely man-interpreted. If God is all-knowing, as every religion says, then how would He not know that different religions would cause so much strife among people? Why would He come up with different holy books and different prophets? Why would He not say all He had to say in one book instead of coming up with the Old Testament, then the New Testament, then the Torah, then the Koran... why would He not have one holy book, one prophet, one set of rules or commandments or whatever you want to call them? Why all the different branches and sects and denominations? Why create all that confusion among people?"

"Why did He?" I ask.

"He *didn't,* honey!" Dad practically screams. "I'm being rhetorical. God didn't create all that. Man did."

"What about all the good things in the holy books?" I ask.

"Those are the only things they have in common," Dad says. "It's only the bad things, the contradictions, the talks about hell and judgment and all that garbage that's different in the holy books. Because that's all man-made. From a time where there were no laws and they created these as a way to scare people into not doing anything wrong or immoral. I thought we had talked about this before, Miryam. When you were little."

"We did," I say. "About there not being any laws in the old days. Not about the ego and the contradictions."

"In the history of the world," Dad says, shaking his head, "nothing has caused more destruction, more wars, more division among men than their interpretation of religion. Do you think God would want that? Don't you think an all-knowing God could have predicted that and prevented it if it really came from Him? It's the way man has interpreted religion that has caused all this."

"That's why in Westernized countries, there's a separation of church and state," I say as if to prove that I do know about this concept.

"There you go," Dad says, slapping my knee. "That's exactly right."

"And I mean this about all religions," Dad says again. "Not just Islam. Who killed Jesus? God? Or a handful of people who judged him? And wasn't it Jesus who when a group of people were trying to stone a woman for adultery under the laws of Moses said 'Let he who has never sinned cast the first stone?'"

A chill goes through me as I think of the literal stones that were cast on Ari. I wonder if that's why Dad brought it up. But I don't ask.

"Now take everything I just said about religion and add politics to the equation," Dad says, oblivious to the sweat that's suddenly dripping down my face. "That's a deadly combination. The combination that killed Ari."

Dad sees that tears are gathering in my eyes and that I'm starting to shake. He moves closer and grabs my hands tightly in his.

"Ari may have died in a car accident and you may have asked me some questions about why God allowed that to happen and that would've been a lot tougher for me to answer," Dad says. "But this...that a government that uses religion as a guise for politics killed him because of something they may or may not have misinterpreted in the Koran and used it to exert their power? Come on!"

Dad brushes away my tears and holds me. He rocks me slowly and gets quiet for a few minutes.

"You should feel sorry for people who are fanatics about religion," he says when he finally lets go. "If someone uses religion to do good, more power to them. But when they use it to cause pain and destruction and actually kill in God's name, for any reason, they may as well be following the devil."

"What if it's someone that God doesn't approve of?" I ask, hoping Dad doesn't think I'm asking about Ari personally. "I mean, what if God really didn't approve of the actions of the person who was killed?"

"Your Hitler example?" he reminds me. "No one would have the right to kill Hitler in the name of God. Who's to say that if you had Hitler's DNA, his brain, upbringing, mentality, a million things that go into what made Hitler who he was, you or I, or anyone else wouldn't have done everything he did." He pauses and chuckles. "I'm not defending Hitler. I'm..."

"No, I know," I say. "I get what you're saying. The government killed Ari."

"Politics killed him," Dad says. "People killed him. Mere mortals. No different from you or me. Or Ari."

Dad gets a distant looks in his eyes and says softly, "God's love is not hemmed in by the doctrine of man." He pauses. "I read that somewhere. And it may not be the exact quote, but Karl Marx said, 'Religion is the oppressor of man.'"

"Karl Marx?" I say. "Wasn't he the guy who...wasn't he the father of communism?"

"I'm impressed," Dad say, raising his eyebrows. "Girl knows her history. Yes, he was. But he was also a brilliant philosopher. And communist or not, I happen to agree with that particular philosophy."

"How do you know all this, Dad?" I ask. "About God, I mean."

"Education," he says. "Education, knowledge, wisdom. All the opposites of ignorance. It's not enough to just know facts. We have to use our brains, the brain God gave us, to gather information from all areas, including religion, and then use common sense."

I nod. Dad watches my face.

"We all have common sense, Miryam. We all have wisdom. We just have to use it. Trust it. I don't believe in religion, but I trust my belief in God."

"I know, Dad," I say. "I know you're not an atheist. That's why I wanted to know what you thought about this."

"I know you've always had a strong connection with God," Dad says. "Ever since you were a little girl." He smiles with a look in his eyes that I know means he just remembered a specific image or memory of me as a little girl. But he keeps it to himself and just says, "You haven't lost that connection because of what happened to Ari, have you?"

I hesitate. "It's been hard. I did at first, a little. But somehow, I still have faith. I just needed to talk about this with someone else. Someone intelligent, but not religious."

He smiles again. "Well, thank you. I'm very flattered. And I hope I helped."

I nod. I lift myself off the bed to kiss him, then I look at him with a slight frown.

"Speaking of feeling flattered," I say. "And no offense, Dad. But you believe that some people are better than others. You think you're better than someone who's not educated, or you think some people are of a lower class than others. I mean, you are pretty judgmental. And your ego just got boosted because I called you intelligent..."

His chuckle interrupts me. "Did I say I was perfect? Did I say I had no ego and was very close to being godly?"

I smile.

"But I've never killed anyone," he says. "And I don't condone killing anyone or think I'm better than someone else because I was born into a certain religion."

"Touché," I say with a smile. "Thank you, Dad. That...I mean, you, actually helped. A lot."

Dad looks at his watch and smiles back. "How much does that psychiatrist charge per hour?"

Chapter 3

Mom watches me to make sure I take the Prozac Dr. Einstein prescribed. "Good girl," she says with a smile.

My parents accepted for me not to see the shrink anymore, but insisted I take the medication. It's a bitter pill to swallow knowing you need to swallow a pill to function. But the masochist in me takes the pill every day, as if begging for more of life's bitterness. So I'm back to living. The kind of living where I don't spend my waking hours waiting for death.

"Miryam," Mom says, "your psychiatrist's secretary called yesterday. Do you remember a young man in the waiting room with you that day?"

I nod and groan, remembering the frustration of being in that room with him for a full 12 minutes.

Mom whispers even though no one's around. "He really liked you." She smiles proudly. "The secretary called and asked my permission to give him our phone number. He wants to go out with you."

I stare at her.

"What do you think?" she asks.

"I think that's the dumbest thing I've ever heard," I say. "Even if he wasn't one of the most annoying people on the planet…two people who need psychiatric help going out. '*Oh, where did you two meet? At out shrink's office.*'"

Mom throws her head back and laughs. "That's what your dad said. He said we don't need two crazies dating."

"Thanks a lot."

"No, no," Mom says, no longer laughing. "He meant the guy, not you. He was there to see the other psychiatrist who works in that office. You were there just because of a little depression, which doesn't make you crazy and…"

"Why are you telling me this?" I ask. "What is the point of this conversation?"

"Maybe he'll take your mind off your problems."

"My *problems*?" I ask with a frown.

"I mean, maybe if you went out with a nice boy, you could, you know…"

"No, I don't know," I say, raising my voice with each word. "What? Forget about Ari? Because of some random crazy guy? I can't even believe you're saying this. How stupid can you be?"

"Now wait a minute, Miryam. There's no reason to get so aggressive. I'm just trying to help."

"Well, you're not!" I scream. "You don't understand what I'm going through. You have no idea. For a while there, I thought maybe you understood. But you have no clue. You said I could go back because of Ari, but what you really meant was 'Oh, just go back and get married.' It didn't matter who the guy was. Well, it matters to me. He's not some *problem* that I can just forget about."

Mom frowns and walks backwards into the kitchen, as if inching away from an assailant.

"I never said that," Mom says quietly, a confused look spreading across her face.

"You see those plates in the dishwasher," I say, pointing behind her. "You can't just rinse them off and let the machine do the dirty work. You have to scrub and scrape and sometimes if you wait too long, it's too late. It gets stuck on for good."

She frowns even more, but doesn't say anything, probably wondering what dirty dishes have to do with what we're talking about.

"You think Ari was just some guy who can be replaced? He was my everything. He was the only one who was always there for me. He was the *one* constant in my life. He was the only one there for me growing up." My voice gets hoarse and I well up with tears. "When you abandoned me. He was the one who helped me raise your kids when I was just a kid myself."

My body goes limp and I slide down the kitchen wall onto the floor. Mom stares at me. Roya walks in from the laundry room. She looks at me, then walks slowly towards Mom. She takes Mom's head and rests it on her shoulder. Mom tugs at Roya's scarf as if it's a shield of armor against my bullets.

I wait for my cries to die down before I continue, switching to English so Roya won't understand.

"I've always blamed myself for everything that's ever gone wrong in our lives. Cyrus has been blaming himself. Even Ari blamed himself. We all blamed ourselves when it was never our fault. It was your fault, but you're the only one who didn't take the blame. All those years of telling you, 'Oh, we're fine, nothing is happening, and I'll just talk to you next week.' Well, we're *not* fine. A lot has happened. And come to think of it, I never could talk to you. How could you not know we weren't fine? How could we be? We were just kids. But you just wanted to believe the lie so you wouldn't have to deal with the guilt. And now you're telling me I can't go back because you're worried about me and you don't think I can take care of myself?"

I feel Mom and Roya staring at me. I avoid their eyes. Part of me wants to crawl over to Mom, hold her leg and already beg her forgiveness. But something stronger, something beyond my control, takes over. Every word feels like a forceful vomit that spews uncontrollably out of my mouth.

"I'm going back, Mom. And I don't care what you or anybody else thinks. You're always worried about what people will think. Their opinion is always more important to you than mine. And I'm *sick* of it. I'm making myself physically sick because of how sick of it all I am. I don't care what anybody thinks anymore because it's my turn to be happy. What prize was I given all those years for being such a good girl? No one even cared. Maybe if I stop caring what anyone else thinks, I'll finally be normal. I've tried to please you all my life. I've tried to make you proud. And you never were. It was just expected. All these sacrifices were expected because I'm a girl. And in your eyes, that's a nothing. Because that's how you've been treated all your life. Like a nothing. This family takes away every ounce of my self-esteem. I'm always reminded that even though I'm important, I'm never *as* important as whatever the pressing concern of the moment is."

I melt completely into the floor. My sobs synchronize with Mom's. I bow my head and stare at the grime between the tiles. The clock above the stove ticks, the dryer in the laundry room adjacent to the kitchen hums. Louder and louder. Once in a while, a button or zipper on a pair of jeans scrapes against the spinning dryer. I concentrate on the sounds of the dryer and the clock until I can no longer hear Mom heaving or Roya's leg twitching nervously.

Chapter 4

A week later, Mom watches me eat my lunch in silence. I peer over at her whenever I feel her staring down. I ache to hold her. I pray that she'll tell me nothing has changed, that she still loves me and knows I adore her.

But I just stuff the spoon in my mouth and struggle to swallow. There are some words you can never take back. And I bombarded her with all of them.

After lunch, Mom asks me into her room.

"Come sit here with me, Miryam," she says, patting her bed.

I smile like a child whose mommy just told her she's the prettiest little girl in the whole wide world.

"Mom," I say, walking towards her. "I'm sorry about the other day. I was just upset."

"Don't be," she says quickly, as if she's been waiting for my apology.

"But I didn't mean it," I say. "You're a wonderful mother. You and Dad did everything for us. And I love you. So much."

I whimper, "I love you so much, Mom."

"Sit down, Miryam."

I do, avoiding her eyes. I grab a throw pillow and look down as I pull the feathers out of its torn corner.

"Miryam, you let out everything you wanted to say to me all these years. And I didn't interrupt you. So show me the same courtesy."

I nod without looking up. Mom takes a deep breath.

"Miryam, since the first hour of the revolution, all that went through my head was my children. *What's going to happen to my children?* I didn't care if they assassinated me and your father the way they did Ari's dad. I didn't care if they threw me in jail for the rest of my life just for being rich. All I cared about was getting you kids out of here so you wouldn't have to suffer for one second. You were just a child. You don't remember what it was like in those days. Children were being kidnapped left and right. Your father and I would get death threats on your lives for bribes. We had tried so hard to give you the best education, put you in the best schools. And everything was taken away from us overnight. So many horrible days. The day I found out Cyrus might be drafted for the war when he turned 13. The day…"

She shakes her head. "Too many days to mention."

She takes another deep breath.

"I told your father that I have to get you kids out of this country even if I died doing it. We decided to start a whole new life in America. Again, you don't remember. You don't know how hard it was for us to even get visas for America. And then, when we finally got there, we thought everything was going to be fine. We were so optimistic. And so naïve to think it would be so simple. Your father and I weren't children. We couldn't adapt the way you kids did. It was much harder than we thought it would be to start a new life at our age. I know you remember how depressed your father and I were. I know you remember him drinking every night."

She looks down for a long time. When she finally raises her eyes, they're filled with tears. Her voice shakes. I go to hold her, but she pushes me away.

"Then one day, I found cocaine in your dad's drawer," she says, ignoring the shock on my face. "He was becoming a drug addict. Fast. We were on the verge of getting a divorce. We tried so hard to keep it all away from you kids. But it was getting impossible. We had to leave, Miryam. We had to come back here, so we could work through our problems away from you kids, so you would be spared being in that toxic atmosphere. I didn't want you to see your father like that. You saw how he got that night with you when he was drunk. You saw how frightened you were? Imagine if you had to live with that every night growing up. As it was, you saw too many of those nights. I had to take him away from you kids. I cried myself to sleep every night the first month I was away from you. I would stare at the phone, just waiting for it to ring and for one of you to tell me something horrible had happened. I was torn between my children and my husband. And I was stupid enough to think that he couldn't make it without me, but you kids could." She shakes her head. "I can't believe I thought that. But it made sense then. I thought I was doing the right thing by staying here, making sure your dad wasn't slipping to a point of no return, getting our properties back from the government and making sure we could send you money so you could have a comfortable life there."

She goes into thought, almost like she's forgotten I'm there. Her voice is a murmur.

"One day I woke up an old woman whose life had passed without seeing her children grow up. And I knew that I could never have those years back. Everyone, every single person, made decisions and sacrifices after the revolution. I made all the wrong ones. And there is no way for me to make it up to any of you. I will die knowing I lived a life that was a series of mistakes. I pray that you never have to make the kinds of decisions I had to make.

"I was so happy when I had all my children with me again these past couple of years. I didn't want to see how miserable you were. I forced us to be a family. I lied to myself saying you'd come around and we would be a family again and that none of those years had gone by. I cannot make it up to you, Miryam. I can just hope that someday, when you're a mother, you will understand. You will see that once children come into your life, you will do anything for their happiness. Or what you think will bring them happiness. Maybe then, you can forgive me."

I reach over and she lands in my embrace.

"I...there's nothing to forgive you for," I say. "I didn't mean what I said that day. I was just angry."

Her body shakes in my arms. "Yes, you were," she whispers. "At me. And you have every right to be. You think I left you there to raise my kids while I was here going to parties every night."

She untangles her body from mine. I look down.

"But that's not true," she says. "I was miserable over here. I didn't let on to what I was going through because I knew you were already so sad and alone."

"Mom, it's not a contest as to who was more miserable."

"I know that," she says almost angrily. "I just don't want you to think I neglected you to come here and live a carefree life. My only real pleasure was doing my charity work. I never just gave money and left it at that. I'd take candy and toys to the kids at orphanages and play with them. Of course, it was also depressing. Playing and feeding animals in shelters and then watching them whimper when the workers put them back in their cages. Holding hands of children with cancer. Talking to battered women at shelters that are more like prisons. But... somehow doing these things helped me stay strong."

I squeeze her hand, as if acknowledging that quiet strength.

I always thought Mom engaged in all her charities out of kindness, gratitude, out of giving back, maybe even boredom. I always rationalized that the reason most of her charities involve stray animals, children with cancer and orphans was to help the helpless, to be around children who are alone and scared. I thought she was subconsciously mitigating the guilt she felt about her own kids and making up for it with other abandoned kids. Sometimes I resented her for it. There were times when I felt so alone in America that days would go by and I'd realize I hadn't talked to a single adult. Meanwhile, children who were strangers to my mother, abandoned at birth by their own mothers, got the gift of my mom's presence, her smile, her hand in theirs. Other times, I thought she did it out of loneliness. She, like me, was lonely on the opposite end of the world, but she found a way to heal her loneliness while helping the truly lonely. Now I realize that they also helped put her problems in perspective. Holding the hand of a pubescent orphan dying of cancer made her problems, and her children's, seem minuscule by comparison.

Mom didn't have the higher education she always wanted. Her parents wanted her to get married after high school instead of letting her go to college.

And as with most men in their generation, Dad wanted her to be a housewife instead of a working woman. But Mom worked through her charities and ultimately got the highest, most valuable education. She learned the lessons no one teaches in school, her teachers being the most downtrodden of us all, telling her what life is all about. I accuse her of having mental scoliosis, hoping books on feminism would seep through her brain while walking with them on her head to cure her physical scoliosis. But she actually knows more than any book could teach. She has heard the stories, gathered all the information and seen the statistics first-hand. She never marched for women's rights, but she has actually given strength and love to battered women. She didn't study psychology, but she's actually heard aloud the voices in people's troubled heads.

And in the big picture, maybe all the people she was there for actually needed her more than her own children did. Like all of us, she leads a semi-double life. But her double life is more noble than most people's. She played the perfect housewife, she threw parties that were legendary, she has more friends and acquaintances than most people ever will. She was a loyal and loving wife to my dad. She played the role of the typical high-society Iranian woman to perfection. But she also lived a whole other life that no one knows about. And it's a shame that she lived in a society where the perfect party, the latest gossip and money were more valuable than her wealth of wisdom.

"Learn from my mistakes, Miryam. Don't let pain win, don't waste your life in regret. That's why I don't want you to let this depression take over you. I want you to slowly move on from it and not let it waste all the love that's inside you. It's normal for young people to think they know everything and that no one understands them. But the older you get, the more you'll realize how little you know."

She squeezes my hand. "Trust an old lady who doesn't know much, but learned everything she does know the hard way. You have so much living left to do. And you can't afford to do it with a heart that's already so heavy. There is so much ugliness in this world. Life is tough enough, Miryam, so don't make it harder than it is. You have to fight. But pick your battles. Life doesn't happen the way you picture it. Life will shock you. People will shock you. You won't make it if you turn everything into a battle and let all that shock and ugliness get the better of you. If you can let go of pain, ugliness, bitterness…if you can keep your heart open to love, you'll be a winner. I'm not saying it's easy or it'll happen overnight. But it will happen, as long as you don't fight it. When you close yourself off to the world because you don't want to let in any pain, you're also closing yourself off to joy."

She watches the tears roll down my face.

"I don't know if you know this," she says without telling me to stop crying. "But I was in love with Ari's father. I didn't want to get married just then. I was only 19. I wanted to go to college. I wanted him to wait for me. But that wasn't my destiny."

I stare at her, but don't say anything. I never knew she was actually in love with him.

She doesn't look at me. She swallows hard, as if feeling the hurt all over again. "Your father was my destiny. And I don't regret marrying him because for the most part, he's been a good husband to me." Pause. "For the most part. And I grew to love him very much. So when I tell you to go out with some other guy, it's not because I don't understand. It's because I *do*."

She grabs a tissue from the box on her bedside table and dries my eyes.

"I never meant that you would ever forget about Ari," she says, crumpling the tissue in her hand. "Or replace him. But you will be able to love someone again. Someday."

She smiles.

"What?" I ask

She smiles wider, switches to English and shocks me that she actually knows the song and the lyrics. She laughs louder with each word as she sings, albeit off-key and with an accent, "You got all your life to live. You got all your love to give. You vill survive."

I stare at her, my sobs spontaneously turning into laughter.

"Yes?" Mom asks.

I'm not sure if she's asking whether I agree that I'll survive or whether she's singing the right words. But I just smile and nod about the lyrics.

Even though I've heard that song at countless parties, even though every girl says it's "their" song, and even though singing it as I looked at Ari is my last memory of him, the song still always reminds of me of Bee, when she would pretend to sing it to all her past boyfriends and change the words to, "I'll more than just survive. I will *thrive.*"

I start to sing Bee's version to Mom about myself, but I stop. I don't think Mom knows what "thrive" means any more than I know if I will in fact survive, let alone thrive.

Mom's smile vanishes and her face gets serious. She squeezes my hand and looks into my eyes. "I have seen your strength, Miryam. I'm sorry if I said anything to make you think otherwise. Because I'm actually so proud of how you handled everything as a child, how you raised your brothers and what a strong and intelligent woman you've become."

Mom watches my face, looking for any reaction, for anything other than the familiar tears gushing from my eyes, hoping everything she just let out had some effect on me. But my mouth is mute, my body frozen. I can't articulate that my tears are no longer of sadness, that rather, a lifetime of exhaustion and a slew of unanswered questions are leaving my body through these tears.

She gets impatient waiting for my tears to stop. She opens her bedside drawer, takes out an envelope with "Iran Air" written across it and hands it to me.

"Your father didn't want you to leave just yet," she says. "But I…I bought your ticket myself."

I look back and forth between her and the envelope. I'm struggling to move, to hug her, to thank her, when Dad walks through the door.

"After I specifically told her not to," he says. "You can use it if you want, Miryam. But you're not ready yet. You can't take care of yourself. I beg of you to stay here a little longer."

I look at Dad's stern face, then at Mom's down-turned eyes. I realize that she never told Dad about my outburst the other day.

"She can take care of herself," Mom says. "She's a grown woman."

"A grown woman?" he says. "Who can barely get out of bed with depression. How can she take care of herself?"

"She *is* a grown woman," Mom says, staring into my eyes. "She's been a grown woman for a long time."

I force myself off the bed. I slip out the bedroom quietly, Mom and Dad's arguing voices trailing behind me.

I close my bedroom door and open the envelope. I study the ticket before putting it in my bedside drawer. I bite down on my lip. I have 12 days left to answer the rest of my whys.

Chapter 5

The sun is barely out, but it already feels like hell. And a mob is already finding its way through the entrance at *Beheshteh Zahra*. Cars are parked even on the sidewalk. Dad tells us to go ahead while he finds parking.

"Is this the only cemetery in Tehran?" Cyrus asks Mom. "Why so packed?"

The graves are all so close together that as hard as we try to have respect and not step on any of them, it's impossible to go two feet without doing so.

"It became like this after the Iran-Iraq war," she says. "They buried all the soldiers here."

She frowns and shades her eyes with her hand. "I need to find that fountain," she mumbles. "Where's the fountain? I've lost my sense of direction."

"I know where it is, Ma'am," Roya says. "My brother is buried close to it. Follow me."

We walk in silence until we reach a large fountain of red water. I squint at the writing on a black banner held up by two poles. I ask Mom to translate.

"It says 'Death to Saddam Hussein,'" she says.

Nader points at the fountain. "What the hell is this?"

"The fountain," Mom says matter of factly.

"What's with the red water?" he asks.

"Oh," she says, realizing it might look strange to us. "It's a symbol of the blood shed by the soldiers during the war."

"You're freakin' joking, right?" Cyrus says.

"It's a symbol of pride," Mom says. "It's supposed to show that they didn't die in vain and that they're martyrs."

"Shouldn't the banner be *thanking* Saddam then?" I whisper under my breath.

"Come on," Mom says. "Let's go to Roya's brother's grave."

We follow Roya until she squats before a grave and closes her eyes. A woman in a chador sits next to her, crying in front of what looks like her son's grave. A man standing next to a nearby grave tells the woman that she should be happy that her son died in the name of Islam.

"Don't cry," he says. "You should be proud. We should all want to die like that. I wish I had been young enough to die in that war."

"You're right," the woman says. "But I just miss him so much."

I stare at Mom in disbelief.

"Miryam, these are simple folk," Mom whispers. "You can't blame them for how they think. They've all been brainwashed to truly believe all this. If you didn't have the benefit of education and your upbringing, you could be one of these people. Try to be a little less judgmental."

Mom hands Roya a few stems from the batch of white roses we bought on our way over. Roya places them on the grave and looks around. She walks a few feet away, to a woman throwing water on a grave.

"Can I have some of your rosewater, sister?" Roya asks.

"Oh, this isn't rosewater," the woman says with a nervous chuckle. She looks around her and lowers her voice to a barely audible whisper. "It's...vodka."

We all stare at her.

"My father loved a good drink," the woman says, still whispering. "Sometimes I bring him the good stuff."

She mumbles an apology and turns quickly around.

"Does anyone in this country have a middle ground?" I ask Mom in English. She ignores me.

A woman to Roya's left asks her if her brother was a *Shahid* (a martyr).

"Yes," Roya says.

"Congratulations," the woman says.

Roya smiles and looks away.

"That darling man was only 24 with a wife and twin baby girls," Roya says to Mom as we walk away. "They drafted him and he died the first day he was on the field. His wife works three jobs just to bring food home. And she tells me 'congratulations.' You see, Ma'am, what they've done to us?"

Mom squeezes Roya's shoulder and tells her to ignore the ignorant.

We pass by people crying, beating their chests and throwing themselves on top of graves. I look at the portraits next to the graves. Some of the boys who died in the war were as young as 12 or 13.

Dad is already kneeling at Grandmother's grave when we get there. He gets up immediately when he sees us. We put down the flowers and sit by the grave. I want to ask my parents to translate the epitaph written in Farsi, but I know that if I open my mouth, I'll cry. I kneel down and close my eyes.

Here I am, Grandmother. Here I finally am. You made sure I didn't leave this country until I came to visit you. I'm sorry I didn't come that first time. I'm sorry I went to see Ari instead. I'm sorry that you gave me Ari and instead of coming to thank you, I just wanted more and more of him. But why did you have to punish me like that? Why did you have to take him away like that? Wasn't it enough that you gave me your disease? Wasn't it enough that you took him away all that time and I was alone, all alone, with nothing but the bottle, suffering just like you had? Wasn't that enough? Why did you have to take him away from me forever? Why? You said

I couldn't have everything I wanted in life. But he was all *I wanted. How was that wrong? How was that too much? Why did you have to punish me like that?*

The tears fall from my face so quickly that it becomes pointless to keep wiping them away with the tissues Roya hands me.

We watch Dad sprinkle rosewater on her grave.

"Maybe we should've gotten some vodka from that woman to throw on instead," I whisper.

Dad stares at me, but doesn't say anything.

"I want to see Ari," Cyrus says softly.

I glare at him. I want to scream at him for uttering his name. I had tried so hard to forget. I was almost home free, but he had to remind me.

Mom looks at me. I turn away.

"Me too," Nader whispers.

"Go ahead!" I yell. "Who's stopping you?"

"Miryam," Mom says, "maybe you should too. We've come all this way and it will really help if…"

I kick the dust around my grandmother's grave and scream, "Ari isn't here!"

I don't know where the beads of sweat end and the tears begin again.

"Let her be," Dad says to Mom as she tries to take my hand. "Come on, Miryam. Let's go."

He grabs my hand and tries to make me walk.

"Ari isn't here!" I wail as Dad strokes my sweaty hand.

"Shhh honey. It's OK. It's OK."

I hold Dad's hand tightly and walk away. I look down at my boots kicking the dust until we reach the car. Dad opens the back door to let out the pent-up heat. I climb inside and sit with my back to the cemetery, my cries slowly dying down.

Dad opens all the doors to air out the car. He paces outside, glancing at me from time to time. When he sees that I've stopped crying, he closes the front doors and gets into the back next to me. He smiles and strokes my hand.

He takes a deep breath, as if he's about to say something, but then looks away. A long time passes before he finally says, "Miryam, I heard what you said. About throwing vodka on the grave. What did you mean by that?"

I bite my lip. "Sorry, I didn't mean to be disrespectful. I…"

"No, no. It's not that. It's just…well, who told you? I mean, how…"

I look down and hesitate. I don't want him to get mad at Mom for telling us.

"Cyrus told me," I say. "A long time ago."

He frowns. "Cyrus?"

He goes in thought. My heart pounds.

"That's strange," Dad says. "I wonder how he knows. Your grandmother stopped drinking a long time before she died. Cyrus wasn't even born then."

"Really?" I ask. "When did she stop drinking?"

"She stopped completely right after your grandfather died."

Chapter 6

I ask Dad to stop the car by the alley so I can walk the rest of the way to my grandparents' house. He parks before he and Mom get out. I look at them and hesitate.

"Can I please do this alone?" I ask softly.

Dad climbs back into the car. Mom stares at me a while, then she, too, slides back into the car. They drive away towards my grandparents' house. I walk slowly towards the bakery Grandfather and I went to when I was 5.

It's still there. Exactly the same as it was 20 years ago. It looked old to begin with, so it doesn't seem any older today. I go closer and smell the breads baking in the ceramic oven. The man behind the counter gives me a friendly wave and tells me to come in. I smile and shake my head. I inhale the scent again and walk away, wishing he hadn't noticed me so I could've stood there longer without seeming strange.

The flower shop is gone, a travel agency in its place, as if all the flowers died and the owner couldn't bear to replace them.

I look down at the asphalt to see the newly mended, shiny black it was that day. But the paved street has relapsed into dirt, grey with age, dented once again with mud-filled potholes. The acorn trees adorning the side of the street look the same. The invisible round rims inside their thickened roots are the only testament to the years gone by.

I retrace the steps Grandfather and I took that morning, kicking the fallen acorns in size 7 sandals instead of tiny blue clogs. I walk slowly, trying to capture the pace he had set on that warm late-summer morning. I talk to him in a whisper. Not so much so passersby don't hear me, but to keep the silence of that day alive.

I reach the green gate and stroke the iron clasp. It melts at my touch and opens to let me through. I walk in quietly as if entering the gates of heaven.

The door to the living room creaks when I open it. I push down the handle and try to close it softly behind me. My shoes clunk on the bare linoleum and echo against the dusty walls. The stench of mildew gets stronger inside each empty room. Dust rises from carpets of what used to be the bedrooms.

It's hard to imagine that anyone ever lived here, that the broken stoves cooked countless savory stews, that laughter chimed where silence now rests, that there were once people who cleaned and cared for this now-decrepit, dirty house.

The last room I enter is Grandmother's sanctuary. Stripped of everything, it looks smaller. I sit on the dirty white carpet of the bare room and remember all the items that used to be here, all the big and small things that comprised Grandmother's life. All those things that, to her, were so private, so precious, but were probably just thrown away after she died.

I think of the last time I was in this room, when Grandmother had tried to teach me a lesson about excess. It would be decades before I would return here. And as many years to understand her message.

After what Dad told me in the cemetery, I realize that Grandmother herself was prone to excess and had tried to shield me from its dangers. She had used Grandfather and alcohol as crutches and learned to let them both go. I must once again follow in her footsteps.

Ari made me feel safe after Grandfather died. And he gave me comfort the night Grandmother died. Alcohol became my solace in Ari's absence. Now I must put alcohol to rest just as Grandmother did. She wasn't trying to punish me by withholding candy when I was a child. Nor did she take Ari away as a punishment when I was an adult. She had tried to teach me about balance as a child. And about letting go as an adult. On Earth and from heaven, her message was the same: nothing external can fill an internal void.

"When you don't appreciate what you have, you'll always think that having more will make you happy. But no matter how much more you get, it'll never be enough. Because you're always going to want 'just one more' of something. And you end up confusing wanting with needing."

And isn't that what addiction is? When more is never enough? When wanting becomes needing?

Grandmother wasn't attacking Mom's parenting or my pleas for candy. She was warning the dormant addict in me not to awaken.

I look around, almost waiting for her to appear, for her voice to come through the walls, for her to smile and say that I had finally understood. But all I hear is a clunk from a chunk of chipped paint falling off the wall. I look around the room one last time and walk out quietly, closing the door gently behind me.

I stroll through the garden trying to find the spot where Grandmother used to plant her herbs. I retrace where I used to run around, careful not to step on her hard day's work. But all I see are stretches of weeded grass.

I look away from the empty pebbled driveway. I lie down on the grass, forgetting that yesterday was farther away than I realize. I close my eyes and let the air's caresses linger on my skin as if my grandparents are stroking me. I'm 8 again, smelling the wild daisies. The tree branches bow and sweep the ground.

But I can hardly feel anything. As if that little girl has separated from me and drifted into nothingness instead of grown into me. As if those grandparents were entities from a dream and those days had only existed in oblivion. Yet at odd moments, watching Dad stroll on the veranda and Mom sit on the old, rusty lawn chair, shielded by the same weeping willows of years past, it feels as if I've gone back to those days, even if for an instant.

But from the distance, I can't see the wrinkles weathering the faces of parents who used to be so full of life, hadn't yet been scarred by the revolution. I can't hear the grandparents call me in when it gets too dark to play outside. They're both dead now, lying beyond the grass, muted sunset after sunset. The trees are no longer bowing, but bending in sorrow. Their branches aren't sweeping the ground, but weeping tears of nostalgia.

The faint sounds of birds and trees swaying in the breeze lull me to sleep. The blades of grass become hundreds of embracing arms from the past, cradling a child they still recognize, whose comfort they still want in their roots. I was meant to fall asleep on that grass, so my mind would shut down and my soul could tiptoe where my body once ran.

Chapter 7

I stare out the taxi window at the familiar route to Bernard's house. An ad for Iran Air has replaced the one for Toyota on the billboard at the corner of Fereshteh Street.

Murky water still overflows in the canals outside his house, as if it's been raining, flooding since I was last here. The house next door is still under construction. The orange tractors are still parked atop piles of dirt.

The taxi drops me off and I watch the driver make an illegal turn onto a one-way street. I walk to Bernard's house and ring the doorbell. I hear the chime echo through the house. The sound of footsteps grows louder until it stops at the door.

"Hello, Miryam," Bernard says, peeking at and around me through a crack in the door. "Come in."

I walk in with a forced smile buried under the hair crowding my face.

The shine from the marble floor guides my down-turned eyes as I follow Bernard to the living room. I take off my uniform and sit on the couch.

"Can I get you something to drink?" he asks.

I shake my head.

"It's nice to see you," he says, sitting down on a small sofa next to me.

I finally look up at his gaunt face swallowing his hallow eyes.

"You've lost a lot of weight," I say.

"And you," he says.

We both know we're not paying each other compliments.

"Miryam, I apologize that I took so long to return your calls," he says softly. "This has been a very difficult time for me as well. I resigned from my post in Tehran. Last year. But it's taken a while to wrap up my work here and I've been very busy. I'll be returning to Austria at the end of the month."

I become aware of the brown boxes scattered throughout the room as if they just now appeared.

I nod, almost implying, "I told you so."

"I hesitated to return your calls," he says. "But I know what you must have gone through. And I want to help you. As much as I can."

I nod slowly and look back down, once again afraid of his eyes.

I wait for him to speak, to tell me everything I want to know.

"What do you want to know?" he asks.

"Everything."

"What *do* you know?"

"Nothing," I say. "I don't know what's real and what's not. You're the only one who knows the truth. I don't know if his mother knows. But even if she does, she's not in a condition that…I…I couldn't put her through the pain of telling me. You're the last person who saw Ari." I look down and almost whisper,

"You're the one who was in the room with him. I need to hear what happened from you."

He nods and looks right at me, letting me know that he's ready for anything I ask. I stare at him blankly. The barrage of questions I've had for more than a year jumble randomly in my head; all the emotions go through me simultaneously. Suddenly, I don't know what to ask. I don't know where to start.

He shuffles impatiently on the armchair for a few minutes, but his eyes never leave mine.

"How close were you and Ari?" I finally ask.

"In the room?" he asks.

"No," I say with a frustrated sigh. "In general."

"Oh," he says, tilting back his head. "I'm sorry. I misunderstood."

He frowns and pretends to think hard. "I don't really know how to answer that. I obviously met him here. At your parents' party."

I nod quickly, emphasizing more frustration at the obvious.

"When I went to visit the States, I saw him in Los Angeles a few times." Pause. "More than a few. Quite a bit. He showed me the sights, took me around, to some parties...more like small gatherings really. A few bars."

My curiosity peaks at who was at these gatherings, wondering if Bee or Paige ever met him. But I don't want to interrupt him.

"I had been to Los Angeles before," he continues. "But not in a while. Never cared for it much. But I did enjoy my time with Ari."

"Why don't you like L.A.?" I ask.

"Not quite my scene," he says, crinkling his nose. "Fake. No culture. No charm. Lots of other cities I've never been to that I'd rather see."

I nod.

"Did Ari ever talk about me when you were with him?" I ask.

"Oh yes," Bernard says with a smile, waving his hand in front of him. "He told me all about you."

He notices the eagerness in my eyes and suddenly realizes what I'm asking. His smile vanishes and his voice is less animated when he continues. "I mean, he told me all about his childhood, about how you grew up together." He clears his throat. "I'm sure you know this better than I do...Ari wasn't very open about his emotions. When he talked about his life, it was more about the events, like a biographical timeline, not his feelings about anything...or anyone...in particular."

His tone is almost apologetic, as if he's trying to reassure me that just because Ari didn't tell him about his feelings for me doesn't mean he didn't have any.

I nod, acknowledging that Ari had trouble talking about his emotions.

"I met quite a lot of Iranians in Los Angeles," Bernard says, obviously trying to change the subject.

"For a change of pace from Iran?" I say.

He chuckles. "Different kinds of Iranians. Nice people, but not quite in the same caliber as the ones here. I find the Iranians in your social class in Iran to be much more...well, classy."

I nod. "Iranians in L.A. are known for being either really over-the-top materialistic and shallow, or low-class and ghetto. They're very..." I squint, trying to find the perfect word. "They're very gaudy. There are exceptions, of course. But for the most part."

"Hmm...," he says, nodding. "Yes, I can see that. Regardless, they're fine people. Especially as immigrants."

"What do you mean?" I ask.

"Well," he says, relaxing on the sofa. "I've met Iranians all over the world. Mass migration after the revolution. I have yet to meet any who weren't upstanding citizens. They all entered their respective countries legally, speak the native language, got higher educations, pay taxes, contribute to society. A lot of professionals."

"True," I say with a smile. "I bag on Iranian immigrants a lot. But I've never known any who mooched off of society. You won't find any Iranians on welfare, committing quote 'high crimes and misdemeanors,' or panhandling for money."

"Too true," he says with a chuckle. "You are a rich people."

"Not all Iranians are rich," I say with a frown. "But if they can't afford to, they don't leave Iran to go to a foreign country to live off of the government."

"Nothing wrong with being rich," he says, noticing my frown.

"Rich Iranians today aren't the same as the ones who were rich before the revolution," I say.

"How's that?" he asks.

"In Iran, I mean. The rich, upper-class people lost their money after the revolution. The ones who are rich now are mostly crooks who stole from people who were rich before the revolution or made their money through this regime. Mostly illegally. Money laundering, Iranian mafia, things I don't really care to talk about."

"You're rich," he says.

I smile and shake my head. "I hope I don't sound spoiled, but we're not rich. Anymore. We're comfortable only because my family got some of their properties back from the government. They've been in court fighting the government for decades. Same with most of the people who used to be rich. I'm talking about the nouveau-riche Iranians, a whole new group of over-the-top rich people who didn't have a pot to piss in before the revolution that are now wealthy. They buy whatever they want and travel everywhere first class. They can buy the first-class *tickets*, but they can never buy actual class."

He nods. "I hear you. New money can only take you so far. Money doesn't buy class. It's obvious that families like yours...Ari's...are, well, in a different class. You have old money."

"Had," I say.

"Well," he says with a slight chuckle, "you're not exactly poverty stricken."

"I never said we were. I just meant that most of our money was taken by this new group of rich people. Illegally. And by legality, I mean the government's whims."

He nods. But I shake my head and say, "You have no idea who or what I'm talking about."

"On the contrary," he says. "Understanding the political system of a country I'm assigned to is part of my job."

"I meant the social structure," I say. "The people who got rich in the guise of helping the poor, but really just helped themselves and made the poverty even worse. I get angry just thinking about them. I...I don't want to talk about it."

He looks at me and sighs. "No," he says softly. "No, you don't. I don't think you came here to talk about Iran's social structure. Or about my opinion of Los Angeles."

We lock eyes and I swallow hard. I look down, trying to figure out how I got sidetracked, wondering if I'm purposely avoiding the questions I came to ask.

I continue to stare down, aware that he's watching me patiently.

"Just tell me, Bernard," I finally plead almost in a whisper. "Just tell me what happened that night."

A torturous silence precedes Bernard's slow speech. "Ari was very tired that night. He still had jet lag and was about to leave the party and go home. He wasn't sure he would have a chance to see me again before returning to Los Angeles the following Monday, so he asked to see me alone."

His eyes drift away and he speaks almost to himself.

"We were in, I think, Leila's bedroom. We heard the commotion downstairs and just when we were about to go out and see what was happening, some Komiteh men barged into the room. I'm sure you know by now, the men that busted the party that night weren't regular Komiteh. They were the *Basij.*"

The Basij, who originally consisted of civilian volunteers recruited to fight in the Iran-Iraq war, are the usually young hardliners of the revolutionary guards. Their very name instills fear in Westernized Iranians. These hard-core morality police believe in martyrdom and have a zero-tolerance policy for anything Western or anti-Islamic. They usually target young people and arrest them for everything from anti-government protests, violating the hijab or engaging with the opposite sex, whether in public or private, or anything else they deem immoral.

Even as I'm looking into Bernard's blue eyes, I can still see the Basij's hate-filled black eyes that trailed me that night.

"I knew they were Basijis right away," Bernard continues. "I can't discuss it, but I know how to recognize them as part of my job. But I don't think Ari knew because he didn't seem the least bit scared. One of them yelled something in Farsi that I didn't understand. Ari answered him calmly. He...Ari walked towards the door, then turned back to me and said, 'Don't worry, just a formality.' Another one of them told him to shut up in Farsi. That part I understood. They yelled something at me that I didn't understand, but Ari told them I don't speak Farsi, that I'm a diplomat. They looked me up and down and didn't say anything else to me. There was a small argument between Ari and one of the guys and I wanted to warn Ari not to get aggressive with them, but the next thing I knew one of them started beating him with a baton. I tried to yank him off of Ari, but two others shoved me away. Big men...all of them, just huge. Even without the batons, they overpowered us. Just one shove and I hit my head on the edge of a table and fell down. Everything happened so fast. I didn't know what was going on and I didn't understand anything they were saying. Suddenly, three, maybe four of them were beating Ari. I was on the floor. Completely frozen and helpless. They acted like I wasn't even there. It *felt* like I wasn't even there. Like I was watching..."

His voice trails off. The tears run down my face, a slew of new questions coming up. But I just stare at Bernard in the same frozen, helpless way he's describing.

"He wasn't scared," Bernard says with a frown. His tone is puzzled, more like he's asking a question instead of making a statement. "He was so calm the entire time. When they barged in, when the first guy beat him, even when he was arguing with them. I remember his face when they dragged him out. I could see pain. Physical pain because of how hard they beat him. But behind that pain, he was… he was just so calm."

Bernard sees me struggling to breathe as I cry. He takes one of my hands and cups it between both of his.

"He was at peace with whatever was in store for him," he says to reassure me.

"Why…" I whimper. "Why was he…"

Bernard watches me, waiting for me to form a full sentence.

"Why was he so calm?" he asks.

I shake my head.

"Why was he arguing with them?" he asks.

I shake my head again.

"Why…" I mumble. "Why was he alone with you in that room?" I finally ask.

Bernard's face relaxes. He lets go of my hand and scoots forward on the sofa.

"Ari had borrowed some money from me when I was in L.A.," he says. "He was paying me back what he owed me. He had a wad of $100-bills in his hand when they barged in the room."

My sobs die down as I concentrate on visualizing the scene in my head.

"The two of you were alone in Leila's bedroom," I say slowly. "And he was handing you cash. In dollars. And they just assumed that…"

He looks down.

"That's what they assumed," he says and fake laughs nervously. "That he was paying me for some…sexual favor."

"*Assumed,*" I repeat.

He nods.

"Even if their assumption was correct," I say, looking carefully at Bernard's eyes for even a hint of the truth. "Why would they kill him based on an assumption?"

He shakes his head. "You're asking me something I've been asking myself every single day. And I haven't come up with an answer."

I whimper and stare at him with frustration and defeat, my eyes almost begging him for an answer.

"There was no reason for them to kill him," he says. "It was completely senseless. It makes me sick to my stomach whenever I think about it." He sighs. "I've been all over the world, worked in all kinds of governments, but what happened to Ari has changed my entire ideology on people. It's shattered my belief in justice like nothing else." He squeezes his temples with his thumbs and takes a deep breath.

"Miryam, I haven't shared this with too many people." He shifts uncomfortably in his seat. "I was raped by different men at an all-boys Catholic boarding school growing up, so I know all about the hypocrisy of religion. Even before I had any sexual desires, before I hit puberty, having sex with men was my normal. Not because I liked it, but because it was forced on me to the point that it became my norm. So, no one despises the hypocrisy of religion more than I do. To me, what happened to Ari was just a different example of a different religion's hypocrisy and senselessness."

"But why would they kill Ari and not you?" I ask, oblivious to his doubtless difficult confession and the bluntness of my question. "I mean, whatever they assumed, they assumed about both of you."

"That's something you'll have to ask your government," he says.

"Ari once told me that diplomats in Iran can literally get away with murder," I say, visualizing Ari in Soraya's kitchen with a basketball in his hand.

"Whoa, whoa," Bernard says, raising his hand. "Are you saying I murdered Ari?"

"No," I say. "You didn't murder him."

"But he was murdered *because* of me," he says with a deep frown. "Is that more correct?"

"Is it incorrect?" I ask.

"Yes, it is," he says, his voice and his body rising. "You're asking me to justify the kind of logic your government uses."

I take his hand as a gesture of apology. He holds it and eases back down in the armchair. He stares at me for a while before smiling weakly at the desperation in my eyes.

It doesn't add up. Something just...

"Something just doesn't add up," I say angrily. "Why would they assume something if it wasn't true and carry it to such an extreme?"

His voice softens back up. "Nothing adds up, Miryam. You're trying to make sense out of something senseless. Maybe they found out about Ari's dad working for the Shah's government. Maybe Ari said something or did something when he was in custody. We don't know. And you're asking me to answer things I just can't answer, Miryam. All your whys are asking the same thing in different ways. 'Why did they kill Ari?' That's really the only question you have for me. And it's the one question I can't answer."

His eyes leave mine; his voice is hushed. "Sometimes our whys don't have answers. And sometimes the answers to our whys will drive us even more crazy than if we didn't know."

I watch Bernard's lips move, but hear Cyrus' voice, telling me on that night before he got arrested, that if I think too much about the whys in life, I'll drive myself crazy.

"Maybe his mom knows…"

I interrupt him and practically scream. "His mom had a nervous breakdown. She was in a psychiatric hospital on suicide watch for six months. And now she's locked up in her apartment with a nurse and refuses to see or talk to anyone."

Bernard looks down. I turn away.

The phone rings and jolts me out of my slouch. We both stare at the cordless before Bernard finally grabs it.

"Excuse me," he whispers as he gets up and walks with the phone towards the bedroom.

I fall back into the sofa and let its too-soft cushions embrace me. I grab the couch's arm tightly, as if my frail body is about to slip into the gap between the squares of cushions.

"Miryam, would you please excuse me for a bit?" Bernard says as he walks back into the living room, cradling the phone to his chest. "I have to take this call. It's important. Regarding my departure."

"Sure," I say, so softly that he has to study my face to realize I've heard him.

He closes his bedroom door, and my heartbeat returns to normal. I'm grateful that he's gone, that there's a forced break in our conversation so I can gather my thoughts and re-think everything I came to ask him.

Instead, I get lost in reverie as I look around the room.

It's just a room, just a house, just furniture and walls. Lots of people have walked into this house. It wasn't just you and him. Stop thinking; stop seeing him.

The sunlight peering through the oversized windows makes the room too bright. The house looks different. So empty and quiet without the sounds of laughter and music, without words echoing off the walls, without the tables' legs dancing to their favorite songs.

These walls, this furniture, this floor, are my witnesses. They remember Bernard's party, the night when Ari and I were just a breath apart.

I stroke the sofa that had cushioned my shaking body and tamed my knees that night. I stare at the floor that had supported my walk, the table that had grabbed the glass before I could drop it. I get up and walk slowly around. With each step, the house comes more alive. The music blares. Ari smiles at me. The floor bounces with our step and the white walls turn pink, blushing when he whispers in my ear, *"I want you."*

I look slowly towards the bedroom. But the closed door traps my memories inside, snickers instead by showing me a shadowy image of Ari in Bernard's embrace. I want to bang down the door, run inside and ask the bedroom if Ari was ever in there with Bernard.

I want the room to tell me that my night with Ari was more special than any night he ever shared in it with Bernard. I want it to tell me that he never made memories with Bernard. That it's all just a misunderstanding.

Or was my night the misunderstanding? Was Ari in such a good mood that night because he was in Bernard's presence? Was I the wrong body at the right time and place?

I thought my competition that night was the blonde girl. That I was the end slice of bread in a loaf that she too was packaged. Or was there a feast laid out for Ari that I hadn't even seen? Was I what he desired least, but devoured in desperate vain? Was Bernard the ideal feast, laid out to a hunger I could never satiate?

Bernard is right that he doesn't know why Ari was killed. He doesn't have the answer any more than I do. Or Dad does. Or even Ari himself would. But he's wrong that it's the only question I have for him.

No, Bernard, I have many more questions for you than that. Did they drag him out and just leave you in there? Diplomat or not, why didn't they confront you about anything? Did they even take you in for questioning? Did they tell you anything about what they were going to do to Ari? How did you find out what happened to him? Were the lights on or off in Leila's bedroom? Were you and Ari laughing together or even smiling at each other?

Actually, none of those questions really matters.

You're right, Bernard. I do have only one question for you. But it's not the one you think. It's not about why they killed Ari. And you're wrong that you don't have the answer. You're the only one who does *have the answer: was there anything going on between you and Ari...ever?*

I bury my head into the sofa's cushions and begin to whimper. Just when I've settled into a slow, steady sob, I startle at the sound of laughter. I turn my head towards the bedroom, where again, Bernard laughs loudly, chillingly.

If only he hadn't done that.

But he did. And with it, determined destiny. That's all destiny is. Random, seemingly meaningless incidents changing the course of life.

I grab my purse and uniform and run out the door. I scurry through the street as fast as my short heels will allow. I throw on my scarf and uniform before I get to the main road. I hail a public taxi and squish myself in the backseat of the orange Peykan with four other passengers. The bearded man in the front passenger seat turns around and stares at me. I avoid his eyes and the dirty looks from the women next to me in the back. I don't look like the kind of person who rides the public taxis. I'm not wearing a chador and my jeans scream upper class. The lady next to me yanks her chador from under me and crumples it on her lap. The stench of sweat is everywhere. I roll down the window and stick my head out. I feel the women's stares; I hear their whispers.

I sit in the cab as different passengers get on and off. The driver looks at me often from the mirror, wondering, but not asking, why I'm not getting off.

I hear Bernard's laugh everywhere. Coming out of the taxi's radio and engine, out the passengers' whispering mouths, through the closed windows of all the cars on the street.

You had no right to laugh, Bernard. How dare you? You, who last saw Ari's face, bloodied and bruised, have no right to laugh within earshot of me. No right to express joy in proximity to someone you know may never again experience joy. If only you had been born in Iran instead of Austria, you too would be dead.

I tell myself not to go back to his house. I don't want to hear the truth come out of that mouth.

The taxi stops behind a red light. I look out the window and see the one-legged boy who was selling cigarettes the night Ari and I were in the cab going to Bernard's party. I watch him hop among the cars stuck in traffic. Just as I'm about to call him over so I can give him the spare change in my purse like I did that night, a girl in the passenger seat of a white Toyota sticks her hand out of the window and waves him over. The sun's sinking rays bounce off the small, but glistening diamond on her ring finger.

She grabs a pack of Winston's from the boy's crate. A man I assume is her husband in the driver's seat hands the boy a small wad of money.

I watch as the girl tears open the pack, sticks a cigarette into her pink-glossed lips and her husband lights it for her with a small blue Bic lighter. She takes a drag and her husband blows the smoke away from his face. Just as the traffic light turns green, the one-legged boy catches my eye and I manage to give him a quick smile.

The taxi drives ahead and I turn my head to watch the boy hop back to the edge of the street, waiting for the next red light, the next row of stopped cars, the next potential customers.

My heart sinks the way it did that night, not because the cabbie is driving too fast, but because thoughts of Ari fill my head in the slow-moving taxi.

I remember his political discussions with the cab driver, the way he held my hand, his voice telling the cabbie to slow down. I remember him under our cherry tree at my parents' party, where he stayed with me as I smoked the cigarette he had snuck in for me. I remember how he would always light my cigarettes even though he hated smoking in general, and my smoking in particular.

That girl and her husband could've been me and Ari.

All the memories flash in front of me, all the big and small things that comprised our relationship since we were children. All the struggles, the bond, the inside jokes, our history, even our fights...everything that built the strong friendship that had brought us to the point of loving each other and wanting to be together as more than just a girl and a guy forced to play house. I feel a pang about what can no longer be, what never had a chance to begin. But even with that pain, I feel a warmth thinking about the fantasy of being together and raising our own children, out of choice, rather than force. Because this time, the fantasy isn't in my head; it's a would-be reality that didn't turn into fruition through events beyond our control.

I didn't run out of Bernard's house just because of the way he laughed. It wasn't just from Bernard's mouth that I didn't want to hear the truth. I don't want to know the truth at all, whatever it may be. I don't want the answer to a question that might drive me crazy.

I don't want my memories with Ari shattered. I want to still picture my life with him, still imagine a future with him, without my illusions becoming a mockery laid bare by the truth.

I need my memories to stand firm as rocks, as stepping stones carrying me to the far-away day when I'm an old lady who can get out of bed, match my clothes, glide red lipstick across my wrinkled lips and walk my white poodle, knowing that I can survive the worst of life.

Chapter 8

"Do you have your passport in a safe place?" Dad asks.

"Yes," I say.

"And your ticket?"

"I've got it all, Baba joon. Don't worry."

I turn away from his pensive eyes. He stands by my door and watches me stuff my last-minute packing into a suitcase. I cram a pair of sweat socks into a corner pocket, I shift my black heels under my pink sweater – I do anything but look up at Dad and the pain I know is fixated on his face.

I want to apologize for how difficult I've been, for how much hardship I caused them. I want to tell him that if only I had one more day, I would make up for all the days of misery I made them live through. But like Mom said, you don't get a second chance.

"Tell me when you're done and I'll come and zip them up for you," Dad says, motioning to my suitcases.

I nod. I grab my handbag and pretend to organize it. I concentrate on Dad's presence. I close my eyes and inhale his cologne. This is my dad. My *Baba*. No one else smells like this, even if thousands of other men wear Paco Rabanne after shave.

I don't hear him move. But I know he's left the room. I turn around just in time to catch a glimpse of his head before he's out of my sight.

I lean against the wall outside my room and stare at the light under my parents' bedroom door. I listen to the quiet and tell myself that this is the last time I'll be under this roof with my whole family.

When their light flickers off, I close my eyes. I take in their breaths, letting them give me life. I fill up my being with their breaths, so I can draw on them in the months to come.

I open my eyes and walk back to my room, my private Bermuda Triangle, where endless thoughts, tears, cigarettes, pills and drops of alcohol have disappeared into the unknown.

I climb over a suitcase and open the closet. Nothing left but dust and scattered tobacco. I stare at the phone sitting in its cradle. I don't pick it up.

I haven't seen or talked to any of my friends in Tehran since the day we were released from jail. The last time I saw them was on that windy fall morning when we walked away from each other with our heads bowed, hugging ourselves not from the wind's lashes, but from feeling exposed to each other.

I watched them climb into their parents' cars, not knowing that the weak smile I gave them was the last one they'd see.

Chapter 9

I wake up in a panic to the calm dawn.

I jump out of bed and open the window. I light a cigarette and watch the street sweeper finish his night's work. I wave at him for an extra-long time, as if he'll understand that it's the last time I'll be seeing him. I return his smile and snap a mental picture of him walking away down the empty street. I wait for the sun's rays to brighten the dark silhouette of the sky.

But the sun isn't out yet an hour later when Dad comes to get me. I stare out into the darkness and draw the drapes on the night one last time.

Maybe if international flights arrived and departed during the day, the ride to the airport wouldn't be as depressing. Maybe then, the quiet wouldn't feel so suffocating, as if we were the only three people left in the world, driving the barren streets looking for even one other soul roaming the Earth.

I remember the last time I was on this road, with Soraya, going to pick up Ari. We were supposed to go down these streets together almost two years ago. He was supposed to be following behind our car with Soraya. We were supposed to get on the same plane, leave together and start our lives anew.

As if to torture myself, I look behind the car through the side mirror next to Mom. But I see nothing but rows of maple trees swallowing exhaust fumes.

My parents are both quiet. The sound of the radio is barely audible. But the guitar's strum drums loudly in my head, humming to the string of thoughts jumbled in my head.

I pinch the fabric hanging below the knot in my scarf, then bring it up to my face. It still smells like Cyrus, Nader and Roya.

"How could you leave your home?" Roya had asked as she watched me say a tearful goodbye to my brothers. "All the love in the world is here for you. Why would you leave it with your own two feet?"

I didn't answer. I couldn't talk. I could barely think. I missed Nader even as I stared at him.

I looked into Cyrus' eyes, then away. I could no longer bear to see the pain that had become a perpetual fixture of his eyes, as much a part of them as his long lashes. And I was once again unable to ease that pain. Perhaps Mom and Dad would ultimately help him more than Ari and I had managed to. I let go of Cyrus' arms, as if admitting defeat.

I dove into Roya's outstretched arms. I didn't even mind her foul breath and the odor emanating from her armpits. This was a woman who was cleaner than anyone I had ever met and it didn't matter that she only bathed once a week on Fridays. Or that it was Thursday and I was being embraced by a week's worth of dirt.

I wipe my tears and force my mind to erase the image of that goodbye. I stare out the dusty car window and tell myself to just take in the final images of the streets instead.

A string of clothes hanging to dry on the balcony of a high-rise waves my eyes over. The clothes ruffle in the wind.

I imagine a woman taking those clothes down from the string tomorrow. She will walk onto that balcony, feel the clothes to make sure they're sufficiently dry, then carefully unhook the pegs clasped to each garment. She'll fold the clothes and take them inside. All the while, she'll be sighing, bored with her mundane life. She won't know, or care, that somewhere on the other side of the world, somewhere she never thinks about, my heart will pound as I walk into a house I haven't been in in years. She will think that taking those clothes off the string is a small part of the destiny that is her significant life. And I will think that turning that knob and walking into that house is the only thing happening in all the world.

If I am to be sane, I have to remember that there are clothes hanging to dry on balconies all over the world. I have to remind myself, maybe every day, that there are women taking their clean clothes off strings without giving my tears, or my laughter, a thought.

In order to survive, I have to remember how truly insignificant I really am.

Chapter 10

My parents and I sip our hot teas in the airport cafeteria, waiting for my flight. The girls at the next table talk excitedly about their upcoming trip to Rome. Their eyes dance with fervor, their smiles bounce quickly into uncontrollable laughter. There is joy in their every gesture. I watch them with exhausted, envious eyes.

The hands on the big clock on the wall seem to be choking me. With every tick, it becomes harder to breathe. I wish it would break down and, as if it were the clock that signifies all of time, everything would stop and I could forever sit feeling the presence of the only two people in the world who will ever love me unconditionally.

Finally, the hands strike 4:45 a.m. Dad rises slowly from his chair and nods sadly. It's time. I bite my lip and look at Mom. She's already crying. I start to tell her to stop, but I, too, start crying. I reach for her and she throws her arms around my neck. The girls at the next table stop talking and look at us.

"Come on," Dad says with a choked-up voice. "Don't do this. We're not even at the gate yet."

He untangles me from Mom and takes my hand. I clasp his hand all the way to where the sign says, "Passengers Only Beyond This Point." My lips quiver and start the torrent of tears in all three of us. I fall back into Mom's arms.

"We'll visit you soon," Dad says.

"It's ridiculous that we're crying like this," Mom says, wiping her eyes. "We'll see each other soon."

But that's not why we're crying. We're crying because of everything that happened, wondering if any of us will ever be the same again.

"Yes, it's ridiculous," I say, feigning a smile.

They watch as two chadori women search my handbag before I get on the plane. The women poke through my purse as if rummaging through a sale at a Friday bazaar. They comment on how nice my wallet is and why the book I have is in English when I should be reading in Farsi. They ask where I'm headed, if I'm a student and what life is really like in America.

"It's so sad how all these young people have to be separated from their families just to get an education," the one with the gap in her teeth says. "Look at her, poor thing. She's just a child."

"Which ones are your parents?" the other one asks.

I point to my parents, who're both standing up on tiptoe, wondering what's going on and if I'm in any sort of trouble. I wave my hand to assure them all is fine.

"Poor souls," the gap-toothed woman says. "They're too old to go through this grief. Why do you young people have to go abroad? Why can't you just live in your own country? It's not that bad here, is it?"

"No," I say. "It's not that bad."

It's worse.

And it's such a shame. Because it's a beautiful country with beautiful people, a rich culture and a history as old as time itself. But under this regime, even with all that, it's worse than bad.

They zip up my purse and I close my eyes, preparing for my freeze frame. I take a deep breath and turn around. Mom smiles and waves. Dad blows a kiss, closes his eyes gently, opens them back up, blows another kiss. Another deep breath. Click. I tuck the images in my mind's overflowing reservoir of intangible snapshots.

I walk through the gate without turning back.

Chapter 11

The plane rises above Tehran at an angle. The streetlights sigh with relief that their shift is over, that the sun is finally here to illuminate the city. I stare down at all the houses. Our house, my grandparents' house, Leila's house, Soraya's house, Bernard's house – they're all down there somewhere, guarding my memories.

I imagine my parents' quiet ride home on that barren road, listening to the radio continue its hum, passing by the clothes on that balcony rustling in the wind, then getting home to my absence.

At least they still have Cyrus and Nader to go home to. I'm headed towards a house where ghosts will greet me.

First, I'll go to Nader's room. I'll see his comic books, his soccer trophies, the race-car-shaped bed he said he was too old for four years ago. I'll glance in the mirror that will no longer watch him growing taller over the years.

In Cyrus' room, I'll stare at the walls he spent years staring at blankly. I'll see his computer, the tree outside that will still shade the room from noon until 2 p.m. everyday. I'll see his bed, the one he never once made after waking up. I'll glance in his mirror and tell it that it will no longer look blurred through his bloodshot eyes.

Then I'll go into my own room, sit on my bed, and think about the last night I had tossed and turned in it, unaware of how long would pass before I would once again put my head on that pillow. I will stare at the phone that hasn't rung in years. I had called Ari from that phone, asking when he would be picking us up for the airport. I had watched Cyrus haul my suitcases out through that door. The suitcase packed with the underwear they yanked off me in jail. The one with the suit I wore to Ari's funeral. I will stare at the mirror on top of my armoire and see myself looking almost exactly the same as when I had last looked in it. Because it only reflects the outside.

And maybe someday, after weeks or even months, I'll have enough courage to walk into Ari's old room. I'll stare at the full-length mirror behind his door, wishing it had memorized his image so it could still reflect what it will never again see.

If I dare, I'll sit on that bed, where it had all began. I'll remember that on it, our bodies had been one. I will thank that bed for giving him so many nights of rest and whisper to it that he is now resting forever.

I will gently close all the doors and let silence live in the rooms like a ghost. When the new owners move in, I will close one last door and walk away without looking back.

And I will not tell them that the house is haunted.

Chapter 12

When I land in Frankfurt, I find the gate for my flight to Los Angeles and decide to sit there for the four hours until boarding time. I don't want to go back to the bar or walk around the airport in this unfamiliar city that cruelly enough, has memories of Ari.

I still feel a sense of belonging as I sit chain smoking on the imitation leather chair, watching people of different nationalities walk hurriedly by. I blend inconspicuously with all the other foreigners. I still have four hours before I head towards a home in which I'm once again an uninvited visitor. I'm still in Germany, my no-man's land between Iran and America, both of which, neither of which, is home.

I drift off to sleep and wake up instinctively when it's boarding time. I walk to the man at the gate and hand him my boarding pass. He smiles and says, "Finally, yah? You've been waiting a long time."

Twelve hours later, the plane's wheels touch down at Los Angeles International Airport. I adjust my watch to 3:12 p.m. local time. I know that Bee and Paige are probably already waiting to pick me up. I feel nothing at their thought. Nothing from that lifetime matters anymore.

I get to the front of the passport-control line and a man at one of the podiums waves me over. I walk quickly towards him and hand him my American passport.

"Where was your original place of departure?" he asks, thumbing the pages.

"Iran," I say softly.

"Excuse me?"

"Iran," I repeat louder, studying his face.

"How long were you gone?"

I'm not sure what I'm supposed to say. Maybe I wasn't allowed to be out of the country for this long.

"Miss?"

"Oh, I'm sorry. Um, around three years."

"Why?" he asks with a frown.

"Why what?"

"Why were you out of the United States for so long?"

"To visit my family."

He flips through my passport again, like something he hasn't already seen is going to appear.

"Where is your home?" he asks.

I start to give him my address in Los Angeles.

"No, no," he says. "I mean, where do you consider your home? Iran or the U.S.?"

He probably wasn't expecting the long pause that follows his question. To him, it's a simple question. To me, it's the equivalent of being asked the meaning of life from someone at the Department of Motor Vehicles.

How do you answer a question that has no answer? How do you explain that children of revolution never really have a home? That we are the world's nomads?

I hesitate.

"Here," I say.

He stamps my passport, as if recording my answer forever. And tells me what I've been waiting to hear my entire life.

"Welcome home."